"It's going to be okay, Bishop. I'll help you."

He looked at me with surprise. "You will?"

"Of course." I reached for his hand.

The moment I touched him, a strong crackle of electricity coursed up my arm.

I gasped.

And then a vision slammed into me as if I'd just been flattened by a truck.

A city in darkness, melting and draining away like water in a bathtub—falling into a dark hole in the center of everything. People, thousands and thousands of them, trying to run away but getting pulled into the vortex. There was no escape.

Bishop was there trying to help. To save everyone, including me. I reached for his hand as he yelled my name, but he was swept away from me before I could touch him.

Then it was all over.

Where there had once been a city, there was nothing but darkness.

dark kiss

Michelle Rowen

NIGHTWATCHERS

Book 1

HARLEQUIN® TEEN

Recycling programs for this product may not exist in your area.

ISBN-13: 978-0-373-21047-3

DARK KISS

This edition published by arrangement with Harlequin Books S.A.

For questions and comments about the quality of this book please contact us at Customer_eCare@Harlequin.ca.

www.HarlequinTEEN.com

Printed in U.S.A.

To Eve Silver…
the journey continues!

prologue

This is going to hurt like hell.

The grim thought was confirmed by the look on the gatekeeper's face, but Bishop didn't want anyone's pity. After all, he'd volunteered for this.

"Are you ready?" the gatekeeper asked.

"Yes, I'm ready."

"And you know your mission."

"Of course."

Bishop glanced over his shoulder at the expanse of bright white behind him. This was as far as he could go before leaving Heaven entirely. He'd left before, many times, but this was different. He pushed aside a sliver of fear. He would return soon—this was not the end for him. It was only the beginning.

The gatekeeper studied Bishop as if looking for any sign of weakness. "You've been warned that there will be pain?"

"I have."

"And disorientation?"

"Yes."

Traveling to the human world was not normally a huge ordeal. However, there was nothing normal about this mission.

An invisible barrier shielded his destination, preventing any supernatural being from entering or leaving the city through normal means. Bishop had been told this gatekeeper had the ability to help him breach the barrier—but it wasn't going to be pleasant. The minds of the others would be protected to prevent any harm, but not his. He was the only one who would remember what needed to be done.

Bishop was positive he was more than strong enough to handle whatever was to come. All the better to prove his worth.

This was going to be very good.

"First you must find the others," instructed the gatekeeper. "If you don't find them within seven days, they'll be lost forever."

"I know this already." He didn't even try to keep the sharp tone from his voice. Patience had never been his strongest virtue.

The gatekeeper pursed his lips and his expression soured. "Do you have it?"

"Yes." A golden dagger was tucked into the sheath he wore strapped between his shoulder blades. It was all he needed to take with him.

The gatekeeper nodded. "Come closer."

Bishop did as he asked. The gatekeeper pressed his pale, long-fingered hand against Bishop's chest. Bishop grimaced as an unpleasant burning sensation sank into him. He gritted his teeth to keep from showing discomfort at whatever protection the gatekeeper was searing into him to help in his journey.

Finally the gatekeeper stepped back. He didn't smile. It was quite possible that he never smiled.

The oldest angels were usually the least pleasant.

"Well?" Bishop prompted. "Are we done here?"

"We are. May your journey be—"

Before the sentence could be completed, the solidity beneath Bishop dropped away. He hadn't had a chance to brace himself.

Bishop had imagined what this might feel like—a cleansing pain that would help him focus on the all-important task that lay ahead.

Instead, it was an agony unlike anything he'd ever experienced. He struggled against it, but it was too much, and he had his very first doubt about his success.

But it was too late for doubts. Too late for fear. Too late for anything.

As he continued to fall with no way to stop his torturous descent, he felt his mind begin to rip away.

The instant he slammed through the barrier surrounding the human city, Bishop realized he'd never before heard himself scream.

What of soul was left, I wonder,
when the kissing had to stop?

—Robert Browning

chapter 1

"This is going to be an amazing night, Sam!" Carly shouted over the music blasting all around us.

"You think so?" I yelled back.

"Best night ever!"

Sure. My throat already hurt and we'd only been here for a half hour. So far it felt like every Friday night at Crave, elbow to elbow with other sweaty kids on the dance floor.

Don't get me wrong, as one of the only all-ages clubs here in Trinity, it was a decent place to hang out—especially with my best friend—I just didn't think it was going to change my life or anything.

Anyone looking at us would think that Carly and I were the polar opposite of each other in looks and attitude. Carly Kessler was a curvy, flippy-haired blonde with a sunny personality whereas I was a skinny, nonsunny, long-haired brunette. And yet we were still best friends and had been forever.

After a few more minutes enveloped in the hot nightclub, Carly clutched my arm, her face flushed with excitement. "Heads up. Stephen Keyes is looking right at you."

I glanced over my shoulder and saw him standing at the

edge of the dance floor. He *was* looking at me. Or, at least, he *seemed* to be looking at me.

I turned back around, my heart pounding.

Everyone has that one crush, the guy they can't stop thinking about even though it's totally hopeless. Stephen Keyes was mine. He was nineteen—two years older than me—and utterly gorgeous with jet-black hair and caramel-colored eyes. We grew up in the same neighborhood, him two doors down from me. He mowed lawns in the summer. I watched from my bedroom window.

It was such a cliché, really. The weird, unpopular chick with the massive crush on the hot, older jock.

As far as I knew, Stephen was supposed to be at university in California, two thousand miles away. I'd even watched his parents help him pack up his car when he left town at the end of August. I wondered why he was back only a couple of months later.

Suddenly he wasn't just lingering at the edge of the dance floor looking distant and delectable. He was standing right next to me. Carly watched, her eyes widening as Stephen leaned close enough for me to hear him over the loud throb of the music.

"Can I talk to you?" he asked.

"Me?"

He nodded and smiled. And I, the girl who shunned and mocked romance in all its forms—movies, books, real life—went weak for a hot guy I had a crush on. Whenever I'd really liked somebody in the past—which, not including Stephen, had been only twice before in my entire life—it hadn't ended in true love. The two other boys I'd fallen for hadn't liked me in return and I'd ended up ignored, brokenhearted and humiliated both times.

However, that hadn't stopped me from liking Stephen. A lot.

Stephen didn't wait for my reply. Instead, he walked away, weaving through the labyrinth of sweaty dancers.

Something wicked this way comes.

The line from *Macbeth,* our current read in English class, flitted through my head. The quote suited Stephen perfectly. He might be the boy next door, but to me he was also wicked. And dangerous.

I didn't do dangerous. Not anymore. Even little dangerous things tended to lead to big trouble. Six months ago, I'd been busted for shoplifting—my dumb way of psychologically dealing with my parents' divorce—although I wasn't arrested for it, thank God. I'd learned my lesson in a very big way that sticking your hands in dangerous places would get them chopped off.

"Go," Carly urged. "This is so awesome!"

She wasn't much help. Carly would storm headfirst into danger if she thought it might mean that she'd have a good time. When she was a kid she'd stuck her hand in a beehive because she wanted to taste the honey. It hadn't turned out so well, of course, but I had to admire her for. . .well, *going for it,* despite all the signs not to. She didn't second-guess herself. She didn't regret anything she tried—even the crazy stuff.

With a last look at Carly, I followed Stephen off the dance floor. I was insanely curious what he wanted to speak to me about. I mean, despite us living very close to each other, he didn't even know me.

He led the way up a spiral staircase to the second-floor lounge, which was surrounded by glass walls with thin, swirling frosted patterns on the otherwise clear surface. Up here, away from the crowd and deejay and loudspeakers, I could actually hear myself think. The lounge had a couple of pool tables and red couches and chairs. Stephen leaned against one of the couches and studied me. He wore a black button-down shirt and dark jeans. His hair was slicked back off his handsome face. My stomach fluttered.

"So..." I began when he didn't say anything. "Do you come here often?"

Oh, God. I was normally proud of my smooth comebacks, my witty one-liners, and *that* was what came out of my mouth? I wanted a do-over.

Stephen grinned, showing straight white teeth. "I'm here every single night, lately. Even weekdays."

"Every night? Really?" I twisted my hair. "Cool."

Cool? Really? I was not handling this well at all. My brain and my voice weren't working in sync.

"Um, what are you doing in Trinity?" I asked. "I thought you were in university now."

He shrugged a shoulder. "I'm taking a bit of a break, trying to decide what I really want to do with my life. Thought I'd come back here for a while."

I just nodded and tried very hard not to say "cool" again.

"You come here every Friday, right, Samantha?"

A flush of pleasure went through me. I was totally okay with friends calling me Sam, but I liked hearing him say my full name.

"Usually."

"You like it here?"

I looked around. There weren't many people in the lounge tonight. It was the first time I'd even come up here, myself. A couple on the far couch glanced over at us every so often as if curious why Stephen Keyes was talking to me. The majority of kids were downstairs on the large dance floor and at the bar area, both visible through the glass wall that circled the lounge. I could even see the top of Carly's blond head from where I stood.

"Yeah, it's okay," I said.

"Just okay?"

I shrugged and rubbed my dry lips together, turning to face him. My lip gloss from earlier was long gone. "Some nights are better than others."

Stephen reached out a hand. "Come here."

If he hadn't made it sound like a charming invitation, I might have resisted. But I walked closer to him, until I was a few feet away. There was something strange in his gaze as he studied me. I couldn't put my finger on it, but a chill slid down my spine.

I cleared my throat. "You said you wanted to talk to me about something?"

"So you're the special one, are you?"

That was the last thing I expected him to say. "Special?"

"That's what she said. That's why she wants me to do this. I normally wouldn't, since you're so young."

She? She who? I frowned at him. "I'm seventeen."

"Exactly. That's young."

"No, it's not."

"Trust me, Samantha. It is."

He slid his arm around my waist so that his hand rested at the small of my back, and he drew me closer to him. His touch sank into me, cool against my hot skin.

It was suddenly difficult for me to breathe. "Who said I'm special?"

He didn't answer. When I looked up at him I realized he was leaning closer to me, closer and closer, and then his lips brushed against mine. I gasped and he pulled back a little.

"Is this okay?" he asked. "May I kiss you?"

My cheeks warmed. "I…um…"

He spoke softly into my ear. "I should warn you, it's a very dangerous kiss. It'll change your life forever, so you have to want it."

If I wasn't feeling so flustered, I might have thought he was being cocky. I mean, *please.* A kiss that could change my life forever?

But I kind of believed him. And after months of trying to be a perfect angel after the shoplifting incident, I wanted to push the edges of my comfort zone just a little bit.

And this *was* special—a boy I liked who might like me in return. I couldn't just walk away.

This time I kissed him, tangling my fingers into his black hair and pulling his mouth toward mine as if I couldn't resist. I hadn't kissed many boys before, so I hoped I was doing it right. It felt right. In fact, it felt *really* right. My lips parted as the kiss deepened. His fingers dug into my waist. This felt like something out of a movie—one of the romantic ones I never watched because they made me feel uncomfortable. I didn't want to try to relate to all of those emotions, those declarations of love and eternal devotion. I mean, spare me the drama.

"You're delicious," Stephen whispered before he kissed me again and my heart felt like it was pounding right out of my chest.

And then it got weird.

The cool sensation from his touch turned icy and spread to the kiss, and I shivered. That iciness slid down my throat to my stomach and branched out to my arms and legs, chilling my entire body. Goose bumps formed on my arms. Dizziness swirled through me. It was jarring, but I couldn't exactly say it felt bad. It was exciting, a rush, like being on a roller coaster in the middle of winter.

I lost track of time. Nothing existed for me except Stephen. His lips never left mine—and I never wanted them to. Minutes, hours, I didn't know how long it was that he kissed me. All I knew was that I couldn't stop kissing him even if I wanted to.

But then, finally, *he* stopped kissing *me*. He held my face between his hands and stared at me for a heavy moment. His eyes looked very dark in the shadows up here. "Sorry, kid. Really."

Then he let go of me and walked away.

Kid?

Time slowed to a crawl as he disappeared down the stairs, the dance music becoming a hollow echo in my ears. My face burned even though my chest now felt like ice.

The scent of sweat mixed with perfume slowly pulled me out of my daze. To my left I could see the multicolored lights above the dance floor. Even up here, the ground shook with the force of all the kids stomping down there.

Carly appeared at the top of the stairs and approached me, glancing back in the direction Stephen had gone. "Sam! What happened?"

I tried to find my voice. "Stephen Keyes kissed me."

Her eyes widened. "Oh, my God! You're so lucky!"

He'd kissed me. And then he'd called me a kid and walked away.

"Lucky," I repeated, just before my eyes rolled back, my knees gave out and everything went black.

chapter 2

In my dream, something moved beneath me, twisting around my ankles like long, cold fingers. I didn't know what it was, but the thought of being dragged down into the black, bottomless hole terrified me. Before it took hold of me completely, someone grabbed my hand.

Frantically I looked up to see a boy. I couldn't see him very well since it was so dark, but he was definitely *not* Stephen.

"Hold on!" His eyes were blue—so blue that they seemed to glow. He was the only thing keeping me from whatever was trying to pull me downward.

I tried to concentrate on his face but still couldn't see him clearly—only his eyes, which burned into me with their strange light.

"They were wrong, Samantha." His voice broke as he said my name. "It never should have been me. This is the proof."

"What?"

"I'm not strong enough for this." His grip on me loosened. "I've failed you. I've failed everyone. It—it's all over."

"No—don't let go! Don't let—"

The next moment, I slipped out of his grasp and fell, screaming, into the bottomless darkness.

"Sam! Wake up!" Carly sounded a million miles away.

My eyelids fluttered open and it took a moment for everything to come into focus. I lay on a red couch on my back and I was staring up at my best friend.

She punched me in the shoulder.

"Don't do that!" Her thin brows drew together. "You just freaked me out! Did you eat today? I have a Snickers bar in my purse if you need it."

"No…I'm okay." I sat up and ran a hand through my hair, forcing my way through a tangle. "What happened?"

"Stephen Keyes kissed you and then you totally passed out for a minute—not that I blame you. That must have been some kiss. Are you really okay?"

How embarrassing. After being kissed by the hottest guy in Trinity, I'd passed out right in front of everyone up here. Several of the other kids had drawn closer to get a look at me. "I was only out for a minute?"

"Yeah. Any longer and I would have called for help." Her cell phone was in her hand, its screen lit up as if she'd been about to make a distress call. She looked over her shoulder at the others gathered nearby. "She's okay now. Back off and give her some air."

They did, their curiosity about the girl who fainted leaving as quickly as it had arrived.

I watched them go back to their couches and chairs, talking amongst themselves. Then I scanned the rest of the lounge with growing dismay at the idea that I'd fainted. I *never* fainted. "Did Stephen see what happened?"

She glanced over her shoulder. "I don't think so. He took off. What did you two talk about?"

Our short conversation was now a blur. "Nothing, really. I don't even know why he wanted to talk to me in the first place. He brought me up here, said I was special or something and then he kissed me."

Her worried look shifted to one of happiness. "So awesome."

I cringed. "It's not a big deal."

"Stephen Keyes kisses you, you swoon like some girl in an old movie and you're trying to tell me it's not a big deal?"

"If it was that big of a deal, he wouldn't have just walked away." I wasn't going to let myself be too disappointed by that, but my throat felt thick and my eyes burned. He'd even apologized. Maybe he was sorry that he didn't find me very interesting or attractive, or maybe he was sorry that I was a lousy kisser. He *had* said that I was too young.

And that dream I'd had about falling and the guy with the amazing blue eyes—that had been seriously disturbing.

"Can we go?" I asked. "Sorry, I—I'm not feeling so hot."

Actually I was feeling cold as ice.

She opened her mouth as if to protest, but then closed it, her expression growing worried again. "You don't look so good. Yeah, we can definitely go."

"Thanks."

"Stupid Stephen Keyes. Who needs him?"

Frankly, I wanted to put the entire experience out of my head. Following the wickedly sexy boy off to be kissed hadn't led to danger; it had led only to the familiar feelings of disappointment and embarrassment. Stephen was the third boy I'd liked who'd made me feel bad about myself. Three strikes. I was out.

If I looked at it objectively, maybe this was a good lesson to learn. I didn't need any more trouble in my life.

I didn't leave my house all day Saturday or most of Sunday and I slept in past noon all weekend. It was highly unlike me to stay in bed so long. I figured I was coming down with the flu. That could explain the passing out and my recent chills.

Late Sunday afternoon, however, I forced myself to go to the movies with Carly. Even though it was only mid-October and the temperature read fifty-five degrees, it felt like it was freezing outside. Carly picked me up in her red Volkswagen Beetle—a gift from her parents for her birthday last month. My dad was generous with my presents and weekly allowance, especially since my parents had split two years ago and he'd moved to England for his law firm, but a few gifts and some cash weren't nearly the same as getting a car.

We paid good money to see *Zombie Queen IV,* which turned out to be possibly the worst movie in the history of mankind. As a self-proclaimed horror movie aficionado—with a deep fondness for all things George A. Romero—it took a lot to impress me.

"I'm so hungry," I said as we exited the theater while the credits rolled over the bloody, severed head of the hero. Even after gobbling down a large popcorn with extra butter, I was famished. It was strange. I'd pigged out all weekend. I didn't normally have such a voracious appetite.

"Maybe you're pregnant," Carly joked.

I eyed her. "Highly doubtful."

"I guess you're right. To be pregnant you'd have to actually be getting it on with somebody."

"Getting it on?" I repeated. "What a lovely way to put it.

Besides, I'm starving, remember? Doesn't pregnancy make you want to throw up?"

"It would make me want to throw up. Actually, I feel sick just thinking about it."

Carly hadn't brought up what had happened—or, rather, *not* happened—with Stephen at the club. It was appreciated more than she knew. If I could, I'd take a pill to forget about the embarrassment of him walking away after our kiss and leaving me standing there all alone. My crush on him had officially been crushed.

"Hey, Samantha!"

I turned to see a boy from my history class waving at me—Noah. He stood in a line waiting to get into the next showing of *Zombie Queen IV.*

"Be warned, that's a ridiculously bad movie," I said as we passed him on our way out to the lobby.

"I'll take my chances." Noah grinned. "You're looking good tonight."

"Oh…uh, thanks."

That was a strange thing for him to say. We'd never really spoken that much before. Maybe he was just being extra-friendly tonight.

Carly didn't say anything until we'd moved out of hearing distance. "So what's up with you getting hit on today? That's the second time since we got here. Am I totally invisible all of a sudden?"

The first time was when a guy named Mike—someone else I barely talked to at school—had sat right next to me in the theater and offered me some of his popcorn after I'd eaten all of mine. I honestly hadn't thought anything of it, but I guess Carly had noticed.

I frowned. "Who said that? I could have sworn I heard a voice, but I don't know where it's coming from."

She swatted me. "You're hilarious."

"I have no idea what's going on. Besides, he was just saying hi. That wasn't exactly an official hit."

"Well, if it doesn't pass, remember to share with your best friend."

I nodded solemnly. "Understood. I promise to share with you the wealth of boys who throw themselves at my irresistible feet."

Irresistible. Right. I already had a theory about why Stephen had kissed me, not that I wanted to share it with anyone, Carly included. I'd decided it had been a dare from his friends to go kiss a weird high school girl who had a thing for zombie movies—not that they'd know that little detail about me.

My stomach growled.

Correction: the weird high school girl who liked zombie movies and was suddenly ready to eat her way through the city. Then again, I'd always been too skinny. "A" didn't only describe the grades I was striving for, but my bra size, as well. Eating eight thousand calories a day would definitely solve that little problem. Pun intended.

Something smelled delicious. My skin tingled and my mouth watered. I closed my eyes and inhaled, seeking the new scent past the salty, greasy odor of popcorn that surrounded us.

Carly groaned. "I can't deal with him right now. I'll just wait over here, okay?"

"What?" I opened my eyes as she wandered toward a movie magazine rack near the concession stand. In her rush to get away, she banged against the island that held the napkins and plastic straws.

"Hope she didn't leave because of me," a familiar voice said.

Oh.

"How did you guess?" I turned my head to see Colin Richards, Carly's ex-boyfriend, standing a few feet away.

Colin sat behind me in English and we'd forged a bit of a friendship since the semester started last month, which was awkward considering how much Carly hated his guts. He'd cheated on her at a pool party this summer and, understandably, she'd been crushed by the betrayal. Colin tended to do crazy stuff when he was drunk. One of the crazy things he'd done was Julie Travis, who'd allegedly had her eye on Colin's broad shoulders, cropped sandy-blond hair and wicked sense of humor since they'd been in elementary school together. However, once he'd sobered up, Colin had realized his mistake, tried to make up with Carly and failed spectacularly. Carly was a lot like me in that way—she didn't get over being hurt easily. She put on a good front, but I knew she was still heartbroken.

"New haircut?" Colin asked.

I touched my dark hair, twisting a long piece around my index finger. "Not lately."

"It looks nice." When he smiled, my gaze was drawn to his mouth. I'd never noticed what nice lips Colin had. Carly had told me many times that he was an amazing kisser. As far as I knew—and, believe me, I would have been told otherwise—that's as far as they'd ever gone together.

I moved a little closer to him. "Are you wearing a new cologne?"

He shrugged. "Just soap."

I pulled myself out of my sudden daze to glance over my shoulder at Carly, who was currently out of earshot. However, she was still giving me the eye. The eye that asked, *Why are you smelling my ex-boyfriend?*

I cleared my throat. "I need to go. Uh, I'll see you in class tomorrow, okay?"

He nodded. "Bright and early."

I turned and walked over to Carly. She put down the magazine she'd been pretending to read. Her cheeks were flushed, which told me she was upset but trying to control her emotions.

"Sorry," I said.

"Don't be sorry." She sent a sneer in the direction of Colin, who'd rejoined his friends on the other side of the theater. "The fact that he's still breathing isn't your fault."

"He really wants you to forgive him."

"Did he say that?"

"Well, not just now, but it's implied."

Her lips thinned. "When he dies, I promise to put flowers on his grave. How's that?"

"It's a start."

I wasn't certain if Carly was still upset because she really loved Colin or if it was something else. Personally I think what had happened stung so much because he was the first guy to pursue a relationship with her. She tended to hide a bit, feeling fat—which she totally wasn't—and not thinking she was good enough to catch a hot guy. I knew at least two other guys who'd be happy to ask her out if she'd give them half a chance. Instead, she wallowed. Which was fine, since I was a bit of a wallower myself.

Carly grimaced, her gaze locked on something over my shoulder. "Brace yourself for impact. Jordan's on her way over here and she looks pissed."

I tensed up.

Jordan Fitzpatrick and I had been friends for three whole weeks in ninth grade drama class, until we'd started to like the same boy—one who hadn't liked me in return and had proven this by laughing in my face when he learned about my feelings. He hadn't liked Jordan, either, so she blamed me for the rejection. She'd then decided that she hated me. Because *that* made sense.

She'd just exited a neighboring theater with some of her equally unpleasant friends and was headed our way.

Nearly six feet tall with flame-red hair and a few scattered freckles on her nose, Jordan was easily the most beautiful girl in school. I knew from our short friendship that she wanted to be a model. A *top* model, of course, following in her mother's footsteps. Her mom currently starred in a soap opera down in Los Angeles, and Jordan had stayed here in Trinity with her father to finish school.

She'd been pursuing the modeling goal every waking moment that she wasn't at school, and so far she'd failed miserably at it. Just because you were gorgeous and tall didn't mean you were also photogenic.

Did I mention she hated me?

"I heard what you did at Crave on Friday night, you slut," she snapped.

"Great to see you, too, Jordan," I said.

"Julie said you were throwing yourself at him."

My stomach sank, but I tried to look confused. "Throwing myself at who?"

Her green eyes narrowed. "My boyfriend."

"Stephen Keyes is not your boyfriend," Carly interjected. "Not anymore."

Jordan's mouth dropped open. "Excuse me?"

Oh, crap. I'd totally forgotten the rumors that Jordan and Stephen had dated over the summer.

Carly might not have a great deal of self-confidence when

it came to standing up for herself, but when it involved protecting me, she did a great impression of a cute blonde pit bull. "From what I've heard, he dumped you last week, right? Sounds like he wanted to start seeing other people. And, FYI, Sam didn't throw herself at him—he approached her. So if you want to blame anyone for your object of lust's lips wandering elsewhere, it would be Stephen himself."

Jordan ignored Carly like she was a mildly annoying insect and focused on me. I could see the confusion in her eyes. "I guess I don't understand why Stephen would want to be anywhere near a nobody like *you*." Her words were sharp as glass as she twisted them into me.

In the answering silence, my stomach growled again. Loudly.

Jordan's expression soured further. "You're disgusting."

"Yeah, well, you're—"

"Go to hell, klepto." She spun around and walked away.

The klepto crack was a familiar insult from her, but it still made me flinch as if she'd slapped me. She'd been at the mall the day I'd been caught and had witnessed my humiliation firsthand.

"What a bitch!" Carly exclaimed. "Just ignore her."

"I'll try." My face felt hot. It sucked to have the subject of the kiss—and my shoplifting embarrassment—brought up by someone I really didn't like.

"She's welcome to Stephen, anyway. But I don't think he's interested in dating redheaded giraffes anymore."

I snorted. "That's the best you can come up with?"

"Give me a minute. I'm sure I can think of a better insult."

Jordan had succeeded in knocking my relatively decent mood right out of me. "I think I'm going to head home. Don't worry about driving me. I need some fresh air."

"You sure?"

"Positive. Besides, I have to make myself a sandwich. Maybe ten. I'm starving."

"If you don't gain any weight with this new diet of yours, I'm going to be mad. I hate being cursed with a slow metabolism." She placed her hands on her curvy hips. "Fine, you go pig out and I'll see you tomorrow. And, Sam?"

"Yeah?"

"Forget about what Jordan said. She's a troll who's just looking to get a reaction out of you to give her pathetic little life meaning. And forget about Stephen, too. Seriously. It doesn't matter how hot he is. If he can't appreciate how amazing you are, then who needs a loser like him?"

I shook my head and finally managed a real smile. "What would I do without you?"

She grinned back at me. "That is an excellent question."

Even when Carly was dealing with her own romantic woes, she still did everything she could to make me feel better about mine. It definitely helped to have that kind of support in my corner.

My stomach grumbled again as I headed for home. I didn't know why I was so hungry now. But I had the strangest feeling that a sandwich wasn't going to help me very much.

chapter 3

McCarthy High was a mile east of the movie theater and I lived a few blocks north of the school. While there were still plenty of shops and businesses in this area, it didn't have the same cold, gray cement look of downtown. Here there were tall oak trees that were turning gorgeous fall colors and well-manicured lawns, still green, lining the side streets.

I'd lived in Trinity, New York, all my life. After my parents' separation, my mother and I had stayed in the same house I grew up in. She hadn't worked when they were married, but since the split, she'd gotten her real-estate license and started a job that quickly took over her life. She loved it, or at least she spent so many hours at it that she *should* love it. I practically felt like an orphan.

A distant rumble of thunder reminded me that a rainstorm had been forecast for tonight. I wanted to get home before it arrived, so I picked up my pace for a couple of blocks.

Then something slowed me to a stop.

A boy sat with his back pressed against the front of an office supply shop, the closed sign in the window just above his head. His long legs lay straight across the sidewalk in front of me. His hands covered his face. I eyed a couple of people as they passed by, but they didn't even glance in his direction.

Typical. Everyone minded their own business in this neighborhood. Especially when it came to someone who looked like he might be a street kid. This boy wore ripped jeans, scuffed black boots and a plain blue T-shirt. No coat. I drew my own black trench tighter around me to help block out the chill.

Just after my parents separated and my father moved away, I'd reacted by running away from home after a huge fight with my mother. I'd been sick of her ignoring me and I'd wanted to make a statement, make her appreciate having her only child around a bit more than she seemed to. Even though I'd known that the world didn't revolve around me, I'd figured that *her* world should. At least, a little.

I'd lived in the heart of downtown for three days, a couple of miles from here. Early on my second day, some street kids had found me sitting on the sidewalk, crying my eyes out as I felt lost and sorry for myself. They'd taken me under their protection and brought me to a local mission, where I'd eaten a hot meal. That night, they'd let me sleep in the basement of an abandoned house they'd found on the west side of the city. Then they'd told me I should go home, since putting up with a mother like mine was way better than anything they had to deal with. Also, after my frantic mother had contacted the police and filed a missing persons report on me, it was only a matter of time before I would have been found. Still, I was on the streets long enough for bad things to have happened if I'd been on my own the whole time.

I'd never seen them again, but I'd never forgotten what they'd done for me. If I could help somebody like that to pay it forward, then I would give it my best shot.

"Hey," I said to the boy on the sidewalk. "Are you okay?"

When I didn't get a response, I leaned over and tapped the kid lightly on his shoulder. I hated to think he might be hurt. "Can you hear me?"

A streetlamp nearby picked that moment to flicker on, and he finally pulled his hands away from his face. He blinked long lashes a few shades darker than his mahogany-colored hair. The most incredible eyes met mine—a cobalt-blue so intense it felt as if he could see right through me to the other side. My breath caught. He was the most gorgeous boy I'd ever seen in my life—and he seemed familiar to me, but I had no idea why.

He was older than I'd first thought. My age, maybe a year older.

His brows drew together. "Who are you?"

"I'm Samantha. Samantha Day. Do you need help? Are you hurt?"

He gazed into my eyes as if hypnotized by what he saw there. I gazed back, unable to look away from him. "I don't know what to do. My—my head. It's not working right ever since I fell. My thoughts are all jumbled together." He grimaced as if he were in pain.

Concern swept through me. "You fell? Did you hit your head?"

"My head?"

I fished in my black leather bag for my phone. "If you want me to call somebody for you, I can totally do that."

"I can't find them." There was pain in his voice, but I wasn't sure if it was emotional or physical. Either way, my chest tightened at the sound of it. "I've been searching night and day. It's my fault. All my fault. I'm going to fail and all will be lost. Everything and everyone. Forever and ever."

He said he'd fallen, but I wasn't so sure about that. If I was placing a bet, I'd say this was either a mental thing or a drug thing.

I studied him. Maybe I'd seen his picture in the newspaper or on TV as his parents searched for him out on the streets, and that was why he seemed so familiar.

"What's your name?" I asked.

"Bishop."

"Okay. Is that your first name or your last name?"

"It's—just Bishop."

"You have only one name?" Unless he was a rock star or a chess piece, it was another sign that he was having trouble thinking straight.

"Right—only Bishop. Nothing else now." The expression on his handsome face was one of deep confusion. "When I volunteered for this, they told me I would be a great leader. They said there might be difficulties, but they thought I could handle whatever happened. It wasn't supposed to be this hard. I thought I'd go back to normal when I arrived. But this—this is *not* normal." He looked angry about "this," whatever it meant. He frowned and rubbed his temples. "Who are you?"

I felt an irresistible urge to help this boy, if I could. "I told you already. I'm Samantha. So you're looking for somebody? Is it somebody from your family—your mom or dad? Is there anyone I can call to come pick you up?"

He pushed himself up from the sidewalk. He was easily a foot taller than me, although I was pretty short at five-two and currently wearing flats. His unexpected physical presence overwhelmed me for a moment and I took a shaky step back from him. The T-shirt he wore fit tight across his chest like it was a couple of sizes too small, but he didn't have an ounce of fat on him. I felt uneasy now that he was towering over me rather than sprawled on the sidewalk, and yet I didn't turn away from him. Those eyes—they seemed to hold me in place. And he smelled so incredible—spicy and sweet—I couldn't even describe it properly. His very presence seemed to sink into my senses.

"Samantha," he repeated.

A strangely pleasant shiver slid down my spine. He cocked his head as he continued to study me with those vivid blue eyes. There was a coldness to his appearance, to the hard lines of his face, but I couldn't look away.

I shifted back again as he drew closer to me. "What are you looking at?"

He held my gaze. "You're…beautiful."

"Uh…th-thanks?" My face flushed at his words and I cleared my throat. "Maybe I should just leave you alone. You look, um, sturdy enough now." To say the least. I felt an urge to move even closer to him, but there wasn't any reason for me to feel that way. Confusing emotions battled inside me. He might be in distress, but I wasn't going to put myself in harm's way. "But you really should call your parents and tell them you're okay. They're probably worried about you. There's a mission on Peterson Avenue. They can help you if you go there."

The chill in the air had gotten worse now that it was dark out. I began to move past him, feeling it time to exit stage left. Besides, my strange hunger seemed to be getting worse by the minute. I needed to eat something soon. Even if it didn't really help, at least it would take the edge off whatever was wrong with me.

"Samantha, wait."

I froze and slowly turned back to the boy who'd just called me *beautiful*. Not something I heard every day, that was for sure. Maybe that was why it knocked me off balance so much, especially given my recent difficulties with the last guy who'd showed a fleeting interest in me.

I didn't move as he approached me again. He smelled warm and clean—I guess he hadn't been on the streets that long. He smelled good...*really* good.

Bishop's expression clouded and he rubbed his temples again. "It's like a million images are hitting me all at once. Even more now that you're here with me. All I know is...it's running out. I have only four more days to find the others before they're lost to me. But...there's no one. Nowhere. Maybe I'm alone. Maybe they're not here. But they're supposed to be, and I'm supposed to be able to find them."

My heart pounded hard and fast. It had done something similar with Stephen the other night, speeding up at the idea of spending time with him. But this was different—it *felt* different. And it wasn't just because Bishop was a very cute, if disturbed, boy whose path had crossed mine. There was something about him—something I couldn't place. So familiar. So compelling. Bishop was strange and babbling, but I felt drawn to him like nothing I'd experienced before. I tried to tell myself he was just a troubled kid I'd found on the sidewalk, not someone I should ever be attracted to.

I need to walk away. Right now.

But I didn't.

"Are you high?" It was a guess, probably a good one. I needed a reason for his odd behavior, to label it so this would make some kind of sense to me.

He looked up at the dark sky. "High, yes. I need to be high above the city. That might help me find them."

I looked up. There were no stars tonight. The heavy clouds were threatening rain. A bright beam of light shone up above the tall buildings, back in the direction of the movie theater.

"Above the city?" I asked, following his gaze.

He shook his head. "I can't fly here. None of us can. And it hurts so much—I can't explain it properly because I can't think properly. I'm damaged." He raked a hand through his dark, messy hair. "Why is it like this for me? I hate feeling this way, but I can't snap out of it and get control. There has to be another way."

He leaned back against the store window, slouching as if it was difficult for him to remain standing. Concern gnawed at my gut.

I didn't want to feel responsible for this guy, but I did anyway. I liked to think I wasn't like the other coldhearted people around here—I refused to let myself be like that. I couldn't sidestep someone just because they were in trouble and saying crazy stuff.

I let out a shaky breath. "It's going to be okay, Bishop. I'll help you."

He looked at me with surprise. "You will?"

"Of course." I reached for his hand.

The moment I touched him, a strong crackle of electricity coursed up my arm.

I gasped.

And then a vision slammed into me like I'd just been flattened by a truck.

A city in darkness, melting and draining away like water in a bathtub—falling into a dark hole in the center of everything. People, thousands and thousands of them, trying to run away but getting pulled into the vortex. There was no escape.

Bishop was there trying to help. To save everyone, including me. I reached for his hand as he yelled my name, but he was swept away from me before I could touch him.

Then it was all over.

Where there had once been a city, there was nothing but darkness.

The horrifying image left me shaking and gasping.

Bishop looked down with shock at my hand in his before I pulled away from him. Thunder rumbled in the skies above us.

"No, wait." He grabbed my hand again.

"Did you see that?" I asked, my voice trembling.

"See what?" He frowned. "I didn't see anything. But when you touch me…I can suddenly think clearly for the first time in days."

I stared at him, finding it hard to catch my breath. The strange vision—had it been my imagination? I was shaking so hard that I could barely form words. "You're crazy."

His expression held deep surprise. "Not anymore."

"You're not making sense."

"But it's still true." There was way more clarity in his gaze now. "I don't understand how you're able to do this, but—do you feel it, too?"

"What?"

"We have a connection. The moment I saw you…I don't know what it is. Maybe you were sent to help me. Maybe they knew I needed you to find me. That has to be it."

The sharp edges of the disturbing vision had softened in my mind like they were nothing more than a remembered dream. Now holding Bishop's hand felt…good. Too good. Touching him had chased his confusion away—although that made absolutely no sense. I suddenly realized it had chased my chill away, too. Warmth slid slowly up my arm and through the rest of me. Yet, despite this newfound heat, his touch still made me shiver.

I looked down at my hand in his but didn't pull it away this time.

"Maybe I'll be able to find the others now," Bishop said.

"What others?" My voice sounded hoarse. "Your family?"

"No. The others. They're…supposed to help me."

"You're still holding my hand."

He raised his blue eyes to mine, and a smile played on his lips for the first time—a really amazing smile that made my heart skip a beat. "You have no idea how good this feels for me."

I had to admit, it felt pretty good for me, too. Dangerously good.

"I don't know what you are or where you came from," Bishop said, "but thank you."

I felt dazed. "*What* I am?"

He nodded. "To make me feel this way you must be very special…and you don't even realize it, do you?"

I almost laughed at that, but what came out sounded like a nervous hiccup. "Trust me, I'm not special. But you do seem better. Not sure I can take the credit for it, though."

"You have no idea what I've been through since I got here. I'm not used to making mistakes, but now it feels like that's all I do. I hope it'll be better now."

He had been horribly confused. And now, suddenly—because he was touching me?—that confusion was gone. It didn't make any sense.

"Who are you looking for?" I asked.

His expression grew pained again, and he craned his neck as he looked up into the sky. "I was told there would be columns of light—searchlights—to help lead my way, but I can't find any. They were to be my guide and I'm lost without them."

I glanced back in the direction of the movie theater. "Uh…you don't happen to mean something like *that* column of light, do you?"

His brows drew together. "I don't see anything."

I frowned and thumbed in the light's direction. "You can't see that bright beam of light over there?"

"No. But..." He hesitated and gave me a hard, skeptical look. "But *you* can?"

"I don't know how anyone could miss it. I thought it was coming from the movie theater."

"Samantha..." Again, as he said my name, I felt that strange shiver course through me. "If you can really see the light, you need to show me where it leads."

I remembered the story about Carly and the hive of bees. She'd been stung ten times and the doctor said she was very lucky it hadn't been worse than that. If it were me, I wouldn't ever have eaten honey again because of that painful memory. But not Carly. She still loved honey. Then again, Carly's always been a little bit crazy.

I remembered Stephen walking away Friday night at Crave, leaving me standing there all alone. That had been my first painful bee sting in a long time, and a recent one, too. I was still recovering from it.

"You said you'd help me," he said. "Did you mean it?"

Bishop wanted me to lead him to the column of bright light that he said he couldn't see. And I was going to do it because...well, I didn't really know why, but I was going to do it anyway.

I let out a shaky breath. "Okay, fine. Follow me."

He let go of my hand as we walked, and the chill I'd felt before began to set in again.

"It's already fading," Bishop said, his expression tense.

"What? The light?"

"No, my sanity. So we'd better make this quick."

"But you feel okay when you touch me?"

He looked disturbed. "Yes."

"Fine. Then, *here.*" I held out my hand to him, and when he entwined his fingers with mine again, I was filled by that incredible, blissful heat—and, thankfully, no disturbing vision this time.

He smiled at me. "Much better."

My face heated up right along with the rest of my body.

I'd been certain the light was coming from the movie theater. Instead, it led us to an alley behind a fast-food restaurant. When we turned the corner, the light disappeared as if someone had flicked off a switch. Weird.

At the end of the short alley, a tall kid with dark blond hair rummaged noisily through an overflowing Dumpster. He looked about the same age as Bishop. I grimaced as he put something in his mouth and started chewing. It looked like a half-eaten hamburger.

Um, *gross.*

Bishop had stopped in place and was staring at the kid with an expression on his face I couldn't put a name to. Confusion, doubt and something else. Something bleak.

"Everything okay?" I asked him.

His shoulders tensed and he looked at me. "It will be."

"Well, good. I assume you know that kid?"

"Don't worry about him." He leaned over and looked deep into my eyes. He took my other hand in his, as well. A breath caught in my chest.

"Okay, I won't worry," I said.

"I really don't understand this."

"Well, that makes two of us."

"You saw the searchlight when I couldn't." He frowned, as if trying to make sense of it all. "You were sent to help me when I needed it most—when I'd nearly given up hope. Thank you."

I couldn't help but grin at how dramatic he was being. "You're very welcome."

His expression turned tense, and he let me go so suddenly that I nearly lost my balance. It helped break me out of my current daze.

"It's strange. I thought for a second that you—" His dark brows drew together before he shook his head.

"You thought for a second…what?"

"Something bad. But it's nothing." He turned to look at the Dumpster-diving kid before returning his gaze to mine. "You need to go now, Samantha."

I inhaled sharply. "What?"

He took a step back as if forcing himself to put some space between us. "I need to talk to him alone."

The distance between us helped to clear my head a little. "But—"

"Just go. And forget you ever met me."

It felt like I'd just been punched in the gut, and it took me a moment to catch my breath. The cold splash of a raindrop hit my face.

He wanted me to forget I'd met him. But I kind of thought that we…

That we *what?* Had a connection because a good-looking but kind of crazy guy had called me *beautiful?* Because he'd said I was *special?*

My second bee sting of the weekend hurt like hell.

"Fine." My chest ached. "I guess you should grab your friend before he finds a dead rat to nibble on."

There was a sliver of regret in his blue eyes—or maybe that was just wishful thinking. He'd gotten what he needed from me and now he was giving me the brush-off. "Goodbye, Samantha."

"Whatever." I swallowed hard, then turned and walked away, forcing myself not to look back.

But even as I left the alley, my steps slowed.

Was he some milk-carton missing kid? Did he need professional help to deal with his mental issues? And who was the garbage-eating boy in the alley Bishop had needed a beam of light in order to find? I couldn't just walk away and forget all about this without having any of my questions answered. Even if he didn't want me around, I had to find out what was going on.

Ignoring the sharp needles of cold rain, I returned to the small alley and peered around the corner. The boys were close enough for me to hear them.

The other kid finally noticed Bishop and abandoned his secondhand meal, dropping the remains of the burger to the dirty, wet ground. "Who are you?"

Bishop didn't speak right away. He cleared his throat first. "You don't know me?"

"No, should I?"

"My name's Bishop," he said evenly. "I'm here to help you."

The other boy eyed Bishop warily. "How are you going to help me?"

"Do you remember who you are? Do you remember anything at all?"

The boy ran a hand through his dirty blond hair, now damp from the rain, his expression tight and uncertain. "I woke up three days ago in a park north of here with no idea how I got there."

"I know how."

Relief flooded the kid's expression. "Yeah? And you can help me?"

Another moment of hesitation. "That's my job. Come closer."

Bishop's voice sounded stronger now, no babbling or disjointed thoughts like before. His shoulders were broad and he stood straight and tall, his back to me, the rain soaking through his T-shirt, darkening it.

The boy moved away from the Dumpster to stand in front of Bishop. They were the same height and build.

"Show me your back," Bishop instructed.

"My back?"

"Please, it'll only take a moment. I can't make any more mistakes, even if I'm absolutely sure who you are."

The blond kid looked bewildered as he turned and pulled up his shirt. It was fully dark now, and the only light came from a single security lamp on a post against the gray brick wall, but I could still see enough. On either side of his spine was a detailed tattoo of wings, so large that it extended down past the waistband of his pants. I squinted a little and noted that the wings were outlined and shaded in black.

It was trendy for some kids to get a wing tattoo—especially the guys on McCarthy's football team, the Ravens. But they usually got it on their arms.

My rational mind wanted me to believe it was just a big version of the Ravens tattoo. However, these wings weren't feathery like a bird's. They were more webbed and...batlike.

Another shiver raced through me and my teeth began to chatter. My hair was now drenched from the icy-cold rain.

"I've seen enough," Bishop said.

The boy lowered his shirt. Just like Bishop, he wasn't wearing a coat despite the chill in the air and the falling rain.

"So now what?" the boy asked.

"Now you need to be brave."

The boy's attention shifted to the gold-bladed knife Bishop pulled from a sheath on his back that I hadn't noticed before. "What are you going to do with that?"

"What I was sent here to do," Bishop said. "My mission."

He plunged the knife into the boy's chest.

chapter 4

A scream tore from my throat. "No! What are you doing?"

Bishop sent a fierce glare over his shoulder at me. "You weren't supposed to see this."

I ran toward the boy and grabbed hold of his arm as he staggered backward. A flash of lightning forked across the sky followed by a crack of thunder, and the rain came down even harder.

"You… You're a—" The boy clutched at me, his eyes widening with pain and shock. I looked with horror at the blood soaking through his dirty white shirt as the boy's grip on me grew painfully tight. "A gray."

"What?"

But then he slipped out of my grasp, dropped to his knees and, with a last hiss of breath, fell face forward onto the pavement.

"Oh, my God! You killed him!" I could barely breathe. My entire body began to tremble. I'd never seen anyone murdered before. Not in real life.

Bishop grabbed me and slammed me up against the brick

wall. I shrieked as he pressed the sharp golden knife against my throat.

"A gray," he growled, and there was nothing remotely confused in his fierce expression anymore. He looked like he wanted to slit my throat right here and now. "I wasn't sure before…but you *are* one of them."

"Let go of me!" I wanted to struggle, but I couldn't move much for fear that the knife would cut me. His body pressed against mine, effortlessly pinning me. His short hair was now slicked to his forehead from the rain and his eyes glowed—literally *glowed*—with blue light. Before, I'd found his eyes beautiful, but now they were absolutely terrifying.

And suddenly, I remembered seeing those eyes before—in my dream, the one I'd had when I passed out at Crave. The dream where he'd let me fall into the horrible darkness.

Something slid behind his gaze, past the fierceness. It looked like bitter disappointment. "How many souls have you devoured since you were turned?"

Tears burned my eyes and I tried to press back against the wall so I wouldn't have to be so close to him. The knife at my neck made it difficult to speak or breathe. "I don't know what you're talking about!"

"You've been kissed. Your soul is lost. You're one of them now."

Kissed.

The bitter taste of bile rose in my throat as I remembered the cold sensation when Stephen had kissed me. At the time it had felt like riding a roller coaster in the winter. Exhilarating and thrilling. It hadn't been a normal kiss. I'd known it then, but I'd tried to pretend it never happened at all. Even though it had.

I should warn you, it's a very dangerous kiss, Stephen had told me. *It will change your life forever.*

Bishop looked pained and the knife eased off a fraction. "I don't understand why you helped me—why you *could* help me. They told me grays would be completely controlled by their insatiable hunger. But when you touched me—"

Oh, I'd touch him, all right.

I drove my knee up between his legs as hard as I could. He gasped and let go of me. I didn't think twice before running away. I ran as far and as fast as I could through the maze of alleys and backstreets we'd taken to get there, before looking over my shoulder. My vision was blurred by tears and rain, but I could see that he wasn't chasing me.

Bishop was insane. A killer. And I'd led him directly to his victim.

I stopped the first police cruiser I saw and ran to the driver's side. "There's been a murder!"

I quickly took the cop back to the alley, but by the time we got there it was empty. Completely empty. The cop looked at me skeptically as I craned my neck, looking for any sign of what had happened here. I knew it was the right alley. The half-eaten hamburger was still lying on the ground in a puddle.

"It happened only a few minutes ago. Please, you have to believe me!"

My insistence seemed to get through to him and he started to take me seriously. He asked me questions about what I'd seen and where I'd been tonight. He told me that there had been a few missing persons cases recently and that I should be careful.

I didn't read the papers or watch the news, so I'd had no idea. If I had, I never would have walked home alone with my head in the clouds, stopping to help out a good-looking kid on the street. Bishop could be the reason behind these disappearances.

"I'll come back tomorrow morning to check the alley again," the cop told me. "Even with the rain, a murder like you're describing would leave blood evidence behind, but I don't see any here." He paused. "Is there any chance this was your imagination? You said you'd gone to see a horror movie earlier, right?"

I opened my mouth to argue with him, but then closed it. He was right. If I said that I'd witnessed a murder, but there was no body, no blood, only minutes after the crime had taken place, then what was he supposed to think?

What was *I* supposed to think?

He drove me home in his cruiser and told me again not to worry about anything, that the police were on top of it. He assured me that the city was safe and that he was quite sure I'd just been imagining things. I nodded, my brain spinning as I felt sick to my core. He walked me to my front door and waited till I unlocked it and went inside before he went back to his cruiser and drove away. I was soaked to the skin from the rain and shaking from cold and fear.

My mother had a business dinner with her real-estate associates that she'd said would keep her out until at least midnight. I didn't often want to spend a lot of time with her—we were so different that we had practically nothing in common anymore—but I desperately wished she was home right now.

I wanted to call Carly and tell her everything. I even went so far as to get my phone out of my bag, but the screen flickered and went out as I scrolled through the numbers. Dead battery. I swore under my breath. Before I went for the landline, I had second thoughts. I had no proof that what I'd seen was even real. I didn't think Bishop had had enough time to pick up the body and carry it away with no trace.

But I'd seen it. I *had.* I wasn't going crazy.

I glanced out the narrow window at the side of the front door, past the blind, to make sure I hadn't been followed.

Grays are controlled by their insatiable hunger.

A sob caught in my chest. I didn't even know what a gray was, other than a drab color. All I knew was that I was hungry all the time. And I knew, down deep, that it wasn't just for food.

The blond kid's face haunted me. He'd looked so alone and confused. I'd seen the hope in his eyes when he thought Bishop was going to help him. Instead, Bishop had stabbed him in the heart.

And then they'd both disappeared.

Despite the fact that I couldn't stop shaking, I managed to eat three slices of cold pizza before I went to bed. My stomach didn't seem to care as much as my brain did that I'd been a witness to murder.

I couldn't get to sleep, staring up at my stucco ceiling and finding scary images of monsters hidden there. I squeezed my eyes shut and tried to block out my thoughts, but what I'd seen in the alley filled my head like a nonstop horror movie marathon. I normally loved horror movies; they were my escape. But they weren't nearly as much fun when you experienced them in real life.

When I finally fell asleep, I had another dream about Bishop. This time I could see him clearly as he approached me on the street, his hand held out toward me as if he wanted to touch me.

I cringed away from him. "Leave me alone!"

His face was strained and haunted. "You know I can't do that. Not anymore."

I realized I had a knife—Bishop's knife—clutched in my hand. "Stay away from me or I'll do it! I'll kill you!"

Despite my warning, he still drew closer as if he couldn't help himself.

I didn't remember stabbing him, but I must have, because the very next moment, he fell to his knees and touched the hilt of the knife sticking out of his chest with shaking hands.

His intense blue eyes locked with mine. "They can't have you—promise me, Samantha. You won't let them have you."

When he fell heavily to his side, the light from his eyes extinguished, and he didn't move again. A cry rose in my throat. Suddenly I wanted to touch him, to heal him. I wanted to make it all better again, make everything go away, but it was too late.

Shadows began to creep toward me from every direction. As they moved over Bishop's body, he disappeared as if he'd never been there in the first place.

"You must come with us now, Samantha," the voices said as the shadows drew closer and closer.

Icy hands gripped me, stripping away any warmth left inside me and leaving only fear behind.

"You're one of us now. You'll always be one of us."

"No!" When I tried to fight them, they began to rip me apart. But instead of blood, darkness spilled from inside me.

I forced myself awake with a blood-curdling scream.

My mother thundered down the hallway and yanked open my bedroom door.

"What's wrong?" Her face was pale, her normally perfect blond hair a mess. She pulled her bathrobe tighter around her. Dark circles cut under her pale blue eyes. She suffered from insomnia and usually got only a few hours of sleep a night. A screaming daughter didn't exactly help matters.

I looked at her from my tangle of light pink bedsheets. "Bad dream. *Really* bad dream."

"A bad dream? That's all it was? I thought you were being murdered in here."

I flinched at her choice of words, wanting to tell her everything but knowing she wouldn't believe a word I said. Why would she? I barely believed it myself. "Sorry I woke you."

She leaned her forehead against the edge of the door. "Better now?"

"I'll survive."

"Warm milk helps me sometimes. Do you want some?"

"No, thanks." Just the thought of it turned my stomach. My new hunger didn't seem to extend toward heated dairy products.

Whenever I'd had a nightmare as a kid, she'd come into my room and read me a story until I got sleepy again. I remembered one in particular about a bunny who got lost in the forest and had to rely on the kindness of strangers—even those who might normally eat him for dinner—to help lead him home. Luckily it had a happy ending. Not all wolves had an appetite for cute bunnies.

For a moment, I had the urge to ask her to read me that story, but I held my tongue. I wasn't a little kid anymore.

"You scared me," she said groggily, rubbing her eyes. "But I'm glad nothing's wrong. Try to get some sleep. Brand-new week starting. Hopefully it'll be a good one."

As she left, she kept my door open a crack. It wasn't as big of a comforting gesture as reading me a bedtime story about rabbits and wolves becoming friends with each other, but it was better than nothing.

I had an old teddy bear named Fritz that had been relegated to the rocking chair in the corner of my room next to my packed bookcase. He was missing an eye, and his left arm was partially detached. I grabbed him and pulled him into bed with me, clutching him to my chest. But whatever comfort he'd given me when I was younger, he failed to deliver tonight.

An hour later, I gave up on sleep. I grabbed my laptop from the floor next to my bed and went to the website for the *Trinity Chronicle,* searching for the latest news to see if anyone had reported any stabbings or murders. There was nothing. Between this and the dismissive "it was just your imagination" reaction I'd gotten from the cop, it was like it never happened.

But it had.

I read up on recent disappearances, but none seemed related to what had happened tonight. Trinity was a big city with a million residents. Bad things happened year-round to people young and old, male and female, beautiful and ugly. It didn't seem to matter who or when or why.

I propped my pillows behind me and gathered my thick duvet closer so I wouldn't feel so cold. Then I did a Google search for *gray,* but that didn't give me anything useful. I mean, it was just a color, that was all. But that was what the blond kid had called me. That was what had made Bishop freak out and look at me like I was a monster, when really it was the other way around. *He* was the monster.

For a moment, I'd thought he was so much more.

I closed the computer, swearing to put him and everything I'd seen and experienced completely out of my mind.

Yeah, right. Like that was even possible.

Monday morning loomed painfully bright and early. I wanted to stay home and hide, but I knew I couldn't. Instead,

I forced myself to get up and get ready for school. My mother had already left for work by the time I came downstairs. I had a breakfast of scrambled eggs and toast—and *more* toast—none of which made a single dent in my hunger.

When I went to the bathroom to get ready, the full-length mirror on the back of the door showed that I looked exactly the same as I ever had—short, skinny, with long, wild dark hair that I pulled back into a ponytail to keep off my face. A smear of peach-colored lip gloss and a swipe of black mascara was the sum total of my beauty regimen for a regular school day. Same as always.

But something had changed. People at McCarthy High were looking at me differently.

I tried to ignore the curious looks and outright stares I got as I made my way into the school. Maybe they were staring at me because I looked like someone who'd hung out with a gorgeous but crazy blue-eyed murderer last night. A murderer who'd disappeared into thin air along with his victim, making me question my sanity and my own damn eyes.

Or, more likely, the news of what happened with Stephen and me at Crave on Friday night had gone viral. Likely Jordan was spreading the rumor that I was a slut, blowing everything out of proportion to make my life even more difficult than it already was.

"Excuse me, Ms. Day," Mr. Saunders, my English teacher, said near the end of first period. His thick glasses made him look like a disapproving owl peering down at me from a tree branch. "Are you paying attention to me this morning?"

I straightened in my seat, flattening my palms against the cool surface of my desk, and tried to pull myself out of my thoughts. "Of course I am."

"Then what did I just say?"

I felt everyone watching me, waiting to see if I'd make a fool out of myself.

"You said—" I gulped and scanned the blackboard for a clue "—something about *Macbeth?*"

"Is that a question or a statement?"

"A statement. Definitely a statement."

"Since that's the play we're discussing this week, I think it's a given that I'm talking about it. But what *precisely* did I just say?"

The walls felt as if they were closing in on me and I suddenly had trouble breathing. I had a very strong urge to get out of there and I didn't have time to explain why. I'd face the consequences later.

I grabbed my leather bag and books before getting up from my seat. "I'm sorry, Mr. Saunders. I—I'm not feeling so good."

"Ms. Day?" He watched with surprise as I left my desk and escaped from the room without another word.

The harder I tried to think about something else, the more the memories of last night clutched me like a giant, monstrous hand. I needed some fresh air. First, I hurried to my locker to drop off my books.

"Hey, what happened in there?" Colin had followed me from class. He held his dog-eared copy of *Macbeth* and his binder casually at his side. "You okay?"

I shoved my books into my locker and closed it, twirling the dial on the lock. "Yeah, I'm fine."

"Glad to hear it."

I crossed my arms to try to warm up. Colin wore short sleeves, which made me think that I was the only one with a temperature problem today. "You left class just to check on me?"

"Well, yeah. Of course I did. I told Saunders I wanted to

make sure you're okay. He seemed concerned, so he didn't have a problem with it. You're lucky he likes you."

No one else had come after me. I didn't have too many other friends in that class. I didn't have too many other friends *period.* "You're so sweet."

I could have sworn his cheeks flushed a little. But it was true. He *was* sweet. Except for his inability to deal with parties without drinking and then making ridiculously bad choices involving stupid, vain cheerleaders, he was basically the perfect guy.

"Listen, Samantha—" He raised his gaze from the scuffed floor to look at me. "I know Carly and I didn't end on good terms. Seeing her trying to avoid me last night wasn't fun."

I tensed at the mention of their breakup. "That's an understatement."

He rubbed his hand over his forehead and looked down at his feet again. "And I know you're her friend—"

"*Best* friend."

"Right. Best friend. But you're still talking to me. You haven't given me the cold shoulder like her other friends have."

Good point. I hadn't. I couldn't help it, I liked Colin. Him coming after me just now to make sure I wasn't going to spontaneously combust proved that feeling was mutual.

"I know Carly doesn't approve," I said with a shrug, "but I make my own decisions when it comes to people I choose to talk to."

"Good. So, yeah, I'm not sure if this might cause some friction between you two, but I just have to ask…"

"What?"

He raised his gaze to mine. "Do you want to go out some time?"

I wasn't sure I'd heard him right. "Go out?"

"You and me, maybe the movies on the weekend. Or we could go to Crave."

Oh, boy.

I suddenly had the very clear image of me telling Carly about this and her not speaking to me for a few decades, even though it totally wasn't my fault. Or maybe it was. I was still talking to Colin after everyone else associated with Carly had collectively decided to give him the death glare whenever he was nearby.

He'd drawn closer to me until there was barely a foot separating us. Too close. Anyone who saw us might get the wrong idea.

I twisted a piece of hair that had fallen out of my ponytail tightly around my index finger and inhaled deeply. "Oh, Colin. I, uh, really like you. Seriously, but—"

I stopped talking.

His scent—I didn't believe it was just soap, like he'd said last night at the movie theater. He smelled…edible. He was too close to me right now. I could barely think straight.

"But what?"

I shivered, now focused entirely on his mouth. "Oh, my God. I'm so hungry right now."

He grinned. "How is it possible that you can make that sentence sound so sexy?"

"Sexy?"

"Yeah." He leaned closer to me.

No, he wasn't *leaning* closer. I was *pulling* him closer, sliding my hands over his shoulders and around his nape to tangle into his hair.

Just as his lips were an inch from mine, I came to my senses. I braced my hands against his chest and pushed him away from me.

He looked at me with confusion. "Uh, what was that?"

"I don't know. Sorry...I need to go." I swallowed hard and walked away from him. Quickly. I didn't stop until I passed through the doors of the school and felt the cool morning air on my face. I gulped it in and tried to push against the hunger that had almost made me kiss Colin. The need was nearly impossible to resist.

But I'd resisted.

Something caught my eye. A blond guy stood at the bottom of the stairs by the path that led to the parking lot. He was watching me.

I gasped. It was the kid from the alley last night.

The one Bishop had killed.

He casually turned and started to walk away. Without thinking twice, I ran after him.

"Wait!" I tripped over my own ankle and almost fell before staggering to a stop on the narrow path that wound through school grounds. The blond guy had sat down on a bench and was watching my approach. His dirty and bloody clothes from last night were gone, replaced by clean blue jeans and a long-sleeved black T-shirt.

"Hi there," he greeted me casually. "Samantha, right?"

"You—" It was difficult to form coherent words. "It's you, isn't it?"

"Depends who you mean by *you*."

"You're alive."

"Am I?" He looked down at himself, holding his arms out in front of him for inspection, then his gaze swept the length of me. "Hey, so are you. What a coincidence."

A cloud of confusion swirled around me, making me dizzy. "But I—I saw you get stabbed in the chest last night."

He got to his feet and closed the distance between us in

only a couple of steps. I staggered back from him and looked around, realizing that we were all alone.

He cocked his head. “Did you *really* see me get stabbed?”

“Yeah, I did.”

“Are you completely sure about that?”

I glared at him. He was mocking me and I had no idea why. “Completely.”

He rubbed his chest. “Funny, because I feel just fine.”

“I’m not crazy.”

He walked a slow circle around me and it felt like he was studying every inch of me. Like, *every* inch.

“Name’s Kraven.” His lips curled into a smile that didn’t look friendly. “I’d say I’m pleased to meet you, but that would be a lie. I mean, things like you are the reason for this little mess, aren’t they?”

My stomach churned and I wrapped my arms around myself, trying not to shiver. “I don’t know what you’re talking about.”

I continued to deny it, even to myself. There wasn’t anything else I could do. The moment I accepted that something was seriously wrong here—and with me in particular—was the moment I believed this insanity was real. And I wasn’t quite ready for the asylum.

“Sure you don’t. You’re just a normal girl, right? And that relentless hunger you’ve suddenly developed—what do you think that is? Just a regular case of the munchies?”

I shook my head, trying to block out how much he seemed to know about me. “Bishop stabbed you. I saw it with my own eyes. So why aren’t you dead?”

Kraven’s mischievous grin widened and his amber-colored eyes began to glow bright red. “Because it takes more than that to kill a demon.”

chapter 5

I couldn't move. Fear crawled through my gut like a fistful of cockroaches. "A demon?"

"Impressed?"

I wanted this to be a movie on TV so I could press the off button and make it all go away. The cold feeling grew deeper, sinking so far inside me I didn't think I'd ever feel warm again. I was sure all the color had drained from my already pale face.

Other than his eyes, there was nothing that made him seem anything other than human. He had a small freckle at the left corner of his mouth. His hair was the kind of blond color people got if they were normally light brown but spent the entire summer working outside in the sun. He looked so normal. Like a boy I might see at the mall, or the movies, or...eating garbage in an alleyway.

Unlike Bishop, there was no madness in his expression. Kraven was totally sane.

Which meant that *I* had to be the crazy one.

"Wh-what do you want from me?" I stammered.

"I want to do my job. The sooner the better."

"What's your job?"

"Why would I tell you my secrets?" Kraven brushed the front of his shirt, straightening out a wrinkle in the fabric, before his gaze, which had changed back to its normal amber color, returned to my face.

A cold line of perspiration slid down my spine and I took a deep breath before speaking. "I swear, I'm not what you think I am."

"A hungry little gray with an appetite for human souls?" Kraven touched my hair and I swatted his hand away. Then he grabbed my wrists and pulled me closer to him.

Sabrina, a girl from my afternoon geography class, passed us and I craned my neck to track her. She was notorious for cheating off whomever was seated next to her, including me several times, and she had the As to prove it.

I'd never been so happy to see anyone before in my entire life.

"Sabrina, help me!" I shouted. "Please!"

She didn't even glance in my direction.

"Why can't she see me?" I struggled to pull away from him, but Kraven held me firmly in place.

He watched the girl disappear down the path. "Because I don't want her to. I cloaked us so we could have a little chat all privatelike." He looked at my mouth for a moment as if mesmerized by it. "Let's get down to business, sweetness. How many have you kissed since you've been turned?"

"None!"

He raised an eyebrow and brought his mouth closer to mine. I could feel his hot breath on me as he spoke. "But you want to, don't you? It's a hunger you can't resist, a raw desire, an…aching need. Tell me the truth. You want to, don't you?"

"No." I clenched my jaw, glaring at him for making it sound so dirty, but inside I felt sick and weakened. I'd ached to kiss

Colin just now, and it had taken everything I had to pull myself away from him. I'd tried to ignore my cravings, feed them with food each time they'd appeared, but nothing had helped.

Kraven knew that. He shouldn't have known anything about me, but he knew what I was feeling inside right now. And he saw the answer on my face even though I hadn't said it out loud.

His smile faded. "Even if I believed you, it's only a matter of time before you can't control it any longer."

He grabbed me by the throat so tight that I couldn't breathe. I scratched and beat at his arms as hard as I could, but it didn't do any good. He raised me off the ground so I was on my tiptoes.

No one could see that he was strangling me right in the middle of school grounds. I strained to get a breath, to scream, but I couldn't. My fingernails dug into Kraven's iron grip.

"Let go of her," someone snarled.

Bishop had appeared a dozen feet away by the bench. My eyes widened, and the fear I'd felt the last time we'd been face-to-face came back in full force along with an almost giddy elation.

The demon finally tore his gaze away from me. "Or what?"

"Or I'll kill you. Again."

Kraven slowly set me back down on the ground, releasing my throat. I wheezed and gasped for breath. "You know, you're a serious pain in the—"

Bishop launched himself at the demon, tackling him to the ground and slamming a fist into Kraven's jaw. Before the next hit landed Kraven grabbed him and twisted his arm away. I recovered enough to leap back as they continued to fight. More students strolled past without glancing at them or at me.

"Some angel you are." Kraven laughed as they finally

pushed apart. "Can't even take a lowly demon like me in a fight?"

"I can take you," Bishop growled. "I can *end* you."

"Thought we were supposed to be working together like good friends and business partners."

"Still up for debate as far as I'm concerned. They shouldn't have sent *you*."

"Too bad. They did. Deal with it."

I'd been a half second from running in the opposite direction, but froze in place at what I'd just heard.

"You're a—an *angel?*" My voice sounded pitchy.

Bishop's gaze shot to me and he took a step toward me. "Samantha..."

I held up a shaky hand. "Don't come any closer or I'm going to scream."

He stayed put, his jaw tight and his fierce gaze focused on me.

On my bedroom wall I had a framed poster of an angel by a fantasy illustrator I really liked—it showed a peaceful, beautiful being of light. If anything, I would have guessed Bishop was a demon, like Kraven, from every horrible thing he'd done so far. Seeing him again had knocked every bit of confidence right out of me.

But those blue eyes of his—they were every bit as beautiful as they'd been last night and able to capture me with just a glance in my direction. It was impossible to even attempt to breathe normally at this point. "If you're an angel, why are you working with a demon?"

His lips thinned. "It's a long story."

"Yeah, a *really* long story." Kraven was studying me again. "Why's she so different?"

"I don't know." Bishop kept his attention on me. "There's

something special about her. When she helped me with her touch—"

"Exactly what was she touching that was so memorable for you?"

"Watch your mouth."

A smile tugged at Kraven's lips and he leered at me in a way that made me feel naked. I fought the urge to cross my arms over my chest. "You're a mystery, gray girl."

"Her name is Samantha," Bishop growled.

Kraven rolled his eyes. "If this is going to work, you really have to loosen up. Like, seriously."

My mind reeled and my stomach twisted from all of this—from what I was feeling to what I'd just been told flat out. I couldn't deny that I hungered for something I couldn't name, and my cravings had been getting worse every hour since Stephen had kissed me on Friday night. When Colin had gotten too close, I'd wanted to kiss him so much that I'd practically attacked him in the hallway. But I hadn't. I *could* control it. I had so far, and I'd continue to do so.

Kraven's smile returned and he moved closer to me again. I froze as he placed a hand on my shoulder. "You know, you're kind of cute. Maybe I won't kill you if you make it worth my while."

"Get your hand off me," I snapped as my fear turned to anger. I grabbed his hand.

Electricity crackled down my arm. Kraven gasped in pain and staggered backward. I stared at him with surprise.

"What was that?" he managed to ask.

Good question. What the hell just happened?

Bishop glared at him. "Just stay away from her."

He frowned. "She zapped me."

"That's impossible."

"I didn't just imagine it. She did." His grin slowly returned, and he eyed me with that hatefully amused expression. "Curiouser and curiouser."

For a second I was reminded of when I'd first touched Bishop and the vision had slammed into me—zapping Kraven had felt that powerful and that uncontrollable. My skin still tingled from the shock I'd given him, as if I was slowly recovering from sticking my fingers in a light socket.

"Ignore him," Bishop said, throwing a look of pure disdain toward the demon. "Samantha, I had to find you again. After what you were able to do last night, I...*we* need your help."

"You need *my* help? You have got to be kidding me. I want nothing to do with you."

His gaze shadowed. "You're different from the other grays—I don't know why or how. But you are. How you found Kraven last night...there are others. I need you to help me find them before they're lost forever."

My ponytail had come loose from the elastic and I redid it firmly. I liked Bishop's voice; it was smooth and deep and it made me shiver. I hated that I liked *anything* about him, after everything I'd learned. "I want both of you to leave me alone."

"I know you're confused, but this is important."

Emotion lodged in my throat, making it hard to talk without sounding choked. "You're the one who's confused, because I don't care what's important to you. I hate you, whatever you are. And I want you to stay away from me."

His gaze began to grow cloudy, like when I'd first met him. He pressed his fingers against his temples. "I don't know what else to say right now."

My heart twisted. Damn it. I had an urge to touch him, to make it better since I knew I could, to erase that pain from his handsome face. But I held myself back. "Say goodbye. You were more than ready to say it to me last night."

"Hey, Samantha!" Carly shouted. "What are you doing out here?"

My head whipped toward her. The shield making us invisible must have disappeared. I turned to look at Bishop and Kraven again, but they were gone.

Just like last night, they'd vanished into thin air.

"Hellooo? Earth to Samantha!"

I composed myself and hitched my shoulder strap higher, and then walked toward her, willing myself to stop trembling. "What are you doing tonight?"

"Me? Nothing. Why?"

I bit my bottom lip. "I want to go back to Crave."

Carly crossed her arms. "Why?"

"I want to see Stephen again."

She gave me a guarded look. "Are you sure about that?"

"I am."

"I just thought…after the other night…" She frowned. "You're not interested in him anymore, are you?"

I gritted my teeth. "Oh, I'm interested, all right."

I was interested in getting to the bottom of what had happened to me and how I could fix it as soon as possible. And Stephen Keyes damn well better have some answers.

chapter 6

I'd burned all day with the need to get back to Crave and confront Stephen, but now that I was here I'd started to doubt myself. I guess I'd focused on my plan—weak though it was—as a way to keep from thinking too much about what had happened with Bishop and Kraven.

I wasn't convinced that I was some sort of soul-devouring monster now. No way. I was still me, nothing had changed that. But something was wrong. Really wrong. And I had to fix it.

"Are you even sure the jerk is here?" Carly scanned the floor looking for him.

"He told me he's here every night lately, even weekdays. He's taking a break from school right now, that's why he's back in town."

"Doesn't he live near you?"

"Two doors down."

"We could have gone there to check."

"I already checked. His parents don't even know he's in the city." I'd called his house after school. I'd had a feeling he wouldn't be there, but his mother's reply that "he's at school" was enough to convince me that if I couldn't find him at Crave, I might not be able to find him at all. Besides, I didn't want to chance being alone with him. I wanted to confront him in a public place.

"Okay, so where is he?" Carly asked. "Let's do this."

She thought my feelings were hurt and I wanted to lash out, and as my best friend, she was ready to back me up.

Just like with my mother, I hadn't breathed a word to her about what was really going on. I wasn't sure what was stopping me, exactly. Carly, of all people, would probably believe there were angels and demons roaming the city.

But still I didn't speak up. She liked to protect me from people who might pick on me. Well, I'd like to protect her from people who might do worse than throw out a few insults. Cruel names might hurt feelings, but sharp golden daggers could kill.

I did wish very hard that I could stop thinking about Bishop. He was constantly on my mind now. If he hadn't shown up today, I had little doubt that Kraven would have killed me.

It was an incredibly sobering thought. I owed my gratitude to Bishop for saving my life, and yet he'd threatened it himself just the night before.

"I need to talk to Stephen on my own," I said. "You should stay here and wait for me."

She eyed me. "Oh, I get it. So I'm just your chauffeur, huh? I don't get a chance to tell him off, too?"

"Believe me, I don't think that. Although, I won't say that you having a car isn't a nice perk." I couldn't help but grin at her mock outrage. "This is just something I need to handle myself. Less embarrassing that way."

She considered this. "So what if he's all schmoozy? All,

'I really want to kiss your delectable lips again'? You're just going to ignore it?"

"That isn't going to happen." Even if Stephen was one hundred percent innocent, his reaction to me after the kiss spoke volumes. I mean, he'd called me *kid*. No, I had more important things to deal with than falling for some self-involved college guy right now, no matter how cute I'd always found him.

It was funny how completely this had doused my crush on him. Like a bucket of water thrown on a lit match.

Also, my immediate and overpowering attraction to Bishop—and the fact that I couldn't get him off my mind—had shown me that my little crush on Stephen had been just that. *Little.*

"You were really into him. What, are you interested in somebody else now?" she asked.

There was a catch in her voice that made me direct my attention away from scanning the dark club to her again. "What?"

She cleared her throat. "Jordan saw you talking to Colin in the hall this morning. She said you were standing really close."

I winced. Damn Jordan. My personal nemesis *and* a total gossip. "It was nothing."

Her eyebrows went up and she finally raised her gaze from the ground to meet mine. I saw relief there. "Really?"

It wasn't nothing, but getting into details about him asking me out and then me wanting to kiss him probably wouldn't earn me any brownie points as a loyal best friend.

"I know Colin's totally off-limits," I confirmed instead. "I promise, there's no way I'd be interested in him like that. But why are you worried that I've been talking to him?"

"I'm done with him. But..." She rubbed her temples. "My brain is going to explode just thinking about this."

"Let's hope not."

"I don't want to be with him anymore, but I don't want him to be with anyone else. Does that make some kind of bizarre, psycho ex-girlfriend kind of sense?"

"Sure it does."

She laughed before sobering. "No, it doesn't. I know that. He's just the first guy who…you know, the first one to really like me."

My heart felt heavy for her. I had to be really careful how I acted around Colin from now on. I didn't want to give him—or Carly—the wrong impression. "Sorry this sucks so much for you. And you need to open your eyes when it comes to other guys. Paul is crazy about you, but you've never even looked in his direction. If you want to start dating again, you should give him a chance."

She frowned. "Paul? Paul McKee?"

"The one and only." He was a friend who always ate lunch with us. A pal, really. But I'd have to be blind not to see the very nonpal way he gazed across the table at Carly on a daily basis. Of course, she never noticed, because she was usually gazing somewhere else.

I scanned the nightclub. It wasn't nearly as busy as it had been on Friday. On school nights it became a restaurant that only looked like a club—like a school cafeteria, but better decorated, with cooler lighting and a sound track. The dance floor was deserted and the place shut down at eleven o'clock instead of 1:00 a.m. A quick inhale brought forth the scent of chicken wings, fries and onion rings. Not healthy, but definitely delicious.

Something else smelled fantastic in here, but I couldn't put my finger on what.

Souls, a little voice inside me said. *You can smell the souls of all the people near you.*

The thought nauseated me. Hopefully nobody would get as close to me as Colin had earlier today. That seemed to be what set me off.

"There's lover boy now," Carly said, snapping me out of my daze. "You're right, he *is* here every night."

Sure enough, looking every bit as gorgeous as ever in black pants and a white shirt unbuttoned at the collar, Stephen walked along the side of the empty dance floor toward the spiral staircase leading to the upstairs lounge.

"Okay, I can do this," I said aloud, trying to summon some inner strength.

"Are you going to talk to him?" Carly asked. "Or just punch him in the nose?"

An excellent question.

He'd done something to me—he'd even warned me about it first. He'd given me this hunger I couldn't get rid of, this craving that now haunted me every moment I was awake and the chill that stayed with me from morning till night.

I was ready to confront Stephen.

Something wicked this way comes.

This time I was talking about myself.

"Wait here," I told Carly. "Please."

"You *sure* you don't want me there for support?"

"I'm sure," I said. Kissing Stephen had led to me almost getting killed. It wasn't something I wanted Carly involved with. Her being here tonight was bad enough.

She nodded. "Good luck. Give him hell."

I grimaced. *Hell* wasn't something I even wanted to consider after meeting a demon today. Slowly, I started up the stairs.

It'll change your life forever, so you have to want it.

I wondered if Stephen said that to all the girls. But I didn't want a kiss tonight. All I wanted was answers.

Stephen sat in the corner of the upstairs lounge on a plush red velvet chair. He watched my cautious approach as if not at all surprised to see me again.

"Samantha Day," he greeted me. "How are you this evening?"

My mouth felt dry. Very dry. I tried to ignore how nervous I was. "I need to talk to you."

"But you didn't answer my question. How are you?"

"Not good," I admitted.

"Sorry to hear that."

"Are you?"

"Of course I am." He gave me a charming smile I couldn't help but respond to. He really was cute, that much hadn't changed since he'd potentially destroyed my life. He waved at the chair beside him. "Please, have a seat."

I swallowed hard, wanting to resist, but deciding to do as he said. I glanced around the lounge as I took a seat on the soft chair. There were about a half dozen other kids in this area, scattered around. Some were reading books, as if this was a relaxing hangout. Some were talking to each other. I didn't recognize any of them.

Doubt clouded my mind when I met Stephen's eyes again. Suddenly, I felt young—really young—and uncertain.

"You walked away after you kissed me," I said, and immediately felt silly. Like some jilted teenager who drew hearts in her binder all day long and daydreamed about boys.

What happened to my decision to be strong and demand answers?

"I'm sorry," he said. "Really."

His answer surprised me. "You are?"

"I needed to—" his dark brows drew together "—take care of something important. And it couldn't wait a moment longer or it would have been too late."

I eyed him skeptically. "What did you do to me?"

"Excuse me?"

"When you kissed me. You did something bad."

"Is that what you think?"

"That's what I *know*."

He leaned back in his chair, studying me as if looking for clues to the same mystery I wanted solved. "It was just a kiss, nothing more. Sorry if you took it to mean more than that. I like you, Samantha, but like I said, you're a bit too young for—"

There was no time for eloquence, so I just blurted it out. "Did you do something to my soul?"

His brows went up. "Excuse me?"

"Just answer my question." Now I sounded impressively strong, considering I was quaking inside.

Stephen stood up and moved toward the glass barrier to look down at the rest of the club. He didn't reply.

After a long moment, with only the boom of the music below filling my ears, I got up and approached him. "It did something, that kiss. It changed me. Didn't it?"

"I did warn you," he said.

I'd wanted him to look confused or annoyed by me talking to him about this. I'd wanted him to not know what the hell I was talking about. But it was all too clear that he knew exactly what I meant. This wasn't a misunderstanding or an epic practical joke. This was real.

I had to be careful with him. My instincts told me that much.

I chanced a look around the lounge to see that our discussion hadn't earned so much as a curious glance from the other kids. "You did something to my soul, I know that much. They called me a *gray.* Why would you do that to me and then just let me walk away with no warning of what might happen?"

"A gray?" He frowned. "Who have you been talking to about this?"

I pressed my lips together. I was the one asking questions here, not answering them.

Stephen went back to the chair and sat down again, grabbed a beer that sat on a black lacquered table and took a swig from it. Suddenly, I wanted to make a joke, maybe something about him having a fake ID. My usual reaction to unpleasant things was to try to be funny. It was a defense mechanism I'd developed during my parents' very unamicable split. Or so my guidance counselor told me when I'd gotten in trouble for snarking on one of my teachers.

Laughing was way better than crying, as far as I was concerned. At the moment, however, I didn't feel like doing either.

"Stephen," I growled. It was pissing me off that he was so unwilling to tell me what I needed to know.

He settled back in the chair, looking like a handsome prince on a velvet throne. "I did what I was told to do, and then I had to leave. I'm not supposed to explain. She'll tell you all about it when she's ready."

I stared at him blankly. "Who?"

His jaw tightened. "You're supposed to be special. She said you were, or I would have at least warned you about the hunger..." He trailed off and then frowned at me, looking into my eyes. "But you're able to fight it, aren't you? Even without me telling you anything about it first. I'm thinking that's exactly what makes you special. You don't seem any different than you were before."

My mind spun. I didn't understand. "I'm hungry all the time."

"But you're not feeding. She didn't think you would."

My shivering increased. I knew he wasn't talking about potato chips or cheeseburgers. "Who the hell is *she?*"

"I can't tell you that. Not yet." He swore under his breath. "I knew you were too young."

"Tell me what you did to me," I demanded. "What is this hunger? I keep eating and eating and I can't get full."

He shook his head, still staring at me as if my admitting the hunger surprised him. "Food won't satisfy you. Not anymore."

My bottom lip wobbled as I started to lose my composure. "What am I?"

He stood up and reached toward me, gently tucking a piece of long, dark hair behind my ear. His expression regained its previous confidence and he smiled. "This is a good thing, Samantha. You're something even more special now. Something amazing."

Bishop had called me special, too, shortly before he'd put that knife to my throat. Call me crazy, but the word put me on edge.

"I'm a—a gray," I said, my throat tight enough that it was difficult to breathe.

His smile wavered and an edge of confusion slid behind his gaze as if he wasn't familiar with the term. But that was what Bishop and Kraven had called it. "What you are isn't a bad thing. It really isn't. But you do have to be careful. There are ways of controlling the hunger through the kiss." He leaned close to whisper in my ear. "You and me—we can practice now, if you like, without doing any harm. Whenever we want to."

Practice kissing with Stephen Keyes. A week ago it would have sounded like a dream come true, but now...

It didn't feel like a dream. Only a nightmare could make me feel like this.

I half expected him to rip off his face to show a literal monster underneath, just before he attacked me. But he didn't do any ripping or attacking.

When Stephen took my hand in his, I yanked it away from him. His skin was cold and it made me shudder.

He blinked. "Our body temperatures are lower now. You'll get used to it. It's one of the side effects of not having a soul."

Finally—confirmation. He'd somehow managed to steal my soul in that kiss.

"How do I get it back?" My voice broke.

He cocked his head to the side. "Why would you want it back? You're better now."

He was infuriating. How could he be so calm about something like this? "Because—because it's my *soul.* You took it and I want you to give it back. Now."

His expression didn't change as he sat down again. "I can't give yours back to you. I gave in to the hunger just as she told me to. And now it's gone."

Panic twisted inside me. My soul was gone. Something I hadn't really thought about as a tangible piece of me had been ripped away and destroyed without my permission.

My hands clenched into fists at my sides. "You can't just steal something so important from me and expect I'm going to be okay with that. Who told you to do this to me?"

His eyes narrowed. "A soul is a burden on a human, an anchor. Trust me...you're better off without it. I never knew how much my soul held me back, but it did. I was miserable—self-doubting, worried, anxious, living a life others planned for me. I had no control over myself. Now I do. The world has opened up to me. It was my soul that held me back. You'll come to see that I'm telling the truth. The hunger can be managed. It's all worth it."

If that was his sales pitch for *Devour your soul? Ask me how!* I was unimpressed, to say the least. In fact, I was so mad I wanted to spit.

But, mad or not, it was too late. He'd done it. My soul was gone. And now I hungered to do the same to others as Stephen had done to me. This wasn't going to get any better; it was only going to get worse. That must be what had happened with Colin in the hallway this morning. I'd been so close…*too* close…

I turned and stalked away. My mind was a jumble of information and I had no idea how to process it all.

"Where are you going?" Stephen's hand closed on my upper arm and he jerked me to a stop before I reached the staircase, wrenching me back around to face him.

I guess he was also done with being pleasant.

"Let go of me!" I snarled, trying to fight the burning sting of tears in my eyes.

Unfortunately, no protective zapping occurred to blast him back from me like it had this morning with Kraven.

I half expected his eyes to glow red like the demon's had, but they remained the same caramel color as always. "I have some questions for you, too, Samantha. You can't just walk away from me yet."

I looked around at the other kids for help, but they still weren't paying attention to us. Considering our heated discussion and the fact he was now physically restraining me from leaving, that surprised me.

"Help!" I called out, loud enough to be heard over the constant musical background to Crave. "He won't let me leave!"

"Don't bother," Stephen said. "They're all with me—my new brothers and sisters. *Your* new brothers and sisters."

A gasp caught in my throat. "But they look so normal."

"They're better than normal."

A second glance showed they were all very attractive, well dressed and had an air of self-confidence. Stephen had said losing your soul was a freeing experience. Looked like these grays agreed with him.

If that was so, then why didn't I feel that way?

"Now, my question..." He pulled me closer. "Who have you been talking to about this since Friday night? I need to know."

"Why do you care?"

"If there's someone out there with knowledge of us, they might not understand. They might try to get in the way. She won't like that." His grip tightened. I tried to pull away but I couldn't. "Answer me, Samantha. Who were you talking to?"

"She was talking to me."

I whipped my head around. Bishop was standing at the top of the stairs. Our eyes met and held for a brief but intense moment before he shifted his focus to Stephen.

"Who the hell are you?" Stephen snapped.

"Let Samantha go and maybe we'll talk about it."

Stephen released me. His tight grip had left a red imprint on my skin. His angry expression shifted to neutral as he eyed Bishop.

"There," he said pleasantly. "I let her go."

"You grab girls a lot around here?" Bishop glanced around the lounge area.

Stephen smirked. "Usually it's the other way around."

"How nice for you. So you're the one who did this to her, aren't you?"

"Don't know what you're talking about."

Bishop's gaze flicked to me as I rubbed my arm. "You okay?"

While I was glad he'd gotten Stephen to let go of me, I wasn't running into Bishop's arms with gratitude. "Did you follow me here?"

"Something like that."

I let out a frustrated groan. "Can't anyone just talk to me straight? Why is everyone avoiding my damn questions tonight?"

Bishop's brows went up. "Okay, fine. Yes, I followed you here. Better?"

"Yes. Stalkery, but better."

"I'm not stalking you."

"Spoken like a true stalker."

"So let me start again." Stephen eyed Bishop with distaste. "Who are you and what do you want?"

There was nothing pleasant about the way Bishop studied him back. In fact, he looked predatory. "You're the one who kissed Samantha, aren't you?"

Again, Stephen didn't seem inclined to answer that particular question, so I did it for him.

"It was him," I said. "Here on Friday night."

Bishop's glare turned into a glower. "Why wouldn't you explain what it meant to her? What she could expect? It was the least you could do."

"Luckily for her, you filled her in on the details. Didn't

you?" Stephen walked an appraising circle around Bishop. "I don't know you. You're not one of us, which makes me wonder what business it is of yours what I do."

"Trust me, it's my business."

Stephen shrugged. "She liked it. She was practically begging me to kiss her."

He was such a jerk. Begging? Hardly.

A muscle in Bishop's cheek twitched. "She didn't understand what it meant."

"She's with me now." Stephen drew closer, as if challenging Bishop to push him back. "You got a problem with that?"

"Excuse me?" I snapped. "I'm *with* you? Not the last time I checked."

He gave me an amused look. "You'll get used to the idea eventually. Be happy about it, even."

"Don't count on it."

"Where's the Source?" Bishop asked evenly. "Is it you?"

Stephen didn't speak for a moment, but then he laughed. "I have no idea what you're talking about."

"Yes, you do. The one who created you. Created all of you. I need to talk to him or her. Soon. We have important things to discuss."

Stephen grabbed hold of the front of Bishop's T-shirt. "No, what I think you need to do is leave now. And Samantha is going to stay right here with me, where she belongs. Give her a few minutes and she'll be enjoying herself. She might be only seventeen, but that's more than old enough for the fun I have planned for her."

The next moment, Stephen gasped as the tip of the golden dagger pressed up under his chin.

Stephen's chest moved in and out as his breathing increased. "Get that thing away from me."

"Why would I? From what you've told me so far, I'm thinking you're just a minion. You're meaningless. You turned an underage girl against her will and gave her the hunger. I don't care if she wanted to kiss you or not. She didn't know what it meant. You didn't explain it. That she isn't now consuming souls all over the city is her saving grace in my eyes. She's different than the rest of you. She's special."

There was that word again in relation to yours truly. *Special.*

Bishop had finally gotten the attention of the others hanging out in the lounge area, but not one made a move to help Stephen. Couldn't say I blamed them. That knife was very sharp.

And—oh, boy. I think it was glowing a little, just like Bishop's eyes had last night. That was no normal knife. And Bishop was no normal guy.

But I already knew that.

The corner of Stephen's mouth turned up in a half grimace, half grin. "You're going to kill me right here? In the middle of a club full of kids? You'll never get out in one piece."

"Nice of you to worry about my well-being. Thanks for that. Now, why don't you make things easier on both of us. Where is the Source?"

"I don't know."

"Then you're not much use to me, are you?" Bishop dug the sharp tip of the knife deep enough that a thin trail of blood ran down Stephen's throat.

Stephen's voice turned pitchy. "She doesn't just stroll in here shaking hands and kissing babies. I don't find her, she finds me."

"At least now I know it's a she."

An edge of defeat went through Stephen's eyes. "Are you going to kill me?"

"And risk opening up the Hollow in here? Not tonight."

Stephen frowned. "The Hollow?"

Bishop gave him a wry grin. "Guess your boss hasn't told you everything, has she? Sucks for you. When was the last time you fed?"

"Friday. With Samantha. The others here aren't feeding."

"And why is that?" Bishop actually looked amused by this. "You know what happens if you feed too much? Have you seen it with your own eyes?"

Stephen's expression shadowed and, if you ask me, went a little green. "The one you're calling the Source tells us what to do. She warned us what could happen if we get too greedy, and most of us believed her."

"Does she come here?"

"No. This is where I hang out. She's never been here before."

Bishop's eyes narrowed. "Don't approach Samantha again."

"I didn't approach her. She came here."

"I don't care. From this moment forward, she's under my protection."

"Your protection? Who the hell are you?"

"Tell your boss that this entire city is now protected by me and others like me and I will find her for that conversation I mentioned. I'm sure she already knows she can't leave—that none of you can. You're trapped. There's an invisible barrier surrounding this entire city that things like you can't breach."

Stephen frowned. "I don't understand."

"That's painfully obvious." Bishop finally let him go and Stephen staggered back a couple steps. His gaze returned to the golden dagger as Bishop sheathed it. "By the way, if I ever see you again, I will kill you, whether you're feeding regularly or not. Have a nice night."

Then he turned, took my arm and guided me down the stairs.

Nobody followed us.

chapter 7

At the bottom of the spiral staircase, I forced myself to pull away from Bishop's firm but strangely comforting grip. I wanted to find Carly and get out of here as soon as possible.

He eyed me. "You're welcome."

A million insults swelled inside me, battling with gratitude and relief. "You think you can just push me around like that?"

He didn't look much friendlier than I felt. "What were you thinking, coming here and seeking him out? Are you looking for trouble?"

"Have you been following me? Hiding in the bushes? Do you have a pair of binoculars trained on my bedroom window, too? Trust me...I always pull the blinds before I get naked." I shivered at how close he stood to me even though his brief touch had filled me with warmth again.

He seemed at a loss for words, as if he wasn't sure how to reply to my "naked" comment. His eyes burned into mine. "Are you always this irrational or is this just my lucky night?"

I took a deep breath. I wondered when the serenity Stephen mentioned might start. Not tonight, that was for sure. "Where's Kraven? Is he stalking me, too?"

His mouth went tight. "I'm not stalking you. Once I met you, touched you, I became able to track you. It's a talent I have—one of the very few I haven't managed to lose."

"Oh, that sounds much better. *Tracking me*. Nothing weird about that." I was wearing heels tonight, but he still towered over me, overwhelming me with his very presence.

"You could have been hurt confronting that thing up there, you know. Not the smartest move."

"Says the guy with the big, sharp, glowy concealed weapon."

"Tell me what happened."

For someone who just last night had turned from confused yet charming to murderous and angry, he now looked genuinely concerned. After guiding me out of sight of the jerk on the second floor, he took a step back from me and didn't attempt to touch me again.

Fine with me. Even though my skin tingled from where he'd had his hand on me and I still had a hard time catching my breath being anywhere near him, I didn't want him to touch me again. No way.

I crossed my arms. "I wanted to know how to get my—my *soul* back. Before that I wanted to know if it was even true, that it was gone. I don't feel any different."

His blue eyes met mine directly. "Yes, you do."

"What, are you in my head or something? I *don't*. I'm hungry, yeah, and I'm always cold, but other than that there's nothing wrong with me."

"Which is one of the things that is wrong. You *should* feel different."

"But I don't."

He scanned the club as if assessing it for incoming threats. I was surprised he hadn't insisted we leave, but I wasn't going anywhere until I found Carly again. He was the one who should leave. Even though it was a weeknight, the music down here—as opposed to the shielded upstairs lounge—was loud. I had to stay closer to Bishop than I liked in order to hear him. Close enough to smell him—and he smelled just as good tonight as he had last night. Warm, clean, spicy. Maybe it was a special angels-only cologne.

I forced myself to take a step back.

"How are your hungers right now?" he asked.

"Bad." They'd ramped up to an impossible-to-ignore level in the past few minutes, actually. I eyed a passing tray of chicken wings. "Maybe I should eat something."

"You think food will satisfy you?"

"I'm not loving the alternative." My attention was irresistibly drawn to his mouth. "Unless you're volunteering."

Immediately my cheeks heated. Where had that come from?

He raked a hand through his short, dark hair. "Sorry, but angels don't have souls. I wouldn't be able to help your hunger very much." He watched me with cautious interest, as if he expected me to burst into flames at any moment.

My face was blazing, and now I had a vivid and unwelcome image of kissing Bishop lodged in my head and couldn't shake it loose. Angels didn't have souls. *Okay.* I added that to my very limited knowledge about him. "I wasn't sure who I hated more, you or Kraven, but I've decided that it's you."

He didn't seem surprised. "And what brought me ahead in the race?"

"The fact that I originally liked you." That seemed to shut him up. Nice to know that the crazy angel had no comeback for once. Speaking of… "How's your head?"

"It's been better. I don't like feeling this way."

"But you're feeling relatively okay now?"

We were tucked into a corner, away from everyone, but he

still looked around to check whether anyone was eavesdropping, even though the music was more than loud enough to shield us. "No. The confusion hasn't gone away. It's still circling. It'll come back…it's only a matter of time."

"Kraven seemed fine."

That earned me a sharp look. "Kraven was protected when he entered the city. I was not. That's why he had to go through the ritual, so his true self could be returned to him."

I stared at the darkly gorgeous but annoying angel. "Your lips are moving but I'm not understanding a word."

"Seems to be the theme of the week."

I glanced around the club for Carly and spotted her chatting with a couple of our friends. I hoped she'd be done soon so we could leave—the sooner the better. Reassured of her safety, I turned back to Bishop. "So the ritual involves you stabbing him with that big, shiny knife of yours."

"Yes."

I shuddered at the memory. "Sounds like the stupidest ritual ever created."

"His temporarily mortal form had to die in order to be reborn with his memories and his true self returned. And, yes, it has to be done with this big, shiny knife of mine."

I swear, most of the time it felt like he was making fun of me. "So demons can be stabbed in the chest and just bounce back from it like it's no big deal?"

"Regular knives won't hurt demons. They're immortal, just like angels. This dagger, however, is very special."

Why was I still talking to him, edging closer to him with every moment that passed? Why couldn't I just turn away and go get Carly?

I shook my head. "I'm officially not a part of this. I'm walking away, going back to my normal life, okay? And that means

I don't want you anywhere near me—tracking, stalking, harassing, whatever."

He hissed out a sigh. "You can't be normal again, Samantha. You're a gray now. It's been confirmed both to me and to you. Even though you're different from the others, it doesn't change what you are. What you need."

To kiss someone. Badly. Even a soulless, dangerous, and frustrating angel. My cheeks now flushed more from anger than embarrassment. "You don't know what you're talking about."

"I know *exactly* what I'm talking about. I'm here because of grays. That's why the others are here as well, like…Kraven." He said the demon's name with distaste. "Grays can't leave the city—no supernatural can. I need to find the Source. She's the one who's responsible for this new infestation. It's like a disease that will keep spreading if we don't stop it. And we'll use force to stop grays whenever necessary."

I didn't think it was possible, but I felt even colder at that. "With that shiny dagger of yours?"

"Grays consume souls. If they give in to their hunger, it can kill a weaker human. Stronger humans can survive losing their soul, but they will become infected—they'll become a gray, too. Being gray changes them, and grays who feed too much, get too greedy, are incredibly dangerous. I've already seen it."

Fear shuddered through me. "Change how?"

His gaze searched mine as if he was looking for more answers there. "Being soulless seems to strip humanity and reason away from the very start. But if a gray feeds, it makes it more uncontrollable."

"But I don't have a soul and I feel the same as I ever did. I definitely know right from wrong."

Bishop's dark brows drew together, still searching my face

as if he couldn't look away. "You're different. I don't know why or how it's possible, but you are. Maybe it's because you haven't fed yet at all. You can't give in to the hunger, Samantha, or it will change you."

I realized I'd moved so close to him that my hand brushed against his. I took a shaky step back. "You're lying to me. About all of this."

"Angels don't lie."

I gaped at him. "I still don't believe you're an angel."

"Do you believe Kraven is a demon?"

"I don't know." I blinked, thinking back to the scene in the alley last night. I frowned. "Do you have a tattoo like he does? Is that some sort of a sign of what you are?"

"It's not a tattoo. Our wings are made of energy that isn't visible or accessible in the human world. But their imprint remains on us."

"Show me."

He just looked at me. "You can't just take my word for it?"

"No. Show me your…your imprint, or whatever it is."

"Will that be enough to convince you?"

"I don't know."

He gave me a stern look. "I don't take orders from anyone. I'm the leader on this mission."

I felt sick and confused, but determined, too. All I could focus on was one thing at a time or I would be overwhelmed. *More* overwhelmed.

"Here's how I see it, Bishop. You were sent here to take care of a problem. I'm part of that problem, according to you. However, you already figured out that I'm different, I'm… special. I saw that light in the sky when you couldn't—and you don't know if you'll be able to. You can't find the others, not without me. And you have only a short time to find them or they'll be lost forever."

He didn't look pleased by the reminder that he wasn't necessarily the one in charge at the moment. That gave me the strength to continue.

"That guy up there." I thrust my thumb in the direction of the upstairs lounge. "No question that he's a total creep, but he also promised to help me. He said I was like him, like the others. That I had a place to belong now. So my question is, why would I want to have anything to do with you—another jerk who nearly killed me last night—when I can go hang out with my new friends?"

It was the last thing I wanted, but currently my only bargaining chip.

He was silent for a long moment. "Because if you say you really haven't changed, then you must see how wrong all of this is."

My jaw tensed. He was right, but I didn't want to let on that was how I felt. Something was off about Stephen. Really off. He was cold, in both body and mind. He said this had freed him from his previous problems, but I wasn't convinced. Something that felt this bad—feeding off other people's souls—just couldn't be right, no matter how he tried to spin it.

It wasn't a matter of becoming a zombie and having a major craving for brains. To my knowledge, a soul didn't have substance. But it existed and it was priceless. It was what went to Heaven after you died. Your spirit that lived on even when the rest of you was dead.

And mine was gone.

I swallowed past the thick lump in my throat and forced myself to stay strong. To not let Bishop think he had the upper hand. I had something he wanted and I still wasn't sure I wanted to give it to him. But I needed something to believe, something that might make all of this remotely okay again.

"Show me your imprint," I said firmly. "And maybe we can talk."

Bishop's blue eyes sparked with emotion as he studied me. Nobody had ever looked at me like that in my entire life, like he could overpower me in an instant but was trying very hard to hold himself back.

When he turned away from me, my heart lurched and I thought he was going to walk away. But he didn't. After doing another sweep of the area, probably to make sure we didn't have an audience, he grabbed hold of the bottom of his shirt and pulled it up. Not all the way, but enough for me to see some skin.

It was fairly dark in this corner of Crave, but there was enough light to see the imprint on his back. It was different from Kraven's black, batlike tattoo. This was more of an outline with some light shading. It looked like actual feathers. Then again, Kraven was a demon and Bishop was…

An angel.

I still wanted to deny it, but that was getting harder with every passing minute.

"You see it?" he asked, glancing at me over his shoulder.

I nodded. He was about to pull his shirt back down, but I wasn't finished yet.

"Wait." I drew closer to him so I could get a better look—was it ink or something else? I ran my fingers over the lines to find it didn't feel like anything but smooth skin. But I felt something else—an energy, a hum, that warmed me being this close to him.

When I'd touched him the first time, I'd had that strange

vision that had since faded. For a while, I'd assumed it was just my imagination running wild, but now I wasn't so sure. Bishop looked like a painfully attractive boy with dark hair and vivid blue eyes, but he wasn't that. Not at all.

"You're an angel," I finally said.

"Thank you for the confirmation. All done?"

Suddenly, I realized that I was touching his back in an intimate way. My cheeks flamed and I pulled my hand away so fast it was comical. Bishop lowered his shirt and glanced at me as if he, too, was surprised I'd been touching him that way only minutes after telling him how much I hated him.

An angel. Here in Trinity.

And I'd just totally groped him in public.

"Sam?" Carly approached us slowly. I guess she was done chatting.

I cringed and turned to look at her. "Uh-huh?"

"Um, what's going on?"

Good question. I wondered how much of that she'd witnessed. By the look on her face, probably too much.

"Nothing." Denial was always a nice thing, even when it didn't help at all.

"Who's he?" She glanced at Bishop.

"Nobody. We should go now." I grabbed her arm and started to direct her toward the exit. I felt a strong urge to get Carly somewhere much safer. And I needed to regroup and decide what to do about my problem.

"Leave? Right when it looks like you're starting to have some fun?" She was actually smiling. My life was falling apart, and she thought it was hilarious.

"No, Samantha," Bishop said. "We're not done here. There's too much to do to wait another day. I need your help now."

Carly waggled her eyebrows. "He needs your help, Sam. That sounds intriguing, doesn't it?"

"It's not like that." I pulled her farther away from the blue-eyed angel. We were so close to the exit. Just another dozen feet to freedom. I stole another glance at Bishop, who'd stopped following and was now staring at me, and ignored my racing heart.

"I knew there was a reason we came here tonight," she whispered. "I thought it was so you could confront Stephen, but it was so you could meet this guy. He's a total hottie. You had your hands all over him just now! And he looked like he didn't want you to stop. Guess you're breaking that no-romance rule of yours, aren't you?"

I grimaced. "It wasn't what it looked like."

"Sure, it wasn't." Her smile faded a little. "I'm all for you finding someone awesome and gorgeous. As long as it isn't Colin."

Oh, yes. Thanks so much for the reminder. I dreaded seeing him again tomorrow. He'd asked me out and then I'd nearly accosted his mouth. There was no way he wasn't going to take that the wrong way. He probably thought I was into him.

For the record, I wasn't. However, just thinking about how close I'd come to kissing him made my stomach growl softly with hunger. That was disturbing.

Carly slanted a glance in Bishop's direction. He stood with his arms crossed, leaning against the wall near the staircase. He wasn't watching me now; his gaze was on the rest of the club as he did another security check.

"Can you give me a second?" I asked Carly.

"Are you going to give him your phone number?"

"Uh, yeah. My phone number. Sure."

Her smile returned. "Go for it."

"Wait here." As I walked toward Bishop, his gaze locked with mine.

Again, my breath caught. He had a way of doing that to me effortlessly. It was kind of annoying. "It's been a long day. I want to go home now."

He shook his head. "You need to come with me."

I exhaled shakily. "I just told you a few minutes ago that I never want to see you again."

Yeah. Right before I'd groped him. Colin wasn't the only one who was getting mixed messages from me this week.

"If I don't find the others, they'll be permanently lost, wandering the city, unsure of how they got here or who they are." Frustration crossed his expression. "I should be able to find them myself, but I can't."

"Why can't you?" I asked.

Bishop shook his head. "The searchlights were my only clue, but they're invisible to me. I must be damaged from entering the city. They told me I might be disoriented, but this is worse than that, and I don't know why. It could jeopardize my entire mission. But there's no way I can get a message to them that things went wrong. I'm on my own."

I twisted a long piece of hair tightly around my finger. "So, the searchlights…why can I see something that you were supposed to see?"

"Good question." His brows knitted together. "Maybe it was prearranged—a plan B nobody told me about. How else could you have found me last night?"

"I was on my way home, that's all. I'm no plan B." I swallowed hard. "I can't deal with this right now. I need time to think."

He touched my arm as I turned away. "You need me, Samantha. Without me, you'll be back here again looking for that gray's help." He cast a dark glance at the lounge over our heads. "Trust me when I say that would be a big mistake."

Tears burned my eyes, but I forced myself to blink them away. I'd be strong. It wasn't like I had many other choices. "According to Stephen, losing a soul's a great thing, but I know this hunger is bad. According to you, I could kill people if I lose control. And I could change into something else, right?"

He nodded. "If you can't control your hunger, you'll become mindless, like a zombie whose only desire is to feed."

"Awesome. A kissing zombie." He wasn't easing my mind, and yet I hadn't pulled away from him. "So what am I supposed to do?"

There was a short hesitation before he spoke again. "Help me. And I'll help you."

My breath caught. "You can help me?"

"I can."

"But…how? My soul, it—it's gone. Stephen said it's gone forever. I can't get it back."

Bishop sent another glance through the club before locking gazes with me again. "He was wrong. I'll help you restore your soul. I believe there's a way."

I felt a sharp, hopeful lurch in my chest. "How?"

"Here's the thing. I'll help you, Samantha, but you have to help me in return. That's the deal."

I looked at him bleakly. "I thought only demons and car salesmen made deals. Not angels."

"I need you to find the others for me. I'll make a deal with you to make that possible. It's that simple."

His controlled expression gave nothing away, but his blue eyes—they told another story. They were filled with worry, with hope, and all of it was directed at me. I held the fate of his mission in my hands—according to him, anyway. And he held my entire future in his.

If I made this choice to help him, my destiny would be irrevocably connected to an angel who frightened, angered and frustrated me, but also intrigued me more than I wanted to admit.

Even though I was essentially one of the monsters, he was willing to bargain with me. If there'd been an outbreak of vampires in the city, I wouldn't blink at the thought of vampire hunters running around with wooden stakes taking care of the problem.

Then again, if I was one of the vampires…

"Would you have killed me last night in the alley if I hadn't gotten away?" I finally asked. "Despite our 'connection,' despite me being 'special'? Would you have?"

His brows drew together and it took him a moment to answer. "I hadn't realized what you were until Kraven pointed it out, so it took me by surprise. I should be able to sense that, too. But you aren't feeding, you aren't putting anyone at risk. You're coherent and thinking rationally. No, I wouldn't have killed you."

"Liar."

His eyes flicked sharply to mine as if I'd insulted him. After all, he had just told me that angels didn't lie. "I can't change what's happened so far or what you think I would or wouldn't have done. The question is, what do you want to do next?"

Again, Bishop was so close to me that our bodies were almost touching. It was as if he was a magnet for me and I couldn't resist his pull. "If I help you find your friends—and you help to restore my soul—you also have to promise to keep me safe, just like you told Stephen you would."

I was revising the contract as we went along. My father was a lawyer, so I supposed it came naturally.

He raised an eyebrow. "Deal. I also have another condition of my own."

Great. Although, I supposed it was only fair. "What is it?"

"When I need you to, you'll help take the cloud away from my mind."

"You need me to...?" I began, but then I got it. "You want me to touch you sometimes, because it takes your confusion away."

"You seem to have that ability," he said, his expression tight as if it pained him to admit it.

I'd twisted my hair so tight that the tip of my finger had turned a lovely shade of purple. "Deal. But I'm not touching you *all* the time." Which was too bad, really....

"No, definitely not all the time." But something slid behind his gaze then. Something that went against his words.

I'd started breathing quicker and hadn't taken a single step away from him, despite how adamant I'd tried to sound about keeping my distance. God, what was wrong with me? He affected me like no boy I'd ever known.

Maybe because he wasn't a boy at all.

I shivered.

Fine. I'd help him. I had no other choice from where I stood, other than going back upstairs and getting cozy with Stephen and his new "brothers and sisters."

Carly must have gotten tired of waiting, because suddenly there she was, stretching her hand out to Bishop.

"I'm Carly, by the way," she said. "Nice to meet you."

Bishop hesitated a moment before he shook Carly's hand. "Bishop."

"So are we leaving or what, Sam? What's going on?"

That was the question of the day. What was going on?

I might not feel like a monster who hungered for human souls, but kissing Stephen had changed me and could eventually take me down a very dark road if I didn't do anything to fix it. Bishop had said he could restore my soul, which would take away the hunger I now constantly felt.

Stephen had offered no such solution.

"You need to go home now, Carly," I said.

She frowned. "But—"

"Please. It's important. Don't ask me why, but you need to get out of here right now."

"Okay, Ms. Dramatic. Are you coming with me?"

"No, I…I have to do something first."

"With him?"

My jaw tightened. "Yeah."

Carly looked confused. "So you're ditching me for some guy you just met?"

I wasn't the kind of girl who ditched her friends for some cute guy, so I could understand her confusion. Giving him my phone number was one thing, but leaving with him was another.

"I'm not ditching you," I said firmly. I didn't have time to argue about this. "Just—please, trust me and go home. I'll call you later." She nodded slowly, and I turned back to Bishop. "Let's go."

"Sam!" Carly called after me as Bishop and I moved toward the exit. "You never told me what happened with Stephen."

"Later, I promise," I told her. Then I looked at Bishop. "You have one hour. That's it."

He shook his head. "That won't be enough time."

"Too bad. That's all I'm willing to give you tonight. Take it or leave it."

He glared at me. I mean, contrary to what Carly might think and any confusing feelings I needed to sort through, I wasn't interested in Bishop romantically. Not a chance. If I'd thought Stephen was trouble, then this guy was trouble times a thousand.

"Fine," he said, his jaw tight. "I'll take it."

I cast one last glance over my shoulder. Standing behind the glass barrier on the second floor, Stephen watched as we left the club.

chapter 8

It was just before nine o'clock on Monday night and I was walking the streets of Trinity with an angel who looked like he could go to my high school.

My mother once read this book that said when she was overwhelmed by stuff she couldn't control, she should focus on what was happening right at that moment. Basically it meant that what happened in the past was over and what might happen in the future was not worth thinking about yet if it was only going to cause anxiety.

Live in the now. Right here. Right now. Nowhere else.

So I focused on doing just that. I didn't think about my missing soul or who'd stolen it from me in a kiss that, for a few fleeting moments, I'd honestly thought had meant something—that the cute boy who lived on my street might actually be interested in me, had noticed me, thought I was worthy of his attention, but instead had turned out to be a monster in disguise.

Nope. Instead, I thought about how tight my shoes felt and how they'd never been meant for long walks like this. And how chilly the wind felt against my face. Instead of thinking about what my swirling hunger meant, I focused on the gorgeous guy walking next to me and how being this close to him made my stomach do constant flip-flops.

Well, maybe I needed to focus on something *else.* Thinking of Bishop like that was dangerous. He'd promised to restore my soul if I helped him. That was the only reason I was with him right now.

Information—that's what I needed. And there was only one way I could think of to get it: ask.

I braved a glance at Bishop. "Can I ask you a question?"

"Sure."

"Why are you working with a demon? Angels and demons…well, I'd assume you should be enemies."

"We are."

"Then…what's going on? I mean, you and Kraven, you don't seem to like each other much."

He hesitated. "We don't."

"You hate him?"

"Angels don't hate."

Bishop seemed to talk like that. Short answers and sometimes a little too formal for your average teen. "How old are you?"

That earned me a look. "How old do I look?"

"Seventeen or eighteen."

He shrugged a shoulder. "Then that's pretty much what I am."

Pretty much? That wasn't exactly a comforting answer, since it basically told me he *wasn't* only seventeen or eighteen.

I cleared my throat. "So, um, the nonhating thing. What about, like, fiery vengeance and smiting the unholy? Angels do that, right?"

This earned me a half grin, which unfortunately drew my

gaze back to his lips. I wondered if all grays constantly thought about kissing people—with or without souls. I really didn't want him to affect me so much, not now that I knew what he was and what he could do.

He didn't look directly at me when he replied. "It's a little different than you might think."

"Okay, then what's up with the demon/angel interaction?"

"Do you see a searchlight yet?" he asked instead of answering.

I glanced around. "Not yet. You're sure there are others?"

"I'm sure."

"Angels or demons?"

"Likely a mix." He was quiet for a moment. "Angels and demons—we're two different but necessary ends of a scale. Demons are on one end and angels are on the other. Balanced numbers—of both light and dark forces—keep everything properly aligned."

I had an image in my head of a huge weight scale with a bunch of demons sitting on one side and an equal number of angels on the other. "Could you tell what Kraven was last night? I mean, if you hadn't checked his back to see the imprint? He looked so normal to me."

His lips thinned. "Here in the human world he could have been an angel or a demon—or a human. I couldn't tell for sure."

Something occurred to me. I remembered Bishop's initial hesitation when we found Kraven in the alley. "Do you know him? Like, from another time?"

He looked at me sharply. "Why would you ask me that?"

I was surprised by his reaction and actually took a step away from him. "I don't know. It just seemed like it to me. I figured that might be why you might dislike each other so much."

He turned his gaze to the direction we were walking. "Angels don't hate demons, but we have a natural aversion to each other. It can't be helped."

That wasn't exactly a direct answer. "Then why work together? Why not just team up with other angels?"

He didn't speak for a moment. I got the distinct feeling that my questions were making him uncomfortable. Well, that made two of us. But I needed answers so I could figure out how I fit into all of this and how Bishop might be able to help me.

"It wasn't exactly in my mission parameters to discuss the situation with one of..." He trailed off before flicking a glance at me, his blue eyes guarded, but I knew what he meant.

"One of the bad guys," I finished for him. A shiver went down my spine—this time it wasn't a pleasant one. "But you know I'm different, right? You said that already. If you didn't, you wouldn't have asked me to help you, no matter what I could do. I mean, you have that knife of yours..." This time *I* was the one to trail off. Some things really didn't need to be spoken aloud.

He watched me carefully and there might have been a little bit of regret in his expression. I wasn't sure. "You're afraid of me now."

I swallowed hard. "Do you blame me?"

"You don't need to be. I mean you no harm, Samantha."

His deep, beautiful voice sent waves of warmth through me, even when we weren't touching. It made me want to believe him. But while words might be warm and beautiful, actions were even better. "Okay. Then prove it."

His eyes held mine. "How?"

"Let me hold your dagger."

He raised an eyebrow. "You think that'll help?"

"It might. I mean, if you let me hold something so important, something that could actually *kill* you, that might give me a bit more confidence." The more I spoke, the more sense it made. At least, to me. "Consider it a symbol of trust between us."

He held my gaze steadily, while his scent—still spicy and delicious and potentially addictive—kept me close effortlessly. It was all I could do to try to keep my expression neutral.

Finally he pulled the dagger out of its sheath. I eyed the hilt with surprise as he held it out to me.

"Really?" I said.

He nodded. "I want you to trust me, Samantha."

I thought about my horrible nightmare, when I'd used this knife to kill Bishop before the shadows pulled me apart. My stomach twisted. "Aren't you afraid I'm going to stab you?"

A glimmer of humor lit up his eyes. "Not really."

"So you don't think I'm dangerous?"

A smile played at his very distracting lips. "Oh, you're dangerous, all right. But not when it comes to something like this. Despite everything, you're a teenage girl. I'm going to take a wild guess that you haven't had much experience with weapons. However, I have. A lot of it."

Despite my lack of experience, he thought I was dangerous to him? That annoying shiver returned, spinning around me and landing right in the center of my stomach. I finally reached out to take the dagger from him. My fingers brushed against his as I did, sending that strange electric sensation through me again. No nightmarish visions this time, thankfully. The knife felt heavy and I held it at my side, close to my leg so anyone who drove past us on the street wouldn't be able to see it. And actually, yeah, it did make me feel better.

I looked at him again with astonishment that he'd agreed to

this. This weapon was incredibly important to his mission and he was letting me—a so-called *gray*—take it for a test drive.

But he was right about one thing—it would take a lot of motivation and strength for me to be able to stab someone in the chest with it. But hurting him was the last thing on my mind right now.

"You are different," he said after a moment, studying me as we passed under the light of a streetlamp. "Different from anyone I've ever met. I wish I knew why."

Ever? I found it difficult to breathe for a moment. "Is that a compliment or an observation?"

He grinned. "Both."

Focus, Samantha, I told myself. I couldn't let myself be distracted by this beautiful, dangerous angel on his mission from Heaven. He was a means to get my soul back; that was the only reason I was here right now. I already had enough painful bee stings racked up this year, I didn't need another one.

I wished I knew what he was thinking. He kept saying things that made me believe he thought of me as more than just a friendly neighborhood soulless monster. He watched me out of the corner of his eye as if he wasn't sure how to deal with me being near him.

But he didn't try to put distance between us. In fact, he was a little *too* close right now—so close I could feel the warmth from his body. My head felt cloudy again.

I inhaled deeply and let the breath out slowly. "So if I'm helping you, then I'm sort of on your team, right?"

He did look at me this time, his eyes an intense shade of indigo in the moonlight. "I don't have much longer to find the others, or the searchlights showing their locations will go out. Then I won't be able to find them at all. They'll wander the streets not knowing who they really are or why they're here. There's not enough time for us to play around."

Again, he was sidestepping my questions. "I'm not feeling very playful at the moment."

"You're helping me find the others, that's all. You're not really a part of this."

The frustration inside me bubbled over. "If I'm not a part of this, why do you need my help? Maybe I should call it a night. I forgot I have some homework to do. Even grays like me need to get good grades if they want to go to college."

It was a pathetic attempt to get him to say he needed me, that I was in this now whether I liked it or not. A small, scared part of me did want to help him, despite everything. I knew this was important.

"You won't be going to college if you don't help me. You're trapped in this city with the others for as long as you're missing your soul."

"Because of this barrier you told Stephen is around the whole city right now keeping grays from leaving."

He nodded. "If it's any consolation it contains angels and demons, too. Anything supernatural. Anything nonhuman."

I gritted my teeth. I didn't want him to see that this possibility had completely floored me. "Fine. Then I'll go to a *local* college." I glared at him. "I guess it's different where you come from, but here if you want somebody to do something for you, you're supposed to be nice to them. Letting me carry your shiny weapon isn't nearly good enough."

He glared back at me. "I'm nice."

I laughed out loud. "Try again. Look, I know you're having issues with relying on me to do these bizarre errands for you. But you do need me, right?"

He pressed his lips together, his gaze sinking so deeply into me that I again found it hard to walk straight. I took that as a yes. That made things simple, really, whether he agreed or not.

We passed a bookstore with several people standing outside smoking. I tucked the heavy dagger under my jacket until we were out of view again. It wasn't the most natural thing to be carrying around.

"So you need me," I said. "And you're telling me I need you if I want my soul back. And I definitely do. I'm still reeling from what all of this means, but when there's a problem, I try to fix it. Seeing as this is the biggest problem I've ever faced in my entire life, I *will* fix it, no matter what it takes."

He nodded. "Then we understand each other."

Bishop was the most infuriating person—angel, whatever—ever. Despite the chill in my body, my cheeks grew hotter the longer this conversation went in circles. "No, I *don't* understand. That's the whole reason I'm asking you questions—or trying to, if you'd stop trying to avoid them. I need to know these things. If you want me on your side, you have to stop treating me like some sort of weird, stinky thing that you don't want anywhere near you."

His lips curved to the side. "Trust me, you definitely don't stink. You smell very good to me."

Again, he managed to render me speechless for a split second. I nearly walked into a lamppost, but I managed to swerve just in time. "Well, okay. Then I'm just a weird thing."

"If you say so." Amusement fading, he scanned the black, star-studded skies. "Anything yet?"

I looked up. "Not yet. Believe me, I'll let you know if a bright beam of light suddenly appears. That is, if you stop being so secretive with me about everything."

He raked a hand through his dark hair, his jaw tight. "Fine. I'll tell you a few things to do with my mission."

"I'm listening."

"Angels and demons have been asked to work together in the past, but only a handful of times. Even though Heaven and Hell are both necessary to keep the balance, we're not friends. We work together only when there's a threat that affects both Heaven and Hell and the balance we need to maintain. And there's a threat like that right now."

Another chill cut through me. "Grays."

"Yes."

"They're—" I really didn't want to say *we're;* despite the ever-present hunger, my stomach felt queasy just at the thought of it "—really a threat to Heaven and Hell? Enough to send a team of angels and demons to stop them?"

When he met my eyes this time, he looked pensive. "There was a similar situation once before, caused by a demon who had the ability to devour human souls. This ability marked the demon as a dangerous anomaly."

"Funny," I said shakily. "I'd think that's exactly what a demon should be able to do."

He shrugged. "Maybe in horror movies, but not in reality. Souls are too important to the universal balance. The original demon who could do this was defeated. But now, with the current rise of this particular problem..." He glanced at me out of the corner of his eye. "The question is, is this a new demon with the same ability? One who can now spread this affliction like a disease through the kiss? Or is it the same demon as last time? But that would be impossible."

"Why impossible?"

"Like I said, she was sent somewhere she shouldn't have been able to return from—somewhere *no one* returns from." His jaw tensed. "But if she found a way, then that's a sign that something *very* bad is on the rise—possibly worse than what we're already dealing with."

I gripped the dagger tighter. "So this demon…that's the Source you were talking about? The Source of the grays? Like Patient Zero?"

He frowned at me.

I shrugged. "It's a zombie movie term. The first one infected who then infects others. And so on, and so on."

"Sounds about right. I'm to personally find her and learn where she came from and what her master plan is—if she has one. My team is here to keep the city safe from grays whose insatiable hunger is putting humans at direct risk."

I thought it through. "So she's like a vampire drinking blood and creating more vampires who want to drink blood, right?" I desperately needed an analogy I could understand. Zombies I understood. Vampires I understood. I'd seen a lot of movies about both. Quite honestly, compared to soul sucking, biting necks might be almost fashionable.

He shook his head as we crossed the street at an intersection. "Blood is not a soul. A soul is the very essence of a human life, a precious and invaluable thing. When that human dies, his or her soul remains in existence—immortal—just as most of your religions believe. It's judged and sent to either Heaven or Hell. Each soul is important to maintain the balance—be it a soul of darkness or of light."

I frowned hard, trying to process all of this. "Wait. So you're trying to say, just like angels and demons, that Heaven and Hell need an equal number of souls to keep this balance? Does that mean that it's a fifty-fifty split? Half of all humans go to Hell while the other half go to Heaven?" Just the thought of this made my heart pound with fear. While I didn't consider things like this very often, I wanted to do everything possible to avoid going to Hell when I got my soul back—now that I knew for sure a place like that existed. "I thought that if you're good in life, you automatically get a ticket to Heaven. But you're saying it's more of a lottery system?"

"No, it's definitely not a lottery." This statement had brought a glimmer of amusement back to Bishop's handsome face. I glared at him. So nice to know that I helped him find the funny side of this incredibly nonfunny situation. "Souls are… How can I explain it so you'll understand? They can change as a human lives life and makes his or her decisions. The better decisions one makes, the lighter a soul becomes. The more evil, the soul grows heavy with darkness. Don't worry, Samantha, more souls do go to Heaven and a human is fully in control of how light or heavy a soul is by his or her actions while alive. Being judged means having your soul weighed."

I blinked, stunned by all of this. "Like, on a scale?"

"It's not quite that literal, but yeah."

I swallowed hard. "So if grays are devouring human souls, then there's nothing left to go to either Heaven or Hell. And that throws off this all-important balance."

"Correct."

I bit my bottom lip and my heart started pounding harder. "So…what does that mean? For me? What happens when *I* die?"

He didn't answer. His focus was on the sidewalk as we continued to trudge along. I grabbed his arm and forced him to stop and look at me.

"Bishop, what does it mean if I die without a soul?"

His jaw tightened and he looked away, scanning the street, before meeting my eyes again. "If you're careful you won't have to worry about that for a long time. Besides, I agreed to help find a way to restore your soul."

That didn't set my mind at ease in the slightest. Fear raced through me. "But—but what if I *am* killed? You're planning on doing that to other grays, right? With this dagger?" I held it up. My arm ached from clutching it for so long, but I wasn't ready to give it up quite yet.

He didn't speak for a moment. "Then it's the end. Just like when an angel or demon is destroyed. You will cease to exist."

I staggered back a step and felt my face blanch. I began to tremble from head to foot.

"No, don't cry, Samantha," Bishop whispered, drawing closer. "It's going to be okay."

I frowned and looked up at him. I hadn't realized that I was crying until he'd pointed it out. He gently stroked the tears off my cheeks. The heat of his skin sank into mine, warming me, and the pleasant sensation made my breath catch. He cupped my face in his hands and looked down at me, his brows drawing together.

"I promised I'd keep you safe," he said. "I promised I'd help restore your soul. I know I haven't shown you much reason to believe in me, but believe it when I say this—I *know* you're different from the others. You're incredibly special—*so* special. And I swear I won't let anything bad happen to you. Okay?"

He leaned forward and brushed his lips against my forehead.

I think I stopped breathing entirely for a moment. His lips left a heated impression on my skin. Talk about living in the now. Everything fell away from me, every worry, every fear.

When he leaned back, something had shifted in his gaze. So far tonight I'd seen confusion, annoyance and a healthy portion of distrust there. But now I was sure I saw…desire.

For just a moment, he looked at me like he wanted me.

My entire world closed in on his lips. Even though he'd said he didn't have a soul, I still wanted to kiss him so desperately it was impossible to ignore the deep need to pull him to me and do just that. The dagger fell from my grip and clanged to the ground as I took hold of his T-shirt, drawing him closer to me. Closer, until our lips were only a breath apart.

I needed his mouth against mine so badly it blinded me to anything else. And he wasn't pushing me away.

Someone nearby noisily cleared his throat. "Sorry, am I interrupting something?"

Bishop stepped back from me, a look of surprise on his face. He bent over to snatch up the dagger and then turned away from me. I felt like some sort of spell had broken with the abruptness of a hand slapping my face.

Kraven leaned against a brick wall, his arms crossed over his chest. He was grinning.

"See, dude? I just knew you could convince her to help out."

"We're searching for the others."

"I'm sure you are. Just taking a little break right now to get to know each other better, right?"

Bishop sent a look toward me, his eyes stormy. Was he angry we'd been interrupted? Or angry that we'd nearly kissed? I hoped it wasn't the latter.

I wasn't sure what had happened just now—why I'd nearly kissed him.

No, scratch that. I did know. That was courtesy of my strange pull toward Bishop, the same pull I'd felt last night when I'd first met him. Something was there between us, and I didn't want it to be.

And yet, I'd still desperately wanted to kiss him just now.

"I think you freaked her out." Kraven studied my distress. "Bad angel breath, maybe?"

"We need to keep searching," Bishop replied.

He still seemed disturbed, but I was composing myself quickly. Something about the demon made that easy. Probably because I despised him so much. Angels might not hate, but *I* didn't have a huge problem with it.

"Surprised gray girl's even willing to pitch in." Kraven lifted one hand and studied his fingernails. "You know, being one of *them*. Are you really sure we shouldn't just kill her and get it over with?"

The only reason I knew he was fooling around was his smart-ass grin, which I wanted to wipe off his face. Preferably with the sole of my shoe.

"Do that and you won't find your team," I snapped. "I'm getting the feeling you two are stuck here together until you finish your job, you jerk."

"Jerk? Is that the best you've got? How disappointing." His grin only stretched wider.

"I need to talk to you for a moment," Bishop said to Kraven.

"Be still my heart."

"Privately." He cast an apologetic glance in my direction.

I let out a shaky breath. "Go ahead. I'll just wait here and think up some better insults."

Bishop followed Kraven around the corner and out of earshot. It didn't take long before the night felt like it was closing around me. The cold sank deep into me even with my coat wrapped tightly around me.

I had to admit, I was curious about what they were currently discussing.

Probably me.

I moved slowly toward the edge of the building until I

could hear them. I pressed my back up against the brick wall and strained to listen.

I was right. It *was* about me. And they were speaking quietly as if trying to prevent me from listening in. It didn't work.

"…a liability to the mission. You never should have brought her in. How much have you told her?"

"Enough for her to understand."

"Great. I didn't think you were a complete idiot, but I guess I was wrong. But I've been wrong about a lot of things, haven't I?"

Bishop's voice turned sharp. "That makes two of us."

"She's one of them."

"She's different."

"Sure, she is. Maybe you can't see clearly since you've got the hots for her. I mean, she's cute enough, but is she worth risking everything over?"

"The mission is all that matters to me." Bishop's voice was tense, and I couldn't tell if he was lying. But he'd said angels didn't lie.

I struggled to breathe. The mission *was* all that mattered to him. I was only a means to help him complete that mission successfully.

Was that really true? Or had I seen something in his eyes before, something real between us? I hated to think it had been my stupid imagination or, even worse, that he'd been messing with me to get what he wanted.

"Yeah, right. You'd never risk anything for a girl. Not you." Kraven snorted. "So what I just interrupted—you weren't about to go at it right here in the alley? Or are you going to try to convince me that as an angel you're totally priestly all the time? All self-denially?"

Bishop hissed out a breath. "I have everything under control."

"I sure the hell hope so." I could hear the sneer in Kraven's voice. These guys really hated each other; I didn't care what Bishop said about angels not hating. Their interaction felt personal, like there was bad blood between them. "I know she works some kind of hocus pocus on your brain when you two touch. Can you imagine what she might do to you if it's full naked-on-naked contact? Maybe you should get it out of your system and just throw her down and—"

The next sound was a grunt of pain after a fist connected with some part of a body. I chose that moment to round the corner and saw Kraven now crouched on the ground favoring his stomach before he slowly rose to his feet. His eyes glowed red in the darkness. Bishop stood with fists clenched at his sides as if ready for the demon to attack. Both their fierce glares turned in my direction.

I faltered for a moment under the heat of those glares, but then forced myself to lean against the wall with my arms crossed, an echo of Kraven earlier. "So…am I interrupting anything?"

"Not at all," Kraven said, regaining that hateful, twisting smile. "Thought you might have run off already."

"Not yet, but it's tempting."

Bishop didn't look happy. Whether he was more upset with the direction of their argument or that he'd resorted to violence to end it, I wasn't sure. Personally, I was secretly thrilled he'd defended me like that. He wouldn't have done that if I was only a means to help him find his team, would he? That had been personal.

Still, I was a little surprised that he'd let Kraven's cheap shots bother him. He'd obviously never gone to a public high school.

I'd known guys like Kraven all my life. All talk. Emotional manipulators. And yes, *jerks*. Just because he was a demon didn't mean I didn't have his number.

Him I could deal with. The angel—well, he was brand-new for me. The whole situation had me so off center that I had to focus on keeping my balance.

That seemed to be the entire reason behind their mission. Keep the balance. Get rid of the threat that was consuming the souls that Heaven and Hell needed to keep their all-important universal balance. I got that. It was insane and scary and way too big for my head to wrap completely around, but I got the gist of it.

"You want to go home now, don't you?" Bishop asked. The question wasn't filled with anger or accusation. He searched my face for the answer, his hands still tight at his sides.

I swallowed hard. "More than you know."

"We need you."

"So you say."

"It's true."

I looked at Kraven before summoning my faltering bravery and moving closer to him. I wouldn't let him believe I was afraid of him. I couldn't give him that kind of power over me.

"Do you need me, too?" I asked.

He sneered at me. "No."

"Can *you* see the lights to find the others?"

He stepped closer to me as if challenging me back, and he reached down to take a tight hold of my wrist. I tensed but didn't try to pull away. "You're kind of bright and shiny, gray girl."

He held my gaze, half his mouth turned up in that patronizing grin.

And suddenly I could read his mind.

I saw past his bravado, past his sneering exterior, down deeper into those amber-colored eyes of his. It felt a little like what had happened this morning, when I'd zapped him to protect myself. This ability drew from the same place. Eyes were the windows to the soul, I'd heard. Since demons didn't have souls, I figured I was just seeing down to Kraven's true self.

I don't know if I can do this. Not with him *here. I didn't know it would be this hard.*

It was his thought, not mine. I knew it. I felt it. It was crystal clear to me.

"You're doubting yourself," I said aloud. "You're worried you're going to fail. You're just like Bishop that way. You two have way more in common than you might admit."

He snatched his hand back from me. The amusement had completely left his expression, replaced with confusion.

"How did you—?" he began.

"They wouldn't have picked you if they didn't think you could do this." If Kraven had been sent on this mission, he must be skilled. Someone who could be counted on to come through in a tough situation. Didn't he realize that?

"You don't know what the hell you're talking about." He cast a dark glance at Bishop, who stood watching us intently.

Bishop raised an eyebrow. "See? I told you she was special."

Kraven turned his fiery glare back on me, and this time it took a lot of effort not to flinch. "Don't do that again."

"You don't want anyone to see the real you?"

"You don't want to see the real me, trust me on that." He shot a look at Bishop. "You don't want her to see the real me, either, do you? Or how about the real *you?*"

"I'll take my chances," Bishop replied evenly.

Kraven's steely gaze met mine again. "How did you do that?"

Whatever it was felt natural. Felt easy. Like it was simply an extension of who I already was, which I knew made no sense at all. "I honestly have no idea."

"I don't believe you."

"That's your problem. And you didn't answer my question." I tried to keep my voice steady. "Not properly anyway. Can you see the searchlights that lead to the others?"

He answered through clenched teeth. "No, I can't."

I nodded. "Well, I can. And I've spotted a new one, so I guess you *do* need me. And if you keep looking at me like you want me dead, I can't say I'm all that interested in helping you out."

"Kraven," Bishop growled. A warning. "Be nice to Samantha."

The demon studied me a bit longer with that disturbed and angry look on his handsome face before a smile finally snaked across his expression. It didn't reach as far as his eyes. "Of course. Welcome to the team, sweetness. Looks like we're going to make a big fat exception for you."

Great. I'd never been much of a team player before and, if I had been, I would never have picked one like this.

I nodded and pulled my coat closer around me, cinching the belt tightly at my waist, and tried my best to swallow my fear. "Okay, then. Follow me."

chapter 9

Bishop's gaze stayed on me as we walked—a heated sensation on the side of my face that I couldn't ignore even if I tried to.

I glanced at him warily. "What?"

"How did you get in the demon's head?"

That was a very good question. I hadn't wanted to do it. I didn't want to have anything to do with him at all if I could help it. "I don't know."

"Can you read *my* mind?"

"I don't know," I said again.

"Try."

We slowed for a moment and he looked into my eyes. I concentrated, but I didn't exactly know how to access this ability, only that it had been really easy with Kraven. With Bishop, his nearness was a major distraction, but staring into his blue eyes did nothing but make my heart start to pound hard and my breath come faster. "I don't think I can. No—there's nothing."

Oh, there was something. But it had nothing to do with reading his mind.

"Maybe there's nothing in his skull to read in the first

place," Kraven grumbled. "Or nothing that hasn't already been all shaken up like a snow globe when he slammed through that barrier."

"Or maybe his mind is stronger than yours," I countered.

"Doubt that."

"Have you had moments of psychic awareness in the past?" Bishop asked, ignoring the demon's jibes.

I shook my head. "Never."

"No mind reading? No uncanny intuition of things that might happen in the future?"

"Like I said, never."

"Only since you've been turned." Bishop and Kraven shared a look. For an angel and a demon who hated each other, their confusion about my newfound skills had finally given them some common ground.

"When I first touched you," I said to Bishop, "I had a vision. And even before I met you I had a dream about…well, I'm pretty sure it was you."

I decided not to mention the dream where I'd killed him.

He was right at my side then, studying me intently while we continued to walk toward the searchlight. I kept my eyes locked on it in the distance.

"What did you dream?" he asked.

"Sex dream, probably," Kraven said with a smirk. "Right?"

"No." Did I mention I hated this guy? I could definitely see why he lived in Hell. I wanted him to return there as soon as possible. "It was a bit fuzzy, but I was about to fall into a black hole and Bishop…well, he had a hold on me until he let go."

Kraven snorted. "Nice. Maybe that was a premonition that he'll come to his senses and kick you straight into the Hollow."

I looked at him. Bishop had used that term in Crave earlier as a threat to Stephen. "The what?"

Bishop glared at Kraven. "Shut your mouth."

"Why? She'll find out soon enough. Thought we were in sharing mode tonight. Or is that only okay when it's you doing the sharing up against a brick wall?"

Again, Bishop chose to ignore the demon and turned his gaze back to me. "What about the first vision, Samantha? What was that?"

"I don't really remember it. At first it was vivid and then it, like, started slipping away. It was bad, though. *Epically* bad. Something about this city—about Trinity." I glanced around at the tall buildings. The darkness tonight felt almost like a living, breathing thing closing in on me. "Destruction. Everything and everyone gone."

Silence was my only answer to that. Even Kraven didn't have a snappy comeback, which wasn't reassuring.

"I figure I was sensing you were going to help save the city. I don't know." I shrugged and shoved my hands deeper into my pockets to try to warm them so I'd stop shivering. I knew one way to get rid of the chill I felt—hold Bishop's hand. But that wasn't going to happen. Not with Kraven around. The thought made a strange longing burrow into my chest. I'd told Bishop earlier that I wanted to touch him as little as possible. I wished that had been the truth.

"But you didn't see that I succeeded," he said. "You saw only destruction."

"I—I don't know. I don't remember. Why? Is that what happens if you fail? The city goes boom?" I said it flippantly, but the looks on their faces was so collectively bleak it sent a deep chill through me. "Will it?"

"No," Bishop said firmly, flicking a glance at the demon. "Because we won't fail."

"Just a gray," Kraven mumbled as if he was talking to himself more than us. "I know you are. I don't get anything else off you. But what's with the sight? Nothing all that special about you that I can sense."

I glared at him. "Then why can I see the searchlights? Why could I zap you before? Why can I read your mind when I look into your eyes?"

The reminder earned me a sour look from the demon. "That is the question of the day, sweetness. But a warning... don't try it again."

"Why? Afraid of what I might find in there?"

He grabbed my arm to pull me to a halt and drew me closer. A shudder of fear ran through me.

"Just don't," he said.

"Let go of me."

He did. I wasn't sure if I could zap him again like I had at school this morning, but I didn't have to try.

I jumped when Bishop took my arm, drawing me away from the demon. The moment he touched me, a wave of warmth flowed through me and my fear faded. A little.

"We'll figure it out, Samantha," he said. "Doesn't have to be all at once."

I nodded and tried to ignore my rapidly pounding heart.

"How much farther?" There was strain in the angel's expression and unless it was my imagination, his eyes had become more unfocused. I didn't need him to tell me that he was starting to feel a bit unhinged. I guessed he hadn't touched me long enough to totally clear his head.

"We're nearly there." I started walking again. The light was just around the corner, in a small park flanked by office buildings. It was like a tiny oasis in the middle of the concrete city, with trees, grass, a walking trail and several park benches. The leaves had mostly fallen off the trees by now and blanketed the ground. It would be very pretty in daylight.

By moonlight, it was eerie.

There was another boy, around the same age as Kraven and Bishop, sitting on a park bench. As soon as I spotted him, the searchlight that led us there went out.

"That's him?" Bishop asked.

Mouth too dry to speak, I nodded.

"I wish I knew how many we're looking for."

"There's supposed to be four of us," replied Kraven.

Bishop looked at him. "Four?"

"Yeah. Two demons, two angels. That's what I was told."

Bishop rubbed his forehead. "I don't remember—maybe I was told that. It's kind of jumbled up. So much to figure out." He pressed his hands to his temples. "Spinning and spinning like a top. Never stopping."

Kraven frowned. "Dude, you okay?"

No, he wasn't okay. Far from it, and he wasn't getting better. He'd said this wasn't how it was supposed to be—that he was more disoriented than he'd expected.

Without thinking about it, I reached for Bishop's hand and felt that breathtaking crackle of electricity between us. Slowly, the confusion lifted from his expression and his eyes cleared of the growing madness.

"Will you be okay?" I asked him.

He squeezed my hand and I saw the frustration in his blue eyes. "Hopefully long enough to do what I'm here to do. When I go back to Heaven it'll be better. I'll be healed immediately."

"When will that happen?"

"After we've found and dealt with the Source. After we've made sure the city is safe. I think I can be extracted a week from now at the most." He looked down at my hand in his and shook his head. His lips curved into a small but devastating smile. "Amazing. One touch and you're able to clear my thoughts. What would I have done if you hadn't found me?"

I didn't even try to answer that. If nothing else, I had a time frame to work with. Roughly a week was how long he thought he'd be here. Then I could have my soul restored, get back to my normal life and try to forget about all this.

Kraven made a snoring sound. "Can we get on with it?"

I cast a glance toward the boy sitting on the bench. I think he'd been sleeping before we arrived, but his eyes were bright and aware as I moved closer to him.

If he was one of the four, then he was a demon or an angel, unaware of where he was or why he was here. He looked totally human to me. Reddish-brown hair with a slight curl to it. Green eyes. A few light freckles on his nose.

He stared at me. "I know you, don't I?"

I pointed at myself. "Me?"

"Yeah. I think I had a dream about you."

I looked at him with alarm. "You had a dream about *me?*"

I exchanged a look with Bishop, whose dark brows were drawn together as he considered this. Maybe this was a sign that I was meant to be a part of this after all, as crazy as that sounded. Maybe Bishop was right—I thought I'd just randomly found him the other night, but if an angel or demon was dreaming about me...then maybe this was meant to help.

I wished I knew for sure.

"Samantha's everybody's dream girl this week," Kraven said. "Except mine, of course. I have much better taste than that."

I wondered if they'd be okay with the team being reduced to only three? I was fine with Kraven being the expendable one. Maybe they could send a replacement.

"What was the dream about?" Bishop sat down next to the kid, but made no immediate move for that nasty golden dagger of his. It was a relief, but I already knew where this conversation was leading. The ritual. The one that still haunted me even though I now knew why it was so necessary.

The boy looked confused but calm. "She was like…guiding me. I was lost and she helped me find my way."

It was shocking to me that he would have dreamed about me. Or maybe it wasn't a sign of anything and he just had me confused with some other short, skinny brunette. "Do you know who you are?"

He glanced around the park. "I don't know who I am or how I got here. I've been sitting here waiting. Hoping somebody would come by who can tell me how to get home."

"Can we just get on with it?" Kraven asked, his arms crossed. "Nobody's here. Tick tock, Bishop. You know? I could be back out patrolling right now. The Source could be doing a song and dance in the middle of Main Street and we're missing it."

Bishop looked at me. "Samantha, maybe you should go now."

"No, please," the boy said. "Don't go. Stay here. Help me."

He reached out a hand to me. There was something in his eyes, something that made me want to stay with him even knowing what was about to happen. I felt a sudden and overwhelming sense of compassion toward him. If I could help him through this, I wanted to do just that.

This ritual was brutal and ridiculous. Was it really the only way they could get here and avoid ending up having the disorientation like Bishop had? Sucked either way, if you asked me. Either you were a clueless kid wandering the city about to get a knife through the chest or you were a crazy kid wandering the city uncertain of what to do or where to go next.

If this was supposed to be a slick mission involving both Heaven and Hell, I would have expected something much better planned out and controlled. There were too many things that could go wrong. Even class field trips were better organized than this.

"Can you do me a favor?" I took hold of the kid's hand. He'd dreamed I'd help him. I would try my very best to do just that.

"What?" he asked.

"Can you show my—my *friends*—" I couldn't think of another word to describe Bishop and Kraven at the moment "—your back? They need to see if you have a certain mark."

He glanced over his shoulder at the two boys. "My back?"

"It's not as weird as it sounds," Kraven said. "Well, mostly."

"Uh, okay." The kid stood up from the bench and raised the back of his shirt up so we could see the imprint he had. It was a lot like Bishop's—feathery, open lines, some shading. Still huge, but not as dark and ominous as Kraven's.

Another angel.

"Disappointing," Kraven murmured. "But, whatever."

Bishop nodded, seemingly satisfied. "Thank you. You can sit back down."

He did, and he looked at me again. "You're going to help me. You promise?"

I nodded, my throat too thick to swallow properly. I felt ill at what was to come.

Bishop glanced at me again and our eyes met and held. "You can go now. We'll handle this."

"No." The kid gripped my hand, keeping me from getting up. "Stay, please."

Just like with Kraven, when I looked into his eyes I had an effortless connection with this kid. He was scared, but he was trying to be brave. And he'd been telling the truth. He'd been waiting here, knowing deep down that help would be on the way. That someone was looking for him.

"You're brave," I told him.

"Am I?"

"Yeah." I tried to smile, but it was shaky. "It's going to be okay. I swear it will."

While I was more than convinced this was all real, it didn't mean I wanted to accept it. My brain kept trying to deny everything I'd been told and everything I'd seen since last night with Kraven and…the knife…

The knife that Bishop now pulled from the sheath while the kid kept his attention on me. Fear swelled inside me.

"Heads up," Kraven said and began whistling loudly as a pair of people strolled past us on the nearby path. They didn't even glance in our direction.

"Are we shielded?" I asked nervously.

Kraven grinned. "We are now."

"Bishop, wait…" I began. There had to be another way to do this.

But Bishop took hold of the kid's shoulder and pushed him back against the bench.

Finally, the kid turned to look at Bishop, his gaze hitting the now-glowing knife. "What are you—?"

It was the last thing he said before the dagger met its mark.

Everyone in a two-block radius would have heard my scream if we hadn't been shielded. But no one could hear me. No one could see this.

"Look away, Samantha," Bishop snapped, but I couldn't. I couldn't look away from the boy who'd just been stabbed in the chest right in front of me. His grip on my hand grew tighter, nearly tight enough to break my bones, before it slackened and fell away. His eyes closed and he slumped backward.

This wasn't real. It was just a ritual that would actually help the kid. Even knowing that, I was still trembling like a leaf. I got to my feet, staggering back from the body.

It looked so real. It was one thing to know in your head that something was a supernatural ritual and that the kid would bounce back. It was another thing to be two feet away from somebody who just got a knife through their chest.

The kid looked dead. Really dead.

Maybe Bishop had been wrong and this had been a mistake and it was my fault because I had led Bishop and Kraven here. I'd heard the horrible sound as the knife sliced into flesh and bone.

"Hey," Kraven said, frowning at me. "It's okay, you know. Same thing happened to me and I recovered quickly, better-looking than ever."

I must have looked *really* bad if he of all people was offering me words of comfort.

The demon reached for me, but I scooted away. "Don't touch me."

He held up his hands. "Okay, okay. Chill out, gray girl. Give it a minute and you'll see it's no big deal."

"No big deal," I repeated shakily. "This *is* a big deal. You… you're both nuts if you think this is remotely normal."

"This isn't normal," Bishop agreed, watching me with concern. "Not to you. Not to us, either. You should have left."

"You're right…I—I should have."

But I kept staring at the kid. Bishop closed his hand around the dagger and pulled it out. The blade was covered in blood that looked black in the surrounding darkness. My stomach lurched and I clamped a hand over my mouth to stifle a whimper. This time Kraven actually touched my arm. I looked up at him to see he was frowning at me, but not because he looked angry.

"Another couple of minutes should do it," he said. "I survived. This angel dude will, too."

I couldn't breathe. I needed to get away from here, away from the blood and death so I could clear my head. I turned away from the angel and demon and started to run as fast as I could.

chapter 10

"Samantha!" Bishop called out to me after I'd run about a block. "Stop!"

I finally did. My lungs felt like they filled with ice every time I took a deep breath. I'd known what was coming and why it had to be done, so I wasn't sure why it had freaked me out as much as it did. Maybe because I'd had a front row seat for the action this time instead of watching from behind a corner.

I'd crossed over a side street. No trees here. Just concrete and tall office buildings, most of their windows dark after a long workday. A car drove up through a tunnel leading from the underground parking, splitting the space between me and Bishop. It would have given me a chance to keep running, but I held my ground. I had a feeling I wouldn't get very far.

Bishop crossed the street and stopped half a dozen feet away from me. A streetlamp shone above us, which made the scene feel marginally better than if we'd been in complete darkness. It was an illusion of security.

"You know I had to do that, right?" he said.

I let out a shaky sigh and nodded.

"I had Kraven wait back there for the angel to wake up. And he will wake up. He'll be fine. Better than before. And he'll remember why he's here in the first place."

"To help you hunt and kill monsters like me."

Bishop's jaw tightened. "We're to patrol the city mostly at night—that's when most of the grays who've lost their reason and humanity come out and threaten humans. We destroy them—there's no saving them. Other grays, like Stephen, haven't given in to their hunger enough to turn completely. I need to find the Source and talk to her."

"And say what?"

"I've been told to give her the choice to retreat—to go back where she came from. If she refuses, I must send her there myself. Then I can figure out how to deal with the remaining grays, and I'll have the team in place to assist me."

His meaning couldn't be clearer. "Deal with" would likely have a lot to do with that dagger of his. "Can grays that aren't feeding, that are in control of their hunger…can you help them like you're going to help me?"

He was silent for a moment. "It's possible. But they would need to be willing to be helped. You are. However, I can't guarantee they will be."

Good point. Stephen said he liked himself better as a gray. If given the option to have his soul restored, there was a strong chance he'd refuse. "I always thought angels were supposed to be peaceful."

He scanned the street. No more activity since we'd stopped to talk. This wasn't a busy area at night. "We do what has to be done. We follow orders. We protect humans from supernatural forces so they never need to know they're being protected."

"You do this a lot?"

"It's my job. And I was honored to be chosen for this mission."

Yeah, honored. Thrown out of Heaven so hard that he landed on his head, and he was honored.

"Are they always this violent?" I asked, trying hard not to think of the kid with the chest wound whom I'd run away from in the park. "These missions?"

He shrugged a shoulder. "Sometimes."

"It's a stupid ritual. Whoever thought of it is…stupid."

His lips twitched as if he was fighting a smile, but his expression remained serious. "I'll be sure to relate your opinion when I return. Maybe they can take it under advisement in future ritual creation."

"You're making fun of me."

Tentatively, he closed the distance between us and took hold of my shoulders, his heat sinking into me. I tensed, but didn't pull away. "I'm not making fun of you. What you did tonight, leading us here…you did it perfectly. Even Kraven can see how important you are. How…"

"Special?" I finished for him.

His smile widened. "Very special."

"I've never felt all that special before." Like, ever.

"Well, you are. To *me* you are."

I swallowed hard. There was a strange longing in his voice, one I found all kinds of confusing. He'd drawn closer still and he held my shoulders gently. Being this close to him made my head spin. I pressed one hand against his chest to push him away, but suddenly realized something very important.

"You have a heartbeat." I wasn't sure why finding something so human about him surprised me so much—enough to knock away some of my previous fear and summon my curiosity again.

He nodded. "Of course. What did you expect?"

"I don't know." I remembered Kraven foraging through the Dumpster. "Do you need to eat?"

"Yes."

"Sleep?"

"More than I'd like to with so much to do."

"I see." I didn't really, but I was faking it as best I could. "Do you look like this where you come from? Same appearance, I mean. Just, maybe, with wings?"

He nodded again. "Except here, sometimes our eyes—"

"They glow."

"It's a little celestial energy. It's what gives us our angelic abilities."

"And the demons…their eyes glow, too, but it's red instead of blue."

"Hellfire. Same sort of principle."

"Right." I felt dizzy. "I—I think I need to sit down."

Bishop slid his arm around my back to help keep me on my feet. I braced both my hands against his chest now. Our eyes met and there it was again—just that easily, my heart did a cartwheel worthy of an Olympic gymnast. I suddenly had the urge to wrap my arms around him and hold on tight—just like I had earlier, before the demon interrupted us. Despite what he was, despite what I'd just seen him do, I felt safe with Bishop.

At least, I felt safe right *now*.

Maybe we were both crazy.

"So now what?" I asked, my voice a whisper.

His gaze had locked on mine as if he was transfixed. He swallowed hard and shook his head a little as if to clear it. "Now you're going home. You said you'd give me an hour of your time. It's been an hour."

"You hold true to all of your promises?"

He grinned a little. "I try."

"I have a question."

"I'm not all that surprised. What is it?"

"Is this how you plan to treat all the grays you come across to make sure they're not the zombie kind? This, uh…personal attention?"

It took a moment before he replied. His eyes burned into mine. "Not really planning on it."

"I'm just special."

"Very."

"Why?"

"I really wish I knew." His hold tightened on my waist and he looked as if he was fighting some sort of inner battle. He let me go, then rubbed his hands on either side of his head. "I must be seriously messed up if I'm feeling this way."

I bit my bottom lip, reminded once again that he might consider me special, but I was still a hungry gray. "I'll try not to take that personally."

"No, I…" He sighed. "This isn't like me, Samantha. Trust me. I was completely and utterly dedicated to this mission from the moment it was put into effect. Nothing should distract me. And now I find I'm all too easily distracted. By *you*."

Okay, that clarification made a huge difference to me, one that made my heart leap. "Oh."

He shook his head. "This is complicated. More than you even know."

"I know. You're going home in a week. It's like you're on a really messed-up business trip, that's all. When you get back you'll be…cured. No more crazy."

He held my gaze. "I promise I'll help you. Anything I have to do, I'll do it."

"Why? I mean, I understand that you're an angel…" I was

still having trouble accepting that as being a real thing, even though I knew it was. "And you're going back home soon. But I'm supposed to be your enemy."

"You're not my enemy. I should have known that the moment I met you. I did, but for a second I doubted my instincts. I won't make that mistake again."

"If I'm so different, maybe other grays are just like me." I thought of Stephen and the others who were in the Crave lounge. "Some of them, anyway."

"It's possible. There could be others who can consistently control their hunger as well as you can—who never feed at all."

My stomach picked that exact moment to grumble. "So what happens if they don't? If *I* don't?"

He blinked and didn't reply for a moment. "I don't know."

I laughed nervously. "Great. That's helpful, thanks." Then I swallowed hard. "It's not easy, you know."

His brows drew together. "Are you having trouble with the hunger?"

"It's a constant issue for me now. I need..." I grabbed hold of a long dark lock of my hair and twisted it nervously. "Why does it have to be a kiss? That is so lame. Now I want to kiss pretty much everyone I come across."

"Everyone?"

I thought about it. "Not everyone. There's only a couple people I *really* feel the urge to grab hold of and kiss really hard, like I can barely control myself."

Something dark slid behind his gaze. If he was a normal boy and I was a normal girl, I might have guessed it was jealousy. "The original demon was said to have an irresistible allure that humans were drawn to. Maybe that's what happened with Stephen. You couldn't help but be drawn to him. And maybe that's what it's like with you, as well."

That would explain why lately I'd been attracting more attention than I normally did. And here I'd thought I was just having a really good hair week. "There was a boy at school this morning. He got too close to me and I nearly..." Well, I didn't have to finish that sentence to make my meaning clear. It did nothing to remove the dark look on Bishop's face. "And...and there's also someone else."

"Someone else you feel the urge to kiss?"

"Well, yeah. But...at least he doesn't have to worry about his soul around me. He doesn't have one."

It took a moment before he understood that I was talking about him. My cheeks heated up. I couldn't believe I was practically coming right out and saying it—like kissing him was all I could think about whenever he was this close to me.

"Then I guess I'm safe, aren't I?" he said, the edge of a smile touching his lips.

My cheeks grew hotter.

I wondered if angels kissed, if they went on dates, or how things worked up there in Heaven. I'd always had an image of them being very clinical, very pure and untouched. Flawless. Then again, Bishop had already changed most of my preconceived notions about angels.

Another car finally drove up out of the underground parking and made a left onto the street. I watched it drive away.

"I should walk you home so I know you're okay," Bishop said. "I'll catch up with Kraven and the other angel later."

I nodded. "There's just one problem."

"What?"

I pointed past him into the night sky where I'd just spotted another beam of light. "I think I've found your fourth team member."

He craned his neck to look then turned back to me with confusion. "You can see another searchlight?"

"Looks like."

My time was up. I'd given him the hour, just as we'd agreed to. The question was, should I stay or should I go? I felt exhausted, but we were one team member away from me fulfilling my side of our bargain. And maybe a little piece of me—or not so little, really—wanted to stay with Bishop as long as I could tonight.

Which was ridiculous. This wasn't a date.

And if I *was* going to date somebody, I certainly wouldn't pick a part-time crazy angel here on a one-week work placement who couldn't wait to get back home to his normal angel life.

If I had a hard time thinking about dating Colin and the problems that would cause with Carly, then that was a walk in the park compared to the complicated nature of being with Bishop.

An angel who seemed so human. Who could eat and drink and had a heartbeat. Who looked at me like he wanted to kiss me as much as I wanted to—

"Samantha?" Bishop prompted.

Yeah, complicated. Definitely complicated.

"Let's go get him," I said firmly. "Then it's done. There will be the four of you, just like Kraven said. My part will be over. Then it's your turn to help me."

"That was the deal."

"It was."

He nodded. "All right, show me where he is."

"What about Kraven?"

He seemed to cringe ever so slightly at any mention of the

demon's name. "He'll catch up. It might be a while before the other angel's back on his feet."

It was another reminder that what I'd witnessed earlier had been horrible, but temporary. "And you trust Kraven to supervise that? He seems like a major troublemaker."

Bishop laughed darkly under his breath. "You have no idea. But for a demon, he's actually not half as bad as he could be."

"That's not all that comforting." Then I jumped a little when Bishop took hold of my hand and laced our fingers together.

He looked at me uncertainly. "Is this okay?"

"Uh, yeah. Fine. For now."

More than fine.

This time he wasn't meeting my gaze. It was probably for the best, given how out of control I'd felt toward him a minute ago. Honestly, the guy could make me forget just about everything, even the important stuff. Was it because he was beautiful and fascinating and exciting? Or was it something else entirely?

I wished I could read his mind. It really might help.

chapter 11

Holding hands with Bishop definitely had its perks, not the least of which was the warmth it brought, a relief from the constant chill I now felt. Who knew a soul worked like a body's thermal insulation?

"The searchlight's moving this time." I watched it as we walked toward it.

"He's lost and wandering aimlessly, trying to find his way. That's all. We'll catch up to him."

And we did. A few blocks away and we were on one of the busiest streets in Trinity, known as the Promenade. The Trinity Mall—the infamous location of my shoplifting incident—was located here as well as the rest of the shopping district. Everything had shut down for the night, but the sidewalks were thick with pedestrians, the streets filled with traffic.

I followed the beam of light through the crowd of people. It shone on the head of one person in particular. Human appearance, check. Teenage boy, check.

"Doesn't Heaven or Hell have any girl warriors?" I asked aloud. How sexist was that? And why did they all look like they could be in my senior class?

"They do," Bishop replied.

"I guess none signed up to be part of this mission of yours."

"Guess not. Do you see him?"

"I see him."

As soon as I locked eyes on this guy, the light switched off. I now had to work hard to keep him in view as we drew closer.

"The kid over there," I said. "Black hair, tall. Leather jacket. Hey, where'd he get that cool jacket?"

This guy was definitely not eating burgers out of Dumpsters or waiting patiently on park benches. Instead, he eyed the crowd around him with a keen and appraising look. I watched as he bumped into a woman who turned to glare at him.

He gave her a killer grin. "So sorry, ma'am. My fault."

Her unpleasant expression shifted to a pleased one. He was extremely attractive, kind of like an actor from a glossy TV show or maybe a male model, with a slightly exotic edge to his tanned skin, dark eyes, and black hair long enough to brush his shoulders. Even though she looked like she was at least fifteen years older, she'd have to be blind not to notice his good looks.

"Oh, don't worry about it," she said.

"Have a nice night."

"You, too." As she walked away, she was grinning.

She didn't happen to notice he'd slipped his hand into her purse during their exchange and stolen her wallet.

"Did you see that?" I asked Bishop with shock. "Not really lost and wandering aimlessly, is he?"

He squeezed my hand tighter. "We can't lose him. Come on."

We picked up our pace and followed the pickpocket down the street, past the crowd and around a corner. The other two had been lost, confused and grateful for anyone who noticed them. This kid seemed like he knew the city like the back of his hand.

He stopped in front of a store window with a display of glittering jewelry, his hands shoved into the pockets of his black leather jacket, which looked new and expensive. Bishop slowed as we approached him, and I sensed his wariness. This boy was different from the others.

"Hey," Bishop said.

The kid glanced at us with disinterest. "Hey yourself."

"Saw what you did back there."

"Oh, yeah? What's that?"

"You stole that woman's wallet."

An edge of unfriendliness glittered in his dark eyes. "So what? Are you a cop?"

"Do we look like cops?" I asked.

He flicked a glance at me. "She was rich, I could tell. She'll survive just fine."

"Is that what you're trying to do, too?" Bishop asked. "Survive?"

"Aren't we all?" His gaze moved to me again and swept the length of me. "Why don't you do yourselves a favor and leave me alone now?"

Bishop finally, and a bit reluctantly, let go of my hand. "Because I need to talk to you."

"I don't feel like talking."

Something was wrong, but I didn't know what. I'd been positive he was the right guy, but now I wasn't sure. I didn't feel anything from him, even when I met his eyes and concentrated. But maybe I wasn't close enough.

Or maybe I'd tagged the wrong person. The real one could still be out there in the crowd.

"Where are you from?" I asked. Bishop shot a glance my

way. He probably thought I'd just be the silent, well-behaved finder of searchlights. It just showed how little he knew about me. Staying quiet had never been one of my greatest strengths.

"Around."

"Around Trinity? Or somewhere else?"

He gave me a tight smile and turned away. "Great talking to you. I'm going now."

"Where?" I asked. "Do you have somewhere to stay? Do you have any friends?"

His shoulders tensed as he glanced back at us. "Don't follow me."

He started walking.

I grabbed Bishop's arm. "Maybe I was wrong about him."

"You weren't."

"How do you know? You said you couldn't tell what Kraven was until you saw the imprint."

"Gut instinct. He's a team member—I'm guessing a demon. Remember how I told you Kraven wasn't as bad as he could have been?" He kept his focus on the departing pickpocket in the leather jacket. "Well, this one just might be."

That sent a chill right down my spine.

Bishop began trailing after the kid. "You should go home now. You've done everything I asked and I know you hate what I have to do now."

For a moment, I considered my options. I could go home and try to forget everything, but just because it wasn't easy didn't mean I should run away with my tail tucked between my legs. This wasn't over until my soul was restored, until my hunger was gone once and for all and I could focus on my normal life again.

So I didn't go home. I followed Bishop as he trailed after the boy with the bad attitude.

As Bishop rounded the next corner, the kid was waiting for him. He grabbed hold of Bishop and threw the angel into an open space, a parking lot in front of a large grocery store. Bishop slammed into a car, setting off the alarm.

Two people wandered past, but they didn't seem like they could see us or hear the blaring noise. I'd be willing to bet, even with his decreased abilities, that Bishop had managed to cloak us.

"What do you want from me?" the kid demanded.

"To talk, for starters. You could have made this easier on yourself." Bishop leaped up from the ground, his eyes blazing with anger. He kicked the car hard, which somehow managed to shut off the alarm.

"It was just a damn wallet. I needed the money, okay? Now you need to leave me alone or I'm going to hurt you." He cast a cold look over his shoulder. "Or her."

Bishop wasn't wasting any time. He pulled the golden dagger out of the sheath strapped to his back. "You're not hurting anyone tonight."

The kid barked out a laugh. "You're kidding me, right? You think you can cut me with that?" He pulled his own knife out of a holder at his waist. "Think again."

Panic gripped me at the sight of the other knife. It wasn't all gold, glowy and supernatural, but it was still sharp and deadly.

"You're lost." I stepped forward, trying to bring some sort of control back to this situation before things went too far. The ritual was bad enough without extra conflict. "We're here to help you."

He moved so fast I wasn't able to scramble away from him in time and he grabbed a thick handful of my long hair to hold me in place, my back crushed up against his chest. I let out a shriek of pain because it felt like he was literally going to yank it out of my scalp. "Maybe your boyfriend needs a louder warning to leave me alone. Drop the knife or I'll cut her."

"I told you we wanted to help you," I managed to say.

"I don't want your help."

"Let her go," Bishop growled. There was dark fury in his eyes.

I grabbed hold of the kid's arm to keep the knife away from me, but he was strong, really strong. Then I tried to summon the same ability I'd used to zap Kraven when I'd felt threatened. I did manage to touch part of that power, as if reaching into a shallow pool of water that I never knew existed within me, but it didn't work. Nothing happened. It was as if I hit a wall and I didn't know why.

"I know it must seem really bad for you." I wanted to keep him talking so Bishop had a chance to stop this. "But you're not alone anymore."

"I am alone," he snapped. "And I'll protect myself no matter what I have to do."

"Have you dreamed about me?" I blurted out. The other angel had said it earlier, so it was worth a shot.

He froze at my words. Bishop drew closer, his eyes still glowing blue. Someone got in the car right next to us, the one that'd had its alarm blaring a minute ago, and drove away as if he didn't see our standoff only a few feet away.

"You have, haven't you?" I continued, craning my neck a little so I could see him out of the corner of my eye. "Maybe it's faded a bit, but you have. You knew I was coming. You know I'm here to help you."

He shot a look at Bishop. "Drop the knife. I won't say it again."

I focused on that invisible wall I'd felt, the one that seemed to surround this kid. With a part of myself I'd never even known existed—a sixth sense, I guess—I managed to find a crack in it and I again sought that pool of power within me.

"Let me go." My teeth were clenched together so I barely got the words out. "Now."

This time, thanks to that crack in his wall, the zapping worked. He let go of me and staggered back as if he'd been electrocuted, his eyes wide with shock.

"What just happened?" he snarled.

"You let her go," Bishop said, striding forward.

And then he plunged his dagger into the kid's chest.

I screamed. It seemed to be my usual reaction to seeing someone get stabbed. The calmness I'd felt a moment ago ripped away, leaving me panicked and uncertain. "Why did you do that? We didn't check his back to make sure he was the right one!"

"He's the one. You proved it yourself by repelling him."

The kid dropped his knife then looked down at the dagger in his chest, which Bishop then yanked back out. He fell to his knees on the hard pavement.

His stunned gaze moved to me. "I did dream about you last night. How did you know that?"

A shiver coursed through me. "Lucky guess."

He fell face forward to the ground. Bishop crouched at his side and looked up at me, his expression grim as he took in the shock on my face.

"Stay," he said firmly. "See what happens next. It'll prove I'm not just doing this to be cruel, even though this one might have deserved it."

I just nodded, shivering. I moved back until I felt a pickup truck behind me, which helped support me so I didn't crumple to the ground, as well. Bishop rolled the dead kid onto his back. I gagged as his leather jacket fell open to show the bloodstain from the knife wound in the center of his chest, soaking through his shirt. Bishop wiped his dagger against his black jeans to clean it off.

Angel. Warrior. Killer. At this moment, I was terrified of him. It took a minute for my natural instinct of fear to back off.

Just a ritual. I kept repeating it to myself. *It's just a horrible but necessary ritual.*

More people arrived and departed from the grocery store, oblivious to the murder scene right in front of them. At the moment, the "I" in CSI stood for invisible.

I had no soul right now, so why did I care? I thought a soul gave a human morals, humanity and an ability for goodness. But now I wasn't so sure. I'd lost mine and I still felt the difference between right and wrong. I hadn't suddenly turned into an unrepentant monster. I felt everything that happened vividly, even when it was happening to someone else.

The kid stayed dead for a long time. Even Bishop began to look uncertain.

I gave him a sharp look. "Don't start doubting this now."

"He is the right one."

"You didn't check him first."

His expression was dark and haunted. "He grabbed you. I wasn't thinking straight. Besides, he never would have shown us his back if we'd asked politely."

He was probably right about that. I slowly moved toward them, looking down at the boy lying on the ground. His dark, glazed eyes were still open, staring straight up at me. Bishop leaned over and finally closed them.

"Great, that's helpful." I fought against my welling nausea.

He eyed me, as if gauging my shifting moods. "You really do hate me right now, don't you?"

"If he doesn't wake up soon, I'm going to have to hate myself, too." I kneeled down at his side. "Check him now. Please."

Bishop rolled the kid over and pushed aside the jacket. I reached forward, my hand shaking a little, and gathered the thin material of his shirt before pushing it up his back so I could see.

I let out a long, shuddery sigh of relief. There was an imprint there. And just as we'd thought, it was a thick, black tattoo of wings, just like the one Kraven—

The kid rolled over and grabbed hold of my throat. He pushed me back and then slammed me down on the pavement, knocking the breath out of me. His eyes glowed red in the darkness.

Demon.

There was no mistaking his intentions right now—he was going to kill me. It had happened so fast, I couldn't concentrate enough to summon my ability to repel him, to find that crack in his wall, and it wasn't coming naturally to me at the moment as it had before. This guy wanted me dead and he wanted to be the direct cause of it.

Then the metaphysical wall he had around him thinned. I was able to easily read his mind as I stared up into his eyes.

Gray…she's a gray. Kill her. Have to kill her. Have to kill all of them.

Bishop had his arm around the kid's throat, trying to pry him off me.

It had all happened so fast. And I still couldn't breathe with his hands tight around my throat as he squeezed the life out of me.

Then I heard a sharp crack and felt intense pain for a white-hot moment before it disappeared completely. The world began to grow dim at the edges. Blurry. Dark. There wasn't even enough time to get scared. It had all happened in a matter of seconds.

Off—get off! They were only words in my head. I couldn't speak, but I forced every bit of conviction I could into them, burrowing into that wall, wearing it away until the crack finally widened and I accessed my inner pool of power. A lightninglike shock exited me and entered him. He literally flew back from me and landed hard, a dozen feet away.

He'd hurt me badly, but I wasn't sure how. I couldn't move, could barely breathe. I couldn't feel my body. My consciousness, my very life, was draining away.

Bishop loomed over me, his expression agonized. He touched my face gently with a shaking hand. "Samantha." My name was no more than a whisper. "This is my fault. Please—no, this can't happen. Look at me. Don't close your eyes."

He pressed his warm hands to my throat, much gentler than the demon had. In the periphery of my vision, I saw Kraven storm up to us and slam hard into the new demon, taking him down to the ground just as he'd started to get up.

"What the hell's wrong with her?" Kraven demanded.

Bishop looked furious enough to kill. "That bastard just broke her neck."

chapter 12

My neck was broken. That would explain why I couldn't feel anything from my shoulders down.

He'd done it…he'd killed me. My life was slipping away. I'd been under the impression they needed the dagger to kill a gray, but I guess I'd been wrong. Maybe the dagger just helped make it a quicker death.

"Why aren't you healing her?" Kraven snapped. "We might still need her."

"I'm trying," Bishop gritted out, but there was a sharp edge of panic in his voice. "It's not working."

"Let me try." Someone else kneeled at my side, nudging Bishop away. Warm hands touched my throat, their heat sinking deep into me. I could barely see anything except for his outline. Reddish hair. Green eyes that began to glow blue locked with mine.

You're going to be okay. Angels can heal if we get to the injury fast enough, even something this severe. This only just happened. Try not to be afraid.

It was his thoughts, and he'd sent them to me as if he already knew I could read his mind. The angel—he was the one we'd found sitting on the park bench.

His touch heated up till it became so painful, I cried out as it burned through me, but then it was gone as quickly as it had arrived. My heart pounded hard—but it was still beating, which was a good sign.

The angel helped me sit up. "Better now?"

I touched a shaky hand to my throat and stared up at him with shock. "You—you healed me."

"I did my best."

"What are you doing?" the new demon snarled. "Why did you save her, you idiot?"

Bishop got up off the ground next to me, walked to the demon currently being forcibly held down by Kraven and slammed his fist into his face. The next moment, he ripped him out of Kraven's grip, threw him up against a nearby SUV and began to beat on him harder. It took both Kraven and the new angel to pull the two apart.

They looked so much alike—angel and demon. I would never be able to tell what they were if I didn't already know.

Blood trailed out of the demon's nose and the side of his mouth, courtesy of Bishop's fists. He also bore a cut on his forehead, marring his movie star good looks, but then the red-haired angel touched his skin and the injury healed instantly with a soft glow of blue light.

"Get away from me," the demon snapped.

"You need to calm yourself," the angel told him.

"She's a gray!"

"She's with us," Kraven said. I was surprised by this admission, given our shaky history. He didn't want me dead anymore, but I knew it wasn't because he liked me. It was because he thought they might need me again.

I'd just come as close as I ever had in seventeen years to seeing everything vanish forever. I'd never given my mortality a whole lot of thought before.

Almost dead. Right here, only minutes ago. But now—it was like it had never happened. I'd had my neck broken by a demon and then been healed by an angel.

I was definitely in shock.

Slowly, I got to my feet and crossed my arms tightly over my chest to try to stop trembling. The cold of the night pressed in on me, even worse than before. My throat, though, it still felt warm, as if I had a thick and comforting wool scarf wrapped around it.

"I'll kill you and send your ass straight to the Hollow, demon," Bishop snarled. He was still being held in place by Kraven, despite fighting hard to break free. "If you touch her again, if you even *look* at her again, I swear I'll do it."

The demon stopped struggling against the new angel and stared at Bishop incredulously. "Why are you defending a gray? I'm just doing what I was sent here to do. You know... the reason you found me and brought back my memories? Stupid bloody ritual, by the way."

Looked like we agreed on something at least.

Bishop appeared to be having trouble getting himself under control. There was a crazy look in his eyes now. My stomach twisted for him.

"That gray over there was able to find us," Kraven explained. "Find you, too."

"She's got some freaky power," the new demon said. "She zapped me."

"Yeah, I know. Doesn't tickle, does it?"

"What is she?"

"A pain in the ass. But bottom line, dude, you need to chill the hell out. Now. Or there's going to be a big problem."

"I'm fine."

"Yeah, looks like it. I strongly suggest you don't give us any more trouble if you know what's good for you. If you screw up this mission, you'll have me to answer to." He flicked a look at the new angel. "We have to keep a close eye on Bishop, too. He's a mess right now."

Bishop laughed then, a broken and humorless sound that made a chill run down my spine. "A mess. Yeah, I'm a mess for others to clean up. Can't see the light, can't find the others. Can't heal. Can't do much except stand and wait and watch and wonder why and where and how and who..."

Kraven eyed him. "Uh, right, whatever you say. Gray girl? You feeling okay enough to help out a bit here?"

What I desperately wanted to do was to leave, to run away and leave them all behind. But I was still here, mostly because what just happened had weakened me to the point that I couldn't do much of anything except wait to see what happened next. And I couldn't turn my back on Bishop when he needed me the most.

Giving the new demon a wide berth, I made my way over to Bishop. His knuckles were red and bleeding. Concern swelled in my chest.

"I'm sorry," he said, shaking his head. "I said I'd protect you, but I failed. I'm sorry, sorry, so sorry."

I was feeling better. Physically, anyway. Mentally—well, I knew I had some brand-new nightmares to look forward to. But right now I just wanted to help Bishop. "Take my hand."

Bishop watched me with glazed eyes, but he didn't move. Finally, I reached for his hand myself. It scared me how quickly he'd lost it, lost his control, his mind, everything. I knew he hated this. But I couldn't be with him all the time to help him out. Thankfully there were the others we'd found to help patrol the city when he wasn't feeling one hundred percent. But was he really going to get better when he went back to Heaven?

I couldn't think that far ahead. I could think only about this moment. Live in the now. The eternal now. If I didn't, I was seriously going to freak out.

When I touched him, the now-familiar energy crackled between us. He squeezed his eyes shut and I glanced over at Kraven, who was watching us carefully.

He nodded at me. "So that went smoothly, didn't it? Awesome plan, don't you think? Who says angels and demons can't work well together?"

I just stared at him dumbly. I guess my shock hadn't totally worn off.

He grinned. "Oh, yeah. *Everybody* says that. With everything that's gone wrong, you'd almost think we'd been set up to fail, wouldn't you?"

I considered that with a gnawingly sick feeling in my gut. "Do you think they knew this would happen to him? That slamming through the barrier would screw up his mind so much?"

He shrugged. "Dunno. Maybe his noggin was weaker than they expected. Not a huge shock there. But luckily, he found you. Can you imagine how screwed we'd all be if he hadn't? Work that mojo, gray girl. Consider me a true believer now. Hallelujah."

I'd take it as a compliment if he didn't sound completely sarcastic. "I don't want anything to do with you. Any of you."

"Any of us?" He gave me a knowing look. "Come on, now.

I think you've picked your favorite. It's adorable that you're so open to caring for those with special needs."

I just glared at him.

"I still don't get it," the new demon said miserably. He'd stopped struggling as if he'd finally accepted that he was outmatched. "Can somebody explain to me what the hell's going on? I thought we were supposed to kill grays, not hold hands with them and exchange valentines. Was there a memo I missed somewhere along the way?"

"Nah," Kraven said. "This is new. Trust me. I had problems with it, too. Still do. But it is what it is. What's your name?"

The demon hesitated, giving Kraven a look that clearly showed he didn't trust him…or anyone else. "Roth."

"Well, Roth, welcome to the team. Unless you give us a hard time, and then we'll have to kill you—for real next time. The crazy angel who nearly broke your nose has the annoyingly self-indulgent name of Bishop. The other angel is Zachary, but he's cool with us calling him Zach."

Zach was the one who'd healed me. I looked over at him. "Thank you."

"You're very welcome," he replied with an easy grin. Where Roth was all fire and hatred, Zach made me feel comfortable just being around him. Plus, the fact that he'd saved my life definitely earned him a few million brownie points and my eternal gratitude.

"I'm better now," Bishop finally said, his voice steady and his blue eyes cleared of any previous madness. My heart lightened.

"Hooray," Kraven said drily.

Bishop did what he usually did and ignored him. He searched my face as if double-checking that I was really okay. "I never meant to put you in this kind of danger."

His heat sank into me through our entwined fingers. I didn't want to let go of him. "I know that."

I wasn't going to say it was okay, because it wasn't. It would take me a while to recover from this.

"You should go home now," he said.

"And then what?"

"Then—lead your life as you normally would. Go to school. Study. Do your homework. Try to be as normal as you can. I think it'll help you deal with all of this."

"Beats wallowing in my misery, right?"

He held my gaze with his. "Kraven will see you to your house."

"He will?"

"I will?" Kraven raised an eyebrow.

Bishop's jaw tightened. "Yes, you will."

"Wait," I said. "Can't you walk me home yourself?"

"I need to talk to the others. I need to try to be the leader I was sent here to be. Kraven will get you safely home."

Kraven snorted. "Are you sure about that?"

Bishop didn't look amused in any way. "You won't hurt her."

"If I do, I'll have you to answer to, right?"

"There won't be enough time for you to answer. Next time I stab you with my dagger, you're dead. Permanently. Remember that." Venom dripped from every word he spoke. "So will you see Samantha home safely or not?"

Kraven's perma-grin faded at the edges. "Whatever you say, boss." He glanced at me. "Let's go, gray girl."

Even though I wasn't afraid of Kraven anymore—although maybe I should have been—I wasn't jumping at the chance to have him as my chaperone. Still, I wanted to go home and I did understand that Bishop, as the leader, needed to deal with the introduction of Roth and Zach into their new group dynamic.

"Go to school, be normal," I said to Bishop. "That's what you think I should do."

He nodded. "I'll be in touch soon."

"I'm counting on it."

With a last squeeze of Bishop's hand, I reluctantly let go of him. It took a moment before I was able to look away from him. His jaw was tight and I knew there were volumes left unsaid between us.

I began to feel cold again the moment I stopped touching him.

I gave Zach a weak smile, but didn't even glance in Roth's direction even though the weight of his unfriendly glare on me was hard to ignore. Finally, I started walking away. Kraven tagged along silently, a few feet behind me, as if he'd prefer no one we passed knew we were together.

Forcing myself to stay strong was harder than it had been before. Roth had very nearly killed me. I wasn't used to dealing with violence. Even when my parents were having problems, their fights were all verbal rather than physical and they tried to have the worst of them away from me. It didn't always work, but while it wasn't pleasant, I was accustomed to words being thrown around as weapons. Not *actual* weapons that could make someone bleed.

I'd dealt with my personal family stress through my snarky sense of humor, and later through shoplifting. I didn't do well with holding it all in. Before too long it came spilling out in one way or another.

Tonight, it felt like it wanted to be tears. I felt a sob building in my chest. When I inhaled, it sounded ragged.

"You okay?" Kraven asked from behind me.

I just nodded and kept walking.

"How much farther?"

I glanced over my shoulder. "Another ten minutes."

We kept walking for a while before he spoke again. "You can tell me, you know."

"What?"

"What you really are. You can tell me the truth." He'd increased his pace so he walked next to me now, and he studied me with a strange look on his face. Confusion, curiosity, a bit of anger—but not all directed at me. Maybe he was mad at himself for not figuring out all of my secrets yet.

I shook my head. "I know you think I'm trying to hold something back, but I have no idea what's going on. Seriously."

"You have power over us and I don't know why. It worries me."

That made two of us. I wish I knew what made me so different. So *special.* It would help. "I don't know what to tell you. I was normal before, so normal that nobody ever looked at me twice, and now I'm not."

"You give the angel back his mind when you touch him, you can see the searchlights to find us when we're lost, you can control the hunger of being a gray so much that you haven't needed to feed yet, you can zap us at will…and the reading minds thing—I don't understand it, but there's a reason for it. And I'm going to figure it out."

"Is that some sort of threat?" I asked, glaring at him.

His jaw was tight. "More like a promise. This mission is too important to let anything trip it up."

"Yeah, I'm sure you can't wait to get out of here, just like Bishop. But I'm not sabotaging anything. In case you've been asleep and haven't noticed it, I've been helping."

"Sorry, but I don't trust that easily." He was silent for a moment.

I swallowed hard. "Look, Kraven, I know you hate me and don't want me to be a part of this. We have that in common. I want this over with. Quickly. And then I want to forget all about it."

"Bishop told you to go to school like normal. Are you going to do that?"

I hadn't really thought about it much yet. "Maybe."

He made a sour expression. "Remember, he's crazy. I think you should stay home. Stay out of trouble. Just fake being sick and hang out in your house and wait it out. You'll be less of a problem for us that way."

I gave him a withering look. "You just helped me make my decision. I'm *definitely* going to school tomorrow, just like Bishop suggested. Thanks for making that easier for me."

I picked up my pace, leaving him a few steps behind me again. He was such a pompous jerk I didn't even know how to handle it.

"Wait, I want to test something. Stop a second."

Reluctantly, I stopped and turned to face him. "What now?"

The light from a streetlamp shone down on his hair, making it seem much lighter blond than it had earlier, a fiery gold color. "I'm thinking of a name. Can you read my mind right now when there's no drama involved?"

There was no humor on his face. He was being dead serious. I hissed out a sigh, met his gaze directly and tried to focus. He wasn't fighting me and there was no wall up around him like I'd felt with Roth in the beginning. What he was thinking about came to me easily, as if I was reading it off a page in a book. In my mind's eye, it even looked like fancy handwriting—black ink on yellowed paper, being written with a quill.

"James," I said. "That's the name you're thinking about right now. Isn't it?"

His brows drew together. "Let's keep going."

He started walking again, his hands shoved deep into the pockets of his jeans. Nothing was said the rest of the way to my house. For a second, I tried to read his mind again, but my attempts hit a wall similar to Roth's. He was shielding his thoughts from me now.

I guess I'd passed the test.

We finally reached my house. As I walked up the driveway, my mother pulled her car up alongside me. Another late night at the office.

I tensed as she got out of her car and glanced at the two of us.

"Hello there." She reached out a hand to Kraven. "I'm Eleanor Day, Samantha's mother."

The smile that had been missing from Kraven's face for the last twenty minutes reappeared as he shook my mother's hand. He sent an amused glance in my direction, no doubt to see how mortified I was at the thought of a demon touching my mother.

"You can call me Kraven," he said. "It's an honor to meet you, Mrs. Day."

My mother smiled back at him, clearly charmed by the tall and handsome blond boy standing in her driveway. I tried very hard not to roll my eyes. Or gag.

"Kraven was just leaving," I said firmly.

"Yes, that's right." He grinned. "Lots to do, worlds to save. You know the drill."

My mother actually laughed out loud at that. It was a light

and joyful sound I hadn't heard in ages. "Well, I'll let you two say your goodbyes. Don't mind me."

She gave me a look that clearly stated that I needed to fill her in on the details the first chance I got. My mother now thought Kraven was my boyfriend. Great. Just what I needed.

When she went into the house, I looked at Kraven. He was staring at the front door.

"Something wrong?" I asked. "Other than everything?"

"Your mom and you..."

"What?"

"Are you adopted?"

I blinked. That was the absolute last thing I would have expected him to say. "No."

"You sure?"

"I think I'd know something like that."

He shrugged. "It's just that you look nothing alike and I didn't really feel any..." He sighed. "Wait. For a second I forgot that I don't care. I'm out of here."

He turned and began walking down the driveway, dismissing me without so much as a goodbye.

"Wait!" I called after him.

He cast an unfriendly look over his shoulder at me. "What?"

"Who's James?"

The demon stared at me for a few seconds as the remainder of the smile left his eyes. "That was my first name back when I was human."

He turned and started to walk away, but I caught up to him and grabbed his arm, looking up at him with shock. "You were human?"

He didn't smile. "Didn't you know? A whole lot of angels and demons began their lives as human."

"No, I—I didn't know that." I couldn't find my voice for a moment. "Even Bishop?"

He snorted softly. "You didn't read that in my mind before? I'm surprised, since you're so fixated on anything to do with him. Would have thought you'd hone in on that info immediately. There's a bunch of memories of him stuck in my brain, whether I like it or not."

"What do you mean? Do you—did you know him? Before?"

"You could say that."

"How?"

"Bishop," he said very softly after a long moment of silence passed between us, "was my brother."

Without another word, he pulled his arm out of my grip disappeared into the night.

chapter 13

Hold on. Did he just say that Bishop was his brother?

His *brother?*

I stood in the driveway staring at the empty street after Kraven had disappeared. I was in complete shock.

This was impossible. And yet…I'd *sensed* there was something between them. Something that went deeper than the expected animosity of a demon and an angel having to work together for a short time.

Bishop and Kraven had once been human. And they'd been brothers.

Yes, definitely in shock.

This was big. Too big.

Bishop hadn't told me. But he knew, it wasn't as if he'd forgotten. From the moment he'd seen Kraven in the alleyway, I'd sensed something—sensed that Bishop already knew him. It had been a subtle hesitation on his part, but it was there. I wondered how long it had been since they'd last seen each other.

How did one brother become a demon and the other an angel?

It hadn't been a heartfelt family reunion between them. There was bad blood simmering just under the surface.

Brothers. Wow. I really hadn't seen that coming. I mean, they didn't even look very much alike. Same build, same height, both gorgeous, but totally different hair and eye colors.

But they were brothers.

I forced myself to turn away from the dark street and go to the front door. My mother was sorting through the mail as I entered the house. She glanced at me with a smile as I closed and locked the door behind me.

"He's very cute," she said. "Have you two been seeing each other long?"

I grimaced a little. "He's just a friend."

"Maybe for now. But boys don't walk girls right to their front doors unless there's some reason behind it. Trust me."

She was right about that. Unfortunately the reason behind it was to get me here in one solid but shaky piece after having my neck snapped like a dry twig by an enraged demon. I shuddered and found myself touching my throat even though it didn't feel injured in the slightest anymore—not even bruised.

"I remember my first serious boyfriend," she said wistfully, not noticing my bleak expression. "The captain of the football team, if you can believe it. I was totally crazy about him, but then I was all about dating and being social in high school. You've been so serious with your grades lately—which trust me, I'm not knocking at all—I didn't think you had time for boys."

I was barely listening to her, still going over everything that Kraven had said to me a few minutes ago. "Am I adopted?"

It took a moment before I realized she hadn't replied; she was just staring at me with surprise.

"What did you say?" she finally said. "Adopted?"

Hearing her say it out loud made me realize how ridiculous it sounded. I wished I hadn't said anything at all. "Forget it, it's nothing."

"What on earth put that into your head?"

"Kraven…he said that we didn't look anything alike. And, well, he's kind of right now that I think about it. You're a blonde. So's dad—although he's a bit darker. Not as dark as me, though."

Bishop and Kraven had different coloring, but they were related. This had to be the same thing.

I'd been ready to put it out of my mind, if it wasn't for the look of shock on my mother's face. She appeared to be at a total loss for words.

"Well, am I?" I began again, starting to feel ill. "You'd tell me something like that, right?"

Finally, she composed herself, running a hand along her hair, currently up in a French twist. "Of course I would, Samantha. Something that important, you'd have a right to know."

"Well…good."

While she'd all but denied Kraven's suspicions, it still didn't set my mind at ease. She'd hesitated when I'd asked her if I was adopted, something that hadn't occurred to me one single time in seventeen years.

I was probably just imagining things. After all, it had been a really tough day.

I didn't sleep much that night. Instead, I stayed awake, staring at the scary shapes the shadows made on my ceiling and playing "worst-case scenario." Not exactly the most fun game at three o'clock in the morning. My alarm clock couldn't go off fast enough.

When it did, I had second thoughts about going to school. For a moment, I wanted to stay home and hide like Kraven had suggested. However, being that *he'd* been the one to suggest it was enough to prompt my butt out of bed and off to school. Hiding was for people who waited for others to save them. That wasn't me. I would face my problems head-on.

I mean, I'd rather not, but I would if I had to.

My future was in Bishop's hands now. Once he got his team organized and did what he had to do to find the Source of the grays, then he'd promised to help restore my soul.

I wondered if I'd ever see him again after that. After he went back to Heaven and life got back to normal for both of us. Maybe he'd forget all about me.

I didn't think I'd ever forget about him.

The thought made something start to ache in the center of my chest.

In the meantime, I'd focus on being normal. If I didn't, then there'd be too much damage to clean up when everything went back to life as usual.

Even after the way I'd been eating lately, I was surprised that I was exactly the same weight as before when I got on the scale. One pound *less,* actually. Carly wouldn't be too pleased about that. I think she wanted me to gain a few pounds to go along with the ton of calories I'd been scarfing down every day since—

Oh, crap. *Carly.*

I'd forgotten to call her last night to make sure she got home okay. Also, to fill her in on the highly edited version of what had happened between me and Stephen. She was going to kill me.

I checked my phone while I sat on the linoleum floor by our lockers, but it was still acting glitchy. It was like it wouldn't hold a battery charge for more than a couple minutes. I had no idea if she'd been texting or calling about how angry she'd been when I'd ditched her last night.

I hadn't really ditched her. Things were just kind of complicated right now. She'd understand. Eventually.

Out of the corner of my eye I finally saw her approach our lockers. She had a big smile on her face, which was surprising on several levels. She wasn't a morning person by any definition of the term. I slowly got to my feet.

"You look happy this morning," I said cautiously.

"I am happy this morning."

If she was happy, then I was happy. Not in the grand scheme of things, but I'd try my best.

"Sorry I didn't call you last night."

That was enough to dim the shiny cheer on her face. She gave me a sideways glance. "Guess you were busy. Did you have fun with…what was his name? Bishop?"

"Sure. *Fun.* That's what I had." I grabbed my books and shut the locker behind me. "You probably want to know all about it. And about Stephen, too."

"We'll talk later," she said. "I promise. Bye!"

And that was that. She was gone, like a blond streak down the hallway toward her first-period art class.

After everything that had happened last night, that she wasn't pissed at me should have made me feel a lot better. One less thing to deal with. But for some reason, her übercheery attitude felt a bit fake. And after being her best friend since we were five, I knew fake Carly from real Carly. This was definitely fake Carly.

Great. She *was* pissed at me, but trying to hide it. Just my luck.

Maybe I should have stayed home today. And tomorrow. And right through senior year.

But staying true to what Bishop had suggested—that I go back to my normal life—I trudged along the hall toward English class. It wasn't long before someone fell into step with me. I knew who it was without even looking.

Yet another problem I wasn't sure how to deal with.

"So you never gave me an answer yesterday," Colin said.

Oh, yes, yesterday. When I'd practically inhaled him through my mouth when he got too close to my orbit of hunger. By the look on his face, I think I'd given him the wrong impression. Couldn't say I blamed him. I would have gotten the wrong impression if some guy seemed to have trouble keeping his hands and lips off me, too.

We passed through the hall thick with other kids, all moving in different directions as the bell finally rang. The sound of lockers clanging shut echoed down the hallway.

"We should probably talk," I told him, trying hard to keep at least three feet between us at all times.

"I totally agree."

Best that I let him down easy. Rip this Band-Aid off nice and quick right now and this wouldn't hurt any longer than it had to.

"This isn't going to happen, you and me," I said.

His smile faded and he slowed his pace only steps from our class. Most of the hall was empty now apart from a few stragglers like us.

Damn it. Maybe I shouldn't have brought this up now, after all. It wasn't like I could just walk away from him. I wasn't that coldhearted.

"You aren't even giving it a chance," he said. "I felt it yesterday, there's something between us."

I couldn't exactly tell him that the reason I'd been so attracted to him was that when he got too close to me, I hungered for his soul. It wasn't something he'd likely take at face value.

I'd been paying close attention to my interaction with other people. And it had everything to do with personal space. In the halls, surrounded by kids, I felt hungry all the time, but I didn't lose my mind and attack anyone with my lips since most people kept their distance. But Colin—he, for some crazy reason—had decided he liked me as more than a friend. That meant he tried to get closer to me. And closer—that was a bad thing. Too close and my brain stopped working normally and my hunger shifted into overdrive.

He was getting too close right now.

Not that Colin wasn't appealing on other levels. Colin *was* very cute. He'd gotten even better-looking since the summer, when he and Carly had been seeing each other. However, his shaggy sandy-blond hair could use a bit of a trim.

Suddenly I found myself stroking that sandy blond hair back off his forehead like I had no control over what my hand chose to do. I stared up at him hungrily.

Bad. This was bad. He'd gotten too close. Only a foot away now and my brain started going blurry at the edges. And his scent, like cinnamon, apple pie—spicy and warm—became impossible to ignore. Bishop smelled even better to me and I was drawn to him like nobody else, but he didn't have a soul to worry about.

Colin did.

His brown-eyed gaze had darkened and he slid an arm around my waist, pressing me up against a set of lockers. "Don't tell me you don't feel it, Sam."

"I don't." I sounded breathless. *So hungry.*

"I know you don't want to hurt Carly. I get that. But just give me a chance."

I was shaking my head. *Too close, way too close.* "I can't do this."

He didn't seem deterred in the slightest. "I want to kiss you so badly right now."

"Me, too."

Why had Bishop suggested I go to school, knowing what I was and what I had to deal with? I didn't feel at all normal right now. All I felt was ravenous.

"I *knew* it." He grinned. "We'll figure this out. Nobody has to get hurt, I promise."

And then, suddenly, he slipped out of my grasp to head in the classroom door. My daze immediately vanished and I inhaled deeply to try to clear my head.

Nobody has to get hurt. I really wished he was right about that.

I knew one thing for certain—even though we were in the middle of the school hallway, I would have kissed him just now, even knowing exactly what that meant. Maybe I would kiss *anyone* with a soul who got within a foot of me.

I wouldn't let that happen again until I got this under control.

Just before I went into class, I noticed somebody watching me. It was my redheaded nemesis, Jordan.

"Color me surprised." A frown creased her forehead. "You're all over *everybody's* boyfriend this week, aren't you? Who knew you were such a slut?"

I gave her the finger and an icy glare then pushed through the door. For the entire hour, I felt Colin staring at me while I struggled to control my insatiable hunger. So much for trying to act normal.

I hated Tuesdays.

All day, it was nearly impossible for me to concentrate, but I couldn't really say I tried all that hard. Still, I needed to keep up my grades to get into my first choice college. If I focused on that, it helped a little. I had come to loathe this city over the years and to escape it was my main goal in life, even before I'd been trapped here by an invisible supernatural barrier. I'd leave the "maintaining the balance of the universe" part to the professionals.

At lunch, I chose to become a total loner and stay away from the tantalizing scent of other kids. I shoved my ham sandwich into my mouth practically whole, kind of like a python swallowing a small, bread-encased pig. Unfortunately, ham sandwiches weren't even making a dent in satisfying my hunger today.

But I managed to control myself. I managed to appear vaguely normal. I guess, if I looked at it that way, it was a successful day.

I avoided Colin and I didn't see Carly at all until school let out. Likely she was avoiding *me.* I stared bleakly at the blank screen of my cell phone as I sat on the steps outside, waiting for her to appear, clutching my leather bag to my chest.

Finally, Carly exited the school. When she spotted me, she made a beeline toward me.

She didn't look nearly as shiny as she had this morning. "We need to talk."

Uh-oh. I had a strange feeling I knew what the subject was going to be. Bigmouthed Jordan had witnessed me practically climbing Colin like a rope this morning. Had she told everybody? I was going to kill her. But first I'd have to get through a very unpleasant discussion with Carly about why I needed to keep my greedy, hungry paws off her ex-boyfriend.

"It's not what you think," I began, when we went down the stairs and stepped onto the path—the same one I'd used to follow after Kraven only yesterday morning. It led to the parking lot. Dry leaves crunched under our feet.

Carly eyed me. "What are you talking about?"

She looked genuinely confused, so before I admitted to something I didn't have to, I took a deep breath. "Okay, well, what did you want to talk to me about? Oh…wait, I know. I said we'd talk about Bishop and Stephen. That's what this is, right?"

"You're acting strange today."

I hitched my bag up on my shoulder, realizing I'd started to sound like a babbling lunatic. "I know. I'm strange. But you already knew that."

"Yeah, but this is extreme even for you. It's that Bishop guy, isn't it? He's got you all crazy."

Interesting choice of words.

The parking lot was up ahead. I could see Carly's red Beetle from here. "You could say that."

She pulled a pair of dark sunglasses out of her purse and slid them on. "Who is he? Where does he go to school?"

"He's—uh, he's not in school right now."

She hopped the curb and sat against the hood of her car. Other kids got in their cars and left the parking lot. I tried to focus my attention on my friend and her questions about the local angel-in-residence.

"How did you meet him?" she asked. "Just last night at Crave, or somewhere else?"

Dangerous subject matter there. I raked my hair over my shoulder and played with it nervously. "I met him Sunday night after the movies when I walked home. We, uh, hit it off."

"Are you dating him?"

I crossed my arms over my chest, making a note to get my

winter coat out of the attic earlier than I normally would. It might help with the chill I always felt. "Dating. No...I really wouldn't call it that."

"What would you call it, then?"

This was getting us nowhere, especially since I wasn't inclined to tell her the truth. "What's with the twenty questions?"

Her lips thinned. "I guess I feel like he should be someone really special in order for you to ditch me last night like you did."

And there it was. Her shiny, happy outlook today was just an act. There was something else about her, though. Something deeper. She seemed different. "I *knew* you were upset about that. But you were acting all 'I'm so happy' this morning."

"I am happy." She pulled her car keys out of her purse. I hoped that meant this conversation was coming to an end. "I want you to tell me more about Bishop."

"He's just a guy." Also, a gorgeous angel who made my heart pound like nobody else, the brother of a demon, and part-time crazy. Not necessarily in that order.

"Just a guy," she repeated like she didn't believe me. Then again, she knew me as well as I knew her. I was certain she sensed something was seriously off with me, too.

"What's the problem?" I asked. "Like, seriously, what's the problem? Is it just the ditching thing? I'm sorry. It won't happen again. You don't know what it was like, though. After I confronted Stephen—"

"You weren't the only one to confront Stephen last night."

My mouth dropped open. "Excuse me?"

"I was mad at him, too, you know. I don't like it when people mess with my friends and hurt their feelings. I wanted to give him a piece of my mind."

A shiver went down my spine and it had nothing to do with the temperature. "Please tell me you're kidding."

"I knew you wouldn't like it, but I had to. After you left the club, I stuck around until he came downstairs. Then I had a talk with him."

I bit my tongue so hard it nearly drew blood as the kid who owned the car parked right next to Carly's got in and backed out of the space. My heart was now hammering in my chest, so loud it made it difficult to think.

"You shouldn't have done that," I said, feeling dizzy. "You don't know what— Oh, my God, Carly. You don't know how bad of an idea that was! When he kissed me—"

"He kissed me, too."

I literally stopped breathing. I just stared at her with horror, feeling the blood drain from my face. "Oh, Carly…no, please don't tell me that. You don't know what it means. He's not just some good-looking guy. When he kisses you, it could mean that—"

"It means that I'm like him now," she said calmly. "Just like you are. I know, he told me everything. Well, first I kind of yelled at him for using you and then walking away, but after he kissed me everything started making a whole lot more sense. Well, after I woke up. I passed out for a minute there, just like you did. He took off on me, too, but he came back." She frowned. "You look like you're going to puke."

That was exactly what I might be doing, if I wasn't so busy trying not to hyperventilate. This couldn't be happening. I was having a nightmare and I was going to wake up any minute. "No, no, please, Carly—tell me you're just messing with me right now."

She frowned at me. "It's okay, Sam. Everything's okay. Stephen explained to me how you're having a hard time with this—that you can't see how great it is. But it *is* great. We're improved now, can't you feel it?" She put her hands to her waist. "I actually feel lighter. Like, at least five pounds. I wonder how much a soul weighs?"

"How can you say it like it's no big deal?" I needed to sit down. Either that or I was going to drop. I found my way to the curb and slumped down heavily on it. All the stress I'd been fighting all day came back in full force. "I'm going to kill him. I'm going back there tonight and I'm going to kill him for doing this to you!"

She sat down next to me and put an arm around me. "No, you're not. What you're going to do is take a few deep breaths. It's okay, Sam. Really."

I stared at her with horror. "This is not okay! And you being all blasé about getting kissed by Stephen—and actually knowing what that means—it's freaking me out even more!"

She grabbed hold of my hand and squeezed it. "Look, I know this Bishop guy has been filling your head with lies. Stephen wants what's best for you, Sam. He was worried when you took off last night and he knows he didn't handle things the right way. Just relax. Everything's going to be fine."

No, this was not fine in any way, shape or form. Stephen kissed Carly. He knew she was my best friend and he'd turned her into a gray as some sort of revenge against me for running off with Bishop and leaving him behind.

I tried to gather myself, to think rationally. At this point, I couldn't fall apart. I'd wanted to protect Carly from finding out anything about this, but she'd stumbled on to the truth anyway. It was all my fault she'd been at the club last night in the first place, and then I'd left her alone and run off with Bishop!

But Bishop said he could restore my soul. If he could do that for me, then he could do it for Carly, too. I could fix this, it wasn't too late. Carly was in control of herself and taking all this crazy information in stride. Now it was out in the open and we could deal with it.

"It's going to be okay, Carly," I finally said, squeezing her hand.

"Of course it is. So tell me…who is Bishop? Where did he come from? What does he want?"

It was on the tip of my tongue to tell her, but I forced myself to hold back. She was too eager for this information, too inquisitive—like an investigative reporter. That wasn't like her. I bet Stephen had asked her to find out everything she could about Bishop from me. Stephen had fooled her into believing he was a tall, dark and handsome guy helping girls free themselves from the burden of their souls.

I hated him more at that moment than I'd ever hated anyone in my life.

Despite the dark feelings swirling inside me, I forced myself to give her a casual shrug. "Like I said before, he's just a guy."

"Okay, fine, if you say so." She got to her feet and helped pull me to mine. "Here's what's going to happen. You and I are going to Crave tonight. There's somebody who's going to be there who wants to meet you."

"Who?" The thought of going back to the nightclub didn't appeal to me in the slightest.

She shrugged. "All I know is she's someone important."

"She?" A shiver of fear went through me. Maybe it was the Source—the one Bishop was searching for.

Carly looked at me with concern. "It's going to be okay, you know."

"Is it?"

"Of course it is." Carly pushed her sunglasses off her face so

I could see her eyes. They weren't glazed or dazed or anything other than totally sincere. She was actually worried right now. About *me.* There was nothing about her that looked remotely like an out-of-control, soul-sucking monster.

Come to think of it, I had yet to see one of these mindless zombielike grays Bishop had told me about. Carly seemed just like me—rational and levelheaded. And not running around kissing anybody with lips.

"Do you trust me?" she asked.

I didn't have to think about it long. "Of course I do."

"More than anybody?"

I nodded. Twelve years of being best friends had to count for something.

"And you want the whole truth about what's going on in this city right now?"

"Yes, of course."

"Then you're going to get it tonight. Stephen was worried I wouldn't be able to convince you to come back. He knows he made a really bad impression on you. I don't think he's half as cool as he tries to pretend to be."

"This is not news to me."

"So come on, come to Crave with me again tonight." She grinned. "Tuesdays are half-price chicken wings night."

I let out a shaky breath and ignored my stomach rumble. "That does sound tempting."

"Thought it might. This hunger—it's not that easy to deal with, is it?"

"You feel it, too?"

"Oh, my God, yes. You should have seen what I ate at lunch. I went to McDonald's. I think they've put up a wanted poster for me as the girl who gulped down four McChickens in one sitting. And two large fries."

"Wow. Impressive."

The only thing that tempted me to return to Crave tonight was the promise of answers. Real ones, this time, not half-truths and shiny sales pitches from Stephen. I needed Bishop to restore my soul, but in the meantime, I might as well do a little research of my own. It could help him, too, if this led me to the Source.

"Fine," I finally said. "I'll go."

She gave me a tight hug then unlocked the driver's side door to her Beetle. "I'll pick you up at eight. Dress up. I think we should try to look really hot tonight."

I frowned at her. "What, you're just leaving me here? The least you can do is give me a ride home."

"You live three blocks away."

"What's your point?"

She laughed. "Fine, lazy. Get in."

Best friends till the end—that had always been our philosophy. Both of us were now missing our souls thanks to a kiss from Stephen Keyes. And so far, nothing seemed like it had changed except our increased desire for chicken wings and fast food.

That was a huge relief.

Maybe Bishop was wrong about grays. Maybe he'd been given some lousy information and this mission was a big waste of time and effort—something had totally been blown out of proportion. Maybe everything was going to turn out okay, whether or not my soul was successfully restored.

No, I didn't think it would be nearly that easy, either. All I knew for sure was that I'd be getting some more answers tonight. I just wished the questions weren't getting so damn scary.

chapter 14

There was no sign of Bishop or the others after school or into the evening. Even if I'd wanted to contact him, I had no idea how.

I couldn't stop thinking about him. From what I'd learned about him and Kraven, to hoping he could help Carly, Bishop was constantly on my mind. Also, I liked being near him—the warmth he gave me, the sound of his voice, his tall and strong presence that made me feel safe and protected. I even liked the way he challenged and aggravated me sometimes.

I missed him more than I ever would have expected.

Instead of focusing on that, I worked on getting ready to go out. I dressed as if it were a Friday night, with a short black skirt, black tights, a sparkly tank top, high-heeled knee-length boots and my thin, knee-length leather jacket. My winter coat would have to wait for a less fashionable occasion. I took extra time with my makeup, going heavy with the black eyeliner, and then I brushed every last tangle out of my hair so it hung in a fairly orderly manner all the way down to my waist.

I inspected the results in the mirror. Not exactly a supermodel, but not too shabby. It gave me a bit more confidence at the thought of facing Stephen and this mystery woman.

Bishop would likely be mad that I'd decided to go to Crave again, but what choice did I have? I wanted answers and I'd been given the opportunity to get more than I already had. I couldn't say no to that.

Carly picked me up right at eight o'clock, and she looked hot, too, in a red dress that hugged her curvy body. Ten minutes later, we arrived at Crave.

As we walked toward the club from the parking lot, I noticed a man sitting on the curb with a cardboard box in front of him and a sign asking for spare change. His face was dirty, his black hair matted and messy, and his beard wasn't much better. His fingernails were caked with grime. He watched me through pale eyes as Carly and I moved past him, close enough to see a handful of coins in the box.

"Greetings on this lovely evening, young ladies," he said.

I felt an immediate surge of empathy for the guy. Some of the people I'd come across during my brief impersonation of a street kid were down on their luck like this and looking for a break or a kind word. Both, if they could get it.

After fumbling in my purse for a five-dollar bill, I dropped it into the box. He smiled as he watched it flutter to the bottom.

"Thank you." His teeth were whiter than I would have expected, given his otherwise unkempt appearance. "Beauty bright like the stars above, it shines in her eyes. Eyes that have seen too much—more than they should. But she's lost and can't find her way. Who to trust…who to trust?"

His ramblings made me think of Bishop and my heart clenched.

"You're welcome," I said. "Go to the mission on Peterson.

They'll give you a good meal and some help if you need it. Although, you probably already know that." This guy had to have been on the streets for years by the looks of it.

He crossed his legs, squinting up at me. "So many speak with forked tongues. But the moon is high in the sky and it won't be long at all until the tides rush in and sweep everything away. Beware, for the time grows closer with every night that passes."

"Um, Sam?" Carly looked uncomfortable. She teetered on her treacherously high heels. "Let's go somewhere a bit saner, shall we?"

"Yeah, okay." I began to move past the man, but his hand shot out to grab my wrist.

Electricity zapped up my arm and, with a yelp, I yanked my hand away from him.

His eyes were wide. "I've waited, watched...so many years. And here you are. Finally. Like a beautiful star sent to save us all."

Save everyone? At the moment, I could barely save myself.

Carly took hold of my arm and began dragging me after her toward the entrance. I stared over my shoulder at the crazy homeless man who'd touched me. That felt a lot like the same electricity as when I touched Bishop.

Who was he?

"Okay, *that* was creepy," Carly said after we entered through the main doors to Crave.

"Yeah." My throat suddenly hurt and I felt sick inside. I'd felt sympathy for a homeless man who rambled about lies and tides and stars.

Was he like Bishop—an angel who'd been damaged from entering Trinity? But touching me hadn't cleared his mind.

I'd seen in his eyes that he'd felt the shock, too, but he hadn't started speaking coherently afterward.

It was nothing. Some static electricity and an overactive imagination, that was all.

"You okay?" Carly asked, putting a hand on my shoulder.

I cleared my throat and tried to compose myself. "Other than being eternally cold and hungry, I'm just fine."

"Talk first. Eat second."

I nodded. Last night with Stephen, I'd had a feeling I'd be seeing him again soon. I just hadn't known how soon it would be.

Carly led the way up the spiral staircase to the second floor lounge, not missing a step. Of the two of us, only I seemed nervous about this. I wished when Stephen had kissed me that he'd given me a little of the confidence he seemed to have given my best friend.

I expected that Stephen would look at me with anger or distaste after his standoff with Bishop last night, but the moment he saw me enter the lounge all he did was smile.

Smile. At me. And it was as amazing a smile as I'd ever seen on his face. One that once would have made my heart flip. But my heart only seemed to do flips for one guy now—and it sure wasn't Stephen.

Still, it didn't exactly set me at ease. I'd been lured off the dance floor last Friday night by a smile just like that.

He glanced warmly at Carly as he approached us. "Thanks for handling this. I really appreciate it."

"No problem." She actually gave him a hug before looking at me. "I'll let you two talk."

"No, wait a minute—" I began.

But she'd already wandered off to join a couple of other kids sitting on a long red couch to the left of the stairway.

Stephen's gaze moved to me again and his grin finally slipped a little. He actually looked awkward all of a sudden. "I'm really sorry about last night, Samantha."

My brows went up. "You're *sorry?*"

"Yeah. I handled it very badly."

"Do you mean before or after you sucked the soul out of my best friend?" My words were cold as ice.

"Soon you'll realize that all of this is for the best," he said. "But I understand why you're upset. Like I said, I handled things badly. I try to be confident, always have, but despite my best efforts, sometimes I come off like I'm a total..."

"Dick?" I finished for him. "I'm just randomly picking words out of the air. Tell me if you think I'm close."

Despite how blasé everyone was being about this life-changing experience, I harbored a high level of rage over what he'd done to both me and Carly. It would take a whole lot of convincing to make me see it any differently.

"Yeah." A grin played at his lips. "I was a total, unforgivable dick to you. Carly let me know in no uncertain terms that my behavior Friday night was unacceptable. She's very protective of you."

"The feeling's mutual." I couldn't keep looking at him—it was making me ill. "She said there was supposed to be someone else here tonight. Someone who might be more open with the truth than you've been. That's the only reason I came back—because trust me, it wasn't to see you again. When do I get to meet this person?"

"How about right now?" someone else said. There was a beautiful girl near the glass barrier overlooking the rest of the club, watching our uncomfortable exchange. She looked about the same age as Stephen, nineteen or so, and had dark hair and brown eyes.

If she was the one Bishop was looking for—the Source—she could be a demon who was able to devour souls. An anomaly, he'd said. One who was now able to create more who could do the same thing and had gotten Heaven's and Hell's attention in so big a way they'd slapped a quarantine over this entire city and sent a team of angels and demons to find her.

She approached and extended her hand to me. "Samantha Day. I'm very glad to finally meet you."

I eyed her hand with trepidation, but made no move to shake it. I wasn't feeling much like being polite tonight. "Who are you?"

"A friend."

Terrific. Yet another person who liked to avoid direct questions. Finally, I forced myself to shake her hand. No spark, no electricity, nothing there but a normal handshake. I met her gaze, trying to at least appear to be brave right now. There was something about her eyes—she seemed kind of familiar to me.

With the way my week had been going, maybe I'd had a vision about her, too, and I just couldn't remember it.

"Do I know you?" I asked.

She shook her head. "We've never met before. My name is Natalie."

"So you're the one with all the answers?"

"First, I wanted to apologize for how things have gone so far. Stephen has been..." She glanced at Stephen, who stood next to Natalie with his arms crossed over his chest, looking more uncomfortable with every moment that passed. "Like you already said, a total dick."

I stifled a nervous laugh at that before sobering immediately. A chill moved down my spine. "You were the one—the one who asked him to do that to me on Friday night, weren't you?"

Natalie held my gaze. "Yes, I asked him to kiss you."

Fear slithered through me, and I took an involuntary step back from her. At first glance, she looked so normal, so pretty...so harmless. But she wasn't. "I—I don't understand. Why me?"

She glanced around at the half dozen other kids up here, minding their own business. Except for Carly, who cast curious glances over her shoulder every few seconds.

"There was no other choice."

"He stole my *soul.*" Anger bubbled up in my voice, even though I was trying very hard to remain calm.

She shook her head. "It might be hard for you to believe, but he actually set you free from it."

"No, he took it without asking. That's stealing. And now I'm cold and hungry all the time and I can't get it back. Explain to me how that's so damn *freeing.*"

She wasn't giving me the same shiny "this is awesome, trust me!" look Stephen had given me last night. She observed my stress and anger and recognized it, rather than dismissing it. "Please hear me out, Samantha. That's why I hoped Carly could convince you to come back, despite your previous problems with Stephen. This is difficult for you, I know that. And I completely understand why you're so upset." She nodded at a nearby table. "Let's have a seat. Stephen, give us some privacy please."

Stephen nodded and wandered off without any argument.

Another surprise. Before, I'd thought Stephen was the one in control here. Now I clearly saw that it was Natalie—a girl who looked like a pretty, dark-haired college student wearing a tight black dress and four-inch designer heels.

I'd give her a chance. One chance, that's all.

I tried to summon up some of Carly's newfound confidence and took a seat across from her.

"Ask me anything you want to know," she said.

I exhaled shakily. "Why me? Why did you ask Stephen to kiss me on Friday night?"

She didn't shift her attention away from me for a moment. "Because you're special, Samantha."

I made a sound then that sounded like half hiccup, half hysterical snort. "So I've been told this week. I don't feel that special."

"But you are."

"Why? What makes me so special that I got tagged to become a gray?"

She looked at me with a sliver of amusement in her brown eyes. "A *gray?* Is that what they've termed it? How…dull. Literally."

I shut my mouth. I didn't want to say anything that might turn attention toward Bishop. "I don't know."

"You can't feel how special you are? You can't feel that you have something inside you that no one else here has? I knew it from the moment I first saw you here on Friday night. It's what makes you stronger than all the others."

I looked at her with shock. "Wait a minute. You saw me on Friday? Have you been watching me?"

"Take it as a compliment, Samantha, not something nefarious. I had to know for sure you were the right one. And you are."

My head began to spin. More double-talk. "I just want my soul back. I don't care about anything else."

"You'd be wise to accept this and make the most of it. You have no idea how incredible this opportunity is for you."

She actually didn't sound cocky when she said it, like Stephen would have. She sounded sincere and matter-of-fact. So much so, I almost believed her.

Almost.

"Stephen told me about your friend Bishop," Natalie continued. "What exactly does he want? Why is he here?"

I couldn't tell if she was a demon. I didn't get any sort of supernatural vibe off her at all at first glance—just like I couldn't immediately tell with the others. I looked into her eyes and tried my best to focus, but didn't sense anything. I couldn't read her mind.

"Samantha," Natalie prompted. "Please tell me what you know about him. He knows about us—about *me*—doesn't he? He thinks I'm a threat."

She knew quite a bit without me saying a word, which made me nervous. All she was looking for was confirmation and some extra details.

"He's a friend of mine," I finally said. "He saw Stephen manhandling me last night and came to my rescue."

"Your knight in shining armor."

"Something like that."

"You don't know who to trust, do you? Him or us?" She gave me a look of concern. "I didn't realize how hard this would be for you. So much has been presented to you in only a few days and you're so young. You're still just a kid."

Stephen had called me a kid, too. The word seemed insultingly dismissive. I didn't feel like a kid after everything I'd been through.

"I trust Bishop."

She shook her head. "If you did, you wouldn't have come here again tonight seeking more answers—answers he's unable or unwilling to give you. But that's smart, Samantha. You shouldn't trust anyone but yourself. Your heart and your gut. They won't lie to you."

"I agree."

"What does your gut tell you about me now that we've met?"

I studied her, breathing in through my nose and out through my mouth, trying to remain calm and controlled. "I don't know yet. You tell me I'm special, but you want me to take that at face value. I have nothing but words right now, no hard proof."

"Words can be both powerful and dangerous. Not as dangerous as a golden dagger, though, are they?"

"Depends on the words, I guess." I chewed my bottom lip, tasting my lip gloss I'd applied earlier. "I want my soul back, Natalie—and Carly's, too. It's all I want."

"Can I tell you the truth about a human soul, Samantha? Will you listen to me before you make any firm judgments about me—about all of this?"

I studied her, trying to see if she was mocking me or humoring me. She seemed sincere, but I wasn't sure. Finally, I nodded. I'd hear her out.

"A soul exists inside a human while they live out their allotted years of life," she began. "When they die, that soul is judged and sent to either Heaven or Hell."

My throat felt tight. "I already know this."

"What you might not know is that a soul, at its very essence, is not actually the spark of humanity. Not the essence of a human's life. Not something immortal that is either rewarded or punished upon death. Not completely, anyway."

I frowned. "What is it, then?"

"At its base level, a soul is the fuel that powers Heaven and Hell and helps them keep their universal balance. Without a steady stream of human souls, both would soon wither and die. Humans wonder why it seems as if they're always left to their own devices—war, famine, destruction, sickness—and no omnipotent supernatural being steps in to help save humans from their own poor decisions and bad luck. The answer to that is simple. It's not human lives that keep Heaven and Hell in existence, but human deaths. Death frees the soul to be sent to one of these places to keep the balance of the universe."

What a horrible idea—a soul as nothing more than fuel. I felt sick with every word she spoke.

"You're lying," I said shakily. I bit my tongue to keep from saying anything that might show how freaked out I was getting.

Natalie's expression was tense, serious, but then a smile spread across her face, which helped her look much less grim, given the subject matter. "I know it's a lot to accept. And I am simplifying it a lot. But the bottom line is, without your soul, you're no longer just an energy source required by Heaven or Hell. For the first time in your life, you're free from those chains."

My stomach twisted. I didn't like what I was hearing at all, but I wanted to learn more. I'd sift through it to see if there was any truth that could help me.

I wrung my hands together on my lap. My palms felt damp with sweat. "How did you learn all of this?"

"The hard way." Her grin faded and she got up from the table and moved to the glass barrier to look down on the rest of Crave. When she turned back to face me, again I was struck by how strangely familiar she looked.

"There's something about you," I murmured. "Something I…I can't figure it out. I feel like I know you."

"Is that what your gut tells you?" she asked. "You should listen to it. It's telling you that you can trust me, that I want the best for you even though my methods might seem harsh. I know it's a lot to grasp, but please try your best. You're important to this, Samantha. More important than you even realize. You're the center of it all. That's why I needed to find you."

"What do you mean, the center of it all?" I shook my head. "I just got dragged into this because Stephen kissed me."

She looked weary suddenly, like she hadn't slept in days. "You know that's not true."

She was right. There were no coincidences here.

"You're the reason the other grays exist," I said quietly. "You're their leader—their boss. You're the one in control here."

"I am," she said evenly. "So you can see why I need to know about your friend Bishop and that very special golden dagger Stephen told me he has in his possession. I know he's looking for me—even now, at this very moment. If he finds me, he'll kill me because he thinks he's doing the right thing. But he's not."

My mouth went dry. I didn't want her to know the truth about Bishop, but at the same time my gut was telling me that Natalie wasn't simply the evil entity I'd expected her to be. There was more to this story, a vital seed of truth here, but the picture was still too blurry for me to see it clearly.

"I don't know what you want from me," I finally said. "I don't have the answers you're looking for."

None that I was prepared to share right now, anyway.

She moved away from the glass barrier and approached me. "You're protecting him."

I shook my head.

"I understand why you're confused. Frankly, I don't really care about Bishop that much, other than concern about my own survival. All I care about now is you."

"But why do you care about me?" I searched for deception

in her expression, but I saw none. She moved away from me to sit back down at the table.

"Have you discovered your psychic gifts since Stephen kissed you?"

My breath caught. "How did you know that?"

"It's part of what makes you so special. You have gifts—gifts you've had since you were first born, but you haven't been able to access them until now. Your soul cut you off from them like a lid on a box. Now that lid is gone, isn't it?"

Before I'd been kissed, I was totally normal. Stunningly normal. But now I wasn't. And it wasn't just the hunger and the chills. It was everything else. Kraven couldn't figure out why I could do the things I could—the visions, seeing the searchlights, my zapping ability, reading the minds of angels and demons, helping Bishop regain his sanity. Was it all related?

"I don't know," is what I ended up saying. "Maybe."

Natalie nodded as if satisfied with that answer—or at least that I wasn't trying to deny it. "I need your help, Samantha."

"With what?"

"Right now, there's a barrier preventing myself or any other supernatural being from leaving the city limits. We've been trapped like defenseless mice for a cat to pick off for entertainment. I think you already know that."

I hadn't tested the barrier theory, but I didn't think she was lying about it. "It's a big city. There's more than enough room to move around here. I've barely left Trinity my whole life."

"We're still imprisoned here. I don't know what Bishop has told you about me, but he's wrong. He's the one you shouldn't trust, Samantha. He's our enemy. *Your* enemy. But he needs you. He's using you for your gifts, isn't he?"

The song playing below shifted to something with a harder

bass thump. I felt it through the bottoms of the tight boots I wore. I'd been so focused on my strange conversation with Natalie that I'd barely felt how much my feet had started to hurt.

I didn't like her accusing Bishop of using me, but I couldn't say she was lying. Bishop *was* using me. He'd even admitted it, which was why he'd made the deal to restore my soul to even things up between us. "So what am I supposed to do?"

"It's very simple." She studied me carefully. "I need you to bring his golden dagger to me."

My heart was pounding right out of my chest. "What for?"

"It's powerful, magical. It's the key to leaving this city. And your newfound gifts will allow you to use it to help save me—save us all—before he finds me and kills me."

I just stared at her, in shock from what she'd asked of me. Steal Bishop's dagger. Save her life. Or she was going to die. We all were.

Bishop had said he wanted to *talk* to her.

After all I'd seen, I wasn't even slightly convinced it would end there.

"Think about everything I've told you," Natalie said. "Think hard. It's very important that you make the right choice now. I mean you no harm, Samantha. I only want you to realize your full potential. I can help you do just that. I know you can feel the truth in what I've told you. Believe in me, Samantha. I can help you more than he can. I can help you accept what you *are* rather than what you *were*. You're better now in every way."

I crossed my arms. I hadn't even taken off my coat since I'd first arrived. My chest felt tight and I literally felt sick to my stomach from everything I'd heard from her. "I want to go now."

She nodded. "I won't try to stop you. I'm leaving now, too. Thank you for coming here and giving me a chance to talk to you. It means more to me than you know."

I turned away from her, half expecting her to tackle me at the top of the stairs and demand that I bring her the dagger right now. But she didn't. I grabbed hold of the railing as I started down the twisting stairs. A few seconds later, Carly was right behind me.

"Did that go okay?" she asked. "You look really pale. Paler than normal, which is a feat in itself."

"Fine. It's fine. Everything's fine."

I didn't sound all that convincing, but considering how swollen my brain felt, it would have to do. I'd wanted answers—I'd gotten them, although I wasn't sure how to deal with what I'd heard. I now had a whole lot of information to sort through.

"So what now?" she asked.

"Forget half-priced chicken wings. I just want to go home."

"Okay, no problem. We'll go."

Part of me wanted to dismiss everything Natalie had told me, but I couldn't. Despite who she was, she'd seemed so genuine. And there was that strong sense of familiarity about her that made me want to believe that she'd been *mostly* truthful with me just now.

What she'd said about my soul holding back the gifts I'd had since birth, like a lid on a box—she was right. It was like a puzzle piece snapping into place and showing me a little more of the mysterious picture underneath. But not quite enough to figure out what it actually was.

If she'd been telling the truth about that, was she telling the truth about how I shouldn't trust Bishop? That he was actually my enemy?

As we left the club, I tried to ignore the frigid air that closed around me. The sky was clear and dotted with stars, and the moon hung low, lighting things up enough to see easily.

As we turned the corner to get to the parking lot, I suddenly found myself face-to-face with Bishop.

chapter 15

I froze. After the conversation I'd just had with Natalie, he was the last person I was prepared to see right now. And yet, when my heart started beating faster, I knew it wasn't just from surprise. I couldn't look anywhere but at him. He was framed by moonlight and his gaze immediately locked with mine. His scent—warm, tempting, addictive—immediately affected me as if he'd just pulled me into his embrace.

Kraven stood next to him. Roth and Zach were nowhere to be seen. Believe me, the first thing I did after getting past the shock of seeing Bishop was to check the area for the demon who'd broken my neck last night.

"Hey, sweetness," Kraven greeted me, his eyes sweeping the length of me with a leering edge. "Looking good tonight. I hope you didn't get all hot just for little ol' me."

Ignoring the demon was becoming a habit.

Bishop didn't say anything at all, which surprised me until I realized that he didn't appear to be completely lucid. It had been a whole day since I'd last touched him to help take the crazy away. I wanted to touch him right now, even after my mind-jarring conversation with Natalie. I wanted so much to help him, to trust him.

But I forced myself to hang back.

He seemed to struggle to hold on to his concentration. His jaw was set as his gaze flicked to the club behind me before it narrowed into a glare. "Why, Samantha?"

"Why what?"

"He means 'why are you here when it's so horribly dangerous and he's worried about his little girlfriend,'" Kraven paraphrased with a smirk. At Bishop's sharp look, he shrugged. "Just trying to help."

I shifted my feet. "Half-price chicken wings on Tuesdays. That's why."

Bishop laughed and the sound made me jump. His gaze twisted into me and suddenly it felt more threatening, almost like how he'd looked at me that night in the alley when he realized what I was.

Natalie's warning about him being my enemy echoed in my mind.

"Shouldn't be here," he said in that broken-up, staccato way of his when he wasn't completely lucid. "Not again. Bad things play here."

"You told me to act normal. Coming here is normal."

That earned me an even sourer look. He opened his mouth as if to argue, but closed it. The heat of his glare made my heart race even faster.

Kraven seemed happy to take over. "It's naughty and you know it. We're here to check the place out. We were here earlier today, too, but there wasn't anything interesting to see."

Of course they were. Even though Stephen had told Bishop the Source never came here, why would he believe that?

"Speaking of dangerous..." Kraven cocked his head, his

attention now on Carly who was studying him back just as intently. "Looks like you're not the only cute gray in the general vicinity."

This wasn't a double date in the making between the four of us. This was trouble. I had a free pass right now with Bishop and the others, but I didn't want anything bad to happen to Carly.

"Who are you?" Carly asked Kraven. She didn't seem either swayed or impressed by the two tall, good-looking guys facing us.

"Nobody you'd want to meet in a dark alley," Kraven replied. "Trust me on that."

She snorted. "You don't look so scary to me."

"You might be surprised." Despite the lightness in Kraven's tone, his glare spoke volumes. He wasn't staring at a girl he really thought was cute, he was staring at someone he considered an enemy. A monster.

I would know, since that was exactly how he'd first stared at me. In fact, he still regarded me that way most of the time.

When he took a step forward, fists clenched, I stepped between them. "Don't. Just don't."

He narrowed a look at me. "Get out of my way."

"Not happening. You want her? You have to go through me."

"Just because we're making an exception for you doesn't mean that extends to your friends, sweetness."

"Carly's not going to hurt anybody. She's just like me."

His expression darkened. "You're not harmless, either, you just don't realize it yet. It's called denial and it won't last much longer, no matter how much your boyfriend might like to think otherwise."

I tried to shove him backward, but he didn't budge. Then

I tried to zap him. That also didn't work. He had a wall up around him and I knew it would take me a while to find a crack in it. "Get away from us. I'm not in the mood for this tonight."

"Leave her alone, Kraven," Bishop growled.

"She's the one doing the shoving." He laughed. "Defending your little girlfriend? Isn't that adorable."

Bishop's gaze had lost some of its previous madness. Either that or he was able to fake it pretty well now that he knew he had an audience.

"Don't try me tonight," he said evenly. "I'm *really* not in the mood."

I eyed Bishop, uncertainty sweeping over me about absolutely everything to do with him. "So this wasn't planned? You came here to try to find the Source? Were you going to try to find me, too? Or..." My mouth felt dry. "Or are you finished with me? I did what you wanted me to do and now I'm just another gray?"

He frowned, as if trying to focus on my voice. "Not just another gray. Special. Don't know why. Wish it were different. Wish I didn't..." He swore under his breath and rubbed his temples. "I hate this. All of it."

I didn't know what to make of his ramblings. Did he want me to just be another gray? Not special or different so I wouldn't cause so many problems for him?

The thought that he wished for something like that made me cringe inside.

Kraven put an arm around Bishop's shoulders and squeezed, but it was more of a mocking gesture than a supportive one. "Bishop's been having a tough night. We've been dealing with some other important business with our two new BFFs.

They're out on patrol right now. Just one big happy family, aren't we?"

"Let go of me," Bishop said. "Or I'll kill you."

Kraven let go of him. "See? Fun, fun, fun."

I looked at Bishop. "He's your brother, isn't he?"

His gaze snapped to mine. "Excuse me?"

I wanted him to deny it. I wanted him to say that Kraven was a big fat liar. Then my trust in him would be restored one hundred percent. "Is it true or not?"

Bishop sent a dark glare in Kraven's direction.

The demon shrugged. "Sorry. Didn't realize it was a big secret. Guess you might have second thoughts now about letting me walk your girlfriend home from now on. All sorts of fun information might come out in the open, thanks to her special little abilities."

Bishop's attention moved back to me and he searched my expression. "I didn't tell you because it's not important."

"Not *important?*" My heart slammed against my chest. "Why would you possibly think that isn't important? He's your *brother.*"

"That was a long time ago. Things change."

"What does that even mean? What's your real name? I know his."

"My name is Bishop. There's no other name for me that matters anymore." There was deep pain in his blue eyes for a split second before it vanished and he searched my gaze. It felt as if he could look right down to my soul—if I still had one.

"I want answers, Bishop," I said as firmly as I could.

"I don't have any for you. Not about this."

He was seriously the most frustrating and secretive person I'd met in my entire life. Ever. And yet I still didn't want to look away from him. I wanted to know everything—who he was, where he'd lived, *when* he'd lived, what his real name was. Because I now knew for sure that it wasn't really Bishop.

"Sam," Carly said. "Can we, like, leave? It's freezing out here."

"Tick tock," Kraven said to Bishop. "Let's get a move on. We check the club and then we have to get back out on patrol with Roth and Zach. Priorities, remember?"

Natalie had said she also planned to leave when I did. For all I knew, she was already gone.

Bishop hadn't looked away from my face. That sliver of madness mixed with something else I couldn't put a name to. He didn't like that I'd found out his little secret—that he'd been a human just like everybody else. And somehow he'd had a brother who turned out to be a demon.

Again, I wished I could read his mind.

And still, despite his strange and unpleasant behavior tonight, I had to keep my hands clenched at my sides to keep from reaching for him. The warmth coming from his body was so tempting that it effortlessly drew me closer to him. I wanted to believe in him so badly, even now that my previous trust had been shaken. It was like an ache burrowing deep into my chest.

"Are you going to hurt my friend?" I asked him softly.

He finally, with effort, tore his gaze from mine to sweep a glance over the blonde shivering next to me. "Kissed anyone yet?"

"No." I looked at her.

"No," she confirmed. "No kissing. Stephen warned me it would only make my hunger harder to deal with."

"He should know," I grumbled.

"Found two tonight so far who met my dagger. Out of

control." Bishop gave Carly another hard look. "Don't kiss or you'll be sorry."

She mock-saluted. "Yes, sir."

I cringed at her fearless sarcasm. I found that I was reaching forward to take Bishop's hand in mine, but I faltered just before I touched him. He hadn't asked me to do this. That was our deal—when he needed me to touch him, he'd ask me.

I met his eyes. *Ask me to touch you right now.*

His gaze sank into me, his dark brows drawn tightly together, but he didn't say a word.

I crossed my arms over my chest and fought against the pull. "Do you have everything under control?"

He seemed to fight for clarity and to find his words. "We're doing our best. For some reason, those with the most severe hunger come out only at night. It'll be better when I find the Source." He gazed past me at the club. "Have you met her yet?"

The truth froze on my tongue. Something stopped me from spilling everything. If Natalie had been an out-of-control monster who was forming an army and wanted to wreak havoc citywide and hurt people, I might tell him everything. But she wasn't. And I needed more answers before I'd know for sure who to trust.

I didn't know her. But I didn't really know Bishop, either.

"No," I said, forcing myself to look into his eyes again. *Give me time,* I thought. *I might be able to find something out to help you.*

Or to help myself.

Hopefully both.

I was book smart, but I had to be street smart now, too. I couldn't give Bishop every ounce of my trust—not when he hadn't been totally open with me in return.

Carly eyed Kraven with distaste. "Let me get this straight. You two run around town killing people?"

"Only the monsters." Kraven gave her a dark grin. "Even if they have bouncy blond hair and pretty blue eyes. So you better stay on your new diet, honey."

"Such a hero," Carly said with disgust. "You think you're doing the right thing? Like you're some sort of savior to mankind stomping out anything that's a little different?"

Kraven let out a humorless laugh. "Nah. I'm way more of an opportunist." When Carly rolled her eyes, he said, "You think I'm lying?"

"Whatever. Come on, Sam. We're out of here." Carly grabbed my arm and started dragging me past them.

I looked over my shoulder at Bishop and my heart twisted. "Wait…I have to…"

"To what? These guys are trouble." She glared back at Kraven. "Unless you're going to try to stop us?"

He smiled, an expression that didn't come close to touching his eyes. "Have a good evening, girls. And nice meeting you…Carly, right?"

Carly physically shoved me into the passenger seat of her car and got in, started it and pulled out of the parking spot. In the rearview mirror I saw Kraven and Bishop watch us drive away. Only then did I realize I was shaking.

"I know that Bishop guy gets to you big-time," she said. "You started losing it there for a second. Thought you might ditch me again and run off with him."

That almost made me laugh. "No, I—I'm not ditching you." He did get to me, though. Even now I wanted to go back and touch him, help him, but I stayed firmly in my seat and forced myself not to ask her to turn around. I played with the edge of my skirt and tried to breathe normally. I had half a mind to go back into the club and warn Natalie that they were there, but she wasn't stupid. She knew enough to be wary of Bishop. I had a funny feeling that if she didn't want him to find her, he wouldn't. Not easily, anyway.

"Not sure why you're so crazy about him," Carly continued. "I mean, he's definitely gorgeous, but he seems like a complete wacko. And that other guy—he's hot, but a total asshole, isn't he? And you said they're brothers?"

"Yeah." I wanted to tell Carly everything, unburden myself of all my problems from the past few days. Tell her the truth about who and what Kraven and Bishop really were, beyond their confusing biological relationship. I mean, I trusted her. And now we were in this together, no matter what.

But I still kept my mouth shut.

She eyed me after a couple of minutes. "Feeling all right?"

"I'm fine." Hungry and cold, but that was nothing new.

"Can I do anything to help?

"Yeah, you can give me a little bit of your self-confidence. Not sure why I didn't get that gift with purchase when Stephen kissed me." I actually managed a smile, remembering how she'd faced off with Kraven. "You're kind of a force to be reckoned with now."

She grinned. "I know, right? Fake it till you make it, isn't that what they say? If I'd been all shy and demure, I think they might have given us a harder time."

"You're probably right." I went quiet, lost in my thoughts, until she finally pulled into my driveway.

She grabbed my hand and squeezed it. "It's going to be okay. Seriously. Would I lie to you?"

"Thanks for being so cool about all of this."

"We'll get through this together like we always do."

"Of course we will." I shook my head, remembering my

strange and confusing conversation with Natalie. Also that odd sense of familiarity I'd had with her. "It's so weird. That girl—Natalie—she reminds me of somebody, but I can't quite put my finger on it."

"Yeah, she reminds me of somebody, too."

I frowned at her. "Who?"

She adjusted her mirror so she could put on a little fresh lip gloss then gave me a sideways glance. "Really? You can't see it?"

My breath sped up. "No, I can't."

"The hair, the eyes? I thought it was kind of obvious. A bit freaky, actually."

"What?" I grabbed her arm. "What's so freaky? Who does she look like?"

She turned to face me, her brows drawn together. "Well, she looks like *you,* of course. You two could totally be related."

I blinked.

She was right. Natalie did look like me. Same hair color, same eye color. Even the shape of our faces was similar.

"Brown hair and brown eyes," I said out loud, rationalizing it all. "Just like fifty percent of the population. I don't have the most unique look, you know."

She shrugged. "I mean, I'm not saying you *are* related, but it would kind of make sense that she was so interested in meeting you, right?"

Right. But it was just a coincidence. It had to be.

I reached for the door handle. "I—I'll see you tomorrow. Thanks for the drive."

"Do me a favor, Sam?"

I looked over my shoulder at her as I got out of the car. "What?"

"Stop worrying so much. It's all going to be okay."

I didn't wait for her to pull out of the driveway before I made my way to the front door and let myself in. It was a little after nine-thirty and my mother was actually home, which was a surprise. She was watching one of her favorite TV shows, so I didn't bother her. I went directly to the kitchen and started eating straight out of the fridge, hoping something might satisfy my current hunger.

Nothing did. Then again, I wasn't really expecting it to.

Wednesday passed without incident.

I know; I could barely believe it myself.

Again, I considered staying home and hiding, but ended up forcing myself to go to school and try to act normal. Carly was there, too, and she was doing a much better job of it than I ever could.

I wasn't sure if it had to do with her lacking a soul or not, but her confidence had blossomed even more. Her extra twenty pounds became a nonissue and she had started dressing better. Sexier. She practically glowed.

I was able to observe how a gray is regarded by other people—especially guys. They checked her out behind her back, murmuring to each other about how hot Carly Kessler had recently become.

For the most part, they seemed to feel the same way about me. I saw it now, the appreciative looks I was getting, even though I wasn't wearing a tight skirt and heels to school like Carly was. Even in my jeans I still received way more attention than I ever had before.

But there was a big difference between the two of us. I wasn't filled with the confidence Carly now had. I felt exactly the same as ever before, apart from the hunger and constant chills, which didn't seem to be going anywhere. Carly appeared to handle those problems way better than I did. Lucky her.

What Natalie told me about souls being fuel had definitely stayed with me. That seemed monumentally important. As if, if it was true, I'd just been told the secret of the universe.

It wasn't a secret I wanted to know.

Colin tried to corner me again, but I managed to slip away before I let him get close enough that I'd become too drawn to his scent. Making the mistake of kissing him and finding out what happened if I actually gave in to my hunger wasn't something I wanted to explore. *Ever,* if I could help it.

And I could. I had control over this.

No sign of Bishop or the others. No sign of Natalie or Stephen. I was either being ignored or I was being given time to process everything I'd been told.

Probably both.

So, really, in the grand scheme of things, Wednesday was kind of awesome. I could almost pretend that all was well with the world.

But then came Thursday.

It all started with a note left in my locker.

> We're squatting in an abandoned church on Wellesley. You can't miss it. Looks like a place nobody sane would ever want to enter. Speaking of nobody sane, your boyfriend needs your very special touch. You might want to drop by for a visit before he totally loses it.

Bishop. My heart twisted at the news that he wasn't doing well. There had been that edge of madness in his eyes Tuesday night, and two days had passed since then. He could only have gotten worse.

The note wasn't signed, but I knew who it was from. Somehow Kraven had managed to find my locker and left me a handwritten note. I guess the demon didn't know how to text. Not that my phone seemed to be working lately.

"I don't know what's wrong with my stupid phone," I said to Carly before class, staring at the blank screen with annoyance. I'd charged the battery again, but it wouldn't stay on for more than thirty seconds. It was practically a new phone, only three months old.

"Mine's the same," she said. "Stephen told me the other night when I was waiting for you that it's like that for all of us."

I looked at her with surprise. "What?"

She shrugged. "Apparently technology doesn't like us. We give off some sort of supernatural vibe now that messes with the signal. Or whatever. I don't really understand stuff like that, but it completely sucks."

I felt myself pale. "That would explain it then."

It had nothing to do with a faulty battery. It was a *gray* thing. Another reminder of what I now was and what it could mean if Bishop didn't restore my soul.

Still, the thought of showing up at that church at the demon's request didn't sit well with me. The flippant tone of the note had left me with a bad taste in my mouth. If Bishop had asked me himself, I might feel differently.

I'd figure out what to do about him later, even though I knew it would be very hard to get him out of my mind so I could focus on my classes today.

"Crave again tonight," Carly said as she shut her locker. "You're in, right?"

I hesitated, stuffing the note from Kraven into the pocket of my jeans. "I don't know."

"Oh, come on. We'll have fun. We can hang out after my date with Paul."

I looked at her with surprise. "Paul? The guy who's had a crush on you for two years? *That* Paul?"

She grinned. "Yup. But it's not an official romantic date or anything. I know that's not a good idea until I figure out how to deal with my hunger properly. I hope he's okay with my current chicken-wing addiction and doesn't think it's too nasty. But we're going to hang out and get to know each other better. No big deal."

"I think it's fantastic. Just…be careful, okay?" I felt a little surge of optimism over this. If Carly's new self-confidence was helping her get over her Colin issues, then it was a very good thing. I'd always thought she and Paul would be perfect for each other, even if there was no kissing allowed until I figured out how to get our souls back and go back to our normally scheduled lives.

Even after my conversation with Natalie, I still hadn't changed my mind about that.

The bell for first class rang and Carly clutched her binder to her chest. "See you later!"

"Yeah, see you." I watched as she scurried down the hall. I really wished I could accept everything as easily as she could. It was as if missing her soul hadn't fazed her one little bit.

I went to English and tried to focus on Mr. Saunders talking about themes in *Macbeth*—and tried to ignore Colin sending constant glances in my direction. I wished very hard that he would get interested in another girl. Soon.

The day dragged on. As I walked home after school, I pulled Kraven's note out of my pocket and read it again. I wanted to be confident and strong, but just reading about how bad

Bishop was getting made my heart ache. I didn't want Bishop to get hurt—but now I didn't want Natalie to get hurt, either.

I was stuck in the middle.

Both Bishop and Natalie had told me different sides of the same story. All I had from either of them at this point was words. Words, even though they weren't daggers, were still dangerous if they turned out to be untrue. Both had their reasons for not being completely straight with me. Could Bishop be leaving important pieces of this puzzle out so I'd continue to help him?

Maybe these zombie grays Bishop told me about didn't even exist—it was like the monster in the closet. Once you opened the door and shone a light into the darkness, you realized that there was nothing there in the first place except for your own fear of the unknown.

Seeing Bishop again would have to wait until I made some sense out of the confusing mess that my life had become. And I had a feeling that Natalie had more answers I needed right now. I just hoped she'd be there again tonight.

Without putting on quite as much eyeliner as Tuesday night, and foregoing the heels for flats, I got ready to leave the house at seven-thirty. My mother was in the kitchen, sitting at the dinette table, a glass of white wine in front of her.

"Hey." I grabbed my bag from the edge of the chair where I'd left it earlier. "Didn't hear you get home."

Her blond hair was down around her shoulders tonight, rather than up in her usual perfect French twist. It was nicer like this, in my opinion.

"I've been working a lot lately, haven't I?" she said before taking a sip from her glass.

That put it mildly. In fact, her flippant way of saying that she'd essentially abandoned me in favor of her beloved new career jabbed at my anger button. "You could say that."

She removed her designer eyeglasses and placed them on the table next to the daily newspaper before rubbing her temples. She looked tired. "Honey, sit down. I want to talk to you."

Between her serious tone and that extralarge glass of wine, I started to worry. We might have our mother/daughter problems, but I didn't hate her. Seeing her so disturbed by whatever it was she wanted to discuss with me...well, it was disturbing.

"What's wrong?" I fought the urge to reach across the table and squeeze her hand.

Her knuckles were white as she took another sip of her wine. Her slightly bloodshot eyes met mine. It looked like she'd been crying. "You have a right to know this."

"Know what?"

"I'd always planned to tell you the truth, but I put it off and put it off. I figured I'd wait till you turned eighteen, then you could do whatever you liked with the information."

I think I stopped breathing. "What information?"

She paused for what felt like a very long time before she finally said it. "You are adopted."

My mouth fell open. *"What?"*

Words spilled from her now like she couldn't get them out fast enough. "Your father and I couldn't conceive on our own, after trying every option. I sometimes felt that it was fate that led us to the agency that gave us you. Like a gift. It was such a wonderful time in our lives and it makes me so, so sad that we've lost touch with each other since your father left. We were supposed to be the perfect family, but I've learned that nothing's perfect in life. But we try. And I've tried, Samantha, I've really tried to be the best mother I could be and provide everything you've needed. I'm sorry I didn't tell you this before and I'm so sorry if it hurts you to hear it now."

I couldn't have been more stunned if I'd just been hit by a truck.

Kraven had been right. He'd taken one look at my mother and me and he'd guessed something I'd never even considered once in my life.

I was adopted.

"Wh-who are my birth parents?" My voice was croaky, like I had to force the words out when they'd rather stay safely inside.

She got up from the table and paced over to the kitchen sink. She clutched it for a moment before turning to face me again, the strain on her face clearly showing her age and weariness. "There wasn't much information on them. The agency did tell me your mother was in her very early twenties. She was desperate to find a good home for her baby. That's all I know. I'm sorry, honey."

Early twenties. Some girl who'd gotten in trouble and needed to fix her mistake by giving her baby up for adoption. The thought made my throat feel thick and my eyes burn.

"Do you know her name?"

She shook her head. "I was told she dropped you off and then disappeared. For years I thought she might come back for you and take us to court over custody, but she never did. I can go with you to the agency. We can try to find out more information together, if you like."

I got shakily to my feet, clutching the strap of my bag over my shoulder. I felt cold now, and it didn't have much to do with missing my soul. This information just wedged into my mind, trying to find space amongst everything else I'd learned this week.

"Yeah..." I cleared my throat and let out a shuddery breath. "I, uh...maybe. I don't know. I need time to think about this. But I—I'm glad you told me. I am."

"Honey, sit down. Let's talk some more."

"No, I have to go out. Carly's waiting for me at Crave. We'll have to talk...later."

I escaped from the kitchen without looking back. I couldn't deal with this right now, it was too much. So I left her there, glass of wine in hand, a woman who'd adopted a baby seventeen years ago and never breathed a word about it. Not even a hint.

But now it was all too clear to me, and I couldn't believe I'd never seen it. I'd never been anything like my tall, blond, blue-eyed, sociable parents—they were like Barbie and Ken, practically. I was short, dark-haired, pale, and had pretty much been a loner all my life.

When my father had moved to England with the promise to see me as often as possible, I'd felt abandoned. I'd tried to ignore those feelings, shove them down deep and let them manifest as a sudden need to shoplift a few items from the mall and hone my sense of humor into a sharp weapon.

This abandonment felt different. I didn't even have words for it. It just made me feel...empty. At least my father—my *adoptive* father—had made promises to see me again since he left two years ago. Which he'd done. Once. Last Christmas he'd held true to his promise and flown here for a week, staying at a nearby hotel. We'd spent a day and a half together. This girl who'd left me behind hadn't done that. She'd given me nothing at all.

A tear slipped down my cheek as I set forth on my way to Crave. The club was a half hour walk along populated, well-lit streets, so my mother never had a problem with it when

Carly couldn't pick me up. I wiped the tear away, mad that I felt any emotion over what I'd just learned. I resolved that it would be the last tear I'd shed over this missing biological mother of mine.

The homeless guy was sitting outside the nightclub again and he watched my approach.

"Facing fate at a fearless rate," he said. "Despite what she's lost, she'll find her way in the dark city, guided by the watchers of the night who protect us from the shadows. Some friend, some foe. But who's who? Who's to know?"

Something resonated in his words, freezing me in place, but I tried to shake it off. I didn't have time for his Dr. Seuss–sounding babble. He freaked me out too much, especially after feeling the electricity when he'd touched me last time. I didn't want to try to wrap my head around what that might mean. Not tonight. My head was wrapped around enough stuff already.

"All is not as it seems," he called after me.

"Not exactly a news flash there," I mumbled to myself.

Ever since my mind-blowing conversation with my mother, I'd known I had to be here again tonight. And it wasn't just to hang out with Carly and eat greasy food by the armful. I needed answers. Real ones.

I scanned the dim interior, searching for her. As promised, she was with Paul, in a corner booth. He stared across the table at her like he'd just won the lottery. She laughed at whatever he was saying. It looked like they were having a great time.

Let them. She'd promised this wasn't a romantic date that would involve kissing. I trusted her. He was safe.

I had other things to deal with.

I summoned as much courage as I could and climbed the spiral staircase to the second-floor lounge. As usual, there was a scattering of other grays—at least, I now assumed that was what they were. I scanned them to see if I recognized anyone from school, but there was no one. They looked older than me, now that I was paying attention. Stephen's age at least. Natalie sat on a red couch in the far corner wearing a tight blue dress, and Stephen leaned against the glass barrier near her.

I walked toward them and ignored my racing heart.

"Samantha," Natalie greeted me with a smile. "I'm glad to see you again."

"Why am I so damn special?" I demanded.

Her dark, arched eyebrows went up. "Stephen, please leave us."

"Yeah, sure." Stephen eyed me warily as he moved to the other side of the lounge and out of earshot.

My heart pounded. My mouth was dry. And to top it all off, my stomach was rumbling. I'd meant to grab a piece of pizza from the fridge before I left the house, but hadn't had the chance.

"Please, Samantha," Natalie said. "Sit down. Make yourself comfortable."

I didn't sit. I didn't want to be comfortable. "Why did you pick me? Why were you watching me in particular? How did you know about my gifts? Who am I? Who are *you?*"

This was why I'd come here. This was what I needed to know now that I'd learned I'd been adopted. I desperately needed another puzzle piece to snap into place.

She just leaned back in her seat and regarded me calmly. "Those are a lot of questions."

"We look alike," I said, when she didn't immediately offer up all the information I needed on a silver platter.

"Do we?"

"I—I mean, we have the same hair color. Eye color." I'd

already started to doubt myself. It didn't take much. "But—is that why you targeted me? Why you told Stephen to kiss me? Why you know there's something special about me? Right now I don't feel very special."

"What would make you think that, Samantha?"

"I'm adopted. I only found out for sure tonight. I'm just reaching, I guess. Maybe I'm wrong. Am I wrong?" My voice caught. "Are we related?"

Natalie crossed her lean legs. Her silver stilettos glinted under the spotlights above the seating area. A small smile played at her lips that ignited both fury and doubt inside me.

"The moment I arrived here I searched for you," she said. "Only you. I knew that you needed me as much as I needed you."

I waited, holding my breath.

She held my gaze before she finally spoke again. "I'm your aunt, Samantha. And I'm the only person in the world who can tell you about your real parents."

chapter 16

The noise from the club swelled in my ears and my head swam. I'm sure what little color I had had drained from my face.

"You're my…*aunt?*" I managed to say after several stunned seconds ticked by.

"I am."

I tried to process this without passing out. We had a family resemblance. I'd seen it before, but this was confirmation that we were related. "But you're so young."

Her brown eyes, so much like mine, began to glow red. "Demons remain the same in appearance as when we died as humans." Her lips curved. "You already guessed I was a demon, didn't you?"

My mouth was so dry it was nearly impossible to form words. "I—I'd had a feeling."

"Just you? Not your friend Bishop? I think he knows too much about me."

I had to sit down or I was going to fall down, so that's exactly what I did, slumping onto a plush red sofa. I forced my mouth to make words again. "Why should I even believe you? You could be lying to me."

She gave me a steady, patient look. "Because I know your gut is telling you that what I'm saying is true."

She was right. It was. It felt as if another piece of my puzzle had clicked into place. I suddenly wasn't totally sure I wanted to see the full picture. But I had to stay strong. I'd wanted the truth. I'd pretty much demanded it.

This was the truth.

Natalie—she was my aunt. And she was a *demon*.

There was so much more I needed to know, I couldn't just stop here. I was in it up to my neck, this swimming pool of truth I'd been thrown into. I'd either sink or swim now.

"My—my real parents," I croaked out. "My father...my mother. Who are they? Where are they?"

Natalie had taken a seat next to me, but she made no move to get closer to me or try to hold my hand. That might have been too much and I'd have run away from this, away from her, before I learned everything I could. Her expression remained serious, but a small smile played at her lips.

"Your father is my older brother. His name is Nathan."

I had to ask the next question, but I was afraid of the answer. "And if you're a demon..."

Then what is he? went unspoken.

She looked me steadily in the eyes. "He's also a demon."

I shivered. It had been possible he was human, of course, but I'd had a horrible feeling that he wasn't. I immediately wanted to push back against this information, but again it settled into me with a soft *click*. "And my mother? Was she a demon, too? Or a human?"

Her lips thinned with distaste. "Neither. She was an angel."

A wave of shock crashed over me. "A-an angel? Wait. My father was a demon...and my mother...was an *angel?*"

"Yes."

"Were they human when they got together?"

"No. Your parents were already supernatural when they met—an angel and a demon."

"Then…what does that make me?"

Her smile returned. "Special."

Snap goes another puzzle piece.

I stood up so quickly I got dizzy. I needed fresh air, but I was frozen in place and couldn't move. It was like there were lead weights in my shoes. I felt numb, but as I forced myself to breathe in and out, in and out, everything slowly became clearer and my heart stopped pounding so hard. It took a while.

"But angels and demons don't like each other," I said, remembering what little I'd learned from Bishop. "They *hate* each other."

"Usually. Personally I despise angels." She shrugged. "But you know what they say…love works in mysterious ways."

How could she be so flippant about this? "What happened?"

She twisted her index finger through a long, dark piece of her hair. It reminded me immediately of my own nervous habit. However, this woman—this *demon*—didn't seem like she got nervous very often. "The same thing that's happening now. A team of angels and demons were sent to take care of a problem. Your parents met. Hate swiftly turned to something else—although, don't ask me how. True love." She said it drily as if she couldn't quite believe it herself. "Problem was, it's forbidden. Angels and demons can't be together like that. Especially not in the human world."

"Wh-why not?"

She gave me a slight shrug, her gaze running down the length of me. "Because there can be a price for such uncontrollable and unnatural passion. Angels and demons don't breed with each other or amongst themselves. *Unless* they're here in the human world. And true and passionate love plays a great role in making the biology click. You are an anomaly, Samantha. An extraordinarily rare result of a forbidden demon/angel love affair." She gave me a bright, wide smile. "And you're rather fabulous, if I do say so myself."

"I'm an anomaly." That was the same word Bishop had used to describe the Source, a demon who could devour human souls. Aka: my aunt. He'd wondered if she was the same one with the ability from years ago. Sounded to me like he was absolutely right about that.

"You're a *nexus,*" she said. "It means the link, the connection. The offspring of a demon and an angel. You were born human—but a special human with gifts that draw from the powers of both Heaven and Hell. These gifts were held back by your soul."

This was why I could do what I did with the other angels and demons. Finding them, repelling them, reading their minds. I had a connection to them, a deep connection that had been born in me. And it was only with my soul missing that I could properly access it.

The powers of Heaven and Hell—angel and demon—in me.

It was a hell of a lot to deal with for a Thursday evening.

"So I'm not really a gray," I said quietly.

Her amusement faded. "I honestly thought that Stephen's kiss would simply get rid of your soul and free up your hidden abilities. It was a surprise to me that you developed the hunger, too."

I glared at her. "So it was just a hunch you had? And you went ahead and did it anyway? Without explaining anything to me first? Without giving me a *choice?*"

She grimaced and had the grace to look guilty. "I am sorry.

I know the hunger is...unpleasant. But it didn't even occur to me that it would cause a problem. For what it's worth, I think it's possible that your hunger will fade as your body adjusts to being without its soul."

"Is that another hunch?"

"You're not like the others, Samantha. You're special."

"Screw you," I spat out. My anger was rising with every new piece of information I got. "You damn well should have asked me first. Because I would have said no."

"The last thing I wanted to do was hurt you." But then her tone turned sharper. "But it's done and there's no going back, only forward. Because of what you are, I believe you have the power to use Bishop's golden dagger as a key to open a temporary exit in the barrier Heaven and Hell created to trap us here."

"Bishop..." I said his name out loud and my battered heart started to ache even more than it already did. I wished I knew where he was right now and if he was okay. I'd tried to be strong, but I wanted to go to him as soon as I could. I just wished he'd come to see me if he needed my help.

"He's an angel, right?" A dim red glow lit up her eyes again as her expression soured. "He's been using you for your gifts from the moment you met."

"Sounds like you're trying to do the exact same thing." It did scare me that she knew what Bishop was without any confirmation from me.

"I'm trying to save both of us. Not just myself. Family comes first, Samantha. Always."

I grabbed hold of the red sofa and squeezed it, as if it might act as an anchor for me. "Where are my parents? Why did they abandon me? Did they just leave me with an adoption agency and take off to Tahiti or something? Why has it been seventeen years and this is the first I'm hearing about any of this?"

Any remaining amusement faded from Natalie's pretty face. She sat down on the edge of the couch again and indicated for me to do the same thing, casting another glance toward the other grays, who continued to keep their distance. No one was within hearing range.

"It's my fault," she said. "All of it. What I can do…what I've done. I'm not proud, Samantha."

"What are you talking about?"

"My hunger." She bit her bottom lip. "My *curse.* It's been hard to control since I first became a demon. The conversion to demon is harsher than the conversion to angel. Lucky bastards. My brother and I…we both had complications. Nathan could absorb life energy—he could kill with a touch—but he had it totally under control. I hungered for a different kind of energy…and I couldn't control it no matter how hard I tried."

I watched her with widening eyes. "Souls."

She nodded, her expression bleak. "It became an addiction, one I knew would lead me to trouble every time I came to the human world. But I couldn't stop. Nathan tried to help me, but I finally ran away. I hid out here and my hungers only got worse. Of course, that meant that I showed up on the proverbial radar screen of Heaven and Hell like a bright blip of trouble. I was destroying what they valued most. I was a renegade that needed to be hunted down. They sent a team of angels and demons to do just that. On that team was my brother whom they'd enlisted in the hope that he could help control me—and your mother, Anna. That's how they met."

Anna. Her name immediately seared into my brain. I swallowed hard. "So what happened?"

"They found me, of course. But it took them many months.

By then, Anna was already very pregnant." She let out a humorless laugh. "Believe me, they were shocked that it happened as much as anyone else could be—at the time, they hadn't even known it was possible. But—" Natalie turned to clutch my hand and looked deeply into my eyes "—they wanted you, Samantha. They loved you even before you were born."

I didn't pull away from her, but my palms were sweating. "Then what happened?"

"Even though they tried to keep it a secret, the other team members figured out they had an illicit relationship. They were torn apart and told they would never be allowed to see each other again. You'd been born and hidden away by then. Anna planned to get you back as soon as she could."

"But she didn't."

"No." Natalie's grip on me grew so tight it was nearly painful. "There was a fight. A big fight. Anna—she was stabbed with a dagger just like the one Bishop carries. The Hollow opened up and swallowed her. Nathan was so devastated at the thought of losing her, he jumped right in after her." Her face tensed. "And the rest of the team made sure to shove me in right behind them. Wouldn't want to waste an opportunity to get rid of three problems at the same time."

I stared at her in shock. My heart was pounding three times as fast as normal. "They killed her?"

Natalie nodded. "I'm sorry."

Grief for a woman I'd never known gripped my throat. Tears welled in my eyes.

I forced myself to hold them back. "Wh-what is the Hollow? I keep hearing that but I don't understand what it is. It's where supernatural beings go when they die. Right?"

Her lips thinned. "It's a black pit where all the unwanted

garbage from Heaven and Hell is tossed—and it doesn't discriminate. It opens up here in the human world only when a supernatural is destroyed—like a vacuum that will suck up anything in its immediate path. Nothing has ever returned from there. It's the ultimate garbage disposal."

It sounded like a nightmare. A horrible, endless nightmare.

But then something occurred to me. "Wait a minute. You said that nothing has ever returned from there. But…you're here. You returned."

The haunted, serious expression was still there, but a small glimmer appeared in her eyes. "I did, didn't I?"

"What does that mean?"

"It means that the Hollow isn't what they think it is. It's changed." There was a large helping of disdain in her voice, and some smugness, too. "They have no idea what's possible now. They dumped me in there like garbage because I was different. Did they think about helping me, like my brother wanted to? No, of course not. I was a problem. And their solution to a problem is stomping their foot on it and kicking what's left into the trash. But I'm back."

I stared at her with cold shock. "You're back and…now you can create more who do the same thing that you do."

"That was a surprise, believe me. It never used to be like this, and I'm sure Heaven and Hell were shocked when that little news item showed up on their radar. When I kiss someone—like I did with Stephen—it changes them. Turns them into something like me. But they need to be careful not to take too much. Their bodies have transformed to become supernatural, but their minds are still frail as a human." She gave me a small shrug. "And humans are traditionally very greedy creatures. Give them a taste of something delicious and they come back for more."

I focused on breathing as normally as possible. "So you kissed Stephen without knowing what it would do to him."

Her lips curved into a genuine, wicked smile. "What can I say? He's cute. I like cute boys. They're fun." She cast a glance across the lounge toward him. "He had a girlfriend, but he dumped her. I vainly thought it was so he could be with me full-time, but I have a funny feeling he wanted to save her. He didn't want to take her soul."

That shocked me. Jordan had been hurt that Stephen had dumped her and had been seen with me. But maybe he'd been trying to save her.

Maybe. I wasn't convinced that Stephen was capable of anything that selfless.

Natalie got my attention again by grabbing my hand tightly and I looked at her with alarm.

"You must get the dagger so that we can escape, Samantha. They can't find me. And if they find out what you are, they'll see you as just as much of an anomaly as I am. My hunger isn't as bad as it was. I can control it now. I'll admit I did some damage here before I realized what was happening. I'm not proud of it." She scanned the lounge with dismay. "But, just like with you, I believe the others' hunger will fade in time if they resist it. Humans can survive just fine without their soul. It's not really needed and it frees them in so many ways. Stephen is a perfect example of this. He's stronger now than he ever was before."

He'd told me the same thing. Having a soul had weighed him down, filled him with doubt and unhappiness. Now he was improved. Better. If Natalie was right and the hunger began to fade, then could it really be okay for grays—unsouled humans—to live side by side with regular humans?

If they felt anything like I did, then I didn't see why not.

"You and I need to get out of this city tonight," she said firmly. "Tomorrow at the very latest. There's no time to waste. No one else needs to get hurt. Please, Samantha. We're family. We need each other, especially now."

"My father..." I whispered. "Is he okay? Can I see him?"

"Bring me the dagger and I'll take you directly to him. He's the one who wanted me to find you again."

"So you're saying that he got out, too? He escaped the Hollow with you?"

She gazed into my eyes and I realized hers had welled with tears. "I can't tell you anymore right now. First you must prove yourself to me. But let me say that Nathan will be so happy to see you, so proud of how beautiful you've become. He'd do anything for you, just as he would have for Anna."

My father. A demon who fell in love with an angel. Who'd followed her without hesitation into an endless black pit knowing that there might be no way back. But there was—Natalie was the proof of it. This Hollow place...it wasn't what everyone thought it was. It wasn't the end.

I would have thought that I'd be afraid of a demon, but I wasn't. I wanted to see him. I wanted to know him.

To do that I had to help Natalie. I had to get Bishop's dagger.

"I want to go now," I said softly.

"Please think about everything I've told you. You're my only hope now, Samantha. And your parents—I know both of them would be so proud of how you've turned out. You are so very special, never doubt it."

Slowly, carefully, I got up off the sofa, testing my legs and finding them solid enough to walk on. Stephen watched as I moved toward the stairs, but he didn't make a move to stop me.

Was it all true, what Natalie had just told me? Grays were

under control except for a few exceptions that Bishop's team could take care of. Their hunger would fade if they didn't give in to it. My gifts came from the powers of both Heaven and Hell combined. And I had the ability to open a hole in the barrier with Bishop's dagger and help my aunt escape before she was hunted down and killed for being different.

I started down the stairs, barely able to focus on the direction I was headed. My conversation with Natalie buzzed in my head, threatening to overwhelm me.

Bishop didn't know what I was. He'd been just as confused as anyone else about why I was able to do what I did. Just as confused as I was about our strange connection and the fact that whenever we were near each other, I couldn't stop thinking about kissing him.

Carly was still with Paul in the booth in the corner. I didn't want to interrupt them, but I did want to say a quick hello before I took off. By the looks of things, their date had progressed at a rapid rate. They'd moved straight from chicken wings to rounding first base.

It was sort of funny, actually. Carly had never been the most forward girl in the world. I knew for a fact she and Colin hadn't kissed until their fifth date. This was only her and Paul's first date and—

Wait a minute.

Carly was *kissing* Paul. Passionately. Didn't she remember what that meant?

I raced over to their table and grabbed her arm. "Carly, wait! You can't—"

When she turned to look at me I almost screamed. Her eyes were black, completely black, and the look in them, like a predator that had been interrupted while feasting on its prey, turned me ice-cold inside.

Paul slumped next to her in the booth. His breath came in rapid gasps, like he was having trouble getting any air into his lungs. His expression was frozen, his eyes glazed and there were strange black, branching lines around his mouth that immediately faded away. His skin was pale, like a ghost.

That wasn't just a first kiss...Carly had been feeding on his soul. Right here in the middle of Crave.

As I watched her with horror, her eyes shifted back to their normal blue, and the cold look on her face vanished. She smiled up at me. "Hey, I didn't know you were here yet."

"I—I'm here." My gaze quickly moved between her and Paul. He was recovering himself enough to pick at the French fries in front of him.

"Hey, Sam," he said. "How's it going?"

"Great," I squeaked out. "Really fantastic. You?"

He shrugged and grinned at me, still looking extremely pale. "I'm with Carly, so I guess I'm pretty happy."

"Yeah." I swallowed. He didn't even realize what had happened. He thought he'd just kissed a girl he liked while they were on their very first date.

I felt ill.

"Join us." Carly scooted over.

She looked so normal now I could almost forget what I'd just seen—a black-eyed monster feeding on a human soul. A monster who, for a moment, had looked at me as if she wanted to tear me apart for stopping her.

She'd said she wouldn't do this. That she had it under control. That I should trust her.

The monster was gone now, without a trace. Carly was back to normal.

But she *wasn't* normal. I glanced behind me, but it looked as if no one had noticed what happened except for me.

"I, um, can't stay. I just wanted to say hi." I looked at the plate in front of her, still half full of food. If that had been my plate, it would have been shiny clean by now.

She frowned and reached out to touch my arm. Her skin felt ice-cold and I flinched away from her. "You don't look so good. You sure you can't sit down for a minute?"

This was not the time for accusations. Maybe she didn't even realize what she'd just done.

I shook my head. "I really need to go."

"Me, too," Paul said. "It's been great, Carly. Sorry I have to take off early. Maybe we can do this again?"

"Absolutely," she said with a big grin. "Thanks so much for dinner."

I didn't think she was only talking about the daily special.

I lingered to make sure Paul got out of the club, watching him walk slowly to the exit as if he was inexplicably exhausted. Carly gave me a big hug then studied my face. A frown creased her brow.

"I know what you're thinking," she said. "But it's no big deal, okay? He's fine. I barely took anything. But...I had to. I couldn't help it. I was so hungry."

I just nodded. "If you say so."

As I headed for the door, I looked over my shoulder to see she was on her way upstairs to hang out with the other grays.

As for me? I headed out to find an abandoned church on Wellesley Avenue.

"Find your answers?" the homeless guy asked as I passed him. "Or just more questions? You saw her, didn't you? She's just like she was last time only worse...much worse."

He knew about Natalie. That she'd been here before. I'd planned to keep walking, but instead I crouched down in front of him so we were at eye level. He looked at me with surprise, as if he'd expected me to ignore him.

I reached out and grabbed his dirty hand in mine.

Electricity sparked up and down my arm—shocking, but not painful. And familiar. I watched him closely and, yes, just the slightest edge of that confusion seemed to disappear from his eyes this time.

"You're an angel, aren't you?" I asked.

He inhaled sharply, his dark brows drawing together. "I screwed up once—according to them. Now I'm punished forever. They have no idea what they did to me."

"Can you think clearly?" I asked, squeezing his hand. "Does this help?"

He looked down at my grip on him. "Nothing eases my pain, not for long. I try and try and try, but I can't escape it. The shackles are heavy. I feel them even now. One day I will be free."

He still sounded crazy. I'd hoped he wouldn't, that I could help him and he could help me in return.

"How do you know about her?" I asked.

He just shook his head back and forth, his lips sealed tightly until he finally spoke. "Tried to help. Didn't matter. She was out of control, had to be destroyed. Couldn't stay, had to go."

Was he a part of the team of angels and demons who'd killed my mother? Who'd sent my father and Natalie to the Hollow? Grief and anger clenched my chest at the thought.

No. I couldn't assume these things. Not now. They were too major to even wrap my head around. "I have a friend, his name's Bishop," I said. "He's like you, I think, but he just got here. Can you tell me anything that might help him?"

"Watcher of the night, angry and vulnerable. Won't be long now. Without you, he'll be lost as his chains grow thicker and thicker. You must help me, beautiful star. You're the only one who can."

"I don't know how."

He was an angel, just like Bishop, but he hadn't gone back to Heaven. He was stuck here for some reason, and his mind had been permanently damaged. Bishop said that when he went back he'd be fixed. This guy—how long had he been here? Natalie said that demons and angels remained the same age as when their human self died, so I knew I couldn't go just by appearance alone.

I didn't have time tonight to help this angel, even though I wanted to.

"I'll see you again," I told him, my chest tight. "And if I can, I'll try to help you, I promise."

He didn't try to stop me as I walked away. I needed to see the other angel, the one I knew I could still help. The one I desperately hoped could help me in return.

chapter 17

St. Andrew the Apostle, the abandoned church I'd been looking for, stood tall in front of me despite being run-down and boarded up. The sign out front was broken, the glass from it scattered on grass that looked like it hadn't been mown in a couple of years. The building was both ominous and sad-looking.

This part of the city had been hit hard by the economy, and most of the stores and businesses had shut down. I guess the same applied to churches.

I approached it apprehensively, eyeing the front doors as if they might swing open and suck me inside. It was difficult to get the image of black-eyed Carly out of my head. One moment a monster, the next the best friend I'd had since kindergarten who'd known what she'd done would upset me. It scared me so much I wanted to run away from it and pretend it hadn't happened.

But it had. And now I had to deal with what that meant. Bishop had to promise me to restore Carly's soul, too. I didn't want her to lose herself to this—to the hunger. As afraid as I'd been of her for that moment, I'd been just as afraid *for* her.

I could fix this. I could. I grabbed hold of that belief with both hands.

Along the side of the building, a door was ajar with a brick placed in it to keep it that way. It was the only indication that the church might not be totally deserted after all. No, a small group of demons and angels had set up camp here.

I wondered if a demon could enter a church that wasn't abandoned.

The need to see Bishop pushed me onward. The door made an eerie creaking sound as I pushed it open farther and I stepped into the cool, dark halls of St. Andrew's.

Voices echoed down the narrow hallway. Keeping close to the wall, I made my way into the church. It smelled old, like mildew and rotting wood.

Even though I was cold, always cold, a trickle of perspiration slid down my spine. Fear was alive and well in this currently soulless body.

"...should be here by now," Kraven said, although I couldn't see him yet. "I left the note first thing this morning."

"This is none of your business." Bishop's voice sounded angry. And shaky.

My breath caught and a shiver went through me.

"Not my business you're in bad shape? You're part of this. You drop your end, that's a quarter more responsibility the rest of us have to carry. And this isn't over yet."

Zach spoke then, his voice calm and even-toned, as if he was accustomed to coming between the two. "It will all work out. I have faith."

"How nice for you," Kraven replied drily.

"I hate this!" Roth snarled, joining the conversation as something crashed to the floor. I glanced around the corner to see the demon kick a stack of chairs at the front of the hall up toward the pulpit. The chairs might have been used if there were extra people in attendance and not enough space on the built-in wooden pews that lined the cavernous room. Two of the large stained-glass windows along the walls were broken, but the one at the very front was still intact and beautiful, even at night.

"What's your problem?" Kraven snapped at him.

"My problem?" Roth grabbed a vase from a side table and looked as if he was going to hurl it at the window behind him. Kraven caught his arm to stop him. Roth pushed the other demon back. "My problem is this sucks. All of it. What are we waiting for tonight? I want out."

"You signed up for this. You were given a choice, remember? You can't go back yet."

"I don't mean back to Hell, I mean *out.* I want to go out on patrol. I'm so bored. I killed three of those soul-sucking freaks last night and I want to find at least as many tonight when they crawl out of their holes. Give me the dagger."

"Bishop's not giving it up," Zach said. "He thinks you'll go after Samantha."

"I don't need the dagger for that. I can kill a gray like her without it, just takes a bit more effort. Nearly did, but you had to go and heal her."

Zach turned away from the demon and moved toward Bishop, who stood with his back braced against the wall as if it was an effort to stay vertical. "What can we do to help you?"

Bishop shook his head. "Nothing. Just—give me time. I'll be fine."

Kraven groaned. "I'll go get her. I'll drag her ass back here myself even if I have to knock her out first."

"No," Bishop replied sharply, glaring at the demon. "Harm her and I swear I'll tear you apart."

This was ridiculous. I put on a brave face, stepped out from behind the corner and walked up the aisle toward them. The other three eyed me with varying degrees of surprise. Bishop slowly raised his gaze up to lock with mine.

Seeing him made my heart skip a beat. I'd missed him so much, but I hadn't realized it until this moment. I wanted to run directly to him, but I stopped myself.

I couldn't seem to be neutral when it came to the angel. What I felt for him was too big to wrap my mind around. It had been wrapped around a lot tonight.

But what I felt for him was real. Seeing him again cemented that fact for me.

"Well, what do you know?" Kraven said. "Were your ears burning, sweetness?"

"A little," I admitted.

The greeting between us was almost friendly, at least compared to the death glare I got from Roth. After all, I was one of the things he wanted to head out tonight and kill to help combat his boredom. If he said he'd killed three last night, how many others were there? How big of a problem had grays become in the city?

There wasn't widespread panic. There weren't cops stationed on every street. They had to have it under control. At least, I really hoped so.

Still, considering what I'd seen Bishop do with that dagger as he performed the ritual on the others, it seemed like an excessively violent end for anyone. While what Carly had done scared the hell out of me, I wouldn't say she deserved a dagger through her heart for it. Paul had walked away, even though he was missing part of his soul now. I just hoped she hadn't done any lasting harm to him.

"What are you looking at?" I snarled at Roth.

A cold smile played on his lips. "Lunch."

I shuddered. "Dream on, freak."

"Every night."

"You need to stay away from me."

He shrugged. "Maybe I will and maybe I won't. Heard what you can do, though. Read our minds. Don't try to do that with me."

I focused on him, holding his gaze for longer than I wanted to. "Too late. Already done."

I didn't need to touch them; I just needed eye contact and an open mind. Tonight it seemed as if his walls were down whether he realized it or not.

His brows drew together. "So what was I thinking just now?"

I felt stronger with every moment that passed. The power of Heaven and Hell—yours truly had access to it, at least according to Natalie. This was just a small taste test. "You're thinking that you hope nobody here can tell how scared you are. How out of your league. How a meaningless asshole like you could have been picked for a mission this important." I forced myself to smile at him. "I'm paraphrasing of course, but am I close?"

He flinched as if I'd actually struck him. Nice. This guy's self-hatred issues made Kraven look like Mr. Well-Adjusted.

I wasn't quite finished, though. "I guess you don't want anyone to know what a coward you really are underneath it all, do you?"

His eyes narrowed. "Be careful, bitch."

"Oh, I intend to."

He stormed out of the room. Yes, I'd definitely hit the mark with him, which I wasn't so sure was a good thing. He was going to hold a grudge against me.

Zach touched my arm and I jumped despite myself. I'd been putting on a brave front, but I was quaking inside just from being here. "Ignore him, Samantha. Are you okay? You recovered from the other night?"

I looked up at him, meeting his pale green eyes. I searched for any kind of deception or cruelty there, but found nothing but an earnest angel who really wanted to know if I was okay.

"I'm better. Thanks to you. If you hadn't been able to heal me—well, I don't even want to think about that."

"I only wish I could help him, too." He nodded toward Bishop.

Kraven watched me a bit warily after my exchange with the other demon. "So are you here to work your mojo with my darling brother or do you want to do some card tricks first?"

I guess the news that Bishop and Kraven were related wasn't a secret anymore. Zach didn't react to it at all.

I approached Bishop slowly, my gaze moving over his tall form, broad shoulders, dark hair. His muscles strained against the sleeves of his T-shirt. He'd barely taken his eyes off me since I'd entered. I'd noticed him tense up when Roth sounded like he was going to get violent with me again, as if ready to jump in and beat the other demon down to the floor, but now he leaned heavily against the wall as if it was the only thing keeping him on his feet. There was a sheen of perspiration on his forehead and his blue eyes were unfocused.

My heart twisted as I shook my head. "What am I going to do with you?"

He let out a short bark of a laugh that made a chill run down my spine. "Good question."

I thought of the homeless guy I'd seen a few times now—the one I was positive was another messed up angel. "Why would Heaven let this happen to you?"

"Got banged up coming here…they didn't know it would happen. Not this bad."

"Is that a guess or a hope?"

He didn't look away from me, but there was a glazed look in his eyes that scared me. "Both."

I clenched my fists at my sides. "Honestly, Bishop. You should have found me before this. Why did you wait till I came here?"

His jaw was tight. "I wanted to handle this on my own."

"Nice thought. But everybody needs a bit of help sometimes." I held my hand out to him. "Well?"

I wasn't going to force him; he had to choose this for himself. He'd asked me in the beginning to help him. It was even part of our deal. But I knew he'd rather find a solution to this problem on his own.

Finally, he reached forward and grasped my hand tightly in his. And—just like the first time we'd touched—it was like lightning struck us. He gasped out loud. The electricity that sparked was even stronger than before. Warmth slid through me, chasing away my chill. Our eyes met and held, and I swear this connection we had felt like magic. Pure magic.

Being so close to him made me dizzy. He was like no other guy I'd ever known in my life. But he wasn't a guy—he was an angel. And I'd *missed* him—missed his scent, his warmth, his eyes, his mouth…everything about him drew me closer and made me never want to leave his side.

Wow—intense. Our connection overwhelmed me with only a touch. My touching the homeless guy hadn't given him sanity, and it hadn't filled me with warmth. This kind of magic—it only happened with Bishop. How could I ever doubt anything this incredible?

Bishop inhaled, squeezing his eyes shut as his grip on me

tightened. When he finally opened his eyes again, they were clear blue and totally sane.

"Better?" I asked.

He nodded slowly. "Much."

I smiled. "I'm here to help."

He didn't let go of my hand. He reached down to take the other, as well. "You still shouldn't have come here. It's too dangerous."

"But here I am anyway. So get used to it. I mean—" I looked down at our hands "—is this so bad?"

His gaze caught mine again and held. "It's good. That's why it's so bad."

When he entwined our fingers, for just a moment I forgot about everything else—it all slipped away and there was only him. When Bishop was totally sane, I wanted to kiss him so badly I could barely restrain myself.

And the way he looked at me, too, with gratitude and something else, something way deeper and more intense…

"I can practically hear the violins playing," Kraven drawled. "So romantic, I could die. Should Zach and I leave the room so you two can go at it, or what?"

I gave him a sharp look. "Are you ever *not* a jerk?"

"Not ever," he confirmed.

"What about when you were human?"

His smart-ass grin faded. "I don't talk about that."

"But you wanted me to know your human name. And that you and Bishop were brothers. Care to share any more about that? Either of you?"

His unfriendly gaze moved to the left as the door clanged shut. Roth had returned from his temporary pity party. He looked at us sullenly but didn't say anything.

"That was just a test of the emergency broadcast system,

sweetness," Kraven said. "Don't let it go to your head that I was trying to get personal with you."

"Wouldn't dream of it, *James*." I think I'd just discovered the demon's Achilles' heel. Talking about his human life was off-limits. But I guess I wanted to test those limits just a little. It had been one of those nights.

My using his real first name earned me a look of sheer disdain. "Sucked any souls out of mouths tonight, gray girl?"

"No. Stabbed any helpless victims?"

"Our victims aren't helpless," Bishop said.

My gaze shot back to him. "Sure, they aren't."

"You haven't seen a gray after they've fed too much."

I frowned as a memory of Carly flitted through my mind.

"Samantha." Bishop squeezed my hand to get me to keep looking at him instead of the jerk of a demon. "What happened? What did you see?"

My throat thickened. "My friend…I think she's in trouble."

"The one you were with the other night?"

I nodded, a sick feeling in the pit of my stomach. "I'm worried about her."

"Did you see her feed?" Zach asked.

I didn't reply right away and they all exchanged a look that made me nervous. I couldn't admit what Carly had done. I couldn't put her in danger. I knew what they'd do to her if they learned the truth. "Bishop, you said you can restore my soul. Well, I want you to restore her soul, too."

"Restore souls?" Roth finally spoke up. "Somebody's living in a dreamworld, aren't they?"

I looked at him sharply. "Excuse me?"

"You can't restore a human's soul once it's gone." He glanced at Bishop who was sending a dark glare his way. "What?"

My mouth was suddenly as dry as the desert. "But Bishop said—"

"Yeah, I'm sure he would have said anything to get you to use that mysterious mojo of yours, right? Good going, angel." A smile stretched across Roth's handsome face. "Nice and devious. I approve."

For the second—or third?—time tonight, it felt as if the floor had fallen away beneath my feet and I was about to fall into a pit of darkness. "Bishop…is that true?"

Bishop gave Roth a dark look that might completely shrivel a weaker demon to the size and consistency of a raisin. When Bishop finally turned his gaze to me his fierce expression had only softened a fraction.

"If there is a way to restore your soul I will find it."

I let go of his hand and staggered back from him. "You lied to me? You—you told me angels don't lie."

"Oh, angels can definitely lie when they need to," Kraven said. "Trust me on that. They just prefer not to since it makes them feel all dirty inside."

Bishop's jaw tensed. "It wasn't a lie. I told you I'd help—that I believe there's a way. And when I go back to Heaven, I'll find it."

Panic gripped my throat. "That's not what you promised me!"

His brows drew together. "Yes, it was."

"Uh-oh. Trouble in paradise," Kraven murmured. "News at eleven."

Despite my other misgivings, I'd had faith that Bishop was being truthful with me about this. And now, to learn that it had all been a lie—that this was it for me and for Carly…

He was no better than a demon.

Before Bishop had a chance to say anything else, I stormed

away from him and back down the dark hallway to the open door. I made it outside the church by the broken sign before I had to take a moment to try to get control over myself. I braced my hands on my thighs and gulped in big mouthfuls of air.

I'd agreed to his deal and done everything I'd promised to do, and all the time he'd known he might not be able to hold up his end of the bargain.

I'd fallen for a guy who'd promised to save me only so he could get something in return. My heart felt like it had broken into pieces, scattered on the front lawn of this abandoned church just like that sign.

How could he do this to me?

I didn't remember his exact words, but he'd left me with the certainty that he had a solution. *The* solution. I wanted to give him my trust—and, yes, my heart, too—but how could I do that now?

Angels might not usually lie, but that didn't mean they couldn't shamelessly manipulate a girl who'd developed a major crush on a beautiful, blue-eyed angel.

"Samantha, stop!" Bishop rushed after me while the others stayed inside. He grabbed hard onto my wrist to keep me from going any farther.

I slapped him as hard as I could across his face. The stunned and outraged look he gave me was almost comical. I guess no hysterical teenage girl had ever hit him before.

I felt something hot and wet on my cheeks and realized the tears I'd been holding back all night were starting to fall. I wiped at them with annoyance. "You led me to believe there was a way to restore my soul, but you were just guessing. Why would you do that to me? You know how much this means to me!"

He let out a snarl of frustration. "What? You think I'm a shameless jerk who gets off on lying to innocent girls? I thought you knew me better than that."

"I don't know you at all! You and Kraven *are* brothers. Maybe you're a lot more alike than I thought. Maybe you should be a demon, too."

His jaw tightened. "You're right, I should be."

My breath caught. "What?"

"A long time ago, I was one of the bad guys." His face was stone. "Real bad, Samantha—you don't know. But I've changed. New name, new job…new existence. Everything's different now."

He'd knocked me totally off balance with this unexpected glimpse into his past. But, really, for all I knew he was just lying again. I glared at him with more intensity than I'd ever felt in my life, our gazes locked on each other. Nothing existed at that moment but the two of us. "You're *still* one of the bad guys, Bishop. This just proves it."

I forced myself to turn away from him, but he grabbed my arm and spun me back around so he could look at me angrily. "Did I knowingly lead you to believe something that wasn't one hundred percent true? Maybe I did. But you said you *hated* me. I had to say something that would keep you around. No matter what."

"I do hate you."

His fingers bit into my shoulders. "That's your decision. But when I go back to Heaven, I *will* find an answer. I will save you."

"Leave me alone." I pulled away from him and started to walk again.

He was persistent, though. He still followed me, which only

made this harder. Having him near me, even now, made it too difficult to think straight.

He said he was one of the bad guys.

I shivered. Who was he? What had he done—and how long ago? And why had he become an angel if Kraven became a demon?

Finally, I stopped and turned to face him. I glared up at his face. Despite the shadows surrounding us, there was a dim, unnerving glow in his beautiful eyes as he watched me.

As I was trying to form words around my racing thoughts, something surprising caught my eye. I stared up into the sky behind him.

He frowned. "What is it?"

It took me a moment to find my voice. "Kraven said there were supposed to be four of you on your team, right? Two angels and two demons?"

"Yeah, four."

I kept staring at the column of light that had just appeared in the night sky. "Looks like you're getting a bonus member."

He turned to look in the same direction. "You see another searchlight?"

I just nodded.

He stayed silent, but I knew what he wanted to say. He wanted me to lead him to the right spot, just as I'd done with the others. Sounded like somebody had their signals crossed—literally—when it came to the total number of demons and angels currently in the city. If there was another one tonight, then there might be even more than that.

My possibility of getting back what Stephen had taken from me had fizzled and died tonight, no matter what the angel was ready to promise me now.

The question was, did I completely blame him for what

he'd let me believe? Would I have done the exact same thing in his position, knowing what was at stake if I couldn't find the others?

Damn it, I probably would have.

It didn't make any of this right, nor did it lessen the anger or betrayal I felt toward him, but part of me did understand.

He wanted to help me. He just wasn't totally sure if he could.

If he'd put it that bluntly, maybe I wouldn't have agreed to help him in the first place.

I hissed out a long breath. "This is it, Bishop. This is *definitely* the last time I'm ever going to help you."

Two of us could play the lying game.

Natalie wanted the dagger so I could help her leave the city. I wasn't ready to do that just yet. My heart ached from hearing her tell me about my parents, but I couldn't do what she wanted me to do. Not yet, anyway.

But I also couldn't lead Bishop to the Source and let him destroy my aunt—the only connection I had to my real father.

Looked like I was still right in the middle. It sure didn't feel like the best location to hang out for very long.

It almost felt routine now, following the searchlight that would lead us to an angel or a demon. I kept several feet between us so I wouldn't feel as drawn to him as I normally did. Didn't help much. Even with my lingering pain over feeling betrayed and lied to, my attraction to him was stronger than ever before as I felt his heated gaze on me while we walked.

So damn unfair.

This searchlight didn't lead us too many blocks away from the abandoned church. It was practically deserted in this neighborhood, compared to where we'd found Roth on the busy downtown sidewalk in the shopping district. Abandoned, empty, lonely—depressing, really. A good chunk of Trinity was like this now, as if any life that had existed before had died off, leaving a shadowy ghost town behind.

The light led us to another boy, not that I was all that surprised about his gender. He was an inch or two shorter than Bishop, which still meant he was at least six feet tall, with cocoa-colored skin and dark eyes. Attractive, of course, no big surprise there, either. He wore ill-fitting khaki pants and a green button-down shirt. His black hair was so short it was nearly shaved.

He had his arms crossed and he trudged along the sidewalk, headed slowly toward downtown.

"That's him?" Bishop said.

The sound of his smooth, deep voice sank into me and made me shiver. I wanted to forgive him, even while memories of his betrayal still swirled all around me.

My conflicting emotions toward Bishop weren't helpful right now. All they could do was distract me.

"Yeah," I finally said. "I don't get it, though. Why would they tell Kraven there's supposed to be four of you and then send another one?"

"No idea." He didn't sound happy about that.

I had a flash of what happened last time with Roth and the worry over us making a mistake and actually killing some innocent kid. "Just make sure to check him first. Don't just, you know, *do it*."

"I will. You can leave now." He paused. "If you want to."

I eyed him sideways while we kept walking and I drew my coat closer to block the chill. Since we weren't exactly walking hand in hand, I felt the cold night all too well. "And miss all the excitement?"

He kept his tense attention on the kid. "I know you don't like this part."

"Bishop, the day I start to like witnessing someone get stabbed through the heart is not a day I'm looking forward to."

He shook his head. "You've been so brave about all of this."

That made me snort humorlessly. "That's not exactly a word I'd use to describe myself."

He finally met my gaze and my heart betrayed me by skipping a beat. I guess it had already recovered from being broken. Fickle heart.

"I just wish I understood how you can do this," he said.

He had no idea what the truth really was—that I was a…a *nexus,* like Natalie said. Since I wasn't ready to share that at the moment, he'd just have to keep guessing.

Bishop pulled me to a stop. The kid had also stopped walking and turned to face us.

"Are you following me?" he asked.

"Us?" I was the first to speak. "Um, maybe. Hi there. How are you tonight?"

He looked at me like I might be a bit crazy. "This is a bad neighborhood, you know. Dangerous at night."

"Your point?"

"What do you want with me?"

Bishop stepped forward. "We know you're lost and we want to help you."

The kid's eyes weren't as dark as I thought they were at a distance. They were a medium brown, flecked with gold. They tracked back to me and his brows drew together. "Do I know you?"

"Me?" I pointed at myself.

"Yeah, you look familiar."

Bishop and I exchanged a glance. “It’s all yours,” I told him, waving my hand and stepping backward.

That earned me the barest hint of one of his rare but amazing smiles. It worked like a lightning bolt right to my heart. My heart honestly couldn’t make up its mind about the angel—it was either broken or doing backflips.

Bishop turned back to the kid. “Have you dreamed about Samantha? Is that how you know her?”

“Dreamed about her? Actually…yeah, I have. Is that strange, or what?”

“Not strange. It was a sign that we’re here to help you right now.”

The boy frowned, but then his attention shifted to something behind us and his eyes widened with fear. “I’ve dreamed about something like that, too.”

I turned to look and a gasp caught in my throat.

A large man was barreling down the sidewalk. He wore a dark blue business suit, which was wrinkled and dirty. I could smell him from ten feet away—like something rotten found at the bottom of a garbage can. His face was so pale white it seemed to glow like the moon in the darkness.

And his eyes—they were black and glazed, with no emotion or intelligence in them. Only hunger.

They were like Carly’s eyes had been. It was enough to freeze me in place with horror.

Bishop shoved me out of the way as the man stormed toward us, and then Bishop was tackled to the ground, landing hard on his back. I shrieked, thinking that this monster was going to hurt Bishop, but I couldn’t figure out what to grab or kick to help him.

But the angel had been chosen for this mission for a reason. I’d only seen a glimpse of his fighting skills before. Tonight I got to see more. He slammed his fist into the man's face and used the leverage to flip him onto his back. The man fought back, but Bishop had taken full control of the situation.

"Can you understand me?" Bishop demanded. "Can you still think clearly enough to answer me?"

A line of drool slid out of the man's mouth as he powered forward, fighting hard and wildly against Bishop, but not making any indication that he understood what he was asked.

"Last chance," Bishop growled, getting to his feet to stand in front of me, as if trying to block me from any harm. "Can you hear me? Or has the hunger taken your mind completely?"

The man was back on his feet and he surged toward Bishop.

Suddenly the golden dagger was in Bishop's hand and he arched it toward the man's chest where it met its mark. I clamped a hand over my mouth to stop from screaming. It had all happened so fast.

A high-pitched screech that didn't sound human escaped the man's throat as Bishop yanked the blade back out. The man fell hard to his knees.

"Samantha, get back!" Bishop grabbed hold of my coat sleeve and pulled me away so there was a dozen feet between us and the monster who'd just attacked us.

The kid we'd been following also leaped by us, just as a swirling black vortex appeared out of absolutely nowhere. Even in the dark of night, this was even darker, a pitch-black hole hanging in the middle of the air about four feet in diameter. With its appearance came a horrible whirling sound, like a tornado, so loud it made it nearly impossible to think.

It felt as if a powerful vacuum was drawing us into it. The three of us slid forward on the pavement toward the vortex. I just stared at it with wide eyes, terrified. Bishop kept a tight grip on me to keep me from moving any closer to it, his rubber-soled shoes braced against the ground as an anchor. I reached out and took hold of the other kid's arm.

The man with the black eyes was closest to the vortex. I felt his gaze bore into me for a long, horrible moment. Finally, the man hissed out his last breath and slumped backward.

The very next moment, it was as if the vortex literally reached out and yanked him back into the darkness. One moment the swirling, thunderous darkness was there, the next it shrank away and disappeared, leaving nothing behind but silence.

My heart thundered in my ears as I stayed exactly where I was for a few seconds, not moving, not breathing. The kid next to me was staring in shock at the space where the black hole had just been.

"What the hell was that?" he managed to ask after a moment.

"That," Bishop said, "was the Hollow."

chapter 18

The kid stared at him. "You killed that guy and he got sucked into a big black hole."

"Pretty much," Bishop confirmed.

"And you're supposed to help me?" He shot a glance at me. "What about you? How can you be so damn calm about what just happened?"

"Do I look calm?" I gripped my hands together to keep them from shaking. "I guess I'm only screaming on the inside right now."

"What's going on?"

Bishop eyed the boy. "Show me your back."

"What?"

"Do it," he snapped like a pissed-off drill sergeant. Whatever small amount of patience Bishop had had earlier had all but disappeared.

The kid glanced warily at the knife Bishop still held. "Yeah, okay. Whatever you say. You really want to see my back so much? You got it."

He turned a little and pulled up his shirt enough for me to

see there was an imprint of wings on his dark skin—and it was just like Bishop's and Zach's mark.

A third angel.

"Crazy tattoo, right?" He pulled his shirt back down. "I can't remember much of anything lately, but I have no idea what would have possessed me to get something like—"

He gasped as Bishop sank the dagger into him. I watched in horror, not expecting it to happen so quickly. I hadn't even had a chance to catch my breath.

The kid dropped to his knees and looked at me with confusion on his pained face. "I thought you wanted to help me."

"I'm sorry," I choked out. It was all I could think of to say. All that I could say.

The boy fell all the way to the ground and let out his last breath.

I braced myself, thinking for a moment the vortex would open again. I jumped when Bishop touched my arm.

"Why doesn't the Hollow open again? He—he's *dead*." I couldn't look at the body.

"It's not the same as a true death. The ritual is specific and the dagger knows the difference. Think of it like an invisible shield surrounding each of the team members, protecting them when they entered the city—enough to fool the city's barrier. It also blocks their memories and any abilities they have. This dagger cuts through that so their true selves can be returned."

The dagger knew the difference?

It could cut through the shield. Natalie thought it could also cut through the barrier surrounding the city—if it was in my hands.

"Okay." I just nodded, stunned. "Talented dagger. Does it talk, too?"

"Not recently." He gave me a half grin and wiped the dagger off on his jeans before sheathing it. He crouched down next to the kid to check his back again. "Maybe Heaven felt that reinforcements were needed already. It's been a week since I arrived. That was as long as I was originally given to find the others."

I just stared back in the direction where the entrance to the Hollow had been. It wasn't something I ever wanted to see again. Natalie had returned from that—from somewhere that was supposed to be one-way only.

"That man was the type of gray you've been telling me about," I said, my voice shaky. "The ones you can't reason with, who have no self-control when they feed too much."

"That's right." He rose to his feet again. "There's no coming back from that."

"He *was* like a zombie." I'd always loved zombie movies, even the really bad ones like the *Zombie Queen* sequel. But that—what I'd just seen—that had been real.

"That's why we're out patrolling the streets every night. This one—" he nodded at the new angel, currently DOA "—can help with that while I focus on finding the Source."

I bit my bottom lip. "Are you close? Any leads?"

His gaze scanned the dark street before it returned to mine. "I'm positive she hangs out at that nightclub of yours. Stephen was lying to me. I think I saw her the other night—she matches the description of the demon from last time. Dark hair, brown eyes, thin, twentyish."

I fought to keep my expression neutral. "You're like a detective."

"The sooner I finish this, the sooner I can go back to Heaven and find a way to help you."

God, I felt so torn. I didn't want him to hurt Natalie, even though he claimed to only want to "talk" to her. I worried what that talk would lead to if he didn't get the answers he wanted.

I paced back and forth on the sidewalk. Not one car had driven by since we'd arrived. It just showed how deserted this part of the city was. At the moment, that was a blessing. This wasn't an unseen alley, this was the middle of the street, and we were currently babysitting a temporarily dead angel.

Since we were stuck here waiting for him to wake up, it gave me a chance to ask all sorts of questions. Bishop had no chance to dodge them.

"If you were to stab that angel again with that dagger, it would kill him, right?"

"Yes."

"And would the Hollow open up? Or is it just for demons and grays?"

"The Hollow takes anything supernatural that dies here in the human world—even angels. It's something to be avoided at all costs. But it happens."

"Wrong place, wrong time. Doesn't seem fair."

"Sometimes it isn't."

He thought the Hollow was the end. But Natalie was proof that that wasn't true.

"You okay?" When he touched my arm his warmth sank into me. When he smiled, it made me light-headed.

I nodded. "I'll be better when that angel stands up again."

"He will."

"You have faith?"

His knee-weakening smile widened. "I try to."

The cold breeze in the air picked up and I cinched the belt on my coat tighter and shoved my hands deep into the pockets.

"I meant what I told you before," Bishop said after a moment of silence passed between us. "When I get back to Heaven, I'll find a way to help you."

"And Carly, too."

He nodded. "Carly, too."

I swallowed past the lump in my throat. More time. More questions. "Why didn't you tell me about Kraven?"

The smile was gone just like that. "Because there's nothing to tell."

"How long ago were you human? You—you said it was a long time ago."

"Not long enough." Despite his vague answers, there was no mistaking the bitter tone to his voice.

"And when you said you were one of the bad guys—"

"I shouldn't have told you that."

"I want to know more. I mean, you're an *angel* so, um…" My mouth felt dry. "You were redeemed, or whatever, for what happened."

His expression grew grimmer. "Sometimes I wonder."

"Tell me more. Tell me—" I was about to say something else, ask something else, when I heard a groan. The angel had finally woken up. It was a huge relief—every minute that passed had made me wonder if he'd be the exception to the golden-dagger shield-busting rule. His eyelashes fluttered open and he slowly propped himself up on his elbows.

"I wouldn't exactly call that a good time," he said, "but it is entirely effective."

Without thinking twice, or worrying that he might react the same as Roth had, I went to his side and helped him up to his feet. Call me Florence Nightingale. I checked his chest to find a tear on his shirt and blood on the fabric, but the wound had healed completely.

"How are you feeling?" I asked.

"Bruised, but intact."

Bishop moved closer to give the new angel his own inspection. "I'm Bishop."

"Yeah, they told me all about you before I left. And what to expect from that dagger there, not that it helped, since I promptly forgot everything, including my own name." The guy grinned and clasped Bishop's outstretched hand. "I'm Connor." He glanced at me. "And you are?"

"Samantha."

Connor looked at Bishop. "You know she's a gray, right?"

"Well aware. But she's different from the others, so take it easy. Without her, we wouldn't have been able to find you. She can see the searchlights. We can't."

"Cool." He still looked a bit guarded now that his senses had alerted him to the fact that I was one of the monsters. "So you have superpowers, huh?"

I tried to smile at him. "I can also read your mind, if I'm so inclined. And zap you if you're mean to me."

Connor cocked his head to the side as he regarded me. "Huh. Sounds a bit like a *nexus*."

I stopped breathing. Then I struggled to keep my expression neutral. It was a secret that I didn't want revealed to anyone.

"Sure," Bishop said with an amused grin. "The daughter of an angel and a demon is standing right here in front of us. I think I'd already know something like that."

"It was just a wild guess." Connor shrugged. "I don't know."

Slowly, the grin faded from Bishop's face and a frown replaced it, as if he was giving the possibility more thought. But when Bishop spoke again, I was deeply relieved it was to Connor. "I'd heard there were to be only four of us. You're the fifth."

"I'm always late to the party. Sorry about that. Feel free to pay me back by stabbing me through the chest." He rubbed the spot over his heart. "Oh, wait. You already did that."

"How long have you been here?"

Connor scratched his head. "A couple of days. Is this a fun city to hang out in? I have been needing a vacation for a while."

"This isn't a vacation."

Connor slapped him on the back. "Sarcasm, my friend. It's my thing. Get used to it. So are you going to intro me to the others, or what?"

Bishop gave him a sidelong glance. "Oh, they're going to *love* you."

The three of us walked back to St. Andrew's in silence, apart from a few random comments from Connor. I knew who the joker of the group was going to be, but I didn't mind. Frankly the fact that he wasn't a demon had already won me over.

He'd made a wild guess and nailed what I was. It had seriously freaked me out.

I felt fragile, like a piece of glass left on the edge of a tall counter, about ready to crash to the ground at any moment. My emotions were hard to control, but that was exactly what I had to keep doing. I couldn't let myself break down now.

Seeing that gray for myself, though, the proof I'd been hoping didn't exist…it had scared me deeply. I'd wanted to believe that all grays were like me. That they thought like me, not wanting to feed. Not wanting to hurt anyone.

But an image of Carly kissing Paul in the booth at Crave earlier haunted me. She hadn't seemed to realize how bad it was and what it could do to her.

But she hadn't seen what I had.

Natalie told me that losing a soul wasn't harmful to a

human, that it freed them. Had that been a lie, as well? Was anyone in this damn city telling me the truth?

The thought was like a clawed hand that took hold of my throat and kept squeezing tighter and tighter. It was best that I didn't say anything right now. Best that I went home and thought about all of this on my own.

"I should go," I said when we got back to the church. "I don't want to go back in there and see Kraven and Roth again."

Bishop turned to me. "I understand. But—wait here. I'll take Connor inside and then walk you home."

I crossed my arms and leaned against the brick exterior near the open door. "Okay."

He looked surprised that I'd agreed without any argument. A smile touched his lips. "Two minutes."

I just nodded, and he and Connor disappeared into the building.

Those two minutes felt like a long time to be left alone in the dark. And my hunger continued to rage. It had gotten worse since I'd left the nightclub, going from a dull throb to a thunderous roar. Maybe I should have had some of those half-price chicken wings while I'd had the chance.

When Bishop returned, the expression on my face must have caused him some alarm. He was at my side in an instant. "Samantha, what's wrong?"

And that did it. The fragile glass was knocked off the edge of the counter and crashed to the ground. I started to cry. Sob. I'd even go so far as to say I was wailing uncontrollably. It was like I couldn't hold it in any longer. The dam had finally broken.

Bishop put his arms around me and pulled me against him. He stroked the long hair back off my face. Through my blurry vision, all I could see was him. It was all dark behind him, cold except for his touch.

"What?" he said again, almost demanding. "What happened? What's wrong?"

"Everything's wrong. I—I'm so scared."

That only made his expression fiercer than it was to start with. "I know I've kept the full truth from you, I've scared you over and over, I've put you in danger so many times." He frowned deeper. "I'm really not helping my case much with this line of reasoning, am I?"

I managed a small laugh through my tears. "Don't become a lawyer."

"What I'm trying to say is that, despite our shaky start, I'm here for you. I'm here for you like you've been here for me."

My heart clenched at his words. "You are?"

He nodded. "You told me earlier that I had to learn to accept help from others. That's hard for me. I've always done my own thing, thinking I was invulnerable. Trust me, I have a whole lot of pride for an angel. It's one of the reasons I was first in line to volunteer for this mission without being shielded like the others. I thought I could handle it, no problem."

"You've done really well," I said.

"No, I haven't. I've been a mess from day one. I was cocky to think it wouldn't be a big deal. It is. I tried to deny it, to fight it, but I can't. Not on my own. Not without your help. And now you need help, too."

The whole time he made his speech, he'd been stroking the hair back off my face, his touch bringing me much needed warmth this cold night.

"I do need help," I finally said. "And it's not because of what happened between us. It's…something else."

"What is it?"

Still, I was afraid to say it out loud. I didn't even know how to get into this and sound halfway cohesive. "What Connor said about me earlier. About me being a *nexus*..."

He searched my face. "It's true, isn't it?"

I just nodded. I half expected him to push back from me, maybe go inside and tell the others, but he stayed right where he was.

"Why didn't you tell me this before?"

I tried to catch my breath, but that seemed impossible right now. "I didn't know, not until tonight."

"How did you find out?"

I hesitated a moment before I said anything else. "I didn't know for sure that I was adopted until earlier tonight. All my life, I had no idea..." I trailed off, looking up at him with uncertainty.

He gazed back at me with undivided attention. "Who told you about this? How did you learn the truth?"

"The Source," I said it so softly it was no more than a whisper. "It's my aunt. My real father's sister—she's a demon."

Anyone else would have reacted with shock or, more likely, total disbelief. But not Bishop. He took it in stride.

"You've met her," he said.

I nodded and it took a moment before I could continue. "Natalie's the one you've been looking for. And you were right...she does go to Crave regularly. That's where I saw her tonight—Tuesday night, too."

"Is she the same demon as last time? The anomaly I told you about?"

I nodded, feeling ill. "She was pushed into the Hollow."

He frowned deeply. "And she's back? How?"

"I don't know how, but she is. And now if she kisses someone—she can create more who have the same hungers as she does. Before, it was just her." My brain felt like it had the consistency of mush as I tried not to make the situation even worse than it already was. "She told me my mother—an angel named Anna—was killed. And my father jumped into the Hollow after her. He must be back, too. Natalie and my father both escaped the Hollow. So it's not what everyone thinks it is. It must mean that if they can, then there are others that aren't killed, that were just sucked in by accident, or whatever, that can escape. It's not one-way—or at least, it isn't anymore."

If my words shocked Bishop or freaked him out, he didn't let on that they did. He braced a hand against the brick wall behind my left shoulder and studied me intently, absorbing every word I spoke. "I'm glad you told me this."

"I was going to keep it a secret, but I couldn't. You needed to know."

He cast a glance back at the door to the church. "Don't tell the others about the reason behind your abilities. I don't want them to know. Connor was only guessing before. Like I said, it's incredibly rare. Heaven and Hell…well, they don't have a great appreciation for anything outside of regulations. And that's exactly what a *nexus* is, especially the ones they're not even aware exist." His eyes met mine again. "They'd view you as something very dangerous."

I took that in. "And how do you view me?"

"*Very* dangerous." His gaze sank into me for a moment, but then his jaw tensed. "I want you to introduce me to your aunt."

I tensed. "Bishop, I don't know…"

"I need to understand what her plan is, what she wants. And if she can stop this before it gets any worse."

"She told me she thinks the other grays' hunger will fade.

That *my* hunger will fade. Then grays won't be a risk anymore. Is that possible?"

His brows drew together. "I don't know. I hope so. This is why I need more information."

My breath caught. "Roth seems to go hunting for the fun of it. Does he care which kind of gray he kills?"

"Roth's...different. The demons view this mission as more of a scoreboard. But I've made him well aware of the rules. And if I can talk to Natalie, figure out some other solution, maybe this can end without anyone else getting hurt."

"Do you think you might be able to help her?"

He nodded. "If she wants to be helped."

"You mean it?"

"I mean it." He stroked my hair back and pushed it behind my ears, keeping his warm hand on the side of my face. His heat sank into me. "When we first met, I thought there was something special about you."

"And what do you think now?" The closer he got to me the more difficult it was to think normally. Or logically. He smelled so good it was all I could focus on.

He raised an eyebrow. "You really want to know?"

I nodded.

"What do I think now?" he whispered. "I think that even though you keep saving me, I'm still in danger whenever I'm close to you."

I could barely breathe. "Danger? How?"

"Like every single time I'm close to you, I want to do this."

When he brushed his lips against mine, I stopped thinking. My hands tangled in the soft material of his shirt, then slid up over his shoulders.

"That's kind of a coincidence," I whispered. "Because I feel exactly the same way."

He kissed me again, soft at first, but it quickly grew deeper and more passionate. Until this moment, I would have had to say my kiss with Stephen had been the best I'd ever had, even though it had ended badly. But this was…*way* better. No wonder I'd never fallen hard for any guy at school before. I'd been waiting for Heaven to send one directly to me.

I pulled him even closer, changing our positions so he was the one against the wall. I had to stand on my tiptoes to keep kissing him, my hands now sliding up into his hair.

"You taste so good," I murmured against his lips.

He did. He tasted good—heavenly. Delicious. My hunger rose up and spilled over and as the kiss grew and grew, my hunger finally started to fade. I'd never experienced anything so satisfying in my life, anything so good, so sweet and intoxicating. I never wanted to stop kissing him.

There were no more worries, no more problems, only him. His kiss. I wanted it all—every delicious piece until there was nothing left…

Suddenly I felt a tight and painful grip on my arm. I released Bishop with a yelp and glared into the face of Kraven. Roth stood right next to him.

I wanted to kill them both.

"What?" I snarled.

I expected some smart-ass reply, but both demons just stared at me with eyes filled with shock before moving to Bishop. I turned to look at him to see he had begun to sink down to the ground, his back still pressed against the wall. His eyes were glazed, his skin pale white, and there were dark lines around his mouth.

Watching through the fog surrounding my mind, I tried to piece together what I was seeing, what it meant, but it didn't make any sense. He looked just like Paul had when I'd stopped Carly from kissing him.

She'd been feeding on his soul.

And, even though it should have been impossible, I'd been doing the exact same thing to Bishop.

chapter 19

Angels didn't have souls.

But I didn't care that it didn't make sense. I just wanted more. I wanted to be left alone so I could kiss Bishop again. There was nothing else I wanted.

Before I could move toward him, Kraven grabbed tightly onto my arms and peered into my eyes.

"Oh, hell, gray girl," he said grimly. "Just couldn't keep your pretty little lips off him forever, could you?"

"Let go of me." It was like I was hearing myself from a mile away. I had to get back to Bishop. I had to kiss him again. I wanted more—so much more. I struggled against Kraven's hold on me, trying to push and claw my way out of his grip.

"Sorry about this," the demon said.

"What?"

He smacked me hard enough to make my ears ring. I yelped and my hand shot to my burning cheek.

And reality set in as fast as a bolt of lightning. The fog surrounding me disappeared and the horror of what I'd done became crystal clear.

"Good, you're back," Kraven said, nodding. "Didn't want to have to knock you out. Or did I? I guess we'll never know."

I stared at him. "What happened?"

"What happened?" Kraven repeated, the mocking tone returning to his voice. "Don't you think that's painfully obvious by now, sweetness?"

Out of the corner of my eye I saw the angels join us and take in the scene. Zach looked shocked, but Connor looked bleak.

Roth, as expected, just glared at me, his arms crossed over his chest.

I shook my head. "But he's an angel."

My gaze tracked to Bishop to see he was slowly recovering. The lines around his mouth had faded to nothing and color was returning to his face. Shakily he got up from the ground, still leaning back against the cold brick wall, and he touched his mouth, staring at me with shock and confusion—a mirror of how I looked at him.

"Sorry to interrupt your romantic interlude," Kraven said. "But we can sense when an attack occurs nearby."

I felt sick right down to my bones.

"But I don't have a soul," Bishop said. He hadn't looked away from me for a moment. While he still looked confused and shaken, there was still desire in his gaze that only continued to grow. I remembered my kiss with Stephen—it hadn't been unpleasant, despite what it was doing to me. It had been exciting, exhilarating and filled with passion. I would have kept kissing him if he hadn't stopped.

And the kiss with Bishop had been so much better than that.

I still ached to kiss him again. And if no one else was here, I think he might have let me.

"Why were you kissing a gray in the first place?" Roth

asked, clearly confused and disgusted by the thought of it. "Some sort of experiment?"

"Doubt that," Connor said. "Bishop doesn't strike me as all that scientific."

"Bishop—" Zach moved toward him, concern on his face. "How do you feel?"

"Angels don't have souls," Bishop said again.

"Fallen angels do." Connor leaned against the wall a few feet away from him, watching him warily.

Bishop blinked at him. "Yeah, it's an anchor to keep them in the human world—a punishment so they have no hope of returning to Heaven. They're cast out forever. But I'm here only temporarily, for the mission. I'm going back."

Connor didn't reply to that, but his expression remained grim. It was different from the sarcastic guy we'd walked back to the church with.

I almost said something to defend Bishop, but I bit my tongue and stayed where I was, shivering in the shadows. There was nothing in the other angel's expression that made me think he was speaking anything but the truth right now.

A soul. Bishop had a soul.

And I'd kissed him because I'd felt that hunger for him from the moment we first met.

This wasn't happening.

"Did you know already?" I asked, my voice barely audible.

Connor looked at me. "Yes."

"How?"

"It's why I was sent here." He turned to study Bishop. "Something went very wrong when you left. Somebody screwed up. They made you fall. For real."

Bishop stared at him, his brow furrowed. "How could that happen?"

Connor's expression tensed. "There are those who want you to fail, for this mission to fail. The gatekeeper who sent you was one of the old guard—the *very* old guard. A zealot who thought the only answer to purge the human world of this new infection would be to destroy the city all Sodom-and-Gomorrah style. But to do that, you'd need to fail. When I got here, I expected you to be in bad shape, but you weren't. So I figured maybe they'd been wrong and didn't say anything. A soul usually messes up a fallen angel's head big-time."

Bishop just stared at Connor with shock as this sank in.

Zach's expression was tense. "The rest of us were protected. But if nobody found us…we'd still be wandering the streets with no idea who we were."

"Yeah," Kraven agreed, eyeing me. "If you hadn't found us, gray girl, we would have wandered the city forever."

"She's a damn gray," Roth snapped. "Is this enough proof for you? She needs to die."

"Back off," Bishop growled at him. "She didn't know this would happen."

"She found us and that gives her a pass," Kraven said. "This time, anyway."

Roth sank back into the shadows. I was surprised they weren't all ganging up on me at this point. I'd just proven that I was every bit as horrible as they thought I was.

I wanted to go to Bishop, to touch him, but I knew that would be the worst thing I could do right now. "This—gatekeeper who did this to him. Where is he now?"

"Punished. I hope he sees the irony when he's cast out of Heaven for his crimes." Connor swept his gaze around the group. "There was no way to know how badly Bishop was affected by this. The barrier blocks nearly all attempts to monitor the situation. So they sent me to help."

I stared at him. "But if he couldn't find the others, he couldn't find you, either."

He nodded grimly. "See, I didn't know he couldn't spot the searchlights. I just knew he'd be messed up mentally. Hindsight's a bitch, isn't it? But now I'm here and I'm in it to win it. Five are better than four, I say. The mission stands. This is just a minor setback."

I gazed around, as if the night might have answers. The only light out here came from the full moon above and a lamp over by the street. A pair of headlights moved along in front of the church from a rarely seen car. I scanned the sky, but it was dark. No more searchlights, just stars.

"Sodom-and-Gomorrah style," I murmured. "Just like my vision."

"What?" Connor asked.

"I—I had a vision that the city was destroyed. Everyone gone. It was...epic."

He frowned. "Do you usually have disturbing visions of the future?"

I cleared my throat. "Not usually. But is that a possibility? If the old guard wants to do that, will they? If the mission fails?"

"The mission *won't* fail," Kraven said. "So it's a moot point. Put that out of your mind, sweetness. We have it covered."

Somehow, his assurance didn't help. A chill went through me then, which was surprising. I thought I'd gone completely numb.

Bishop raked a hand through his hair, his posture slumped as if he'd grown very tired. What I'd done to him had weakened him. "I can't go back now."

"Don't say that." I moved toward him, but stopped myself from getting too close. Even a few feet away his scent made me dizzy and triggered my hunger again. I wanted to kiss him so badly it was like I was going into withdrawal from keeping my distance. He affected me now even more than ever before. I clenched my hands until my short fingernails bit into my palms. The pain helped clear my mind.

"Why? It's true. I might be crazy a lot of the time, but I'm not stupid." He held my gaze, his face strained as if he might feel the same need to get closer to me, but then he tore his attention from me to look at Connor. "I was supposed to be extracted early, once I dealt with the Source. I got in through the barrier, so I could be pulled back out. That won't happen now. And with this soul inside me, I might not get back at all, not if they can't reverse this."

"I'll do what I can when I get back," Connor said.

"Have you ever heard of a fallen angel returning to Heaven?"

Connor didn't speak for a moment. "No."

"Exactly my point."

My heart twisted. It sounded as if he'd already accepted that this was the end.

Going back to Heaven and being cured of the madness that plagued him—it was all he'd wanted since he'd arrived, his beacon. If he couldn't go back, he'd be like the homeless guy I'd met. I realized then that I didn't even know what the guy's name was. I hadn't asked.

"I met someone," I said, breaking the silence. "A homeless man who hangs out near Crave. He was kind of out of it, rambling. When I touched him, I felt the spark similar to when I touch Bishop. He's an angel, too."

A fallen angel.

"Not surprised," Kraven said. "There are plenty of fallen angels in the human world. Heaven has a way higher fail rate than Hell. When a demon stays in the human world, it's usually a reward, not a punishment. Unless he's been officially exiled."

Bishop stared at me and I saw the pain shadowing his eyes as he absently touched his lips again. His gaze flicked to Kraven. "Did you know this?"

"Which part?" the demon asked. "I'm having trouble keeping track."

"That I was fallen? That what was wrong with me wasn't just disorientation caused by the barrier?"

Kraven's lips thinned. "I saw the signs. And yeah, I thought it could be this. I wasn't sure."

"Why didn't you say anything?"

There was nothing compassionate in Kraven's harsh expression. "It's not my fault you didn't do your homework. I guess it's just like old times, huh? Trust the wrong person, you end up screwed."

With no warning, Bishop attacked him, grabbing the demon and slamming him down hard on the ground. If Kraven had been a human, it probably would have broken his back. Bishop even got a couple punches in, directly to the demon's face, before Zach and Connor forcibly pulled him back and tried to restrain him. He looked completely crazy right now, and it scared me. I was frozen in place—all I could do was watch and try to make sense of all this.

"Get control over yourself," Zach warned Bishop. "You're only making things worse."

It was the first time I'd heard an edge of anger in the angel's voice. Maybe he wasn't always the kindhearted healer.

Kraven wiped the blood at the corner of his mouth and pushed up off the ground. His eyes glowed red. "Yeah, I know. It sucks. But you can't blame me for this. It's not my fault."

"You should have told me," Bishop hissed.

"Why? What good would that have done? Your brain is toast. If it wasn't for her—" he thrust a thumb at me "—you'd be off in a rubber room somewhere, drooling and rocking back and forth and the rest of us would be eating out of Dumpsters and sleeping on park benches. Just before the city was wiped off the face of the planet with us in it, like in your girlfriend's vision."

The pain on Bishop's face tore me up inside. "What can I do?" I asked.

Kraven shot a dark glare in my direction. "You can stay the hell away from him."

"I didn't know this would happen." A sob rose in my chest.

"I believe you. But it doesn't change anything. You got a taste. Would you have taken it all if we hadn't stopped you?"

My breath caught. I'd felt it—tasted it. Bishop's soul. I'd sensed it leaving him and entering me. And I'd wanted more.

Roth eyed Bishop as if he were damaged goods that should be taken directly to the dump. "He'd probably like that. Suck the whole soul out, and maybe he could flutter back to Heaven without that ball and chain around his ankle."

"Or, more likely, it would destroy him completely and he'd be taking a nosedive right into the Hollow," Connor said without even an ounce of humor. "Got a front row seat for that earlier. Not fun."

"Why would you think something like that?" I asked, alarmed at the very thought of it.

He looked at me. "We're not human. Well, not anymore. When we're given the chance to be an angel or a demon, we're changed on a base level." He flinched. "It hurts, trust me on that. But once we're finished with the conversion, we function without a soul. Having one—"

"Would screw us up," Kraven finished. "But it's a lose-lose.

Without a soul, a fallen angel or an exiled demon would perish in the human world. With it, you risk getting your eggs scrambled."

"Maybe," Connor said with a shrug, "maybe not. When it comes to Bishop, anyway. What happened to him was a mistake, not a punishment. Maybe he'd be okay without it."

Maybe. That word didn't sound like something I could put even an ounce of my trust in.

Bishop had sunk back down to the ground. But he watched me, his expression raw, his eyes filled with something else—something I couldn't name. Something aching and bottomless and filled with need. All directed at me. It scared me, because I felt like I was looking back at him exactly the same way.

He should hate me right now. But he didn't.

Just the opposite.

I realized I was moving toward him again when Kraven yanked me back, his grip painfully tight on my wrist.

"Don't go near him," he growled at me.

Zach crouched next to Bishop, a hand on his shoulder as he'd begun to rise. It was to hold him back from meeting me halfway. He was the moth, I was the flame. Right now I knew I could burn him very badly. Despite a nearly overwhelming urge to struggle against Kraven's grip on me, I stayed back.

"I feel it now," Bishop said, pressing his hand against his chest. "My soul. It's heavy inside me."

"Lighter than it was, though," Kraven added, giving me an unfriendly sneer. And here I thought we'd almost become pals. Guess not. "After all, you were just dinner for your new girlfriend."

I hated everything about this. And there was absolutely nothing I could do to make it better.

Kraven yanked on my wrist.

I shot him an angry look. "What?"

"I'm taking you home."

"I can get there by myself."

"Nah. Consider me your chaperone to make sure you don't sneak back here and try to stick your tongue down his throat again." He looked over his shoulder. "Roth, go with Connor on patrol. Zach, you take care of my darling soulful brother. Make sure he doesn't follow after us. Looks like he wants to."

"Wait a minute," Connor said. "Bishop's your *brother?*"

As Kraven dragged me away, I craned my head over my shoulder to look back at Bishop, anguished at the thought of leaving him like this. His blue eyes burned into mine. Confusion, madness, anger—and desire—all mingled together there in his gaze.

Mix in an extra helping of guilt, and that was exactly how I felt, too.

I wanted to cry, but my tears had dried up. Now my eyes just stung. I wanted to close them and try to shut out every memory of what just happened.

When I first found him, sitting on the sidewalk, lost and confused and unable to find the searchlights, I'd helped him then.

I'd helped destroy him tonight. Less than a week to go from one extreme to the other.

"So you finally got a taste of angel cake," Kraven said after a few minutes of walking. Each step away from Bishop felt heavy and forced. "Was it worth it?"

"I didn't mean to do that."

He finally loosened his grip on me and put some space between us. We'd exited the run-down area of town and entered a neighborhood with tall trees, manicured lawns and fashionable condos. Like night and day in the space of a couple of blocks.

"Right. You're just an innocent teenager looking for love in all the wrong places."

Kraven had a truly amazing talent for pissing me off. "You knew about this and you didn't say anything before. You could have warned him."

"It was just a hunch. He got the fuzzy end of the lollipop by being the one to enter the city without being shielded. The crazy easily could have come from that. What am I, psychic? That's your job, sweetness."

"Will he be all right?"

"From your first kiss? Yeah. He'll recover. Pretty sure it would have taken a lot longer for you to suck the whole thing out. As for the future…I don't know. He's a survivor. Kind of like a cockroach. Just when you think he's finally dead, he'll pop right back up again and start flapping his wings."

All I could do was concentrate on putting one foot in front of the other. My arms were crossed tightly over my chest and I kept my eyes on the sidewalk stretching in front of me. My throat felt so thick it was nearly impossible to swallow. "So what about me?"

"Good question. What about you?"

"Are you really walking me home? Or are you walking me to my doom?"

He eyed me. "Your doom? Sweetness, you watch way too many movies."

I let out a shuddery breath. "So what do I do now? What you said before? Stay home, close the blinds and hide from the world?"

"Nah. I'm sure you'd end up getting in trouble even there." He grinned darkly at me. "Go to school like a good girl and keep an eye on that little friend of yours. Also, I'd suggest you stay away from Bishop until this is all over."

That actually made me laugh sharply.

He frowned. "What's so funny?"

"You sound like you might just give a crap about what happens to your brother. And here I thought you two hated each other way more than just angel/demon animosity."

"I feel nothing for him." His jaw tensed. "Whatever you might think about us is wrong. We had some biology in common once upon a time. That was a long time ago. There's nothing between us except some bad memories."

"So you don't hate him?"

"Hate can be a useful emotion."

That wasn't really an answer, not that I was expecting one. I concentrated on him for a moment, surprised that his walls were down. "You do hate him. But not nearly as much as you hate yourself, right?"

I was sorry I said it as soon as the words left my mouth. Due to the lack of a snappy comeback, I thought I'd struck a nerve.

"You shouldn't feel that way," I said. "I mean, I don't know what happened between the two of you when you were both human, but—"

"Just shut up, gray girl. Is that even remotely possible for you?"

I flinched. I took it back: he didn't just hate himself down deep. He'd made plenty of room in there for me, too.

Twenty long minutes later, when we reached the end of my driveway, I finally chanced a look at him, but he'd already turned and started walking away.

I quickly let myself in the house. The only indication that my mother had been there earlier was the empty wineglass in the sink. As I stood in the dark kitchen, feeling utterly and completely alone in the universe, I noticed something important.

For the first time in nearly a week, I wasn't hungry at all.

When my mother got home at a little after ten o'clock, she guessed that my bleak mood was due to the fact I'd finally learned I was adopted. She was so guilty about keeping it from me, it was hard for her to look me in the eye.

I was upset about that, but not as much as she might think. It had been a shock, but it had also helped many things start to make some sort of sense. I wondered what she might think if she found out who my biological parents were.

She wouldn't believe it. And neither would I, if our positions were reversed. She might be my adoptive mother, but I'd always been a realist and a skeptic just like her.

I wish I could say I had a great plan to make everything turn out okay. I didn't. And after another restless night when I doubted if I got more than a half hour's sleep, I trudged to school once again. Happy Friday.

My thoughts weren't clogged only with my own woes. No, I couldn't stop thinking about Bishop.

It was torture thinking about him, thinking about what happened. And the look on his face when he learned he was really fallen. He immediately assumed that meant he couldn't go back to Heaven—even if it was a mistake on their part. But this wasn't his fault. He'd given up so much to lead this mission. There had to be a way.

The homeless man was fallen, too. That meant he also had a soul. My heart clenched thinking that could be Bishop's future—full-time madness, wandering the streets alone. I drew in a ragged breath and tried not to break down in the school hallways.

I didn't want Bishop to be hurt. I wanted him to get better, not worse.

He was so brave. He'd volunteered to lead a mission to help save the city from destruction—to help maintain the balance of the entire freaking universe. And now he might have to stay here forever. And go crazier by the day.

It was so desperately unfair.

I wanted to help him, to touch him and make the madness all go away, but Kraven didn't want me anywhere near him again. But Bishop needed me—despite what had happened between us.

I needed to find him again. I needed to be close to him, to hold him…to kiss him…

Damn it, Samantha, don't think about that. I rubbed my forehead so hard it felt raw.

But that kiss—it wasn't just a kiss. It was a free sample of crack cocaine given to an addict. I desperately needed more. I needed him. I wanted him. Now. Tomorrow. Forever.

But I couldn't have him. And that thought felt like a sharp golden dagger slowly slicing deep into my chest.

My running shoes squeaked on the linoleum as I made my dazed way through the busy halls toward my locker. My leather bag felt heavy on my shoulder today, even though I hadn't taken any books home this week. Hadn't done any homework at all—it was the last thing on my mind.

I twirled the lock on my locker to open it up and stared inside. I couldn't do this. Why was I even here today?

To keep an eye on Carly.

I peeked past the edge of my locker to see her headed straight for me. For a moment, I thought she might look guilty, but, no, she didn't. In fact, she looked extremely happy.

The Carly I knew might like to stick her hands into beehives, but she definitely felt the sting. This wasn't her. Not really.

"Hey." She greeted me with a big smile. "How's it going?"

Hazardous question. I was afraid to answer it with the truth. Everybody had been lying to me, so I suppose it was only fair for me to join in.

I pushed a smile onto my face. "Pretty good. You?"

"Great."

"And you and Paul…?"

"Oh, my God." She beamed. "He's so amazing. I can't believe I never gave him a chance before."

"Yeah, me, too. But—" how could I approach this in a way that wouldn't do more damage? "—you kissed him."

She dug in her locker and pulled out some supplies for her art class before closing it and leaning her shoulder against it. "I know you're mad at me for that."

"I'm not mad, I'm…concerned."

"He's fine. You saw it yourself. And I feel fine. Let's not make this a big deal, okay?"

"Why did it happen? And…has it ever happened before?"

A little of the happiness disappeared from her face. "That was the first time. I couldn't help it. He smelled so unbelievably good, I couldn't stop myself. And he wanted to kiss me. I didn't force him or anything." Instead of looking guilty, she looked wistful. "He was so delicious, I can't even explain it."

It made me cringe at the reminder of my kiss with Bishop, which had been both amazing and horrible for different reasons. "You need to promise me that won't ever happen again."

Her smile faded. "I don't know if I can promise that."

"Carly—"

"Look." Her voice went from bubbly to sharp in two seconds flat. "I have it under control. I got the warnings—don't feed too much or I could totally lose control. I *won't* feed too much. But I can't not feed at all. Not anymore. So just get off my back about this, okay?"

I faltered. "I'm just worried about you."

"Don't be. Paul's fine. I already saw him this morning. He's *fine.* So stop trying to make me feel guilty, because it's not going to work. Maybe you should focus a little more on yourself rather than me. You're the one with the problem."

"I am?"

"Yeah. Two of them. Around six-two, gorgeous, dangerous as hell?"

Well, one of them was. The other was just six-two, gorgeous and dangerous.

My stomach sank further the longer this conversation went on. Carly seemed different today. She didn't see that what she'd done was that bad. I had a feeling that if I kept pushing her, it wouldn't get her to promise me not to kiss Paul—or anyone else—again. It would only make her angry with me.

"Let's forget about all of this," I said. "I trust you."

"Good to hear." Her smile immediately returned in full, shining force. "We need to go back to Crave again tonight. Just because I'm seeing Paul doesn't mean I have to be exclusive. I swear, not to sound full of myself, but guys are flocking to me now. *Flocking.* I've never felt this good about myself in my life."

I wanted to cry. The old Carly would see there was a problem here. A *big* problem. This Carly, the one missing her soul—she'd changed. *I'm so sorry. I'll do everything I can to fix this. Fix you. I promise.*

"Crave, tonight," I said, nodding enthusiastically. "That sounds great."

"Oh! I almost forgot. I have a note for you from Natalie." She dug into her purse and pulled out a sealed envelope.

My shoulders stiffened. "That's from Natalie?"

"Yup." She handed it to me. "We'll talk more at lunch, okay?"

"Yeah, sure. Okay."

She took off down the hall and I stared at the envelope for a long moment before I finally opened it up and read the handwritten note inside.

Samantha,

There's not much time left. I need the dagger and I need it tonight. Bring it to me at Crave as soon as you can. I trust you to do the right thing.

—Natalie

Sure. No pressure there.

Not much time left? What did that mean? The angel who'd sabotaged Bishop's entry into Trinity had wanted to destroy the entire city to squash the threat of the grays. He saw grays like a virus and the barrier was acting like a quarantine tent so no one infected could get out. Did more angels feel the same way? Demons, too?

Or did she mean that Bishop had nearly found her? I knew he'd seen her but hadn't approached yet. She feared for her life—that must be it.

My loyalties were still torn. She was my aunt—I believed it. I didn't want her to die. She was the only way I could find my real father.

Bishop claimed that he could help her, if she wanted his help.

This could still be okay in the end. Nobody had to die. Not if I had any say in the matter.

So what was my immediate plan?

English class. Yes, that seemed like a good idea. Listening to Mr. Saunders drone on about Shakespeare sounded better than anything else I needed to face right now. In English, I could zone out, recharge, and figure out my next move in peace.

"If I may have your attention," Mr. Saunders said. He adjusted his round glasses as I sat down behind my desk.

He wrote something on the blackboard. It took me a second to clue in to what it said and what it meant.

SURPRISE QUIZ.

Oh, crap. There went my chance to zone out.

Mr. Saunders looked evil with delight at the groans that rippled through the class. Nobody did surprise tests anymore. It was so unfair, especially considering how little I'd paid attention this week. Even though my life had fallen apart and I didn't know how to put it all back together again. I didn't want to jeopardize my good grades. I'd worked damn hard for them and they represented a potential scholarship to get me into my college of choice. And the chance to get out of this city for the first time in my life. To my…future.

Out of this city, even though there was a barrier around it keeping in all supernatural beings—including yours truly.

Mr. Saunders placed the multiple choice quiz in front of me as a million questions sped through my mind, none of which were about *Macbeth* and could fit neatly into an (a) through (d) choice.

I scanned the questions, but didn't really read them. Time ticked by, but my mind was elsewhere.

If Natalie managed to leave the city—with or without my help—she could eventually infect the whole world. No more souls. Which was why Heaven and Hell had stepped in as soon as they realized Natalie was in town.

If Bishop and the others failed, then there were those who wanted to destroy this city just like I'd seen in my vision. To them, a million people were expendable, but six billion weren't. After all, they'd still get the souls of the dead either way.

To me, even one person lost was too many.

I longed to talk to Bishop. He could say something that might help me figure out what to do next. And it wasn't just advice I wanted. I ached to see him again. I needed him. I missed him. Without him, I felt like I didn't know what to—

Snap!

A vision slammed into me, making me gasp and clutch at the sides of my desk. My eyes went wide as the blackboard and the rest of the classroom before me flicked to a totally different image.

It was…the church. The abandoned church.

Kraven and Zach were both staring at me. Roth sat off to the left in a wooden pew inspecting his fingernails. Connor paced back and forth behind the pulpit. Light streamed in through the stained-glass window behind him. In the daylight I realized it was a depiction of Noah's Ark.

"You need to stop feeling sorry for yourself," Kraven snapped.

"Who me?" I asked, confused.

"I'm not feeling sorry for myself," Bishop growled back at him. It was his voice, but I couldn't see him anywhere.

Kraven rolled his eyes. "You are. Just like old times, bro. It's really pathetic."

"Go to hell."

"Been there, done that."

A pair of hands moved over my eyes—Bishop's hands, as if he was trying to block out the world, and then—

Snap!—I was back in my classroom.

That was Bishop. I'd just seen through Bishop's eyes.

What the *hell?*

Suddenly I realized everyone was staring at me. A few looked back at me as they handed their finished quizzes in to Mr. Saunders at the front of class. What had I said or done just now to draw this much attention to myself?

Class was almost over. A glance at the clock told me there were only five minutes left.

"Ms. Day," Mr. Saunders said with a frown. "Are you all right?"

"I—I don't think so."

I thought he was going to get mad at me for interrupting the end of the test, but instead he looked concerned. "Do you need to leave?"

I just nodded, scrambled to get my things and bolted from class as if I was being chased. It kind of felt like I was.

chapter 20

When I got to my locker, I collapsed to the floor and clutched my binder to my chest.

I'd just seen through Bishop's eyes. And I had no idea if it was a vision of the future or something that was happening right now.

I could read the others' minds if they weren't trying to block me out, but not Bishop's. I'd tried and it hadn't worked. But this—it wasn't like reading his mind at all. I couldn't sense any emotions or thoughts from him, I'd just seen and heard exactly what he had.

And it had given me a major headache in return. I squeezed my eyes shut and rubbed my temples while I tried to breathe. When I opened my eyes again, Colin was kneeling next to me. I stifled a shriek.

So much for avoiding the ongoing problem he presented.

"Sam…hey," he said cautiously. "Are you okay?"

I looked up at him. "I think I have a small chance for survival, but I'm not totally sure about that."

"You're funny." He grinned a little, but a frown still drew his brows together. "What's wrong?"

"I have a bad headache."

"I'll try to be quiet."

"You don't have to stay with me."

"I don't mind." He sat down next to me and reached over to brush the hair off my forehead. Not good. He was way too close to—

Snap! The hallway disappeared and suddenly I was back in the church.

"I need to find her." Bishop sounded angry. "You can't keep me here forever."

"You're not going anywhere near her," Zach replied calmly. "Not when you're feeling like this."

"I'm fine. I'm thinking straight."

"Doesn't look like it from where I'm standing. The demons—well, they don't understand why it's such a big loss to know you're cut off from Heaven—especially like this. But I do. To think there's a chance it could be taken from me forever would be too much to bear."

Bishop barked out a short, humorless laugh. "Are you trying to help or make this worse?"

Zach grimaced but moved closer to put a hand on Bishop's shoulder. "Sorry, really. All I'm saying is you can confide in me, anything at all, for as long as I'm here. And when I go back, I'll do whatever I can to help you. Connor feels the same way. I know you think she can help you, but she can only make this worse. Samantha's dangerous, Bishop. You just need to stay right here and—"

Snap!

I was back in the school hallway as if someone had changed the channel on a television. Colin gripped me by the shoulders, and he looked confused and concerned. My head was seriously throbbing now and my heart pounded hard and fast. I pressed back against my locker, feeling the cold metal through my thin blue shirt.

Bishop wanted to find me. My heart swelled. I thought he might hate me now that he'd had time to process what happened last night, but he wanted to see me again. But they weren't letting him.

"You're so pale. Do you want me to take you to the nurse's office?"

"No, I'm fine." I made myself get to my feet. After opening my locker, I shoved my binder inside and pulled out my bag.

Zach was right. I was dangerous to Bishop. If I kissed him again, I could destroy him completely.

Colin stood up, too. "I'm worried about you."

"Thanks, but…you don't have to be." I really didn't want him involved in any of this. I was dangerous to more than just Bishop.

He sighed. "Look, I know you've been trying to avoid me all week."

And here I thought I'd been all sneaky and subtle about it. And also, based on this conversation, a total failure.

He continued, "I'm sorry if it seemed like I was pushing you for an answer. I understand that you don't want to mess up your friendship with Carly, but I do feel like we have something between us."

I eyed him, wishing for the time when a high school love triangle might have been my biggest problem. "You think so, huh?"

"Well, yeah. Don't you?"

I reminded myself that none of this was Colin's fault; he was just an innocent bystander. But having him near me only made everything more difficult. My hunger had been MIA ever since I'd kissed Bishop, but it was beginning to make its thunderous return the longer Colin stood here. He smelled so good, I couldn't help but notice.

Even though Colin being close to me did trigger my hunger, it was still nothing compared to what I felt when I was with Bishop. Colin smelled good and I felt that lure—but he wasn't Bishop.

Nobody affected me like Bishop did.

Still, Colin was a serious distraction and another reminder of my hunger and what it could mean if I gave in to it.

"Oh, Colin," I said, shutting my eyes for a moment before opening them again to look at him bleakly. "You're making everything worse just by being around me."

He blinked. "Oh."

I shook my head, my heart clenching. I didn't want to hurt him, but I didn't see any other way to keep him safely away from me. "I have to go."

"Where are you going?"

"Home, probably. I…I don't know. I just need to get away from here."

His expression tightened. "You mean, away from *me*."

I hissed out a breath, hating that my hunger made everything so much more difficult than it had to be. I had to end this right now.

"God, Colin, just take the hint, would you?" I forced the words out. "I'm not interested in you. I'm sorry if I made you think differently, but I don't like you that way. I don't like you at *all* after what you did to Carly. So just stay away from me."

I tried not to flinch as the pain slid through his eyes. "Yeah, no problem. I think I can take the hint when it's delivered that loudly."

He walked away as students filled the hallway after class.

I sighed and leaned back against my locker, bashing the back of my head gently against it.

"Nice," somebody said. I turned to see Jordan standing

there with her arms crossed, her long red hair like a curtain over her left shoulder. "Let 'em down nice and easy, huh?"

"You heard that?"

She shrugged. "Couldn't help it. You were practically yelling at him. You actually had me fooled after being all over him the other morning. Thought you liked him."

"Get lost," I mumbled. I didn't have the energy to deal with her this morning and she was just making me feel worse about what I'd said to Colin.

It was for his own good, I reminded myself. But that didn't make it any easier.

"Get lost?" Her eyebrows went up. "Is that the best you've got for me today? Pretty pathetic."

"That's me, pathetic. But you already think that so what the hell do I care?" A lump was growing in my throat at a rapid pace. It hurt to swallow past it.

Jordan eyed me. "You're kind of a freak, you know that? I don't know how you managed to keep any friends at all. First with the klepto thing, then with the boyfriend-stealing thing. It's almost like you're completely losing your—" Her voice broke off and a frown creased her brow. "Hey, you don't look so good."

My bottom lip was wobbling of its own free will; I had nothing to do with it. "Just leave me alone."

"You told Colin you're going home. How are you getting there?"

"I'll walk. It's not far." I pushed at a tear that had managed to escape, annoyingly enough, and turned away so she couldn't see it.

She groaned. "No, forget it. I'll drive you myself. You can't go anywhere like this. You're a total wreck. You'll probably walk out in front of a bus."

I shot her a look. "*You're* going to drive me home."

"I guess I am."

"Why?"

"You want a ride or not? Stop overanalyzing, Samantha. It's really unattractive."

I felt too tired to overanalyze at the moment. Or even just analyze.

Going home sounded good. So I ended up trudging after Jordan out to her car—a white Mercedes SLK convertible—expecting her to take this opportunity to be cruel, cutting or a general bitch.

She didn't, other than looking put out by her own suggestion to drive me home.

"Nice car," I observed as we got inside. "Let me guess, it's a present from your parents?"

"Just my mother. She's in Hollywood, you know, doing her soap opera." She didn't say it with much pride, more like resentment. "This was my birthday present to make up for the fact she'd rather be there than here these days."

"I have a father like that," I said. "He usually sends fifty-dollar bills and emails, though, not luxury sports cars."

I also had a mother who'd barely noticed me for two years and now could barely look me in the eye. But my personal family drama would have to take a backseat right now. Not that this car had a backseat.

Jordan reversed out of the parking spot and shifted into Drive. "Maybe we have more in common than we thought."

Absentee parents aside, I sincerely doubted that.

Although, I couldn't help but eye her a little, curious about her and Stephen.

"Can I ask you a question?" I said.

"What?"

"Why did you and Stephen break up?"

She glared at me. "You're seriously asking me that?"

"Did he want to see other people?" Or had he done it so he wouldn't be tempted to kiss her—and take her soul?

Her face paled and her knuckles were white on the steering wheel. "He didn't give me a reason. He sent an email and then refused to take any calls from me. The one time I saw him after that, he started walking in the other direction. Happy now?"

It didn't give me any information other than the fact that he was a jerk who wanted to avoid confrontation. "I'm sorry."

"Sure you are. Now shut up."

I did as requested.

As Jordan pulled away from the school, I felt guilty about leaving early, or rather, leaving Carly there. It felt like I was abandoning her. But I wasn't. Not for long, anyway.

I'd see her again tonight. I knew exactly where she'd be.

No catastrophes happened on the short drive to my house. None at all, which was a bit surprising. Bracing myself for the worst did take some effort.

"Thanks for this, but I don't understand," I said to Jordan as I stepped out of her car after she arrived in my driveway. "You don't like me. I don't like you. Why did you bother to drive me home?"

She rolled her eyes. "Because I'm nice, stupid."

She pulled away and I watched the car disappear into the distance.

Jordan Fitzpatrick had been nice to me today. Well, *her* version of nice, anyway.

I'd take it.

When I let myself into the house, I felt an overwhelming wave of exhaustion, plus the headache from earlier hadn't let up yet. I tried to tell myself I'd only imagined seeing through

Bishop's eyes because I'd been thinking about him nonstop since the kiss last night. It really was too bad I was such a realist. I believed what I saw with my own two eyes.

Besides, if it had been my imagination sending forth a fantasy, I would have much preferred to see *him*. Not everybody else.

When I lay down on the couch in the living room, I planned to close my eyes for about five minutes before I got up and dealt with everything. But when I opened my eyes again, I realized one very important thing.

It was dark outside.

I sat bolt upright. The house was eerily quiet, except for the soft tick of the clock on the mantel above the fireplace that gently informed me it was after seven o'clock.

The stress that had kept me awake the past few nights must have caught up to me. Or maybe the vision of being in Bishop's head had given me a bad headache *and* exhausted me.

I hurried into the kitchen to see that my mother hadn't come home from work. She'd scribbled a note this morning and tacked it to the fridge to tell me she had a client meeting. She'd be home by around nine o'clock and—

Snap!

I was outside of the church, on the overgrown front lawn.

Despite the glass being broken on the sign and it missing a few letters, I could still make out the last message it had to give: Down in the Mouth? Time For a Faith Lift.

"You don't understand," Bishop said, his voice quiet but steady. "I have to do this."

Kraven stood in front of him as if blocking his path. "You don't know what will happen. Getting the rest of your soul sucked out could kill you."

Bishop snorted. "Didn't think you'd care so much. Brotherly love? After all this time? Who are you trying to fool?"

Kraven glared at him. "Screw you. The only thing I care about is this bloody mission. You going off and doing your own thing is not for the better of the team."

"Somebody like you lecturing me on leadership. Fantastic. I'm surprised you'd try to stop me at this point. If I'm gone, you get to make all the rules. You're second-in-command here."

Kraven's expression didn't change. "I'll take over if you're gone, but Roth still shouldn't have put that idea into your scrambled-up head."

"He speaks his mind."

"He's an ass."

"He's a demon."

"Touché. But we're not all that stupid. It's not worth the risk you're taking."

There was a heavy pause. "Speaking of risks, what deal did they make you to agree to this mission? I know Hell offers up a lot of temptation. Money, prestige, power...women. All your weaknesses."

Kraven glared. "Funny, I always thought those were your *weaknesses."*

"What did it, James?" Bishop's voice twisted unpleasantly. "Why do you give such a damn if this mission is successful? And did you have any idea I'd be part of this or were you as shocked to see me as I was to see you?"

A car drove by, the headlights illuminating Kraven's light hair. It also showed that his expression had darkened. He crossed his arms, walked back toward the sign, kicked at the broken glass, before turning back to look at Bishop. "If those bosses of yours decide to go old school, we'll all get wiped off the map if we fail. Sounds like a good reason to succeed."

"Exactly. Which means you're risking your very existence to be a part of this. But for what? What's the shiny reward?"

"If we're successful?" Kraven said grudgingly after a moment. "I don't have to go back to Hell. I get a fresh shot here."

Bishop let out a soft snort. "Right. A fresh shot. You're addicted to making bad choices. You think that will ever change?"

Kraven shot a dark glare at him. "Like I care what you think. I want a second chance and I'll do anything to get it."

It took Bishop a second to respond. "Then maybe you should have one."

A huge grin slowly spread across the demon's handsome face. "Oh, dude. You're so pathetic—that much hasn't changed. You actually believed me. What a joke. Yeah, I'm willing to sacrifice my entire existence for the chance to stay here in this pathetic city. Sure."

"You were lying?"

"Yeah, I was lying, idiot. I signed up for the babes and the power, of course. Can't wait to collect my reward. It's going to be a major party—no crazy, self-involved angels invited."

I didn't know if he was lying. But the flat look in his amber-colored eyes did hold a glimmer of something else there. Longing, envy...I wasn't sure. And then he turned away so I couldn't keep trying to figure him out.

I didn't particularly want to figure Kraven out.

"This has been a fun talk." Bishop's words were tinged with anger and something else—familiarity. This kind of joking around by Kraven wasn't new to him.

"So much fun."

"Are you going to try to stop me from leaving?"

Kraven looked over his shoulder. "Nah. You go face your destiny. Roll those dice to see if you get a trip back to harp-land. I guess I'm in charge now. Feels good, actually."

"Good luck."

"Yeah, whatever. Go find yourself a gray willing to suck out the rest of your soul. I think that Carly chick was giving you the eye the

other night outside that nightclub. Go let her stick her tongue down your throat. Party on."

"Maybe I'll do that." Bishop stretched out his hand. "Give me the dagger."

The sheath Bishop normally wore was now strapped to Kraven's back. "And risk this falling into the Hollow? Not a chance. With you gone, I need this to help me do my job so I can reap my rewards. Now why don't you go find yourself a deadly blonde babe and get out of my face? And try to make it forever this time."

Kraven walked away from him, back toward the church, and—

Snap! I was in my kitchen again, leaning heavily against the counter while my heart hammered against my rib cage.

"Bishop, no," I whispered.

If he found a gray to remove the rest of his soul, he might have a chance to go back to Heaven if that was all that kept a fallen angel anchored in the human world. In Heaven, he'd have his mind fully restored and he'd be able to investigate a way to restore my soul—which he'd promised me he'd do.

However, losing his soul could also kill him outright. And then the Hollow would open up and swallow him whole.

Natalie had returned from the Hollow, but she admitted she was an anomaly—in more ways than just her demonic hunger. There was no guarantee that Bishop could do the same. And Natalie hadn't been killed first: she'd been shoved into the vortex still alive.

The thought of Bishop dying was a deep pain that spread out from the center of my chest. I heard a strange, mournful sound and realized that I was sobbing at the thought of losing him. Last night was close enough.

Kraven had suggested he find Carly to kiss.

My hands were shaking when I dialed Carly's house, hoping she hadn't left for Crave yet. Even though my cell phone didn't work, thankfully the landline still did.

After the fifth ring, her mother answered to break the news to me that Carly wasn't at home. She'd gone out, and I knew where.

"I don't know what's wrong with her," Mrs. Kessler said. "She's acting so strangely this week."

My stomach sank. "Really? Like how?"

"She seems…different. And there's something in her eyes—something vacant, like her mind's a million miles away. Is she dating someone new who might have caused this? She won't tell me anything."

I exhaled shakily. "I—I really don't know what's changed."

"But do you see it, too?"

I clutched the phone tight enough to hurt my hand. "Yeah, but I'm sure it's temporary."

I hated to lie. This wasn't temporary, but I hadn't accepted that it was permanent. I'd do anything I could to help her and make sure this didn't get any worse.

"I don't know, Samantha. The look she gave me tonight when I tried to stop her from going out—well, it's been every single night this week!—it chilled me. She won't even tell me where she's going or with whom. I'd hoped it was with you."

The kitchen counter cut into my back as I leaned my full weight against it and I just tried to breathe. "I'm sorry."

"It's not your fault. Teenagers, well, they can change in an instant sometimes. I know that. But this…" Her voice quavered. "I hate to think my Carly's changed forever."

My heart broke. "Me, too."

I ended the call, feeling sick inside, but at least I knew where Carly was. Crave. With Natalie. With Stephen. And with a wide selection of tantalizing teens to trigger her hunger and slipping control.

I headed out of my house at a fast clip. I had to get to Bishop before he reached Carly—if, in fact, that was his plan. I didn't know where else he'd go. I couldn't lose him like this—not when he wasn't thinking right. Not ever. I couldn't let him kiss Carly.

My heart also twisted for another reason entirely—jealousy. It was irrational, I knew that. This wasn't a romantic kiss. He would be doing it because he didn't think he had another choice.

Bishop belongs to me.

It was a fierce and scary thought that overcame me for a moment, stopping me in my tracks on the sidewalk.

I'd known him less than a week.

But that didn't change a damn thing. He'd quickly worked his way into my heart. He *was* my heart.

Maybe he was my soul, too.

The romance-soaked thought didn't make me roll my eyes like it might have in the past. Instead, it scared me. It was the truth—plain, bleak and heart wrenching. I'd fallen for him so hard that I'd been left shaken and bruised.

I would save him. Even from himself.

And if Carly even thought about kissing him, I was going to punch her in the face.

"Beautiful star." A voice sank through my cloudy thoughts. "She's come out tonight to battle the world. To save us all from the darkness."

The homeless fallen angel stared up at me from his seat on the ground, legs splayed across the sidewalk. Dirty, ripped blue jeans and a gray sweatshirt that had seen better days completed the look. It was disconcerting how much seeing him tonight reminded me of when I'd first found Bishop. It worked just like a hand reaching in my chest and squeezing.

"You've picked a different spot tonight," I said. I was halfway to Crave.

"I move," he replied. "I have legs. They help."

"Yeah, I'm sure they do." I frowned down at him and studied his face as if trying to find clues there to help him—help Bishop, too. "What's your name?"

He sighed. "I had a name a long time ago."

"What was it?"

"Seth," he said after a moment as if he had to concentrate very hard to remember it. "Rhymes with breath. Rhymes with death. Two sides of the coin, breath and death. Lose one, gain the other—a gift or a curse, but I guess that's up to you. Or them. Or him. Or anybody."

I wanted to know more about him, but I didn't have time for this right now. I had to hurry or I wouldn't be able to stop Bishop from finding Carly. "I have to go."

"Your lost love walks the dark night without watching where he's going. Another pair of lips he seeks, but he wishes they were yours."

A breath caught in my chest. "You know about Bishop? You can see what he plans to do?"

Seth pressed his fingers to his temples. "I see things. Jumbled, together and apart, can't sort through them all. Past, present, future. Don't know what's real and what's false. What's good and what's evil. Here, black and white become gray. And the mouth is open, always hungry, feeding on everything." He reached forward to clutch my hand, and electricity sparked up my arm. "He doesn't want you to stop him. He's chosen this dark path so he can end this."

A chill went down my spine, making the night even colder than before. "I need to stop him even if he doesn't want me to."

This close to the fallen angel, I could sense his soul—now that I knew he would have one. It triggered my hunger. But there was no way I'd be tempted to kiss him, and it wasn't just because he was dirty and old. I mean, gross.

"The dark mouth is already open and waiting," he said. "Just a crack, but it leaks its poison slowly, slowly. It's changed. It's grown. It hates as much as it loves. It's how she returned."

The Hollow. It wasn't one-way. It wasn't endless. How did Seth know?

I'd have to tell Bishop and the others. When I fixed this mess tonight—and I refused to think that I'd fail—I'd tell them to find Seth. Despite talking crazy, he had information that could help them.

I had to get to Bishop. If he didn't want me to stop him? That was too damn bad, because I was going to do it anyway.

When I turned the next corner, something was blocking my path. Something with broad shoulders, blond hair and a sour expression.

Kraven.

chapter 21

Clouds had rolled in overhead, blocking the stars and moon. More rain was scheduled for tonight. I felt a mist start to come down, not enough to drench me, but enough that the cold sank into my skin.

Now that Bishop had abandoned his position as leader to go off on his personal mission, his word wasn't enough to protect me anymore if Kraven decided to start treating me like any other gray, especially now that he was in possession of that sharp dagger.

Or maybe I was being paranoid.

"Get out of my way," I said as strongly as I could.

"What? No greetings for a good friend?"

"If I saw one, then maybe."

"Are you taking a stroll over to our new digs to see your boyfriend again? You need to stay away from him."

I hissed out a breath, but decided to change my approach. Kraven had tried to stop Bishop earlier. Maybe, just maybe, he could help me. "I know what he's planning to do. I want to stop him."

He frowned. "How do you know anything? Have you been reading my mind again?"

There was no way he could guess how I'd know something like this. I didn't want him to know. Bishop had warned me not to tell the others about the origins of my abilities, and this might tip him off. "Don't flatter yourself. I'm not all that interested in your thoughts."

"Bishop's gone AWOL. But don't worry…I'm extending your grace period for the time being. Who knows? We might need your mojo again before all this is over."

"I need to find him."

He raised an eyebrow but didn't budge one inch from his place in front of me. "Wow, you're all determined. Is my angelic brother really *that* good a kisser? Somehow, I find that hard to believe."

Did he honestly think that was all this was? God, he was so frustrating to be around. "Kraven, just do me a favor and step—"

Snap!

Bishop entered the front doors of Crave. He scanned the dark interior, his gaze moving across the sweaty faces of kids already on the dance floor, a sparkle of colored lights hitting them. Compared with other weeknights, Fridays were the busiest by far. There had to be a couple hundred teens already here. The deejay played a remix of Britney Spears's old song "Toxic" with a bass-heavy throb.

I couldn't read his thoughts, but I knew he was looking for her. Looking for Carly—

Snap!

Back on the sidewalk, I stared at Kraven who regarded me with confusion.

"Where did you just go?" he asked.

"Nowhere."

His frown deepened. "You were here, but your mind wasn't. Do you have more tricks up your sleeve that I don't know about, sweetness?"

Panic filled me. I had to get to Crave now. "I need to stop him."

The demon took a few steps closer to me, and his hard expression finally softened a fraction. "I know you think I'm the bad guy here, but I'm not."

Great, now was the time he picked to get chatty. "You're a demon. That's bad."

"Depends who I'm dealing with, really." He blew out a breath, his attention staying fixed on me. "You really want to stop him, but getting kissed again is what he wants."

"He doesn't know what he wants. He's crazy, remember?"

"He made his choice. You barging in is only going to complicate matters."

"Tough. Because I'm going to barge. Now get the hell out of my way."

He still didn't move. Why would he? I wanted to stop Bishop from destroying himself. If I succeeded, Kraven wouldn't get to be the leader and tell the others what to do.

It was night, so I assumed the others were patrolling the city right now. I hoped so, anyway. After seeing that zombie gray last night, I knew this city needed some serious protection.

"He doesn't deserve your devotion," Kraven said evenly.

"Why? Because he used to be a 'bad guy' when he was human?" I watched for something in Kraven's eyes and succeeded in getting a spark of interest from the demon.

"Told you that, did he? Got to say, I'm shocked."

This was only more confirmation, and it made my stomach churn. "What did he do? What did *you* do? Why are you a demon and he's an angel?"

His lips stretched into a sinister smile. "Because he was willing to do what I never would."

I could barely breathe. "And what's that?"

His grin only grew wider. "It's a secret, sweetness. And I'd never betray my little brother's trust."

My cheeks burned with frustration. "Please move."

"Or what? You'll zap me?"

"Maybe."

He raised an eyebrow. "You know, I still haven't figured out your secrets. You're a complete enigma to me."

"What do I have to do to get you to get out of my way?"

He cocked his head and glanced toward the street as another car drove past. I was so close to Crave, only two more blocks to go. His gaze tracked back to me. "Angels can heal while they're here in the human world. They can also influence minds—get humans to change their behavior in subtle ways or think differently on a subject."

"Why are you telling me this? I don't care." Still, my ears perked up.

"Sure you do. You're fascinated by anything to do with my little brother." He moved even closer to me. "Demons, we're different, of course. We can throw a bit of fire around if we're so inclined, but it's a major energy drain here. We can't mess with minds, though, apart from shielding small areas from a human's senses. Too bad, mind-messing might make this easier."

Kraven reached forward to brush my hair back over my shoulder and then slid his warm fingers down the side of my neck.

I swatted his hand away. "What do you think you're doing?"

His eyes moved to mine again and his grin widened a little. "Maybe you don't hate me as much as I thought you did. A slap's not the same as a zap."

"You have about three seconds before I do just that."

"Uh-huh. Anyway, like I was saying, demons can't influence minds. If I could, then I would stop you from chasing after him. So I'll have to do this the old-fashioned way. I learned this little trick back when I was still human. It's very helpful sometimes."

He reached for my neck again and pressed hard. Before I could do anything to stop him, the world faded to black all around me.

I woke in an alley, staring up at the dark night sky. A raindrop splashed directly into my eye and I scrambled to get up off the damp ground, blinking hard and rubbing my face.

"Huh," Kraven said. He leaned against the brick wall next to a Dumpster. "You weren't out nearly as long as I thought you'd be."

"How long?" my voice creaked out.

"A couple minutes."

I staggered a little, feeling dizzy but mad enough to spit. Panic swept through me. "Why did you do that to me? Do you want to be the leader so bad that you have to knock me out to stop me from going after him?"

He shrugged. "It's better if he's gone."

"How can you say that? He's your brother. Don't you care what happens to him?"

He cocked his head. "Sweetness, you really don't know a thing about us if you're asking me that question."

Heartless bastard. I glared at him as I touched my throat. He'd cut off the blood to my brain to make me pass out like he was some pointy-eared character from *Star Trek*. Why had

I let him get close enough to touch me? It wasn't as if I even liked the jerk. He repulsed me.

"I guess you think you're protecting the mission by trying to stop me right now," I said with disgust. "Got to complete it successfully if you want to stay here in Trinity and seek your redemption. That's what you told Bishop, right?"

"How did you—?" Surprise shot through his amber eyes before they narrowed. "Wait a minute…this is different from you reading my mind. You're listening in on private conversations."

"Maybe I can do things you don't even know about."

A cold smile turned up the corners of his mouth. "Tricky, gray girl. Very tricky. I think I'm finally getting it. Somehow, someway, you're able to get in Bishop's skull now and listen in. Is that it?" He must have seen me pale a little. I didn't like how good he was at playing the guessing game with me. "Interesting. Can't imagine that would be much fun, though. A demon would show you a way better time than an angel."

"You offering?" I asked sharply.

He snorted. "Sorry, not tonight."

I gave him a withering look. "You are so incredibly—"

Snap!

Bishop had finally spotted Carly hidden away in a corner booth. My heart sank to see that she was kissing someone else—a guy I didn't even recognize this time. Oh, God, what was she doing? Couldn't she stop herself anymore?

Bishop approached her table and stood there until she saw him out of the corner of her eye. She disengaged from the boy, who then slumped back in the booth, his eyes glazed. Those strange, scary lines branched around his mouth for a second before they started to fade. She turned her black, predatory gaze on Bishop.

Seeing her like this again chilled me to my core. Especially now that she was looking at Bishop.

"Well, well," she drawled. "Look who's here."

"Carly, right?"

"Present and accounted for. Where's your tall, blond and handsome friend tonight?"

"Not here."

She pulled a hand mirror out of her purse and checked her face, applying some more lip gloss while her date recovered from losing part—or all—of his soul. "You're a popular guy around here, Bishop. Everyone wants to know your story."

"Not much to tell."

"Samantha's not here."

"That's okay. I wanted to see you."

Her brows went up. "Really? Why's that?"

"Because I want you to kiss me. I want to be like you."

She studied him curiously for a moment. By now her eyes had shifted back to their regular cornflower-blue. "What about Sam?"

"She's not here."

Carly rubbed her lips together and swept her appreciative gaze over Bishop, from his eyes and then downward. "She'd be mad at me if I did that."

"Do you care if she is?"

"I'm not sure."

"Do you want to kiss me?"

She gave him a wicked grin. "Oh, yes."

Jealousy twisted inside me. Even though I knew what the kiss was for, I wanted to be the one he asked. And I hated how my so-called best friend was looking at him. She wanted to consume him, body and soul.

But Bishop was mine. *If she touched him I'd kill her.*

Irrational. I hated how irrational I'd become when it came to Bishop.

But even now, after everything I knew about me, about him, I wanted him. I wanted to kiss him again.

Carly slipped out of the booth. She wore a tight black dress tonight that showed a lot of leg and plenty of cleavage. She oozed sexiness like I'd never seen before.

But Bishop barely spared a glance at Carly's curvy body. He looked over her shoulder and up to the second-floor lounge. Natalie stood by the glass barrier looking down at him.

"Can you introduce me to Natalie?" he said.

Carly nodded. "I can do that. I know she really wants to meet you."

There was something in the way Natalie stared at Bishop that made my blood run cold. It was a look I hadn't seen in my aunt's eyes before. Curiosity turned to cold hatred. Deep malevolence. She knew who and what he was. And she looked like she wanted to kill—

Snap!

Back in the alley, I was gasping for breath, clawing at the brick wall behind me to help keep me on my feet. Kraven now had a hold of my arm and I yanked it away from him.

"What?" he asked, frowning. "What did you see?"

I had to get past him. I had to get to the club and stop him from going upstairs to that lounge. Stop him from kissing Carly or getting anywhere near my aunt.

I hadn't seen a pretty demon with a supernatural eating disorder just now—one who wanted freedom, wanted help with her problem. One who wanted to reunite me with my real father and tell me tales of my parents' doomed love affair.

No, this demon wanted to kill the angel who'd been sent to find her. And I knew with a clear and cold certainty that she would take great pleasure in being the direct cause of his death.

I'd given her the benefit of the doubt, feeling some sort of important family bond with her. But it was lies. All lies. I was so sick of being lied to.

Natalie might very well be my aunt, but she was evil. And now she was going to kill Bishop.

The problem was, Bishop was already on a suicide mission.

Wait a minute.

A suicide mission. That was it—that *had* to be it.

I looked at Kraven with wide eyes. He studied me back cautiously. "What's up, gray girl?"

Bishop had set out tonight to lose his soul—that was true. But it wasn't because he felt sorry for himself and believed this was his one chance to go back to Heaven. It was because he knew destroying himself would open up a passageway to the Hollow.

And he wanted to take Natalie with him.

No, I had to be wrong. This was too crazy of a plan.

Then again, Bishop *was* kind of crazy to start with.

"Samantha, talk to me," Kraven said after I went deadly silent for a moment, lost in my thoughts.

Funny, I think this was the first time he'd ever used my real name.

I turned my attention back to the tall, blond demon. That he was looking at me with concern etched onto his handsome face almost made me smile.

I had a plan now and I really hoped it would work.

"You know," I began, "before all of this, the last time I got in major trouble was when I was caught shoplifting."

Kraven looked surprised at the abrupt change in subject matter. "Thou shalt not steal. I approve. What did you take?"

"A scarf, a bottle of nail polish. Nothing major."

"Why did you do it?"

"I saw something I wanted, so I took it." I shook my head.

"Also, because I was dealing with some family drama and it was a way to get attention. It was stupid."

"We all make mistakes."

"You, too?"

His jaw tensed. "Trust me...compared to some of the things I've done, shoplifting is no big deal."

I pushed a slow smile onto my face. "I think you're right. You're not so bad. In fact, you're kind of charming when you want to be."

He eyed me cautiously. "Oh, yeah?"

I nodded. "And you try to hide it, but I think you sort of like me, don't you?"

"Don't flatter your—" His words cut off when I threw my arms over his shoulders and gave him a tight hug. He didn't return it, instead standing there rigidly, until I finally let go of him. He just stared at me, stunned. "What was that for?"

"Good night, James." I turned and walked out of the alley, sliding the dagger I'd just stolen from him into my leather bag. I guess I'd really taken him by surprise with that hug. He hadn't felt a thing.

Maybe I was a better thief than I thought I was. This wasn't a scarf or a bottle of nail polish, though. No, this was infinitely more important to me right now.

I made it an entire block before I felt a hand clamp down on my shoulder, stopping me in place.

Crap.

A cold smile played on his lips while his eyes glowed red in the dark. "Cute trick, sweetness."

I decided to play innocent. "What do you mean?"

"Give me back the dagger."

"What dagger? Oh, you mean that shiny gold one?"

His eyes narrowed. "You're devious and manipulative. You're right, maybe I do like you."

I tensed. "I need to borrow it."

"Then you should have asked me nicely."

"May I borrow the dagger? Pretty please?"

"No. Give it back."

"I'll return it later, I promise."

I turned away from him, but he grabbed my wrist tightly. "I'm still trying to be nice, which isn't all that easy for me," he said. "Give it to me."

I spun around to face him and pressed my free hand against his chest. "You need to remember not to get too close to me. I'm dangerous, remember?"

If he had any walls up, they didn't get in my way this time—I was too driven to get away from him. The electricity came to me in an instant and flowed through my arm into the demon. He looked shocked—literally—before he flew backward and hit the window of a darkened office. It cracked as he slid to the ground unconscious.

Bishop had told me angels and demons needed to sleep and eat. By the looks of it, they could also be knocked out cold when necessary.

Kraven had done his Vulcan neck squeeze on me without a moment's hesitation. This just evened things up between us.

"Sorry," I said as I passed his still form, feeling guilty about what I'd had to do regardless of whether or not he deserved it.

I started running toward Crave, praying I didn't arrive too late.

Natalie wanted me to bring her the dagger so I could help her escape the city. Well, I was bringing it to her, but for a different reason entirely.

I knew it was the only way I could kill a demon.

chapter 22

I might have partially accepted that I was the daughter of a demon and an angel, but as I pushed through the entrance of Crave with the dagger weighing heavy at the bottom of my bag, I just felt human and scared.

Maybe I should I have told Kraven what I was and what I knew. Bishop had said not to, but the demon could have helped. He was part of this mission, too. But there was no time to go back and get him. For all I knew, he'd be unconscious for hours after the amount of power I'd put behind my last zap.

My searching gaze fell on a familiar face. Colin stood off to the side of the dance floor about twenty feet away from me. I almost waved at him, but I stopped myself. I'd hurt his feelings this morning. By the look on his face right now, I wasn't sure if he'd ever speak to me again.

Colin looked away first, plastering a smile on his face as he talked to a pretty girl I recognized from school. Maybe he thought it would make me jealous, but instead I hoped he was interested in someone else. Someone safe. One thing I knew for sure was that I wasn't safe anymore.

Snap!

Carly slid her hands over Bishop's shoulders and was gazing up at his face.

He flicked a glance at the other side of the lounge. Natalie waited a dozen feet away, watching them carefully, her legs long and lean under the short skirt of her tight, midnight-blue dress. Her lips twisted into a dark smile of approval.

"Kiss me," Bishop said.

"Okay." Carly smiled at him and tightened her grip on the front of his T-shirt, drawing his face closer to hers. Her eyes fixed on his mouth.

Snap!

There was no time to waste. Heart thundering, I took the stairs two at a time until I got to the top and, ignoring everything and everyone else in the lounge, I made a beeline for them. Just before their lips touched, I grabbed hold of Carly's arm and wrenched her away from Bishop. I guess I was stronger than I looked because she staggered back toward the glass barrier where she stared at me with shock.

"Wh-what the hell?" she stammered. "Where did you come from?"

"That seems to be the question of the week." I stood in front of Bishop, blocking him in case she got any more ideas. I felt his angry gaze burning into my back. He was close enough that I felt his breath warm against my skin. "Stay away from him."

She narrowed her eyes. "I heard you've been all over Colin this week. Isn't it only fair I go after the guy *you're* interested in?"

I glared at her. "Don't try to justify this."

"I thought we were best friends."

"I thought so, too." My heart ached. She had a glazed look

in her eyes and I knew I couldn't get through to her right now. She didn't understand this was wrong.

Bishop finally spoke, a low growl. "Damn it, Samantha. You shouldn't be here."

I forced myself to turn enough to look at him and my chest tightened. The last time I'd looked into his eyes, I'd desperately wanted to kiss him again.

Nothing much had changed since last night. I still did.

A little of the steely resolve faded from his gaze and his dark brows drew together. I guess my emotions were written all over my face.

The girl who'd tried to ignore romance because she was trying to avoid painful stings had basically made a permanent move right into the beehive.

"I shouldn't be here?" I let out a shaky breath and tried to sound calm. "But I love this club. I come here almost every night lately. Good times."

When in doubt, scared to death, and fighting a truly fatal attraction, it was best to tap into a little sarcasm.

"This isn't your business." Despite his words, something slid behind his eyes. Something vulnerable. He hadn't expected me to come here, to try to stop him. He thought this was the end for him. Seeing me again had shocked the hell out of him.

But he wasn't looking anywhere else. He'd asked Carly to kiss him, but now his gaze was only on me.

"I guess we're not exclusive, you and me, huh?" I desperately tried to sound flippant. It didn't work very well. "You want to see other people. I get that. I mean, I don't blame you. Last night…it shouldn't have happened."

The same pain I felt twisted in his expression, and his gaze slid to my mouth.

Our kiss—it hadn't just been addictive to me.

I couldn't kiss him again. If I did, I could destroy him completely. So, of course, it was all I could think about now.

"You shouldn't be here," he said again firmly.

"Neither should you."

He hissed out a frustrated sigh and raked a hand through his dark hair. "I'm exactly where I need to be."

I'd kept Natalie in my sight since I'd come up here, afraid to turn away from my aunt in case she managed to escape. But she hadn't even tried. She watched my exchange with Carly and Bishop with growing interest.

Stephen was also there, standing close to Natalie like the good and obedient minion he was. Other grays were up here as well, eight of them—six guys and two girls who were all watching us with vacant expressions. The other times I'd been here they seemed like regular kids. Tonight, they didn't.

I realized that their eyes had all turned to black.

I turned my widening gaze to Bishop's.

His expression was grim. "Leave now, Samantha. This doesn't have to involve you."

He sounded commanding, but there was the slightest catch in his voice. I didn't have to be able to read his mind to know what he was thinking right now. He knew if I walked away it would be the last time we ever saw each other.

"I know what you're trying to do," I said quietly, for only him to hear.

His jaw clenched and he gave me an almost imperceptible shake of his head. "Please, just go."

"I can't do that. There's another way."

"No, there isn't."

He didn't know that I had the dagger. I had other plans for tonight. And I wouldn't let him die like this, no matter what.

Natalie finally approached. Her gaze moved between me

and Bishop. Carly stepped back, now giving me a sullen look. "It seems rather dramatic over here. Everything okay?"

"Never better," I lied.

I looked into her eyes and tried to read her mind, but it felt different from the others. With them, I could feel when they had walls up. With her I felt nothing. And I sensed nothing.

"Did you bring me what I asked you to?"

"I'm still working on it." It was a lie, of course, but I had no intention of handing the dagger over to her.

Disappointment skittered across her pretty face, but then she nodded at Bishop. "You care about him, don't you?"

There was something in the way she said it. It wasn't the curiosity of an aunt wondering which boy her niece was currently interested in. There was an edge of unpleasantness that hadn't been there before.

A shiver went through me. "Are you asking as my aunt or as somebody who wants to use my feelings against me?"

She raised an eyebrow, regarding me with amusement now. "I feel like something's changed between us, Samantha. I thought we were establishing a close bond. Was I wrong about that?"

My throat felt tight. "You said they're under control." I thrust my chin toward the group of grays watching us creepily. "And that losing a soul is more freeing than harmful to a human, other than having to deal with the hunger."

"I did say that."

"But Carly's changed." I struggled to keep my voice from breaking. "I want my best friend back. The one who still knows the difference between right and wrong like I do."

Carly groaned. "Oh, brother. Give me a break. The universe does not revolve around you, Sam. Get over yourself."

I flicked a glance from her back to my aunt. "See what I mean?"

"So you don't think it's for the better? She's kind of sassy like this, don't you think?"

I didn't reply. She was baiting me and I didn't want to play into it. She found all this amusing. My pain was amusing to her.

Even still, the longer I was here, the more I doubted my original plan. Even if Natalie revealed herself to be a totally evil demon without a chance for redemption, could I really kill her?

Maybe not. But Bishop could.

I'd seen him wield this dagger without hesitation. It was his mission to come to this city and find the Source. To stop her because she was a dangerous threat to the balance of the entire universe.

I had to get the dagger to him. But that might be tricky.

Also, the fact that he was so close to me right now that I could feel the heat from his body sinking into mine—that his addictive scent had wrapped itself around me and made it nearly impossible for me to concentrate—my mind wasn't working right. It never did when he was this close to me.

"What do you want?" Bishop said. It was directed toward Natalie.

She moved her attention from me, her face pinched and displeased now, but it shifted into something else. I recognized that look in her eyes. I'd seen it in Carly's.

Predator.

"Oh, I don't know." She moved closer to him. Her gaze slid down the length of his body. "Happiness, wealth, true love. Just like everybody else."

"That's all?"

"What else is there that matters?"

He shrugged a shoulder. "Destruction, vengeance, power, world domination."

Her smile stretched, but it didn't reach her eyes. "Those are fun, too."

"How did you escape the Hollow?"

She regarded him in silence and it seemed as if she was fighting to hold on to that calm and amused expression. "You know, Samantha, that dagger your friend Bishop carries—or *usually* carries—is one similar to what was used on your mother."

Pain twisted inside me.

"Your father really did love her, but their relationship was forbidden. Nothing that threatens the perfect universal balance is allowed to exist, you see. Unfair, isn't it?"

"Where's my father?" I asked, trying very hard to keep my voice steady.

"I told you I'd take you to him if you helped me." Her brown eyes, so much like mine, moved to me. "He'll be disappointed that you failed to bring me what I asked for."

"You want the dagger," Bishop said.

Her smile returned. "I do."

"What happened to you all those years in the Hollow? What's it like in there? It's not supposed to be like anything. It's supposed to be the end of everything."

Her eyes flashed red. "Maybe that's how it is if you're dead. But I was thrown in there alive, just like my brother was."

"He wasn't thrown, he jumped," I said. "You told me he followed after Anna."

"Same difference."

"I'm sure you weren't the first ones who entered the Hollow that way. It sucks in anything within its radius, not only the dead."

"You're right. There's lots of garbage inside that Heaven and Hell didn't think would ever see the light of day again. Everyone assumes that Hell is where that darkness and true evil end up. But even they have standards. Anything unacceptable, anything problematic or anomalous that can't be properly categorized or used, gets tossed." Her lips thinned. "But it's not the end. It's not a black hole of nothingness. It's so much more than that now."

"Since when?" Bishop asked. "When did it change?"

She laughed…an unpleasant sound. "Were you sent here to ask me these questions before you killed me? I guess they know something's up with the Hollow. They're afraid of what that might mean to their precious balance."

He shook his head. "They're not afraid."

"They should be. Actually, they should be terrified. If I got out, other things will, too. I can promise you that. Other things that will make me look like nothing more than a pretty girl who likes to kiss pretty boys. All here in Trinity."

"So it's open here, but nowhere else. It's stuck, just like you are. Because of the barrier."

Her pleasant expression washed away, leaving behind something ugly. "I need your dagger, angel."

Bishop's face was all cruel, hard lines as he regarded her. Nothing soft. "You think Samantha can help you escape because of what she is."

She flicked a look at me. "He'll kill you, you know. It's only a matter of time. You're an anomaly, just like me. A threat to the balance. Be careful with this fallen angel, Samantha. Soul or not, he'll steal your heart just before he slices a sharp blade into it."

Even though I didn't trust a word that came out of her mouth, a chill ran down my spine. I braved a look at Bishop, but he kept his attention fully fixed on my aunt. His fists were clenched at his sides, the muscles in his arms tense.

Stephen stayed behind Natalie, his brows drawn tightly together as he listened in on the conversation. Carly moved to stand next to him. Her eyes moved back and forth between us as if she were watching a tennis match.

I hated that Carly was here and had become a part of this. My best friend since kindergarten—my closest ally and confidante. I wanted to save her so badly, but I didn't know how. I couldn't accept that she had changed forever from this. Losing Carly's soul felt even worse than losing my own.

There had to be another way for this all to end. What had Natalie experienced while being in the Hollow for all these years? How had it changed her? I couldn't hate her for this, I felt sorry for her. And if I still could, I wanted to help her.

"How did you get out?" Bishop asked Natalie again.

"You," she purred, "are very tenacious. You're the leader, aren't you? There are others in the city like you who run around every night killing my brood. I don't like that very much."

I scanned the faces of the people around me. Carly stood next to Stephen with a blank look on her face. Stephen's expression was unreadable, too, but his gaze was now fixed on me rather than Natalie.

It made me shiver.

And the others...

I glanced behind me and nearly shrieked when I saw they'd all gotten to their feet and taken a step closer, their expressions as blank as sheets of paper. They blocked my path back to the staircase.

Not one normal teen had ever tried to climb those stairs to come up here. This had become a grays-only section. It scared me to think what would happen if anyone did venture up to this second-floor lounge.

"Did you make a deal to leave the Hollow?" Bishop persisted. "With whom? And what was it for?"

Her gaze traveled leisurely over his tall, muscular body and broad shoulders. "It was really more of a favor."

"Why did the Hollow change? It hasn't always been this way."

"No, it hasn't. Only for about seventeen years."

Seventeen years. Since I was born. Since my real mother was killed and my father and Natalie followed her into the Hollow.

I still clutched the strap of my heavy leather bag, my palms damp with sweat. Throughout this, Bishop had remained sane. But even now I sensed his struggle to keep his focus.

He glared at her, frustration etched into his handsome face. She wasn't answering his questions; she was only making everything more confusing.

I knew I was right about his ultimate plan for tonight to open the passageway to the Hollow and drag Natalie back into it with him. And now that I'd arrived, I'd complicated things for him. No, scratch that. I'd totally screwed up his chance to sacrifice himself for his mission.

I knew why I'd done it. Even though I knew I couldn't kiss him again, I refused to lose him. Not like this. No matter what that meant.

The song blasting below us shifted to something frenetic with a driving beat. My heart rate increased right along with it. Bishop drew closer to me until his arm touched mine. It was enough that I felt the spark between us, and a pleasant ribbon of warmth slid through me.

His nearness did crazy things to my head, made me dizzy. I fought to maintain my concentration, but I didn't make any move to put distance between us. Being close to Bishop might be more distracting than I wanted it to be right now, but it also helped to give me extra courage.

"However you returned, you're now putting the world at risk by your very presence," Bishop said to Natalie.

"You say that like I should care."

"How can you not care?" I asked.

"I know you don't understand, Samantha." She gave me a winsome smile. "But you don't have to. All you need to do is help me get out of this city."

I shook my head. "Sorry, I can't do that."

She closed the distance between us, grabbed hold of my wrist, yanking me forward. "You will."

Her grip grew so tight I couldn't help but whimper as I fought to break her demonically strong hold on me. Bishop took her hand and wrenched it back from my arm hard enough that it would have broken a human's wrist. She shrieked in pain.

Bishop's eyes glowed with blue light. "Hurt her and I hurt you. See how it works, demon?"

Natalie's upper lip curled back from her teeth in a half smile, half grimace. "You're still weaker than you should be with that soul stuck in you. Good to know."

"It's been a difficult week."

"I'm sure. But you got the chance to meet my lovely niece. And it's obvious to me that you do care about her—probably much more than you should. So do I."

"You had your underling suck the soul out of her mouth in a single kiss. Doesn't sound like a caring aunt to me. It sounds like a self-involved demon who only wants to serve her own interests."

"It was the only way for her to discover her true full potential. It was my gift to her."

Bishop glared. "You are one cold, deluded bitch if you really think that."

"Maybe I'm a cold bitch, but I'm not deluded." Natalie's amused expression had returned. She liked that she was able to push Bishop's buttons and get a tangible reaction from him. "I made an exception for Samantha because we're family. I gave Stephen very specific instructions when he took her soul—for him to take it all in one kiss. That isn't easy. But my Stephen—" she cast an affectionate look at him over her shoulder "—he's got a very talented mouth."

Stephen remained silent, his brows drawn close together.

Bishop's expression tightened. "What does that mean?"

"Samantha's soul—" a smile curved her full lips "—it was taken all at once, not in pieces. That means it can be saved."

My breath left me in a whoosh like I'd just been punched in the stomach. That was the last thing I expected her to say. "You mean it's not gone forever?"

"He brought it to me when he was finished with you." The demon's smile held. "I have your soul, Samantha. And if you ever want it back, you need to do exactly what I tell you to do."

chapter 23

A wave of dizziness swept over me as I tried to process this. "Where is it?"

"Somewhere safe," Natalie replied. "Not here. Only Stephen and I know where it is."

"That's why he ran away right after he kissed me, isn't it?" I asked breathlessly.

"Stephen?" Natalie prompted, flicking a look at him.

Stephen's throat jumped as he swallowed and he opened his mouth to speak. It seemed like a struggle for him for a moment. "That's right."

I met Bishop's gaze. He looked as surprised as I felt, but there was cautious hope in his blue eyes.

"And what about Carly's soul?" he demanded. "Did you hide that somewhere, too? That would be the perfect insurance to get Samantha to do as you wish."

Carly watched us, her expression still glazed and uninterested. But she was paying close attention. I wasn't sure I even wanted to know what was going through her mind. She liked how she was without her soul—her new confidence, the attention she got from boys at school and at Crave. She might not want it back even if that was an option. But I had to know the truth.

"Well?" I said, looking at Stephen instead of Natalie. "Did you or didn't you?"

Stephen nodded. "I still have it."

Relief and fear crashed over me. Maybe Carly could be returned to her former self. But at what cost?

Natalie crossed her arms and nodded at a couple of the grays behind me and Bishop. "Restrain him."

Before Bishop could move, two male grays grabbed hold of his arms to hold him in place.

"My boys are extra strong," Natalie said. "When I create the grays myself, they have that extra something special. They can hold your weakened angel in check quite easily."

Panic shot though me. "Natalie, what are you doing?"

"I'm moving this along. I have places I need to be. Stephen?"

Stephen was at my side in an instant and he took tight hold of my arm.

"Her purse," Natalie instructed.

Before I had a chance to struggle, or to even realize what was happening, he'd ripped my leather bag off my shoulder and pushed me back from him so hard that I stumbled to the floor and landed on my butt.

Bishop growled with rage and fought against the grays. "I should have killed you the other night when I had the chance, you son of a bitch."

"But you didn't," Stephen replied. "Your mistake."

He thrust my bag out to Natalie. She took it, unzipped it and then reached inside and drew out the dagger. The gold glinted under the pot lights in the ceiling above us.

Bishop's eyes had widened. I'd surprised him. Too bad my

plan hadn't worked out—not that it had been that solid to start with. I'd waited too long, hoping for a chance to convince Natalie to change her mind. Hoping there was a way that everyone could survive this.

Now she had the dagger.

"I knew you were lying, Samantha," Natalie said as she inspected the blade. "When you said you didn't have this, the lie was clear in your eyes. You're a very honest person. That weakness must come from your mother's genes."

I hated her. At that moment, I'd never hated anyone more.

"Interesting. This could be the very same dagger that killed Anna." Natalie glanced at the restrained fallen angel before her. "How many of these are there?"

Bishop's teeth were gritted. "I don't know."

"Even if you did know you wouldn't tell me, right?"

"Good point."

"Does it have a name? All of these fancy magical weapons usually have names."

Bishop glared at her. "Yeah. I like to call it Goldie."

"You're funny for an angel."

"Not really. I'm just inspired at the moment." Bishop's gaze flicked to the dagger. "You planning on killing me with that thing? Take revenge on me for the others who shoved you in the Hollow seventeen years ago and forgot you existed?"

My stomach clenched. What was he doing? Egging the demon on to kill him right now?

"You wanted Carly to kiss you earlier." She drew so close that their faces were only inches apart. She slowly slid the tip of the dagger down the center of his chest and back up. "Your soul smells so good to me—even better than a human's. How does my little niece manage to keep her lips to herself around you? It must be torture for her."

She cocked her head as she studied him. "But you don't have your *whole* soul, anymore, do you? I can sense that. I guess she did have a nibble. Can't blame her for that."

"Are you going to finish it off? Kiss me and suck the rest of it out?"

"Would you like me to? Or is it only Samantha's mouth you want on you now?"

I pushed up to my feet and surged toward her, wanting to claw her eyes out, but Stephen blocked me.

"Stay back," he warned.

"Why are you doing this?"

"Why not? There's nothing else that I care about anymore. Might as well align with someone as powerful as Natalie."

"What about Jordan?"

He flinched as if I'd slapped him. "She's history. And if she comes anywhere near me again, she's in serious trouble."

God, why hadn't I told Kraven about this? Why had I knocked him out? He could be storming in right now to stop this. Or— I didn't know for sure. Maybe he'd let this play out just as it was, sacrificing his brother in order for the mission to be successful and he could get his reward. It wasn't as if there was any love lost between them.

But still, some storming in would be really nice right about now.

Where are you? Come on, demon. This is your chance to save the day.

But nothing happened. I hadn't really expected Kraven to suddenly appear in a blaze of glory. We were on our own. A quick glance at Carly told me she wasn't going to be any help, either.

"I *could* kiss you," Natalie said to Bishop. "Or I could kill you outright with this dagger. But neither option works for me. I need you."

Bishop's expression darkened with understanding and his attention moved to me. As our eyes locked, my heart twisted.

My skin crawled the longer she kept talking with that dagger in her hand while Bishop was held in place. His soul zapped his strength as easily as I'd zapped Kraven earlier. He couldn't break free.

"Please don't hurt him." My voice cracked on the words.

She glanced at me. "Will you use this dagger to cut through the barrier and help me escape this city?"

I shivered. "I—I don't even know if I can do it."

Natalie turned back to Bishop and stabbed the dagger into his shoulder. Bishop let out a sharp gasp of pain as blood welled around the weapon. Natalie yanked it out and Bishop's red blood now coated the golden blade.

It happened so fast that I could barely register what she'd just done. I tried to move, but Stephen shoved me back so hard it knocked the breath out of me. "What are you doing? No, Natalie, don't—please, don't hurt him!"

She smiled without humor. "See? I knew you cared for him. That should speed this up."

Bishop's forehead gleamed with perspiration and his teeth ground together. "Think about it, demon. Even you must see the problem of leaving this city with what you're capable of doing. You'll destroy everything."

"I'm sure you have a point. Somewhere." She thrust the blade into Bishop's stomach this time and twisted it sharply. He grunted in pain, but didn't scream.

But I did. I screamed so loud that I couldn't believe no one immediately thundered up those stairs to see who was being tortured up here.

Stephen's attention shifted away from me for a split second and I took the opportunity to drive my knee up between his legs. He let go of me and staggered back. I rushed across the lounge to grab hold of Natalie's arm before she sliced into Bishop again.

"Stop it!" I managed to say, my eyes blurred with tears. "Please, stop!"

"Then agree to help me. It's that simple. I can do this for hours. I've cloaked this lounge. No human will see or hear a thing no matter how loudly you scream for him." Her gaze searched mine and her eyebrows drew together a fraction. "It doesn't have to be like this. Desperate times call for desperate measures, Samantha. I'm desperate right now. I'm just trying to survive. So end this."

Tears splashed onto my cheeks. "I hate you."

"Hate makes you strong, love makes you weak. I learned that from my brother. He's strong now, Samantha. You have no idea how strong. He wants to meet you, to know you. I can take you to him. This is your chance to have a family who'll accept you for who and what you are—no matter what."

A family who didn't ignore me or treat me like a burden. Somewhere I belonged, with people who wanted me around. Once upon a time, that might have been enough to tempt me. But not tonight.

I dug my short fingernails into her arm. I had no doubt that she could easily bat me away and go back to hurting Bishop in an instant, but I held on as tight as I could. I tried to access my abilities, to zap Natalie like I'd done with Roth and Kraven, but I wasn't able to summon so much as a spark. She hadn't just cloaked this lounge, she'd cloaked herself, as well. Her walls were stronger than anything I'd felt before. I couldn't break through.

I glanced at Bishop to see that he'd slumped down after his injuries and was being held up only by the strength of the grays. Blood dripped from his wounds to stain the hardwood floor.

Carly stayed quietly behind Stephen, who was slowly recovering from what I'd done to him. I didn't have time to mourn the loss of my friend or deal with the thought that to save her I had to help Natalie escape from Trinity so she could destroy the rest of the world.

I had to play along. I had to make her believe. For me to cut through the barrier—and I wasn't even sure if I could—I'd need the dagger in my hand. And when it was, I would summon up whatever courage I needed to end this once and for all.

"I—I'll do it," I whispered.

"Samantha, no," Bishop rasped.

Natalie cocked her head. "You mean it?"

"Yes, I mean it. Don't hurt him. I'll do whatever you want me to do." I held out my hand. "Give me the dagger."

Her gaze met mine and held it for a long moment, during which I held my breath. "I knew you'd change your mind."

"I guess you know me."

"Yes, I think I do."

For a moment, I thought that I'd done it. I'd convinced her that I was ready to do as she asked.

Unfortunately, my aunt wasn't stupid.

"Yes," she said softly. Any warmth fell away from her gaze and her eyes narrowed and glowed red again. "Definitely your mother's genes. You are such a horrible liar, I don't even know why you bother."

"Forget Samantha," Bishop snarled. "You were thrown into the Hollow for nearly two decades. What horrors did you face in there? Blame me for that. Kill me for that. If I'd been on that team, I would have been happy to shove you in."

My stomach lurched. "Bishop, no!"

Rage flashed in her eyes. "Don't mistake me for a fool, angel. It won't be long before my niece won't be lying when she says she'll help me escape. I'll know when that moment comes. I'll see it in her eyes."

She moved as if to thrust the blade into him again. I didn't think, I just attacked. I grabbed hold of her right arm to keep her from stabbing Bishop. I had no *nexus* abilities to use against her, nothing except the sheer will to stop her from hurting Bishop.

I might not have been as strong as a full-demon, but I was quick and small and I darted around her, punching and kicking her with one goal in mind—to get her to drop that dagger. Finally, with a well-placed kick to her wrist—which cut my shoe when it edged against the blade—I knocked the dagger out of her grip and it fell heavily to the floor. Natalie grabbed me by the front of my shirt and drew me close to her.

"You're a bad liar, but you're ruthless like a demon," she growled. "Maybe you are like your father after all. He'll be happy to hear that."

Then she backhanded me so hard that I think I blacked out for a second. Pain reverberated through my head and I tasted the copper tang of my own blood. I spun back from her with the force of the blow and landed hard on my back. All I could do was stare up at the ceiling and try to breathe. It wasn't easy.

"No!" Bishop roared. "Samantha, run!"

But I couldn't run. I could barely move.

"I didn't want to hurt you," Natalie snarled as she loomed over me. "But I will. Now you will do exactly what I say or I will start cutting the angel into pieces right in front of you until you agree. I'll do the same to your best friend and then to you, as well. With your dying breath, I promise that you *will* help me escape from this city."

She placed the sharp stiletto heel of her shoe over my throat and pressed until I was sure she'd puncture a hole right through my larynx. I wheezed in pain and panic ratcheted through me. She wasn't trying to kill me, just hurt me. She wanted me to see that she wasn't playing games anymore.

"I'm going to kill you!" Bishop's voice was filled with rage.

"No, you're not. You can barely get to your feet, angel. It's over. I win."

So much for trying to save his life. I couldn't even save my own. I was completely at her mercy.

She was right, it *was* over. She'd force me to do what she wanted. And after the horrible threats she'd made, I knew I would do it to save Bishop. To save Carly. To save myself.

It would be my fault that the world was destroyed.

"Um, excuse me?" Carly said.

Natalie hissed out an annoyed breath and looked at the curvy blonde now standing next to her. "What is it?"

"Nobody gets to hurt my best friend," she said evenly. "Not even you."

Carly sank the golden dagger deep into Natalie's chest.

chapter 24

Natalie staggered back and stared down at the dagger. She took hold of it, pulled it out with a grunt and dropped it to the ground. As she raised her gaze to meet mine, her brown eyes were wide—so wide—and filled with shock.

She'd thought she'd won.

Bright red blood welled from the wound, staining her dress. "It didn't have to be like this. You should have wanted to help me. We're family."

I hadn't wanted it to end like this, but now I saw there was no other way it could end. There was still something I needed to know. The carrot she'd dangled in front of me all this time. "How can I find my father, Natalie?"

This earned a sharp, pained bark of a laugh from her. "I'm sure you'll meet him soon. He has big plans for this world… and for you. This isn't over. But it could have been different. I could have protected you. We could have been a family. Now you only have yourself to blame when everyone turns against you. And they will. I guarantee you that."

Her eyes glowed bright red for a moment as pain twisted on her face. Then she fell heavily to her knees. The scary black vortex opened up behind her, accompanied by the tornado-like roar, and fear crashed over me to see it again arriving right on schedule as it sensed the demon's impending death.

I scrambled back from her as fast as I could. And then, before I could say anything, scream anything, the dark hand of the Hollow reached out and grabbed her, pulling her back into its gaping mouth.

It had happened so fast.

Carly was at my side, clutching my arm, as the storm continued to rage in front of me. "What the hell is *that?*"

I stared at the spot where Natalie had disappeared with utter and complete shock even though I'd been expecting this. "You don't want to know."

Her familiar form blocked the swirling, roaring vortex. "Are you okay?"

"Not even close." I forced myself to look at her. She hadn't changed totally back to her former self, not that I'd expected she would. She was still a gray, which meant she wasn't nearly as petrified about what had just happened as the old Carly would have been. "Why did you do that? Why did you save me?"

She frowned. "Because she was hurting you."

"Thank you." Gratitude welled within me and I grabbed Carly and hugged her fiercely. Maybe she wasn't lost to me after all. I pulled back to look into her bright blue eyes.

"You're welcome." She smiled. "We're still best friends forever. Right?"

She was still here. She was still Carly underneath it all. And I could get her soul back and fix her. I knew I could.

"Forever," I confirmed.

Suddenly, I felt a pair of strong arms come around my waist

to pull me back from her. It was Bishop, who now had me in his tight grip.

"What are you doing?" I demanded.

"Look at her," was all he said.

I looked at Carly and a scream caught in my throat.

Tendrils of darkness had begun to move over her shoulders like black fingers. The Hollow hadn't closed after taking Natalie. It had moved closer. It sensed another supernatural entity nearby, and it was still hungry.

Terror gripped me, cutting off my breath. I couldn't find the air to scream.

The sound of the vortex grew louder, so loud I couldn't think. Carly stared at me with wide eyes as the Hollow's grip tightened on her, covering her with its darkness. She reached a hand out to me, confusion written all over her face.

"Sam?" she asked, her voice trembling.

And then the Hollow yanked her backward into its swirling black mouth, just as it had Natalie.

"No!" My scream cut past the roar of the Hollow.

I was hallucinating, I had to be. Horror filled every cell of my body, freezing me, but I knew I had to do something. I had to try to save her. She'd only just disappeared. I couldn't accept that—I could never accept that.

She'd just saved my life. I had to save hers.

I fought against Bishop, but he held firm. I struggled, I squirmed…I had to get out of his grip. My focus was completely on that black hole. If I could get to it before it closed, reach into it and grab her hand—

I couldn't lose her. Not like this—not when I'd just realized that she could still be saved.

"Samantha, stop!" Bishop yelled at me as I scratched and clawed against him. "She's gone!"

"No, she's not. I have to help her!"

I finally managed to slip out of his grasp and scramble away from him. My eyes stung with tears, but I fought to see past them. I'd gotten away from Bishop in order to try to save my friend, but he'd been holding me back so the Hollow wouldn't sense that I was in its path.

And, just like a gray, its hunger had no end.

The vacuumlike suction I'd felt last night with Bishop and Connor began to draw me closer to the black hole and I stared at it with horror. I lost my balance and fell hard to the ground. It was as if the world had tilted and I was now sliding feetfirst toward the Hollow's hungry mouth.

My shock over losing Carly so suddenly and horribly was replaced by icy fear. I'd thought I could save Carly—fight this monstrous thing that raged mere feet away from me. I was wrong.

Bishop grasped my wrist before the vortex could gobble me up, but its dark fingers reached out to wrap around my ankles and pull me toward it.

"Hold on!" Bishop's eyes glowed blue in the darkness that swirled around me.

Something about this sank into my mind, past the fear, past the shock. This was my vision—my very first vision. The one I'd had before I'd even met him, after Stephen had kissed me. I thought I'd been falling into darkness, but in reality I was being pulled sideways into it.

This was how it ended for me. I was bound for the Hollow just like my aunt, my father, my mother…and my best friend. It was my fate—the inevitable end to everything I'd been fighting against.

"They were wrong, Samantha." Bishop's voice broke as

he said my name. "It never should have been me. This is the proof."

"What?" He'd said this to me before. And in my dream he'd also let go of me. He didn't think he deserved to be leader. He thought someone else could have done a better job—even with a fallen angel's soul meant to sabotage the entire mission.

"I'm not strong enough for this. I've failed you. I've failed everyone. It's—it's all over." Even though he tried hard to hold on to me, I still started to slip away from him and I shrieked. The Hollow was incredibly strong and I was so scared I could barely function. He'd given up hope. The sight of me slipping away had finally broken him.

But I wouldn't accept that. There was still a chance to change this; I felt it deep inside myself. What I'd seen was only a possibility—a worst-case scenario. Visions were previews of the future, but the future hadn't happened yet. Carly was the one who believed in fate and destiny, not me. I was the realist, the cynic. Even now.

I didn't want to give up. I didn't want to stop fighting, not yet. Not *ever.*

"No, Bishop! Listen to me. You *are* strong. You *are* a leader. I believe in you and I trust you with my life."

His face was strained. "Samantha, no…"

I stared into his pained gaze. "Yes! You're amazing and I'm so happy I met you, no matter what happens now. Do you hear me? I can't lose you, not like this. If you let me go right now, we won't be able to get my soul back and I won't be able to kiss you again. So don't let go of me. You hear me? Because I really want to kiss you again!"

His dark brows drew together and he stared at me, surprised by what I'd just said to him. But I saw the spark of determination strengthen in his eyes.

"Then hold on! I won't let go if you don't."

Which meant we'd both get sucked into the Hollow together in mere moments if it continued to pull on me this hard. But my words had given Bishop the strength he needed to keep holding on.

Long enough for a very tardy demon to get his ass up here and help us out.

Through my watering eyes, I caught a glimpse of Kraven moving toward us, his gaze registering shock at the sight before him.

"Need some help?" he asked.

"Yes!" I yelled at him. "Help us!"

"What's the magic word?"

"Now!"

"Close enough." He edged toward me, eyeing the swirling blackness wrapped around my ankles with uneasiness.

"Don't get close to it!" Bishop hissed. "You'll get sucked in, too."

Kraven swore as he assessed the situation. "Then just hold on to your girlfriend, little brother."

I was only a few feet away from the dark vortex and I fought against the intense suction with every ounce of strength I had left. True to his word, Bishop didn't let go of me, but our grip wouldn't last much longer.

Kraven moved behind Bishop and grabbed the angel's ankles. With effort, he pulled. It felt like a tight rope, with Bishop and Kraven on one end and the Hollow on the other. I was in the middle, about to be torn in half.

Bishop kept his hold on me and Kraven kept pulling on his legs until slowly, slowly, I found that we were moving away from the vortex. Once Kraven got some traction, we moved faster until the black tendrils that had wrapped around my ankles receded into the darkness. I looked over my shoulder, and I swear the Hollow was staring at me with malevolence.

I shuddered.

But then, a moment later, the dark swirling hole closed up and disappeared as if it had never been there in the first place. I stared at the spot where it had been, a hungry mouth with an insatiable appetite. It had swallowed Natalie and Carly right before my eyes. It had very nearly taken me, too.

I'd escaped from it, but my best friend hadn't. I'd lost her right when I'd learned there was a possibility of bringing her back completely, restoring her soul…

She'd saved me, but I couldn't do the same in return.

The painful realization was like a blow, stealing my breath and shattering my heart into a million pieces.

"Carly…I'm so sorry," I whispered as tears streaked down my cheeks. I began to sob and Bishop pulled me against his chest. I clung tightly to him. I let myself sob against Bishop's shoulder—I didn't even know how long. I already thought I'd lost her, but it hadn't been like this.

But a small glimmer of hope remained. I was a realist, yeah, but I'd already seen my share of miracles this week. She hadn't been killed, just taken. Natalie had found a way out. If that was possible, then maybe Carly could do the same.

Finally, I looked up at Bishop through damp eyes.

He held my face between his hands and looked at me with concern. "I'm sorry, Samantha."

I clutched the front of his bloodstained T-shirt. His knife wounds were still deep, still bleeding. "Will these heal?"

He grimaced. "I'll need Zach's help."

I glanced around the lounge, surprised to find that there were only three of us up here now. "Where's Stephen?"

He was the one who knew where my soul was. Where Carly's was, too.

"Gone. Must have taken off after Natalie was stabbed. The others are gone, too." He stroked my hair back from my face. "He can't leave the city, so all he can do now is hide. We're getting very good at finding grays in this city. We'll find him, too."

I nodded and drew in a ragged breath. "So I guess you believe in miracles."

He gave me a smile that warmed me inside. "It kind of comes with the job."

I chewed my bottom lip, again looking back where the vortex had been. I swallowed past the lump in my throat, feeling ready to curl up in a ball somewhere and keep crying. Instead I ran my hand under my nose and decided to be as strong as I could for as long as I could. "So now what? Natalie's gone. What happens now?"

"Heaven and Hell sensed her presence nearly two weeks ago. They will sense that she's gone. But they won't remove the barrier yet. Every gray is still a threat—but they're not nearly as strong as Natalie was."

I stared up at him. "So when you said you thought you'd be all finished in a week…?"

"Wishful thinking." He grimaced. "I was originally told I'd be extracted after the Source was gone so I could be healed if there were any side effects of breaking through the barrier. That's when I planned to find a way to help you—while the others were still here on patrol. But that's not going to happen now. I'm not going anywhere. I'm officially fallen."

"And officially crazy, depending on the day." Kraven appeared to my left. "By the way, you're welcome for saving both your butts. Now, can we go? I'm not in the mood for dancing with teenagers tonight. Maybe tomorrow."

Natalie was gone, but there were still grays in Trinity. And something else was bothering me, something that Seth had said just as we'd parted ways earlier tonight.

"I told you about the homeless guy, the other fallen angel," I said to both of them. "He sees things, visions, sort of like I do. He said to me that the dark mouth is already open. Just a crack, but it leaks its poison. Is he talking about the Hollow?"

They exchanged a glance.

"Sounds like it," Bishop said with a nod. "Natalie made it clear that it's changed. It's not a place of nothingness. It's a *place*. And if it's leaking, then that's all the more reason for the barrier to remain right where it is."

"But that puts Trinity even more at risk, right?" I asked as a shiver went down my spine.

"Good job we're here," Kraven said with a smirk. "More potential things to kill. Fun, fun, fun."

If the Hollow had sprung a leak, and that was how Natalie had originally escaped, that meant other things could, too. Which was a very scary thought. However, it gave me more hope that Carly could return. In the meantime, anything supernatural was stuck inside the city until future notice.

The demon snatched the gold dagger off the ground then swept his gaze over Bishop. "You don't look so good, brother."

"I'm fine."

Bishop had been so strong when he'd tried to hang on to me so I wouldn't slip into the Hollow, but I knew he must be hurting after being brutally stabbed twice.

I stared at the dagger in Kraven's grip. Seeing Carly thrust it through Natalie's chest—she'd killed her to save me.

I'd known Carly since kindergarten. Spoken to her every

day. Shared everything with her, good times and bad. Secrets I wouldn't tell anyone else, tears, heartbreak, hopes, dreams, wishes. Now she was gone and I had no guarantees I'd be able to find her again.

Bishop went down the stairs first. I followed slowly, passing Kraven as I went.

He watched me warily. "You knocked me out, gray girl."

I let out a shuddery breath. "I had no choice. For what it's worth, I regretted it after I got here. We could have used the help."

"Obviously. But I'll have to watch you carefully. I can block your mojo if I concentrate."

"I know." I swallowed hard. "Listen, I know we've had our problems, but thank you for saving me and Bishop."

I turned and started down the stairs, but Kraven caught my arm, making me look back at him.

His expression was tense as his eyes met mine. "Who says I was trying to save him?"

He let me go and I continued down the stairs, unsure of what he meant. He hadn't wanted to specifically save Bishop, his brother with whom he shared some unpleasant history. History that neither one wanted to talk about. But he'd come here after I'd knocked him out. He'd come here not to help push us both into the Hollow, but to save us.

To save *me.*

Whatever his motivation, I was grateful to him. I wouldn't forget that. But I didn't think I'd ever trust him completely.

After what just happened on the second floor, I was surprised that everything looked like just another Friday night on the main level. The cloaking on the lounge had worked perfectly, since nobody down here had any idea what had happened. The music hadn't let up for a moment and multicolored lights flashed across the kids on the dance floor.

That was me a week ago. It felt more like a lifetime.

Stephen was nowhere to be seen. I wanted to believe that what they'd said about my soul wasn't a lie, but I'd been lied to so much this week that I didn't know what to believe anymore. Just what my gut told me, I guess. And my gut told me he'd been speaking the truth. My soul still existed—somewhere.

And if it did, then one day very soon I was going to find it again.

I would never give up on the possibility of rescuing Carly from the Hollow, but her absence had to be dealt with. And, again, the truth wasn't going to be much help to anyone right now.

First, we met up with the others.

After Zach tended to Bishop's wounds, healing them with a touch, Zach went with me to Carly's house. I tried to hold it together, to be strong, but I felt weak and tired and sick with grief as Zach gently explained to Mrs. Kessler that Carly had run away from home with a boy she'd met at Crave.

A runaway teen. Not exactly a new story. With a bit of angelic influence from Zach, Carly's mother believed what he told her one hundred percent.

She gave me a big hug, knowing that I would miss Carly every bit as much as she would while she was off on her rebellious romantic adventures.

"I'm sorry," I choked out as she clung tightly to me. "I'm so, so sorry."

"It's not your fault, honey." She let go of me and wiped tears from her eyes. "She'll come back. I know she will."

I hoped she was right about that.

When we finally left Carly's house, I went with Zach to join the others at the north edge of the city so I could see it for myself. I was told the barrier stretched around Trinity's circumference like a silver dome on a room service dinner. Most of it was invisible, even to me, but in certain places, like here, patches of it could be seen—a shimmering transparent wall reaching up into the darkness.

"Don't get too close to it," Kraven warned. "It gives a hell of a zap. Reminds me of what you can do."

"You tried it?"

"I like to test my limits whenever possible."

Bishop came to my side and reached down to take my hand in his. A spark slid up my arm at his touch. It kept him sane and me warm, and I wasn't in any hurry to let go of him. He felt good, he smelled good. Too good. The heat of his skin sank into me. I avoided looking at his mouth. Way too tempting, even now.

He squeezed my hand. "How are you holding up?"

"I'm still here." I braved a shaky smile. "That's a start. How about you?"

"Better. My wounds are gone, but my head—it's still not as clear as it was before I arrived. I guess I should get used to it." He said it calmly, but I could see the pain in his eyes.

I wished I could take his pain away. All of it.

"So things still suck here," Kraven drawled. "And we're all still stuck working together. But we got the Source and we know there's something wonky happening with the Hollow. And none of us are wandering the city, Dumpster-diving. It could have gone a hell of a lot worse."

"Such an optimist." Bishop shot him a look. "Color me surprised."

"Bite me, little brother."

"I'm still not understanding how you two are brothers," Connor said. "I mean, even apart from the angel/demon thing, you don't look much alike."

"Same mother," Kraven said. "Different fathers. *Very* different fathers. But enough about that." He shifted his gaze to me. "Looks like you saved your boyfriend's ass tonight, sweetness. Maybe you should give him a big, juicy victory kiss to celebrate."

I shot him a look that I hoped would wipe the grin off his face. It didn't work.

Nice of him to rub it in.

Unless I wanted to risk destroying Bishop completely and sending him to the Hollow, I couldn't take the risk of kissing him again. Not until I got my soul back.

"So now what?" Roth said as he glared at the barrier. "We're stuck here forever? I think I'll go crazy, too."

"Come on, it's not so bad." Connor slapped the demon on his back and Roth flinched at the friendly contact. "It's a big city. And we're here to protect everyone and keep them safe and sound at night while they're asleep in their warm beds. Sounds pretty damn noble to me, even if it might be forever. And I'm sure it won't be."

"I didn't sign up to be noble," Roth growled. "And what about her? She's still a gray. Shouldn't we kill her? One less gray and we're closer to getting out of here."

"If you come anywhere near Samantha," Bishop said, "I'll be happy to reduce this team back to four members."

Roth rolled his eyes. "Whatever. She's your problem, not mine. I'm out of here."

He turned and started walking away.

Connor shrugged. "I should probably keep an eye on him. Demons, you know."

He took off, too.

"I'll leave you two lovebirds alone in case you want to start making out. Come on, Zach." Kraven started off in another direction, his hands stuffed in the pockets of his jeans, without another glance in my direction.

"Keep an eye on him," Bishop said to Zach.

"You got it." Zach grinned at me. "Glad you're part of the team, Samantha."

"I am?" I asked with surprise.

"Sure, you're our honorary sixth member with mysterious abilities and visions of the future. The Snow White to our motley group of dwarfs. Plus, you're way better looking than the rest of these guys."

If I could have summoned the ability to laugh at the moment, I would have. "Thanks, I think."

"See you!" He ran off after Kraven.

The walk home with Bishop was a silent one, both of us lost in our thoughts. What happened haunted me. It would be a long time before I could make sense of any of it. When we finally arrived at my house I turned to look at Bishop. He searched my face before he spoke.

"You changed it," he said.

"Changed what?"

"The future. You got me to keep holding on to you. You told me that in your original vision, I let go of you."

"That's right." He looked pained, but not from madness at the moment. His mind was currently clear. I squeezed his hands in mine. "I meant it, you know. Everything I said. I believe in you."

"I was set up to fail by that gatekeeper. I knew that how I felt was more than what I should have expected. I expected pain and disorientation from breaking through the barrier, but nothing like this. *This* is how a fallen angel feels because it's a punishment. I understand that now."

"It shouldn't have happened to you, but you're still here and so am I. That means that things can still change for the better for both of us. It's been one hell of a week, Bishop, but I'm so glad I met you."

He raised his gaze from the ground and our eyes locked. "You are?"

My breath caught. "I'll admit things are a bit complicated between us now."

"That's an understatement." He frowned. "How did you find me tonight? How did you know what I planned to do?"

I hesitated, trying to figure out how to tell him. "I seem to have developed a new ability. I can see through your eyes sometimes, like I'm in your head."

His dark brows drew tighter together. "In my head?"

"I can't seem to control it, and it happens only with you. It was enough to show me where you went tonight—but I don't know why I can do it."

"I do," he said. "You touched my soul when we kissed. It connected us."

My heart swelled. It made sense, I had to admit. "So we're soul mates now?" After I said it, heat crawled onto my cheeks. "I mean, you know. You're an angel and I'm, uh, I'm—"

"Special." A small smile played at his lips. "Very special."

As we stared at each other, that connection grew even stronger than before. "You should probably go now."

He raised an eyebrow. "Yeah?"

I nodded, my gaze moving to his lips. "I'm getting really hungry again."

"That sounds dangerous." He didn't budge, nor did he ask me to clarify if I meant for food.

For the record, I didn't mean food.

"Definitely dangerous." I swallowed hard. "I'm so sorry for what happened last night. I'm so sorry I did that to you."

"Don't be sorry." His eyes remained serious. "Believe me, Samantha, that kiss—it was enough to prove something very important to me."

"What?"

"That I'd do anything to find a way to kiss you again."

He leaned forward to brush his lips against my forehead.

My heart swelled. It wasn't a real kiss, but it would have to do.

Before he walked away, I had to ask him one more thing. "Bishop, I know you don't want to tell me much about what happened when you were human. Not even your name back then, but...I need to know something. Will you answer just one question for me?"

"One question?" he said, holding my gaze.

I nodded.

"*Only* one question," he said again. "You promise?"

"I promise." *For now,* I thought.

He was quiet for a moment. "Fine. Ask your question."

"Kraven told me that you're an angel and he's a demon because you were willing to do something that he'd never do." I let out a shaky breath. "What was it?"

Silence fell between us and stretched for so long that I never thought he'd answer me.

"What was I willing to do to become an angel when I'd done more than enough in my life to become a demon instead?" he asked quietly.

My mouth was bone-dry. I just nodded.

His blue eyes flicked to mine and they were now haunted.

"I killed my own brother and sent him to Hell. *That's* what I did to become an angel."

I didn't speak. I didn't think I *could* speak. My mind swirled around and around with this new piece of information. I didn't know what I'd expected him to say, but *that* was definitely not it.

Stunned, all I could do I was watch him walk away and disappear into the night before I forced myself to finally turn toward my house. My mother stood by the open front door, watching me with a curious expression.

"New guy?" she asked.

I cleared my throat. Thankfully, she didn't seem to have heard what we were talking about. "Fairly recent."

"He's cute. You like him?"

"Yes."

"A lot?"

A fallen angel. Dangerous as a demon. Once one of the bad guys. Responsible for killing his own brother. "More than I probably should."

Her face was strained, and I didn't think it was because of my confusing love life. "It's been tearing me up about what happened. I should have told you the truth years ago."

I shook my head. "Now I know. I'm adopted."

She sniffed and ran a hand under her nose. Her blond hair was down tonight and spread around her shoulders. Instead of her usual business suit, she wore jeans and a sweatshirt. Comfortable, nondesigner clothes for a change. Very unlike her. I approved. "All I can say is I'm so sorry. I know we've had our problems lately, but I think we can work through them if we want to. I love you, honey. I have from the very moment I was lucky enough to welcome you into my life. We all go through hard times in order to make us realize what the important things really are. My work's not important. *You're* important. You hear me? And—and I want us to be a real family again, if you'll allow it."

She looked exhausted from getting all of that out at once. It made me smile a little. "Have you been rehearsing that speech all night, waiting for me to get home?"

She exhaled shakily. "All day, actually."

I processed what she'd said. I believed she meant it, every word. "It was a good speech. And I agree. Yeah, we've had our share of problems, but…family's not always about biology, it's about love and support through good times and bad. You might not have given birth to me, but you're my mother and I love you, too."

A slow smile spread across her face. "When did you get so wise?"

"Recently. Very recently." I gave her a tight hug.

Natalie told me that hate makes you stronger, love makes you weaker.

I couldn't have disagreed with her more.

"Well, good." Her voice trembled as she stroked my hair. "Because that all could have just gone very badly. I imagined several outcomes, you know."

"This outcome is a good one."

She nodded and gave me another quick hug before we both went into the house. I closed the door behind us.

"Feel like pizza?" she asked. "I'll order one. It's not too late."

"Make it a large? Can we get wings, too?"

"No problem. Pizza and wings." She turned toward the kitchen to grab the phone, but looked over her shoulder at me. "Lock the door while we're waiting. Can't be too careful. This city is getting more and more dangerous every day."

A chill went through me as I turned the lock and pulled the safety chain over. "You're right. You can never be too careful."

She had no idea what was lurking out there. No idea what her adopted daughter really was. But she was safe from me. With everyone else—there were no such guarantees.

I needed time to deal with what had happened to Carly. I needed to find Stephen and get the chance to recover my soul—and hers. I had to figure out what it meant to be an honorary team member in a group of angels and demons who were currently trapped in Trinity and tasked to protect the city.

I also had to deal with the fact that I'd fallen in love with a fallen angel—one with an extremely scary and deadly past—and if I ever kissed him again I could destroy him completely.

Yes, those were some serious problems I had to deal with very soon.

At the moment, however, all I really wanted to think about was pizza.

★ ★ ★ ★ ★

Don't miss the next NIGHTWATCHERS *story*
WICKED KISS.
Only from Harlequin TEEN.

CRAVE

Book one of *The Clann* series

Bloodlust. Magic. Forbidden secrets.
THE CLANN
CRAVE
Melissa Darnell

Vampires and powerful magic users clash in a contemporary tale of forbidden love and family secrets. Outcast Savannah doesn't know why she's so strongly attracted to Tristan, Clann golden boy and the most popular guy in school. But their irresistible connection may soon tear them apart and launch a battle that will shatter both their worlds.

Available wherever books are sold!

HTCRTR